# Lindsay Buroker's

# Blood and betrayal

## An Emperor's Edge Fantasy Adventure

# FOREWORD

Thank you, good reader, for continuing on with the Emperor's Edge adventures. Maldynado hopes you'll find his story entertaining and that you'll be solidly in the Maldynado-needs-a-statue camp by the end of the book. Oh, and he'll allow that you may be curious to catch up with Amaranthe as well.

Before you jump into that, please allow me to thank my wonderful beta readers, Kendra Highley and Becca Andre, for perusing early versions of the manuscript and suggesting improvements. Thank you, also, to my editor, Shelley Holloway, and cover art designer, Glendon Haddix, (they're also wonderful!) for continuing to work on the series. Now, I'll let you get into the story, since it seems someone left you with a cliffhanger at the end of the last book…

# CHAPTER 1

SMOKE SMOTHERED THE DIRIGIBLE'S NAVIGATION cabin like a dense fog. Murky water seeped through the spider web of cracks in the viewing window, dripped off the smashed control panel, and pooled on the floor in front of Maldynado Montichelu's nose. Awareness of the puddle—and the fact that his left nostril was swimming in it—came abruptly. When Maldynado jerked his head out of the water, pain sharper than any woman's tongue stabbed his skull from the inside out. He winced and grabbed his temples. His fingers brushed a bump larger than any of the mountains they'd just flown over. He didn't know if it'd been thirty seconds since the crash or thirty minutes, but he'd liked things better when he'd been unconscious.

Maldynado sat up and examined himself to see if any important body parts were missing. Everything seemed to be intact, though more than one crimson stain marred his ivory shirt. The fringes dangling from the hem hung in a dirty, snarled mess. He sighed when he spotted his latest fur cap wedged beneath a warped metal panel, blood and grease stains competing for prominence. When Maldynado had agreed to join Amaranthe's team, he had assumed that the mercenary life would include perils to his body, but he hadn't known how devastating it would be to his wardrobe. Ah, well, Sergeant Yara had thought the raccoon-tail cap silly anyway.

Yara! She'd also been in the navigation cabin, alternately yelling advice and cursing at him, when the dirigible crashed. Maldynado spun about, looking for her.

She lay crumpled in the corner. With her broad shoulders and strong jaw, nobody would call the six-foot-tall woman fragile, but at the moment…

Maldynado crept toward her, a hand outstretched. Eyes closed, neck bent awkwardly, Yara wasn't moving. He wasn't even sure if she was

breathing. For that matter, he wasn't sure if *anyone* was breathing. The only sound coming from the rest of the dirigible was the trickling of water.

Maldynado touched Yara's shoulder. "Lady Gruff and Surly, are you awake?"

Her eyes didn't open.

"Are you… alive?" Maldynado asked more quietly. The woman was terse, rude, and utterly lacking in femininity, so he had no idea why he cared; nonetheless, a feeling of concern wormed its way into his belly. He shook her shoulder. "You better not be dead. This team is already overflowing with ankle spankers. I was looking forward to having more women around."

Yara's eyelids fluttered open. She blinked a few times, focused on him, and frowned. "*Ankle* spanker? The only thing you've got that'll reach that far is your ego."

"Now that we've reunited with the others, there's no need for you to continue as Chief Maldynado Insulter." He offered her a hand. "Books has been fulfilling that role for the last nine months."

Thinking of Books reminded Maldynado that the rest of the team was back there somewhere and might need help. He huffed in exasperation when Yara refused his hand. She rolled over, braced herself on the wall, and found her way to her feet on her own. As soon as she tried to take a step, she tottered and almost pitched over, so Maldynado ended up grabbing her arm to support her anyway.

"What a crash," Yara muttered without thanking him. "Is it common for people to try and blow up your team this many times?"

"Not in the same week, no."

They were angling for the corridor leading to the cargo bay and the dirigible's exit when a dark figure stepped into the hatchway. Sicarius.

On any given day, Sicarius, with his death-black attire, humorless face, and dozen-odd daggers and throwing knives, cut a grim figure, the sort of figure that people crossed the street to avoid—at a dead sprint. Today, dirt and blood smeared his face and body, more of the latter being revealed due to numerous tears in his shirt and trousers. Anyone else would have looked weak and haggard; *he* looked like an angry ancestor spirit from one of the old stories, the kind of spirit who slew the populaces of entire towns to avenge the deaths of family members.

When those dark flinty eyes focused on Maldynado, his gut clenched and he took a step back. He might be six inches taller and possess a broader build, but it didn't matter. He wouldn't provoke Sicarius under any circumstances, and circumstances were worse than usual.

"Amaranthe is missing." Sicarius's hard gaze never left Maldynado's face.

"*Missing?*" Maldynado squeaked, then cleared his throat in an attempt to reclaim a normal register.

"She was thrown out when the craft lurched." As always, Sicarius spoke in an emotionless monotone, but Maldynado was fairly certain there was an accusation in those words.

"It's not my fault," he blurted. "I did my best *not* to crash. Or to lurch. They hit us with something. Anyway, I was only piloting because Books was helping with the surgery. How'd that go anyway? Is the emperor…"

Sicarius had turned his back while Maldynado was speaking, and he stalked down the corridor without a word.

"Do you always tinkle down your leg like that when he looks at you?" Yara asked when he was out of sight.

Maldynado squelched a flicker of irritation and the urge to respond defensively. Growing up with a pile of older brothers had long ago taught him that confrontations ended before they began when one let insults ricochet off one's skin like slingshot pebbles clinking off an armadillo's shell. "Nah," he said, "only once or twice a week, when I can tell he's in a real ornery mood and might thump me."

"Has he ever actually touched you?"

"Oh, yes." Maldynado left the navigation cabin, heading into the dented and warped corridor where even more smoke thickened the air. "He calls it training. It's painful."

Thanks to a tilted floor, Maldynado had to climb up a slope to reach the cargo bay. Voices came from beyond the open rear hatch, so he hurried. If the boss truly had fallen out, they needed to hustle to find her before those Forge minions, or whoever had been flying that bizarre black aircraft, found her first.

As it turned out, the hatch wasn't simply open; it had been torn off. He was about to step outside, but the back end of their craft hung several feet above water clogged with cattails. The vegetation-filled

wetlands stretched several hundred meters until the foliage ended at the edge of Lake Fenroot's blue depths. Above Maldynado, the huge, decimated dirigible balloon blotted out the sun as it dangled amongst moss-draped trees edging the shallows. Many trunks had snapped under its pull, or perhaps from the metal cabin ramming into them during the crash. Despite the water everywhere, copses of trees were burning at various points around the lake. A smoky pall smeared the horizon, a reminder that the enemy craft had torched large swaths of earth before finally striking the dirigible.

A cough and a nearby splash drew Maldynado's attention. Books, Basilard, and Akstyr, weighed down by their weapons and rucksacks, were wading toward a muddy beach hemmed in by trees with large, gnarled roots. Maldynado felt a twinge of irritation that nobody had come to check on him and Yara, but he supposed one could say Sicarius had been doing that, albeit without any expressions of concern or inquiries to their health.

The emperor, his neck bandaged and blood staining his pale brown hair, had already reached the beach. He stood next to a couple of rucksacks as he gazed toward the lake. He might have been trying to spot Amaranthe, or he might have been watching for their attackers to return. Nobody was talking, and any birds or critters that might call the wetlands home were staying quiet in the aftermath of the crash. Only the splashes of the wading men disturbed the silence. The smell of skunk cabbage and decaying vegetation mingled with the smoke, adding to the place's utter lack of charm.

Sicarius strode through the thigh-deep water with more alacrity than Books and Akstyr and climbed onto the beach ahead of them. He set a footlocker down next to the emperor. Maldynado was about to hop into the water when Sicarius's voice froze him.

"Did you get your weapons and gear?"

"I'm not even sure where my gear *is*," Maldynado said. "It's probably one of the myriad things that belted me in the head during that landing."

Yara came up beside him and peered through the hatchway. She was blinking and seemed to have trouble focusing her eyes. The whole team needed a doctor. And an alcohol-drenched vacation.

"Get your belongings," Sicarius told Maldynado. "We can't remain at the crash site." His gaze tilted skyward.

"Is he second in command?" Yara asked quietly.

Maldynado rubbed his aching temples. "Dear ancestors, I hope not."

Back in the cabin that he'd never had a chance to sleep in, Maldynado found his rucksack jammed under a bunk, the flap still tied shut. His rapier and utility knife were another matter. In the chaos, they'd separated themselves from their sheaths, and he had to crawl all over the cabin to retrieve them from amongst pillows, bed sheets, and blankets that had flown everywhere during the haphazard final flight.

Yara beat him out of the dirigible and already waited on the beach when Maldynado hopped into the water. He gave a sad salute to the craft as he slogged away. He noted its location, so he could tell Lady Buckingcrest where they had crashed her property. It would take a lot of hard work to win her favor again after destroying her prize dirigible, but maybe the craft—and their relationship—could be salvaged.

"Are you going somewhere?" Books was asking someone when Maldynado reached the beach.

Sicarius had shouldered his rucksack. "To find Lokdon. Where did she fall out?" This time, Books was the recipient of the icy gaze, as if Sicarius blamed him for letting her go.

"I'm not positive." Books gnashed his lower lip between his teeth as he scanned the wetlands. Blood streamed from a cut beneath one of his graying temples, and the wrinkles creasing his brow seemed more pronounced than usual. He eventually pointed toward Lake Fenroot. "I think we were over the lake."

"You *think*," Sicarius said.

"Yes, *think*. At the time, our dubious pilots—" Books waved toward Maldynado and Yara, "—were hurling the craft to and fro. When Amaranthe slid through the door, I was struggling to keep from being flung out myself. I didn't have time to peek out a porthole to triangulate our location."

Maldynado propped his fists on his hips and was about to argue that there'd been nothing dubious about the piloting—there was only so much one could do when being shot at by a craft with superior firepower—but he noticed Yara standing a few feet away in a similar hands-on-hips pose, her lips curled as if also poised to retort. Something about

the similarity disoriented him. He dropped his hands and said nothing. She looked at him at the same time as he was eyeing her, frowned, and seemed to forget her retort too.

*The west side of the lake*, Basilard signed, his pale-skinned fingers flying. *We tried our best to help her, but it happened too quickly. It's possible...* When Sicarius focused on him, Basilard's fingers faltered. He glanced at Books and ran a hand over his bald, scarred head before squaring his shoulders and continuing. *We were high and near the shoreline. Shallow water. It's possible she is... injured.*

Maldynado swallowed. He'd been trying to stay above the treetops, so they'd been at least fifty feet up when the other craft struck.

Without a thank you or even a nod, Sicarius said, "I will recover Lokdon." Then, as he started walking toward the lake, he added, "Sire, come with me. I can best protect you."

The emperor, who had heretofore been quiet, blinked and stared at his back. "Uh, thanks, but I'll take my chances here."

Sicarius halted and turned slowly, pinning the emperor with his stare. Emperor or not, Maldynado expected the young man to squirm under those dark eyes—everyone else did. Sespian lifted his chin, though, and returned the stare. There was even the faintest hint of an eyebrow raise, as if to say, "That's right. I'm refusing to obey you. What're you going to do about it?"

Though Maldynado wanted to hunt for Amaranthe, too, he felt compelled to wink at the emperor and say, "Don't worry, Sicarius, we can take good care of him. We're fine pugilists." If Sespian had been anyone else, Maldynado would have thrown an arm around his shoulders as he spoke, but there were protocols against touching the emperor. In battle, congratulatory shoulder thumps from trusted warrior-caste brethren might be appropriate, but, alas, Maldynado was neither trusted nor warrior-caste any more.

Sicarius's face never changed—someday Maldynado wanted to see the man lose his temper, or at least sneer in frustration—but he did take a step toward the emperor, as if he might force the issue. He froze before he'd taken more than that one step though. His hand dropped to that nasty black dagger of his, and he swiveled, his eyes shifting toward the sky—or at least what they could see of it. The balloon and lingering smoke obscured the view.

"What is it?" Books asked.

"Trouble," Akstyr muttered, pushing a snarl of hair out of his eyes. Dampness had flattened his usual spikes and made his mismatched clothing appear even baggier than usual. If he had to flee, he'd be lucky if his trousers didn't drop to his ankles.

*A likely guess*, Basilard signed, and glanced toward the trees, as if seeking a hiding spot.

Though numerous minutes had passed since the crash, the birds hadn't started chirping again. Maybe it was the smoke and the flames still dancing in some of the trees. Or maybe it was something more inimical. Maldynado found himself scouring the sky as well. Their attackers had prematurely left them for dead once before—in the tunnel cave-in. They might not be so quick to leave the area this time.

"Get off the beach," Sicarius said. "Into the trees. Hide."

Nobody decided to use that moment to question whether Sicarius was second-in-command or not.

Maldynado grabbed the end of the footlocker and waved for Basilard to help him with it, but Sicarius barked, "Leave the gear."

Yara, Books, and Basilard sprinted for cover in the forest. The emperor hesitated, as if he meant to wait to make sure the others were safe before running.

Sicarius strode toward him, spun him toward the woods, and pushed. "Go, Sire."

Maldynado caught up and ran at Sespian's side. Emperor or not, the young man could use an ally, especially since Sicarius seemed to have—ancestral spirits save the boy—made "protecting" him his project. Even if it was well meaning, Sicarius's attention wasn't something a person should have to face alone.

"Here, Sire." Maldynado hopped a stump and slid into a nook formed by a tightly packed copse of trees.

With his broad shoulders, Maldynado had to turn sideways to squeeze into the spot, but he wagered nobody in the air over the wetlands would be able to see him. He waved, inviting Sespian in beside him. Being of slighter build, the emperor slipped in without trouble. Sicarius paused behind him.

"Sorry," Maldynado said brightly. "No room for three."

Sicarius opened his mouth, but, before he could speak, a great cacophony shattered the stillness of the wetlands. It pounded at Maldynado's eardrums, and a stunned moment passed before he could identify the noise as wood snapping, a *lot* of wood snapping. A tremor ran through the earth, and ripples shot across the nearby water. The smell of something burning singed the air.

Sicarius disappeared from view. Maldynado wanted to sink low in his nook and bury his head, but he peeked around the closest tree instead.

All around the beach, trees had been felled or were falling. So many branches and bushes burned that it seemed like one huge inferno spouting flames into the sky. Even in his protected copse, the heat battered Maldynado's face.

Every trace of the dirigible, including the metal hull, had disappeared. Incinerated.

Maldynado groaned. "So much for salvaging the craft." Not only would Lady Buckingcrest never forgive him, but she might even send men out to hunt him down.

Nothing but smoldering black smudges remained of the footlocker and abandoned gear on the beach. Beyond the crash site, a massive dark shape cast its shadow over the water. The solid dome hovered a few meters above the wetlands, its smooth, unadorned hull so inky black it appeared as if a semi-circular hole had opened up in the sky, revealing empty nothingness within. The craft seemed to be waiting.

"That cannot be good," the emperor murmured.

Maldynado pulled back and leaned his forehead against fuzzy, damp moss growing up the side of his tree. "I hope Amaranthe was able to get out of the water and find a place to hide before they saw her."

"They're probably not looking for her," Sespian said. "They'll want me back."

Back or *dead*? Maldynado kept the thought to himself. Sespian had enough on his mind. "If they stumbled across Amaranthe while looking for you, I'm sure they'd be happy to pick her up—or shoot her outright. We've caused a lot of trouble for them, and she's our fountainhead."

Sespian winced. "I would… deeply regret it if harm came to her because of me."

The words weren't hollow ones. Maldynado could tell from the new layer of concern that weighed down Sespian's face. So much for not putting more on his mind.

Maldynado fidgeted, eager to hunt for Amaranthe. If Forge *hadn't* found her, and she was holed up somewhere, incapacitated from her injuries, she'd be waiting for her team's help. Actually, incapacitated or not, she'd be scheming up some way to help herself, but she wouldn't be too proud to accept assistance.

"Is it gone yet?" Maldynado whispered.

From his spot, Sespian had a better view of the water. "It's moved closer."

"Wonderful. They must be hoping we'll stroll out and volunteer to be flambéed."

"Or maybe it's going to torch the entire wetlands to ensure we're all dead."

"Cheery thought." Maldynado said. Maybe Sespian knew Forge didn't want him "back" after all.

A tree snapped. Branches broke, and leaves rattled as it fell, landing with a noisy splash. Maldynado gripped the mossy bark of his own tree and leaned out, trying to keep his body hidden as he observed the craft.

Still hovering, the floating dome crowded the shoreline. Trees standing next to it appeared as thin and frail as toothpicks. Its convex top rose higher than their canopies. Nothing on the flat black bottom of the craft caused ripples in the water below, nor did the leaves in the trees near it stir, so Maldynado couldn't imagine how it flew or stayed in the air. It did drift from side to side as it hovered, occasionally bumping those "toothpicks," causing them to crash to the ground as if they were rootless dowels capable of being knocked over in the faintest breeze.

Maldynado expected the craft to tire of waiting and to send some of those deadly beams out to raze the entire forest, leaving nothing but a smoking crater. But, after hovering for several more moments, it floated upward. Once above the canopy, it headed south.

Long before Maldynado thought crawling out of hiding would be wise, Sicarius darted past him. He leaped ten feet into the air, caught the side of a stout pine, and scrambled up the trunk. He skimmed upward, zipping around branches like a squirrel before disappearing from view.

"That man is exceedingly odd," Sespian observed.

"Oh, you have no idea," Maldynado said.

"Why does Corporal Lokdon employ him?" Sespian asked lightly, as if he were simply making conversation and the answer didn't matter, but intensity sharpened his brown eyes.

"He can thump everyone else into pawpaw pulp, and he does what the boss asks." As soon as Maldynado said that, he thought of Sicarius's recent string of assassinations and grimaced. "Most of the time anyway." That might not be all that accurate either. "Often enough that she finds him useful," he amended.

"Hm. And I suppose she must find you useful too." Sespian raised his eyebrows.

Maldynado vowed to be careful what he said. If his brother, Ravido, truly planned to usurp the throne, Maldynado might be presumed guilty by lieu of having the same parents. "Oh, I'm all sorts of useful." He touched his chest and offered his most disarming smile—it worked wonders on women, though a nineteen-year-old emperor might be less enamored. "I'm tolerable good at thumping folks, too, and I can get great deals from the many female clerks and businesswomen in Stumps."

Sespian mulled that over for a moment before saying, "You're the group shopper?"

"Technically, yes, but don't forget the thumping part." Maldynado lifted an arm and flexed his biceps.

Sespian's measuring gaze remained on him long enough that Maldynado started to feel silly holding his arm aloft. He lowered it, but kept the affable smile. He didn't have anything to hide, but he'd prefer it if the emperor saw him as a simple man, the sort who couldn't string together a coup if he wanted to. Or maybe the sort who, even if he *could* string together a coup, couldn't be bothered to make the effort. Nobody worried about men like that.

Sicarius dropped out of the tree, bending his knees to soften the landing. "Books."

Foliage stirred somewhere behind Maldynado, and boots crunched through the twigs and dead leaves. Grumbling accompanied the footsteps, something about, "being summoned like a hound."

When Books stopped in front of him, Sicarius dropped a compass into one pocket and pulled a folded piece of paper out of another. Curi-

ous, Maldynado wriggled out of his nook. With the dirigible nothing more than a memory, it seemed unlikely the enemy craft would return.

"I need a pen," Sicarius told Books.

Annoyance flickered across Books's weathered face. "You think gathering writing utensils was my first priority after that brawny toad—" Books pointed at Maldynado, "—crashed us? I was hurrying to get out before the engine exploded, something I assumed would happen given that Maldynado had been flying. I didn't even have a chance to grab my sword."

"Come now, Booksie," Maldynado said, "we all know you could be set upon by a platoon of Nurian soldiers and you'd always grab writing utensils first. You can only fight one man at a time with a sword, but, with a pen, you can compose a lecture to bore legions of enemy troops to death."

Books glared at him. Sicarius held out his hand.

Sighing, Books pulled out his journal and unclipped a pen. The journal was the compact, leather-bound one that had disappeared the day before the team left the capital. Maldynado hadn't realized he'd gotten it back.

Sicarius took the pen, unfolded his paper, and laid it on the ground. It was a map of the satrapy. Sicarius marked a couple of topographical features, scribbled coordinates under them, then started drawing lines. Maldynado scratched his head.

By now, the others had gathered around. Books and Basilard were nodding as they watched, and, after a moment, Sespian seemed to get it too. Akstyr and Yara didn't show any signs of enlightenment, but they didn't seem to care either.

"What are you working on?" Maldynado asked. "I ask because the boss could be out there, bleeding to death somewhere, and unless this is going to help us find her, I think it should wait." He gazed out toward the lake. At least a half hour must have passed since Amaranthe fell out and the dirigible crashed. If she were able, she should have joined them by now, or at least signaled.

Sicarius was using the back of a knife to draw a straight line down the center of the map, and he didn't respond. Maldynado huffed in exasperation. He was tempted to take charge and divide up the group for a search, but he didn't know if anyone would listen to him.

Sicarius circled two towns alongside the line he'd drawn.

*He saw which way the craft flew away,* Basilard signed. *I think he's trying to figure out where it might be going from the bearing.*

"Yes," Books said, "though we have no guarantee that it's flying in a straight line in the direction it departed. Or that it's heading to a destination within the satrapy."

Maldynado stamped his feet. "Does nobody else care that the boss might be dead or dying somewhere and need our help?"

Basilard frowned at him.

"We *all* care," Books said.

"Then why aren't we—"

Sicarius stood, the movement abrupt enough that Maldynado stepped back and shut his mouth.

"Fifteen minutes," Sicarius said.

Maldynado frowned. "You want to wait fifteen minutes to search?" He shook his head and started to say more, but Sicarius spoke again.

"Fifteen minutes passed between when the craft shot us down and when it came to check on us." Sicarius pocketed the map. "We'll split up and circle the lake to check for her anyway."

Realization dawned on Maldynado. "You think they got her during that time?"

"Books, Basilard, Akstyr, and Yara, go east around the lake," Sicarius said. "The emperor, Maldynado, and I will go west until we meet."

Maldynado bristled at having Sicarius give orders—this wasn't an exercise session, after all—but they could vote on who the ersatz leader would be later. Besides, he was sending Yara and Books, the two people most likely to heckle Maldynado, off in the other group.

Everyone else must have also decided this wasn't the time for arguing with Sicarius, for they trooped off in the indicated directions without a word, though Sespian did pause to gaze to the east. He had an urgent reason to reach Sunders City, Maldynado recalled. But, when Maldynado jogged after Sicarius, Sespian fell in behind them, apparently willing to help look for Amaranthe first.

Good kid, Maldynado decided. At least that's what he thought until Sespian started peppering him with questions about his family.

They had scarcely started down a muddy trail weaving through ferns and trees on its way to the lake when Sespian asked, "How do you get along with your brother, Maldynado?"

"I assume you mean Ravido, though I don't get along with any of my siblings, Sire."

"Yes. Have you communicated with him lately?"

"I haven't communicated with anyone in the family since the old man disowned me over a year ago."

Sespian ducked a branch stretching over the path. "Would you admit it to me if you were in regular contact with your family or… with anyone else?"

Anyone else? What "anyone else" was out there that the emperor thought Maldynado might contact? "I imagine not, Sire. But, given that some of my family members are apparently up to seditious activities, it wouldn't behoove me to be in contact with them." Behoove? Had he actually said behoove? Wandering around with Books was having a tedious affect on his vocabulary. The rest of the words sounded stilted too. He hated having to be careful about what he said. If Ravido got anywhere near the throne in the Imperial Barracks, Maldynado hoped he tripped over it.

"You're honest about that much at least."

Maldynado was honest about *everything*. Occasionally he might *exaggerate* when it came to exploits involving women, but that was natural. "Uh, yes. Does colluding against the throne still carry a death penalty?"

"I believe so. Though… if you *had* been colluding and were to decide that helping me is a better option, we could waive any head-removal penalties."

"I'm not colluding, Sire." They'd reached the lake, and Maldynado shielded his eyes with his hand to exaggerate the fact that he was searching for Amaranthe. Maybe Sespian would notice and decide question-asking time could wait until later.

"I wonder if Ravido always had an interest in ruling," Sespian said.

Maldynado managed to keep his sigh soft.

"Back when you *did* have regular contact with him, did he talk of the family's glory days? Of when the Marblecrests used to rule?"

"Sire, he's more than twenty years older than me. I never knew him well." Maldynado wished Sicarius had split him off into the other group, heckling notwithstanding. Or that the emperor would ask *him* some questions. Not that Sicarius would answer. Maldynado didn't think he could get away with that. Silence could condemn him.

Sespian climbed on top of a log on the path and paused before stepping down. "Am I premature in asking questions?"

"What?"

"Corporal Lokdon suggested I have a few drinks with you before discussing family matters. Unfortunately, this swamp is lacking in purveyors of alcoholic beverages."

Maldynado, climbing over the log himself, almost fell into the ferns on the side. "*Amaranthe* suggested you question me?"

"She assured me you weren't conspiring with your brother and said you might be a source of information on him and any other friends or family members who are assisting him with his dubious goals."

"Oh." It stung that Amaranthe had suggested Maldynado might betray family members, but he supposed she'd been watching out for his backside. The next time the group wandered past enforcers or soldiers, the emperor could order him killed with a wave of the hand. "I don't know what Ravido is up to, Sire. Has he already passed the point of no return?" Maldynado thought of the weapons delivery outside of Fort Urgot. His brother might be in the incipient stage of an uprising, but if blood had not yet been shed… "Or is it possible he might be talked into giving up his wayward plans?"

"I'm behind on events, thanks to being ushered all over the empire to inspect military installations, but the last I heard, he hadn't killed anyone. It's possible banishment would be punishment enough. But… if he's put things into play while I've been gone, then the law and hundreds of years of imperial precedent would demand his death, yes." Sespian frowned, perhaps not liking the idea of killing Ravido, or killing people in general.

Ahead of them, Sicarius had disappeared around a bend, and Maldynado nodded that they had better hurry up. He could use the short jog to give himself a moment to respond as well.

Distracted, he misjudged a step and his boot caught on a root. He recovered his balance, but not without cracking his elbow against a sapling. Another bruise for the collection. What a day. "Yes, Sire, drinks would have been appropriate before asking me to share information that could result in my brother's death."

Sicarius looked back at Maldynado with an extra dose of coldness in his hard eyes. That surprised Maldynado. Why would Sicarius care one way or another about Ravido's doings?

"So," Sespian said, "though you don't particularly like your family, you're not willing to betray them." He seemed to be mulling the fact over, rather than judging Maldynado for the choice.

Maldynado pushed a hand through his hair, tucking a few loose curls behind his ears. "I don't want to be flushed down the wash-out with them, but I'm not ready to volunteer to be the trap that ensnares the bear for the hunter either. I'm already... I already betrayed the family once. If I did that to my mother again, she'd wring my neck herself."

"I see," Sespian said as they continued along the path. Softly, perhaps more to himself, he added, "Loyalty may be an admirable trait in men, but I do wish more of them would direct it in my direction."

With Forge scampering around the capital, infiltrating the Imperial Barracks, Sespian must have trouble knowing whom he could trust. Maldynado felt for the kid and wanted to help, but—

He stopped a hair shy of crashing into Sicarius.

Sicarius had stopped to face the emperor. Though it was always hard to tell with him, he looked like he had something to say. He glanced at Maldynado, didn't utter a word, then strode ahead several paces where he knelt to examine the ground.

Sespian's forehead crinkled. Maldynado gave him a shrug. He couldn't explain Sicarius either.

"Fresh tracks." Sicarius stepped off the trail they'd been following around the lake, touched the broken tip of a thin branch, and veered into the foliage on a short peninsula.

Maldynado pushed past ferns to follow him, wondering how Sicarius managed to move through the same vegetation as he did, but without making a sound. After he ducked a branch growing a mossy beard so long it'd make the hairiest old men in the Veterans' Quarter jealous, the water came into sight again. Sicarius had stopped on a muddy bank at the end of the peninsula. Maldynado didn't need to be a tracker to spot

all the prints. Many different sizes and styles of boots were represented. If Amaranthe had come ashore here…

Sicarius knelt and touched the ground. He brought a finger to his nose.

"Blood?" Maldynado asked.

"Yes."

"Amaranthe's?" It was a dumb question—people's blood didn't have an identifying smell, did it?—but Maldynado somehow hoped that asking would lead Sicarius to say, "No, she's fine. This belonged to the bloke she punched in the nose." It was an unwarranted hope though. Maldynado would bet on Amaranthe in a one-on-one match-up against almost anybody—even if she wasn't stronger or faster than her foe, she'd scheme up some plan to defeat him—but against the ten or twelve people responsible for these footprints?

"Likely," was all Sicarius said.

He touched one of the footprints. From where he stood, Maldynado didn't see anything special about it, but Sicarius grew still. "Major Pike was here."

Maldynado put a hand on the nearest tree for support. "The Major Pike you described as Emperor Raumesys's master interrogator?"

"Yes."

A twig snapped as Sespian pushed his way out of the foliage behind Maldynado. He took in the scene with a grim set to his mouth.

"They must have seen her fall." Sicarius pointed to a mark near the water. "When she came ashore there, Pike was waiting."

"She *came* ashore, as in her broken, battered body floated up to the bank, or she *walked* ashore?" Maldynado asked.

Sicarius strode back into the underbrush, quickly disappearing from view.

"Oh, no," Maldynado said, "no need to answer our questions. We're just speaking to give the wildlife something to listen to."

A crow squawked on the other side of the trail.

"Yes, like that."

Sespian hadn't said a word, and he didn't react to Maldynado's sarcasm. His eyes were cast downward, toward the trampled mud where Sicarius had found the blood. Maybe he felt partially responsible for Amaranthe's predicament. Did emperors have the capacity to worry

about commoners? Not a lot of Maldynado's own warrior-caste brethren did, but Sespian seemed a sensitive sort. Too sensitive maybe. If he had the brawny assertive mien of his predecessor, Emperor Raumesys, he might not have so many people picking on him as someone easy to remove or shunt aside.

"We'd better go after him." Maldynado pushed into the foliage, figuring he'd lose track of Sicarius if he didn't follow immediately. As it was, he reached the trail and didn't see anyone. He searched for fresh boot prints, but the ground was harder packed there, and he couldn't decide which way the kidnappers had gone. He listened for a rustle of leaves or snapping of twigs that would announce Sicarius's passage, but of course that never came. Near the water's edge, a frog started croaking, but nothing stirred in the underbrush.

Sespian, making less noise than Maldynado would have expected, stepped back onto the trail. "Which way?" he asked.

Uhm. Maldynado pointed into the woods opposite of the peninsula and headed in that direction. If Sicarius had stuck to the path, Maldynado should have seen him. Besides, he didn't want to appear clueless in front of the emperor.

Maldynado pushed through dense, tangled undergrowth for several minutes and was about to confess that he'd been guessing when the crow cawed again. Complaining about assassins passing nearby? He angled toward the call.

Up ahead, the trees thinned. Afraid he'd simply walked in a circle and returned to the lake, Maldynado almost turned around, but curiosity or perhaps intuition prompted him to continue.

Between one step and the next, the trees ended. Maldynado found himself squinting into autumn sunlight slanting down from a swath of open blue sky. A huge circular expanse stretched before him with all the trees, bushes, grass, and moss cleared. No, not cleared, he realized as he walked off an edge, almost tripping because of a height difference from one step to the next. The entire circle, easily hundreds of meters in diameter, was a foot lower than the surrounding earth. The foliage hadn't been cleared; it'd been smashed. Compacted beneath a weight so great, even stout trees had crumpled beneath it, their trunks flattened into the ground.

"Bloody bears," Sespian breathed. "They landed here? I didn't realize how big that craft was. Or how heavy. How could something with such mass fly?"

"I don't know." Maldynado tilted his head. "Bloody *bears*?"

Sespian flushed. "When I was growing up, one of my bodyguards always said, 'bloody balls.' I adopted it until my mother heard and said it wasn't appropriate for young princes to say balls. 'Bears' was my work-around. The word still slips out at times."

That story did little to change Maldynado's mind that Sespian might be a tad soft for the position of emperor. "Do yourself a favor and don't say things like that around military men, Sire."

The flush deepened.

"The tracks end over there," Sicarius said from behind and to the side of them.

Surprised by his soundless return, Maldynado nearly spat a, "Bloody bears," himself.

"Lokdon was walking, hemmed in by soldiers," Sicarius said. "The tracks disappear fifteen feet from the shelf." He pointed at the foot-deep depression ringing the circle. "The boundary marks the hull of the craft, presumably."

"How'd they get inside?" Sespian asked. "A ramp?"

"Unknown."

"So, they have her." Maldynado sank into a crouch, his elbows on his knees. Curse his dumb ancestors, why hadn't he done better at piloting that dirigible? If he'd gone straight ahead toward Sunders City at top speed instead of trying to lose their pursuers in the wetlands, they might have made it. The enemy might have broken away to keep from being seen by outlying residents. "We have to go after her."

Sicarius had moved away from Maldynado and Sespian and stood on the compacted earth, his gaze toward the south. The direction the craft had gone.

"How will your team find her?" Sespian asked.

*Your team*, he said, not *we*. Of course. What did some outlaw mercenary leader matter to him?

Maldynado caught himself before he said something snide. The emperor's own mission called to him, that was all. And that mission might save the entire empire. Sespian couldn't cast it aside to help rescue one person.

"I don't know, but we will. Somehow—" Maldynado snapped his fingers and spun toward Sicarius. "That map. Is that what you were doing? Figuring out where they're taking Amaranthe and where they might land?"

"Books was right," Sicarius said without looking at him. "There's no way to tell if they'll continue in a straight line or if their destination is within the satrapy."

"Of *course* they're going somewhere in the satrapy," Maldynado said. "We think Forge people are flying that thing, right? Well, if we're figuring right, Forge's priority is the capital. They're trying to back the next heir to the empire—no offense, Sire—right? If they're acting soon, they're not going to suddenly decide to take a vacation on some tropical beach down south. Maybe they're not going far at all."

For the first time, Sicarius met Maldynado's eyes and seemed to be interested in what he had to say.

"We can catch them," Maldynado insisted. He had to believe that. "What cities were near the line you drew?"

"Markworth and Deerlick Wood lie along the bearing I calculated."

Erg, Markworth was over three hundred miles away, and Deerlick Wood, at the edge of the satrapy, even farther. Deerlick Wood was a derelict mining town and Markworth a resort town on Lake Seventy-three, a spot where wealthy warrior-caste families vacationed, extending their summers when the weather grew cooler up north. Maldynado's family had property in the area. He'd even visited as a kid, but that didn't help him come up with a reason for Forge to go there. As far as he knew, there weren't any natural resources, manufacturing facilities, or business opportunities. It was a destination for fun. Nothing more. Forge didn't seem to be all that interested in fun.

"Even if they're not going to those towns," Maldynado said, "they were heading south along the river, right? The river is populated all up and down in that area, so people would be likely to see that monstrosity flying overhead. People like to talk. They'd mention something like that, and we could tell if we were on the right track."

Sicarius had stopped listening, or at least he wasn't looking at Maldynado. His eyes had turned toward Sespian, who, to his credit, wasn't

squirming under the attention. Maldynado always felt like a schoolchild being taken to task when Sicarius gave him a look that lasted more than two seconds.

"You will go to Sunders City next?" Sicarius asked.

"I must, yes," Sespian said.

"Your absence in the capital will allow schemers to strike."

"I *must* know what exactly Forge plans. There is someone traveling through Sunders City that I… must find."

"You could send someone else," Sicarius said.

"There's no one else I trust."

"You sought out our team."

"Because of *her*." Sespian waved toward the sky in the direction the aircraft had flown. "If she's gone now…" His voice cracked, and he cleared his throat. That surprised Maldynado. Did the emperor care about Amaranthe? Why would that be? "Your team has done all that I requested. I thank you, but I'll go my own way now. You need to find your missing comrade."

"Your mission," Sicarius said, as if Sespian hadn't spoken at all. "It will be dangerous? A risk to your life?"

Sespian lifted his hands, palms up. "Probably. That doesn't change anything. I'm prepared to go on my own."

Insects droned in the wetlands. A second frog joined the first, starting up a croaking chorus. Sicarius looked to the south again. He had the appearance of a man facing a hard choice, though Maldynado couldn't understand why. They *had* to go after the boss.

Finally, Sicarius said, "I will get her. Sire, Maldynado and the others will accompany you to Sunders City and act as your bodyguards, or lackeys if that is what you need. They will protect you."

"I don't need lackeys *or* bodyguards," Sespian said at the same time as Maldynado lifted his hands and said, "Wait, I'm going after the boss too."

"You will accompany the emperor." As he spoke, Sicarius issued his favorite dark glare, the one that could make a man's love apples shrivel up faster than a nude streak into the snow on Solstice Day.

Maldynado usually avoided that stare, but this time he crossed his arms over his chest and stared back. "I'm going too."

Maldynado knew that Sespian's safety should be his first priority—disowned or not, he was a son of the warrior-caste, and thus sworn to defend and protect the emperor and empire—but he wouldn't turn his back on Amaranthe. Besides, Sespian was standing in front of them, safe for the moment. Amaranthe was the one who'd been captured by some torture-loving goon with a passion for molesting people. Maldynado didn't trust Sicarius to go after her alone. He might do some obligatory hunting, but he didn't care about Amaranthe the way the rest of the team did. He didn't care about *anyone*.

In the face of Maldynado's stubborn response, Sicarius strode across the field toward him, each step firm and deliberate. Maldynado prepared to defend himself, even if it meant ending up compacted into the earth alongside the smashed trees, but Sicarius stopped a pace away.

"Amaranthe would wish the majority of the team to help the emperor," he said. "That is what we came down here to do."

The argument surprised Maldynado—Sicarius didn't have a history of using words to sway people—and he almost caught himself nodding. He turned the head movement into a shake and a scowl. "That was before she got captured. She'd—"

"Want the team to help the emperor," Sicarius repeated. "I will go after her. I can travel faster on my own."

Maldynado wanted to deny the statement, but he knew Sicarius spoke the truth. *If* he gave it his full effort, Sicarius could go farther and faster than anyone.

"I'll get her," Sicarius repeated softly. There was a determined intensity to his eyes that Maldynado hadn't noticed before. He was always so pragmatic and seemed indifferent to feelings and emotions, but that look in his eyes...

"Fine," Maldynado sighed. "If you promise to do everything possible to find her and not give up."

Sespian cleared his throat. "While it's nice that you two are in agreement, I never said I'd take any of your people with me. The security and continuation of the empire as we know it is at stake. I'm not willing to bring untested mercenaries along."

"Untested?" Maldynado touched his chest. "*Untested*? I've been tested by swords, rifles, bows, giant krakens, man-eating makarovi, and

don't forget all the man-slaying machines powered by wizard magic. That's just in the last six months."

Sicarius and Sespian were eying each other and ignoring Maldynado. Nothing new there.

"You promised payment," Sicarius said.

"What?" Sespian asked.

"In your note. You promised payment for your kidnapping. You said the money is in Sunders City."

"Corporal Lokdon said she's not interested in payment."

"She's not here," Sicarius said, his tone hard.

If Maldynado hadn't known him—and known money was even less likely to sway him than an eyelash-batting from a girl—he would have believed Sicarius wanted the coin.

"I see," Sespian said, his jaw tight. "Very well."

Maldynado wondered if Sicarius had chosen the best method for ensuring the team got to accompany Sespian. Wouldn't they be better served by Sespian believing they were in this for altruistic reasons? Or at least reasons that weren't as shallow as craving coin?

Sicarius pulled out his black knife and strode toward Sespian. The young man tensed but stood his ground.

Seeing them face-to-face gave Maldynado a start. For one thing, he hadn't realized they were the same height. Sicarius always seemed taller than his six feet while Sespian, lacking the ever-present glare and body full of lean ropy muscle, seemed smaller. What really struck him though was the similarity of the determined, mulish expressions they each sported. Huh.

Sicarius flipped the knife and extended it, hilt first, to Sespian.

"What do I do with that?" Sespian looked at it, as if he thought he was supposed to examine it for some secret about the otherworldly technology.

"Take it," Sicarius said.

Sespian grasped the hilt, though he simply held it out, brow furrowed in askance.

"I have often found its properties useful," Sicarius said. "You may find the same."

Standing a few feet away, Maldynado could only gape. Sicarius was giving up his knife? His *favorite* knife? He didn't even let Amaranthe use that.

If Sespian knew the magnitude of the gift he'd been given, he didn't show it. In fact, he continued to hold it out, as if he were thinking of rejecting the gift.

Sicarius spoke again without giving him a chance. "Maldynado and the others will accompany you to pick up the money. I've delayed long enough." He glanced toward the southern sky again, then started past Maldynado, apparently intending to head off in that direction immediately. He didn't even have any supplies beyond the knives he wore and whatever was in his rucksack.

Sicarius halted beside Maldynado long enough to say, for his ears alone, "Make yourself indispensable, so he chooses to keep the team around. If I return with Lokdon and find you've lost the emperor…" Sicarius's eyes had never been fuller of threat when he said, "*Don't* lose him."

# CHAPTER 2

IT HADN'T TAKEN MORE THAN FIVE SECONDS INSIDE the enemy aircraft to convince Amaranthe Lokdon that falling out of her team's perfectly good dirigible and being captured had been a very bad idea. The cold, unadorned black walls lacked charm, but, more than that, the cavernous corridors branched and branched again, forming an asymmetric layout that made her feel like a field mouse being dragged into the bowels of a fox's den. Even if she escaped, she might never find her way out. The proportions were odd, too, with high ceilings above narrow, confining corridors. In a spot where they climbed stairs, she found herself tripping over the steeply spaced treads. She remembered Sicarius's claim that this technology had come from a non-human race. For the first time, she truly believed it.

The white-haired man walking behind Amaranthe, prodding her whenever her step slowed, added to her unease. At first, she had hoped her first guess wrong and that this *wasn't* Pike, the old emperor's Master Interrogator, but one of his men had addressed him by name. And rank. Apparently, he'd kept the "Major," even though he'd been booted from the army for raping recruits. No doubt Emperor Raumesys and Commander of the Armies Hollowcrest had found those sadistic tendencies useful and encouraged the ex-officer to further develop them.

Had Major Pike been the only one accompanying Amaranthe, she might have tried to surprise him and escape, but a dozen other men marched ahead of and behind, hemming her in. Having her wrists tied behind her back didn't encourage athletic feats either.

"Should I feel flattered that so many people came out to capture me?" Amaranthe asked over her shoulder. Since talking had always been her best way of gathering information, stirring up a conversation

might be to her advantage. If nothing else, she wanted to know what had happened to Sicarius and the others. If this aircraft had succeeded in shooting down the dirigible, they could be wounded. Or worse.

Something hard pounded her between her shoulder blades. The pain, when compared to some of the injuries she'd received in the last twenty-four hours, was minimal, but the blow did cause her to stumble and bump into the men walking in front of her.

"Sorry," Amaranthe said when one glared back at her. "Uneven flooring."

The man's over-the-shoulder glare continued for a long moment, and, as Amaranthe righted herself and resumed walking, she scrutinized him, trying to decide where he might have been recruited from. He had short hair, a clean-shaven face, and an athletic build, as did the other men escorting her. Soldier, her mind proclaimed, though she had no proof. They wore civilian clothing—factory-sewn wool trousers, sturdy cotton vests and dusters, and a variety of workman's boots. None of the garments suggested uniformity, though her guards did have a tendency to walk in step with each other.

"Are you General Ravido's men?" Amaranthe asked. She didn't expect anybody to answer, especially not with the boss five feet away, but maybe she could surprise an eye flicker out of them, something that might confirm her guess.

Before that happened, Pike grabbed her elbow. Amaranthe expected another blow to land between her shoulder blades, and braced herself, but he yanked her back instead, then propelled her face-first into the wall. If she'd had her hands free, she might have caught herself, but without that recourse she smashed into the unyielding black alloy. Pain burst through her cheekbone. She bit her tongue, and blood flooded her mouth.

Amaranthe tried to pull away, but Pike leaned into her back.

The grip remained on her elbow, but knuckles or something else hard dug into a tender point near her kidney. She sucked in a pained gasp of air. Her first instinct was to squirm away, but there was nowhere to go. She tried to lift her leg for a backward kick, but his own legs trapped hers, forcing her knees against the wall.

Hot, fast breaths whispered across her swelling cheek. Had the effort taxed Pike? No, despite his age, rock hard muscles pressed against Ama-

ranthe's back. He was fit. He was just... excited. She swallowed and tried not to dwell on that idea, but his face came in close, beard stubble scraping at her skin. Fresh fear arose in her heart. All along, she'd been concerned for herself, but she hadn't figured pain would be applied so soon. Surely, they should reach a nicely appointed torture chamber first?

"Too much talking?" Amaranthe asked, trying to sound brave, or at least unimpressed by the attack.

"Talking is allowed," Pike said, his voice raspy from some old throat injury. Or maybe the promise of tormenting someone had excited him into hoarseness. "But only to answer questions. One question specifically."

Again, Amaranthe tried to push away from the wall, but she couldn't find the leverage. A detached part of her mind, the part avoiding thinking about Pike's unpleasant closeness, analyzed the cool smoothness of that wall. It wasn't porous like stone or brick, but it didn't feel like metal either. It *felt* like the same material as Sicarius's dagger.

Thinking of him reminded her that she should only have to endure Pike's torment temporarily. Assuming her team had survived that crash—and surely they were too tough to die that way—they'd come looking for her. They'd find a way into this black behemoth, stick Pike full of daggers, and help her escape. She just had to survive until then. Then again, maybe her certainty was unfounded. The emperor needed help, and Sicarius... He'd admitted to caring for her, but Sespian was his *son.* Protecting him would have to be his priority. And, with Amaranthe gone, he'd likely take charge of the group. It was possible nobody would come for her. She tried to firm her resolve before the new thoughts could bring despair. If the team didn't come, she'd simply have to escape on her own.

Pike mashed her harder against the wall, apparently expecting a response.

Amaranthe forced her aching jaw to move so she could ask, "What question might that be?"

"What," Pike murmured, as if they were embracing lovers engaged in a tête-à-tête, "is the emperor to Sicarius?"

Though the question surprised her, Amaranthe kept herself from reacting outwardly. No amount of torture would make her give up Sicarius's secret, but it would be better for her if Pike didn't figure out

there was a secret to be had. She found it encouraging that Pike wanted information on Sicarius and the emperor; that had to mean they'd survived the crash and eluded capture. She hoped the others had too.

"What are you talking about?" Amaranthe asked.

"After a year of simply reacting to Forge's plans, last week, he slew as many of the members as he could reach. Days later, he risked his life, leading your team to kidnap the emperor. Why?"

*Sicarius* led the team? Amaranthe kept the thought to herself. Barely. The taste of blood in her mouth reminded her that arguing with the man had repercussions. If he thought she was some underling and Sicarius was in charge, things might go easier on her.

Fingers gripped the back of her head, nails digging into her scalp. Amaranthe had barely registered that pain when Pike rammed her face against the wall again. She gritted her teeth to keep from crying out. Blood flowed from her nose.

"You will find," Pike said, "that prompt and truthful answers result in less discomfort." He lowered his voice to a whisper to add, "Though I do not mind employing copious amounts of… discomfort to coerce information from you."

"Oh, I'm sure of that," Amaranthe muttered.

"Sicarius must have found out that the emperor wasn't meant to make it back to the capital. For some reason, this prompted him to take aggressive action. What I want to know is why."

Amaranthe felt her eyes widen, and she was glad the wall was the only thing looking at her face. All along, she'd suspected Forge had been planning to get rid of Sespian, a fact that had been confirmed when Books explained that the deadly neck implants were never intended to come out. What she *hadn't* known was that they planned to act so soon. They must not need Sespian on the throne any more. They had a replacement ready. Ravido. Maybe that weapons shipment had been delivered so the general and his loyal soldiers could march into the city, take the Imperial Barracks, and declare the Marblecrests the new rulers of Turgonia. It wouldn't be that easy—there were others who could legitimately bid for the throne, but it'd be hard to mount a campaign if Ravido and his men were already ensconced. And if Forge was a part of things, throwing its support behind him…

Emperor's warts, what if all of her musings had already happened? What if, while she had been out of the city, Ravido had already been making his move? What if he already had the Barracks?

"You hesitate," Pike murmured, "even though I hold you helpless. Are you foolish or loyal?"

"Both, probably," Amaranthe said. "Look, the emperor sent us a note offering a hundred thousand ranmyas if we got him away from you. As far as I know, that's all Sicarius was interested in."

"Sicarius has never been motivated by money."

"That might have been true when you knew him, but it's been a while, hasn't it? People change, even assassins. He doesn't have anyone paying for his room and board any more. Maybe he's tired of all the people hunting him and wants to escape our long, snow-smothered winters. Maybe he's fixing to retire in some tropical paradise devoid of bounty hunters."

There, that might give Pike something new to muse upon.

Hoping she had him distracted, Amaranthe tried to step away from the wall, to alleviate the pain of having her face ground into it. Pike's hand, still tangled in her hair, dropped. The movement ripped strands of hair free, but that was the least of her concerns. His fingers wrapped around her neck. Panic surged through her limbs, urging her to fight. But, with soldiers everywhere, she couldn't possibly escape. Besides, she told herself, trying to will calm into her body, Pike wouldn't kill her there. He'd stopped to pick her up for a reason. Logical though her thoughts may be, they failed to keep her heartbeat steady and unconcerned.

The strong, calloused fingers tightened around her neck. With his lips to her ear, Pike whispered, "I sense fear beneath your evasiveness. You know why Sicarius is protecting the emperor, and you *will* tell me."

\* \* \* \* \* \* \*

As the team hiked away from the lake, the trail turned into a road and the wetlands faded, replaced by farms and ranches. Sheep nipping at grass and weeds near the fences didn't bother to lift their heads to acknowledge the passing of the emperor over all of Turgonia.

Maldynado hoped any people they encountered would be just as busy with their inner thoughts. Sespian, he imagined, wanted to stay incognito. He didn't have a costume beyond torn clothes, an unshaven face, and dirty nails, but he was being careful to walk between Basilard and Books, with Akstyr ahead of him and Yara lagging behind. Somehow Maldynado had ended up leading the yawning and beleaguered team toward the Goldar River and Sunders City. It was a little thing, but it made him uneasy. He did not want the responsibility of leading. As he'd learned long ago in life, people who let themselves be put in charge got blamed when things went wrong. Unfortunately, he'd let Sicarius do just that, and now he had to keep track of Sespian.

Maldynado eyed the rustic houses and outbuildings on either side of the road. If he remembered the area correctly—he hadn't been through town since those childhood trips to Lake Seventy-three—the main bridge across the river and into the city core lay only a few miles away. The group would reach Sespian's money stash by nightfall, and then what? He'd have no more reason to stay with the team. Not unless someone convinced him they were indispensable.

Every time they passed people walking in the opposite direction, Maldynado hoped they'd turn into a covey of highwaymen who would leap out and give him a chance to protect the emperor. Unfortunately, the pedestrians walking, cycling, and riding past on mule-drawn carts only regarded the team with wariness. Even if any of them had highwayman aspirations, they'd probably prove smart enough to leave this group alone. Though tired, grimy, and missing half of their gear, the men—Yara included—had the tempered-in-blood look of war veterans. These days, even Books managed to look moderately dangerous when he rested his hand on the hilt of a weapon.

Sespian lacked the mercenary visage, but his face *did* earn a few second glances from passersby. That was a cause for concern.

"Sire," Maldynado said, struck by inspiration, "would you like me to go into the city first and acquire a costume for you? Even though you're a touch scraggily at the moment, your face *is* on the ranmya bills. People might recognize you and report you to local Forge minions." Maldynado had no idea if Sunders City *had* local Forge minions, but it sounded good.

"Hm." Sespian stepped around a pothole in the muddy road and kicked aside a few soggy brown leaves. They might have left the wetlands, but no one would call this part of the satrapy dry. Plenty of moss carpeted the stumps in the farmers' fields. "You *did* say you're the group shopper, didn't you?"

"When it comes to clothing, yes. Fashion consciousness is one of my gifts, and I *always* stay abreast of the latest trends. I can make sure people are so busy admiring your outfit that they won't notice your face." Maldynado paused, not certain that had been a good selling point.

"Sire," Books said, "I strongly, no, *vehemently* suggest you don't let Maldynado purchase clothing for you."

"Vehemently?" A hint of a smile touched Sespian's lips for the first time since the crash.

"*Most* vehemently."

"Don't listen to him, Sire." Maldynado was glad the emperor couldn't read Basilard's contribution—he was back there signing, *Tell the emperor I agree and that letting Maldynado choose a costume would be unwise.* Maldynado dropped back, butting Books out of the way and waving for Basilard to tie his fingers together. "I've often chosen appropriate ensembles for the boss," he told Sespian. "She trusts my taste and understands my value in this area."

Books made a choking sound, but Akstyr was the one to say, "Has she ever worn one of your costumes for more than two hours?"

"No," Books said. "In fact, she was distinctly put out over that... minimalist ensemble you acquired last spring. The glares she hurled about rivaled some of Sicarius's best ones."

Maldynado waved at the men, trying to shush them. For once, he had a serious—life-threateningly serious—agenda to pursue, and these jesters insisted on fooling around. Sergeant Yara, battling fits of yawns, had been tagging along several paces to the rear, but she was drawing closer now. Maldynado did *not* want her to join the chorus of critics.

"Ignore them, Sire." Maldynado turned his back on the others and waved toward the road ahead, inviting Sespian to focus in that direction rather than to the rear. "They wouldn't know fine fashion if it sashayed up to them in the form of a beautiful woman inviting them to an evening of debauchery."

"Did he just say *sashayed*?" Akstyr asked. "Men aren't supposed to use words like that."

"I'm surprised he knows what it means," Books said.

Keeping his back to them, Maldynado said, "I'm certain I can find something dignified and appropriate for a bookly sort such as yourself, Sire."

Sespian's lips flattened at the word "bookly," and Maldynado realized that might not be considered complimentary.

"It's true that, when given a chance, I do acquire alluring costumes for the boss," Maldynado went on, hurrying to cover his blunder, "but it's intentional. I wish to encourage male interest. She spends entirely too much time plotting and scheming and training with *Sicarius* of all people. One shouldn't spend that much time alone with someone like that. It could stunt one's social skills." Maldynado had wandered away from his target topic, but maybe if Sespian saw that he cared about Amaranthe's happiness, he'd realize Maldynado was an all-right sort of fellow.

"Training with Sicarius?" Sespian lifted his eyebrows.

"Sure, fencing, sparring, calisthenics, running obstacle courses." A thought occurred to Maldynado. "You didn't think I meant anything… venereal, did you? There's nothing like *that* going on between them." He glanced back at the others. "There's *not*, right?"

To Maldynado's surprise, Sespian glanced back too.

Books opened his mouth, but before he could speak, Basilard pointed at the road ahead. No, at the bridge, which had come into view, though it remained a mile or so away. A wagon sat atop it, and there seemed to be a knot of people around it.

Maldynado squinted. "Anyone have a spyglass?"

"We lost most of our gear along with the dirigible," Books said.

*They're soldiers*, Basilard signed. *They're stopping people.*

Maldynado was about to translate for the emperor, but he was looking at the bridge, too, and he'd slowed his pace.

"Soldiers," Sespian said.

"You have good eyes, Sire," Maldynado said.

"For a bookly sort?"

"Er, yes. Do you… want to be seen by soldiers?" Maldynado hoped not—what good could he and the team do if Sespian could simply walk up and fetch a team of grunts to follow him around and keep him safe?

"Not particularly," Sespian said. "I don't have any way to know which ones are—" He caught himself with a frown, and repeated, "not particularly."

Maldynado had no trouble seeing through the gap. Sespian couldn't be sure who might be loyal to Ravido.

"Is there another way across?" Sespian asked. "The place where I arranged to have funds stashed is south of downtown, on the other side of the bridge."

Good, Maldynado thought. "Not for many miles. My costume idea might be necessary, after all." Technically, they could filch a boat, but if soldiers were guarding the bridge, they'd be watching the docks too.

Sespian sighed, as if whatever plan he'd meant to pursue had been dashed to the ground, and he was being forced to pluck a new one from a barrel full of rotten apples. "Do you think you can get past the soldiers without attracting notice?" he asked.

"That's asking a lot of Lord Flamboyantcrest, isn't it?" Sergeant Yara asked. Thanks to the slower pace, she'd caught up and joined the conversation. Wonderful.

"So long as the soldiers aren't female, I'm sure they won't look twice at me," Maldynado said. "You can all camp out in one of the parks on this side of the river. I'll go on my own, so you needn't risk yourself on my noticeableness."

"Noticeability," Books corrected.

"That too."

Books muttered a comment that included the word sashay, but Maldynado didn't pay attention. Sespian was scrutinizing him. His gaze had a weight to it that made him seem more formidable than his age and size suggested. Maybe it was simply the fact that he could order Maldynado beheaded with a wave of his hand. Even soldiers loyal to Ravido would have no qualms about complying with that order. Maldynado *was* an outlaw with a bounty on his head, after all.

"Very well," Sespian said.

Maldynado blinked. Distracted by the idea of axe-toting soldiers chasing him, he'd momentarily forgotten his proposition. "You'll wait while I go in? And get you a disguise? Do you want me to collect your belongings too? If your business is elsewhere, maybe there's no need for you to go into town at all."

"I'll fetch them myself," Sespian said, his tone cool.

Maldynado winced. He'd sounded too eager. If the emperor's "belongings" included the hundred thousand ranmyas he'd promised the team, he might think Maldynado wanted to make off with it. As if Maldynado needed to steal when he could find female patrons to finance his desires. But Sespian had no way to know that yet.

"Whatever you wish," was all that Maldynado said—an indignant proclamation about his trustworthiness would sound suspicious. "Does anyone else want a costume?" He propped his fists on his hips and eyed each of his teammates. "Never mind. You all look like you've been wrestling in a particularly muddy pigsty. I'll bring everyone clothing."

"Gee," Yara said, "a chance to be dressed by a fop who thinks a blue-dyed fur cap is stylish."

"Do you have any money?" Books asked.

Maldynado fished in his pockets and came up with a quarter-ranmya coin. He displayed it for the team and winked. "Far more than I'll need. You'll see."

"Good." Books plucked the coin from Maldynado's fingers. "I need a recent newspaper. Who knows what chaos has ensued in the days we've been out of the capital?"

Maldynado's shoulders slumped. The last person he wanted to go shopping with was Books. He could take the joy out of anything.

"Actually," Sespian said, "I'd prefer it if you stayed and talked with me, Professor Mugdildor. I have a few questions on finances and economics, and I believe you may be able to help."

"Oh, no." Maldynado lifted a hand. "You're new around here, Sire, so nobody's told you, but you do *not* want to ask Books for a lecture. You don't even want to ask a question that might lead to a lecture. It's bad for your health. And the wakefulness of those around you."

Maldynado smiled, expecting a chuckle from his warning, but only Akstyr smirked. Books scowled at him—nothing unusual there—and Sespian's lips turned downward too.

Basilard waved for attention and signed, *The soldiers may have spyglasses and wonder why a group of men are dallying by the side of the road.*

"Yes, yes," Maldynado said, "I'll go do my task. Where will you be waiting?"

"Crow Landing," Sespian said. "Take Sergeant Yara with you."

Speaking of taking the joy out of things…

Yara frowned, but she squashed whatever objection might have leapt to her tongue, and bowed toward Sespian. "Of course, Sire. I'll watch him."

"*Watch* him?" Maldynado asked. When had he become someone who needed *watching*? He'd been one of the first people Amaranthe recruited for the team, and he'd never failed to follow orders. Not like Akstyr. He could understand Sespian questioning his loyalty, but Yara? She wasn't even officially *on* the team. Maldynado looked to Books and Basilard for support.

Books cleared his throat and avoided Maldynado's eyes as he said, "I have voiced a concern over the fact that you went out of your way to arrange that dirigible for our transport, a dirigible that came with spies and a pilot who was happy to see us dead."

Maldynado gawked at him. Books was accusing him of betraying the team? And he'd already *voiced the concern*? In front of the *emperor*? It took a gargantuan effort for Maldynado to keep his fingers from clenching into fists, fists that could launch themselves into Books's nose. Didn't he know what a tenuous line Maldynado already walked, thanks to his family's plotting? "You think *I* had something to do with that?"

"You were quite insistent on Lady Buckingcrest," Books said.

"Because we needed to *fly* for the boss's scheme. Lady Buckingcrest is the only person I knew who could make that happen."

"Amaranthe did not request flight," Books said. "No sane person would. In fact, we had a lorry at our disposal that would have worked fine."

Maldynado wanted to argue. He wanted to explain that the main reason he'd been desperate to keep his distance from Amaranthe that night was because she'd had the look of a hound on the trail of a raccoon. She'd wanted to chat privately with him so she could finagle information on his brother out of him. But if he said so now, everyone would think he had a sly reason for not wanting to talk about Ravido. He hated his cursed brother, that was all, and talking about family history was painful. Why didn't anyone *get* that?

Maldynado looked to Akstyr and Basilard. He couldn't believe the entire team was suddenly suspicious of him. After all this time together? After so many battles fought and so many near-deaths?

Akstyr looked… indifferent to the conversation, or maybe tired. Either way, he wasn't patting Maldynado on the back in a gesture of support.

At least Basilard met his eyes. A crinkle furrowed his brow, as if he weren't sure why everyone was turning on Maldynado either. Good, but that might only mean that he wasn't from the empire and didn't care what Maldynado's relatives were up to. Still, Maldynado found himself asking, "Bas, you know I'm honorable and trustworthy, right?"

*I believe you would not intentionally harm the team*, Basilard signed.

Intentionally? So, Basilard just thought Maldynado was inept and had been fooled by some woman?

One of Akstyr's surly whatevers wanted to find its way to Maldynado's lips, but, no, he wasn't going to let them know how much this upset and rattled him. And he certainly wasn't going to give anyone another reason to believe him untrustworthy.

"Fine." Maldynado plucked his coin out of Books's fingers and handed it to Yara with a flourish. "The new person fetches Books's newspaper." Pretending he had no worries, he gave her his best smile. A sane woman would find it gorgeous and irresistible.

She scowled at him.

# CHAPTER 3

MALDYNADO CONSIDERED THE HAT-FILLED nook in Madame Mimi's Evenglory Boutique, lamenting the limited selection and the fact that most of the clothing in the shop featured the previous year's styles. He plucked at an orange-feathered scarf. It was unforgivable, really. Sunders City wasn't *that* small or *that* far from the capital. He was on the verge of walking out when a black hat, half-hidden on a stand bristling with garishly colored yarn beanies, caught his eye.

"Huh." Maldynado plucked it from its unseemly perch. "This might do."

This was the hat of a killer, a serious no-nonsense hat for serious no-nonsense people. Black, low, and sleek, it possessed the finest brushed velvet and represented quality craftsmanship. Maybe with this hat, Sespian and everyone else would take him more seriously. It oozed menace and whispered of blood-soaked deeds carried out by dark men of sinister purpose. Yes, this was *the* hat. He was vaguely surprised Sicarius didn't already own one. It could use an accent though. Maldynado tapped his lip thoughtfully, then added a large, bright pink plume so that it stuck jauntily out of the side. There. Perfect. He placed the hat upon his head.

"Can I help you, mister?" the shopkeeper asked.

*Mister*? Women usually took one look at Maldynado and assumed the title was "my lord." He supposed, in his swamp-bathed clothing, he *did* have the appearance of street riffraff. He'd have to disavow the woman of that notion.

Turning, Maldynado swept the hat from his head and offered a deep warrior-caste bow. The aging female shopkeeper wore so much lip paint and rouge that he was surprised her face hadn't fallen off under the weight. That didn't keep him from offering his brightest smile.

"Actually, my lady," Maldynado said, granting her the title, though he knew from the shop's name that she wasn't warrior-caste, "I may be able to help you. I see that, despite your prominent location on the River Walk, I'm your only customer."

"It's normally busier than this, but the hour grows late."

Now that Maldynado faced her, she gave him a more appraising look, perhaps noting the quality of the tailor-made garments beneath the grime of the road—and far too many crashes for one week.

Maldynado assumed a pose that showed off the breadth of chest. "As busy as you'd like? My siblings and I were robbed by riverboat pirates, and I'm in dire need of clothing that will hold us until we return to our estate in the capital."

She'd been taking note of his physique while he spoke, though she frowned when he mentioned needing free clothing.

"This, of course, would be a hardship for you, but in exchange for your generosity, I'd be willing to talk up your shop in my circles. Many of my comrades travel downriver to Markworth in the spring, and I could suggest they stop here, the wonderful boutique where I received exquisite service." He gave her a conspiratorial wink.

"I…"

It wasn't much of an offer, but she seemed flustered beneath his gaze. Good. The middle-aged ones tended to be more wise to the ways of men and could represent more of a challenge than the younger ladies, but all that war paint had to be hiding a few features that made men scarce. Judging by the flush of her cheeks and the number of appraising glances she stole when he wasn't looking, she appreciated his attention. A hint of calculation entered her eyes, though, and he started to grow concerned.

"You're offering free advertising, you say?" she asked.

"Essentially."

"I must see how you'd look in my store's clothing. Naturally you'd need to be a good representative if your recommendation were to leave an impression on people."

Maldynado wanted to snort and proclaim that he looked good in *any* store's clothing, but she was already bustling about, assembling an

outfit. She laid a stack of garments in his arms and smiled. Maldynado waited for her to direct him to a fitting room. She didn't.

"Do you have a changing area?" Maldynado asked.

"Alas, it's closed for repairs." Her smiled deepened.

Ah, so she wanted a show. Maldynado shrugged, set the clothes down, and unbuttoned his shirt. He'd undressed for far less noble purposes. Besides, when a man had a flawless physique, he really owed it to the world to share it in all its glory. While he changed, he glanced at the front door a few times, hoping Sergeant Yara would wander in. She'd chosen to wait on the street—keep watch, she'd said—but maybe she'd grow bored and check on him.

The shopkeeper assisted Maldynado in putting on her clothing, doing more touching than the act required. She also made him try on five different ensembles before finding one that he'd "represent well." Maybe, for enduring this, he'd barter for *two* outfits for everyone on the team.

A half hour later, the dressing and shopping were done. Unfortunately, Yara never came in. Maldynado was on his way to the door when the shopkeeper glided to a stop in front of him with a large stack of business cards in her hand.

"Here you are, my lord." She stuck them in his pocket. Pockets, actually, as the sizable stack required dividing. "You promise you'll hand them out to those in your circle, right?" She tilted her head back, gazing into his eyes with her own imploring ones.

A twinge of guilt ran through him, and, he knew as soon as he nodded his head that he'd actually have to do it. A fib now and then was one thing, but a promise? He couldn't break that, even if the "circle" he ran in now wasn't terribly likely to shop on the River Walk at Sunders City.

When Maldynado stepped outside, his arms laden with bags, the setting sun gleamed orange on the water. Despite the reluctant promise he'd given, he felt good. The sexy new hat perched atop his wavy curls, and his dirty garments had been replaced by practical travel wear: a leather duster, suede shirt a touch snug across the chest so that it emphasized his musculature, and fitted trousers that emphasized… other things. If Yara still had that quarter-ranmya coin, he might arrange to accidently bump it from her fingers, so he could take a while picking it up in front of her.

But where was Yara? He searched for her amongst the handful of pedestrians strolling down the shop-lined cobblestone street. The area wasn't as busy as he remembered from his youth, though the chill in the air might explain that. A nippy breeze gusted down the river, hinting of rain, or maybe snow. Smoke billowed from a stack on a steamboat chugging upstream, making Maldynado think of warming his hands by a fire. A fire in a suite in a fine inn preferably, but he supposed he needed to return soon with the clothing if he didn't want Sespian to grow weary of waiting and go off on his own.

Maldynado finally spotted Yara in an alcove of a brick building, her back to the wall as she alternately watched the street and read a newspaper. Ah, too bad. She must have spent the coin.

"Good evening, my lady," Maldynado drawled as he approached. "Enjoying the view?" He extended a hand toward the water.

"No, you useless fop." Yara thrust the front page of the newspaper out for his perusal.

With his arms full of bags, Maldynado couldn't easily grab it, but he leaned closer to read the headline in the fading light. "Emperor Sespian Savarsin Missing. Huh, that's a newspaper from the capital." In fact, it was *The Gazette*, the paper Deret Mancrest's family owned. "They couldn't possibly have gotten the news about the kidnapping yet." Unless someone had *known* Sespian wouldn't be coming back from his train trip. Deret couldn't be involved with the plotters, could he?

"Keep reading," Yara said.

"Due to our missing emperor, as well as last week's deaths of prominent businessmen and women, a military contingent from Fort Urgot has been deployed to occupy the capital and the Imperial Barracks. These forces will protect the citizens and ensure peace while Emperor Sespian is sought."

"Ensure peace." Yara snorted. "More likely they want troops loyal to your brother to be in place when they decide the emperor is no longer missing but dead."

"I wish people would stop calling Ravido *my* brother, as if I'm responsible for his actions." A half mile downriver, soldiers were still stationed atop the bridge, stopping people as they passed. On the way across, Maldynado hadn't been delayed long enough to learn why the men were on guard—dropping the Marblecrest name had earned him

and Yara prompt passage into the city—but now he understood. Garrisons all over the empire would be alert after an announcement of a missing emperor.

"Yes," Yara said, "it's clear you don't want to be held responsible for anything. I'm surprised you volunteered for something as crucial as shopping."

"People who take responsibility get blamed when things go wrong. No responsibility, no blaming. That's how this old chap prefers it."

Yara folded the paper and stepped away from the wall. "You'll never get your statue."

"What? Why?"

She had already turned her back and was striding down the street. Maldynado hustled to catch up with her, his shopping bags tangling with his legs.

"I'm a good fighter, and I've helped the boss out a lot. She's going to be all right. She's probably escaped already and is figuring out how to deal with all this." Maldynado waved at the newspaper tucked under Yara's arm. "She'll come up with a plan to get Sespian back to the Barracks and to stop Forge for good. I'm trustworthy and loyal, despite what the others think right now, and I'll be with her, ready to fight. I'm behind her until the end."

"They don't make statues of people who walk behind others. You have to walk out in front." With those words, Yara increased her pace and pulled ahead, as if to let him know she was done with the conversation. And him.

Maldynado caught himself slowing down. She'd been derisive, and his first thought was to brush off her words, but he grudgingly admitted there might be something to them.

On her way by, Yara brushed past a pair of pretty young women, giggling and pointing in windows as they strolled down the sidewalk. They noticed Maldynado, exchanged whispers, and one gave him an inviting smile. The idea of accepting that invitation teased his thoughts. It'd be nice to forget Yara, the emperor, and the suspicions of the team for a night. But he kept walking. There was too much at stake, including Sicarius's threat.

Sighing, Maldynado passed the pair with no more than a nod. When the inviting woman's smile turned into a disappointed pout, he almost changed his mind. He hated to be the cause of feminine dismay.

While he gazed back with those second thoughts, something else drew his eye. Across the street another pair of women had walked out of a single-story antique shop bestowed with mildew-covered shingles and a multi-paned window so old one would have to press one's nose to the glass to see any of the wares inside. The structure seemed out of place on the street of sleek, modern buildings that overlooked the river, but that wasn't what captured Maldynado's attention. One of the women, the shopkeeper perhaps, withdrew a keychain and bent to lock the door. The second woman... was one of Maldynado's cousins.

If he'd taken the time to think about it, he would have remembered that he had kin in Sunders City, but seeing her surprised him. Cousin Lita was his age and, with thick brown curls that tumbled about her shoulders, possessed the family good looks. She and her two brothers had come up to stay on the main Marblecrest estate a couple of summers when their parents had been traveling.

Maybe he should stop, say hello, and try to inveigle gossip out of her. When the emperor had suggested Maldynado might be a source of information, he'd balked at the idea of betraying his family, but that had been before he knew everyone was suspicious of him. Maybe a few choice tidbits about Ravido would placate Sespian and the others. Lita had always been a gossip and a chatterbox, so, if anyone had choice tidbits on the family, it'd be her. Of course, if Maldynado *did* extract and share crucial details, he'd have to live knowing he'd turned snitch on his kin. That didn't sit well with him.

Before he'd decided whether to cross the street or not, Lita's head turned in his direction. Her hazel eyes widened, and her mouth dropped open.

Maldynado lifted a shopping-bag-laden arm in a wave. After waiting for a group of young women to cycle past on elaborate tricycles burdened by baskets bulging with purchases, Maldynado crossed the street and bowed to the two ladies. Lita held a yellowing ivory box in her hands.

"Good evening, Lita, and..." He gave his cousin a chaste smile, then offered the shopkeeper a sexier one. Though she was an older woman

dressed in unrevealing clothing more appropriate to a dusty library basement than River Walk Street, Maldynado had long ago learned to be gracious to all ladies. Some of them were like rose buds, simply needing a little sun and encouragement to blossom into attractive flowers. And, those who weren't like that… tended to know others who were.

"Ms. Pealovetch." The woman looked him up and down, sniffed once, and walked away.

Then again, some women were simply grumps who weren't worth the effort.

"Maldynado!" Lita blurted. "I'm surprised to see you here." She eyed his bags. "Well, not surprised to see you shopping, but surprised to learn you're in Sunders City. Did you take your father up on his offer?" She must have seen his brow furrow, for she added, "Or, if you've been out of town, maybe you haven't seen him lately? Did you *know* about his offer?"

"I haven't talked to Father in over a year. Is there something I should know?" Maldynado couldn't ask for a better lead-in to family gossip.

"He's been looking for you. Didn't you hear? He wants to invite you back into the family."

"He what? I mean, he was rather adamant that I'm a worthless leech who doesn't deserve any portion of the family lands or money."

"Yes, Uncle Brodis has always seemed… tough, but I heard he was willing to forgive you for past transgressions if you'd return home and help the family with, oh, I'm not sure what it was. A business endeavor perhaps? Your sister-in-law, Mari, has grown quite entrepreneurial of late."

"Has she?" Since Mari was Ravido's wife, Maldynado tucked the detail away for later examination. The news about his father interested him the most. Could his parents want help for Ravido? Were Father and Mother supporting his throne-usurping enterprise? Maybe Maldynado's kin had learned that he'd gone from unambitious duelist to veteran warrior in the last year. Maybe Ravido wanted Maldynado on his team. Though it seemed unlikely. All of Maldynado's experience suggested that, even if he single-handedly turned back a Kendorian invasion in front of all of his kin, they *still* wouldn't believe him more than a dandy.

Lita released her box with one hand and gripped his arm. "I do hope you'll consider it, Mal. I know your parents are strict and hard to love,

but it's been fifteen years since Tia… passed on. Your mother has for-given you, and your father… I'm not sure he'll ever forgive you, but I think he forgets sometimes."

Mother had *forgiven* him? Since *when*? Maldynado found that news harder to believe than the rest of it, and, for the first time, he eyed Lita with suspicion. Even if she did live in Sunders City, what were the odds that they'd randomly run into each other here, in a town of fifty thousand?

Perhaps noting his suspicious mien, Lita shrugged and said, "Is it so hard to believe? They can't hate you forever. Old wounds may always ache in bad weather, but sometimes you forget there was a time when you didn't have them, and you lose your bitterness over the cause. The dull ache becomes a part of your life."

"I guess," Maldynado said neutrally. Nothing about Lita's face or words seemed duplicitous, but he'd known many women with a knack for convincing fibbing.

Lita squeezed his arm and let go. "If you prove to the family that you care, that you're willing to help out, they'd be more amenable to you. Especially your parents. I'll be the first to admit that some of your brothers are nettlesome and perhaps not worth the effort."

Maldynado snorted. Yes, Lita had suffered numerous dunkings in the lake at the hands of her older cousins. And they hadn't even *disliked* her. They'd been worse to Maldynado, but that was the nature of older brothers, he supposed.

"All you'd have to do is talk to your father and let him know you're interested in taking some responsibility."

Maldynado lifted his arms skyward, bags rustling. "What is it with women? Always nattering in a man's ear about responsibility."

"As a warrior-caste scion, you're expected to—"

"I know, I know." Maldynado stretched his hand out, palm facing her. "I'm just feeling set-upon by your sex of late. The only woman who doesn't—" He caught himself. He was supposed to be getting details, not giving them. She didn't need to know about Amaranthe, though an uncomfortable lump formed in his throat at the thought of her. Lita was the only woman who simply accepted what he was willing to offer with-out making extra demands on him or bemoaning the fact that he wasn't "responsible." Cursed ancestors, he hated that word.

"It's just that they had such high expectations for you, Mal," Lita said when he didn't continue. "Aside from Ravido, most of your brothers had respectable but not exemplary military careers, and even he, I've heard, used bribes and favors to ensure he eventually advanced to general. For another family, respectable sons are fine, but for Marblecrests? For a family with a history full of fleet admirals, legendary generals, and even Turgonian emperors?"

"It's easy to get buried under that much history," Maldynado said.

Lita sighed at him, as if they were speaking in two different languages, and she couldn't get him to understand. "If you'd had mediocre talent, it would have been one thing, but you were so good with a blade. And, when you were younger, your grades were all above average, especially when it came to military studies. Uncle Brodis was sure—"

"I know what he was sure of." Maldynado noticed his shoulders were hunched up to his ears. He hated talking about this stuff. He'd wanted the family's current gossip, not a rehash of old history. His earlier suspicions that Lita had been planted in his path disappeared. She wouldn't be *nagging* him if she wanted to talk him into something. "It doesn't matter. I'm not interested in reuniting with them." Maldynado tipped his hat. "It was good seeing you, Lita. Give my good regards to your brothers, please."

"Mal, wait." Lita must have forgotten she'd been holding the ivory box, for, when she stretched out with her hands, it slipped from her grip.

Maldynado squatted and caught it before it clunked onto the cobblestones. The lid flopped open, and a small black sphere fell out. It took another quick snatch to keep it from falling to the ground and rolling down the street. Maldynado gaped at the cool, smooth object. Utterly devoid of symbols, it appeared to be made of the same material as Sicarius's knife. And, if Sicarius was right, that'd mean it was made of the same material as that flying craft too.

Lita laughed. "What fabulous reflexes. See? That's what I mean. You're not mediocre at all when it comes to innate talent."

Maldynado tore his gaze from the sphere, lest his interest strike Lita as odd. He stood and cleared his throat. "Mediocre? Me? Naturally not. The ladies have known of my innate talent for ages." On the outside, he waggled his eyebrows and launched a speculative look at a passing woman; on the inside, his pounding heart threatened to leap out of his chest and sprint a few laps around the block. After Lita finished rolling her eyes, Maldynado asked, as casually as he could, "Say, what is this thing?"

"The box or the ball?" Lita asked.

"The ball. I've seen enough dust-collecting knickknack holders to not need an explanation on that thing."

Lita laughed again. "Oh, Mal. You're so silly. That's an antique ivory snuff box from the Tarovic Era."

"Yes, as I said, a dust-collecting knickknack holder. And the black doohickey?"

"I have no idea, but your sister-in-law sent me to pick it up for her. She's collecting them, I gather."

Lita reached for the sphere. Maldynado stifled the urge to snap his fingers shut about it, and she plucked it from his grasp.

"It's interesting, I'll admit," Lita said, "but I don't see why one would want a collection."

Not unless that collection included a super powerful aircraft with firepower that would make Turgonia's best warship roll over and cower under the waves. "I have six sisters-in-law. Which one did you say is collecting?"

"Mari."

"Ah." Ravido's wife again. Maldynado might have found his information for the emperor. "You know, Lita, I think you may be right. If there's a chance to reunite with the family, I *should* take it. After all, one never knows how long one's parents will be around. You don't want to later regret missed opportunities to make amends."

Lita blinked a few times and peered up at Maldynado's face. Maybe he'd slathered too much icing on the cinnamon bun.

"I'm not going to rush to do as Father pleases, but maybe I'll stop by the estate when I return to Stumps." Maldynado gave the sphere an indifferent wave. "If you wish, I could give that to Mari in person. You were simply going to post it, I assume?" Inwardly, he shuddered at the idea of a potential weapon going through the mail.

"Actually, Mari's on her way down," Lita said. "I'm expecting her to arrive on the *Glacial Empress* in a couple of days."

Maldynado's fingers twitched. He wanted to get that sphere. If he could give it to the emperor along with this information, it could prove

that he had good intentions. But if he seemed too desperate to snag it… The last thing he wanted was for some cousin to tell Ravido that he might be angling to thwart his plot. He had enough to worry about already.

"Is she?" Maldynado asked. "And Ravido is coming as well?"

"No, he's busy with something in the capital. Did you hear? He was reassigned to Fort Urgot recently."

"I *had* heard that. I wonder why they moved him. Wasn't he a post commander somewhere down south?"

"The machinations of the army are beyond me."

Maldynado had a feeling he'd gotten as much information out of Lita as he would. As it was, she'd probably relay the details of the meeting to Mari, who might mention Maldynado's appearance to Ravido. Maybe he should have kept walking and pretended not to see his cousin after all. Still, he might be able to find out more about these black artifacts from Mari. If he was brave enough to visit her. The last time they'd been alone in a room together, she'd tried to take his pants off, no matter that her husband had been in another part of the house.

"As long as she's going to be in town, I'll have to stop by and visit her," Maldynado said.

"Do you know her well?"

"Not as well as she'd like," Maldynado muttered.

"What?"

"Nothing. Where'd you say she'd be staying?"

"Rabbit Island. The *Glacial Empress* stops there upon request, so that its warrior-caste clientele needn't mingle with the commoners at the city docks."

"Yes, of course."

Maldynado exchanged a few parting words with Lita—and foisted a couple of the boutique's business cards on her—before walking away, but he was already thinking of the ramifications of their meeting. With the luck he'd had lately, he might end up in more trouble than ever. Busy worrying over that possibility, he almost crashed into someone standing in the middle of the sidewalk.

Yara. After her dismissal, Maldynado had assumed she'd left town without him. He hoped she hadn't been close enough to hear the conversation—he hadn't been so oblivious to his surroundings that he

wouldn't have noticed her leaning against the wall behind Lita—but she might have caught a few words. And seen that black sphere.

"That was my cousin," was all Maldynado said. "Ready to rejoin the others?"

Yara considered him through half-lidded eyes.

"Or—" Maldynado hefted the bags, "—did you want to try on your outfit first? It's quite alluring. If you have curves under those bulky sweaters and unflattering enforcer uniforms, these garments will show them off."

"You're incorrigible."

"Yes, yes, I am." Maldynado smiled as they started walking, relieved that he seemed to have distracted her from whatever she'd been thinking about as she studied him. But they'd gone only a few dozen paces when she spoke again.

"Who's Tia?"

Maldynado stumbled. If Yara had heard Lita mention Tia, then what else had she heard? He'd been planning to share some information with the emperor, but now he'd be forced to divulge every detail. Grandmother's hairiest wart, his role as family snitch was assured. If they didn't sculpt statues of men who walked behind others, he was even more certain tattletales didn't earn them. He couldn't keep himself from glowering at Yara.

"I didn't know they taught eavesdropping tactics at the Enforcer Academy." Maldynado straightened his bags and continued down the street toward the bridge.

"Corporal Lokdon has never eavesdropped on you?"

"She doesn't need to. She always knows what I'm thinking whether I talk about it or not."

"So she knows about this Tia and the details of the estrangement from your family?"

"No, she's not as *nosey* as you." Maldynado gave Yara a pointed look. In truth, Amaranthe was nosier than anyone he'd ever met, but she hadn't dug into his history, at least not that he knew about.

"Perhaps, given your current predicament, you'd be wise to share everything you know with the emperor."

"You think it's within me to be wise?" Maldynado said it jokingly, but at the moment he had doubts himself.

"Less foolish might have been a better word choice." For once, Yara's face wasn't hard or condemning. Maybe it was the soft light of the sunset, but she actually seemed… sympathetic.

Maldynado's lady-wooing instincts kicked in, and he realized that he might win some sympathy from her if he shared his story. Almost as soon as she'd joined up with the team in Forkingrust, he'd been mulling over ways to get her into bed. Oh, she wasn't the sweet, voluptuous sort he usually went for, but she was handsome enough in her own square-jawed, hard-eyed way, and challenges always enticed him, at least when it came to women. Much like taming a tiger, there was an exhilaration in winning over someone determined to ignore, or even loathe, him. He'd never used Tia's story to win anyone over though, and he shied away from the idea. It would be disrespectful to her spirit. Besides, it wasn't as if the story would guarantee him sympathy. His family had condemned him over it, and maybe Yara would too. He'd certainly never forgiven himself.

"I'll keep your advice in mind," Maldynado said.

"Was this Tia one of your lovers?" Yara asked as they continued to walk. "Was there some scandal that embarrassed the family?"

The fact that she was asking questions surprised Maldynado. So far, all she'd done was throw insults at him. Why change now? He searched her face, wishing he was as good at reading people's thoughts as Amaranthe was. Yara seemed to be… looking for confirmation that he'd messed up his life because of some stupid affair. Maybe she'd have an easier time continuing to dismiss him that way. Why not? Most others did. He'd come to accept that, but the idea of someone thinking Tia had been some throwaway female roused his hackles.

"She was my little sister," Maldynado said.

The base of the bridge had come into view, and he quickened his step, leaving Yara to trail behind. He'd shared as much as he cared to that day.

\* \* \* \* \*

Amaranthe had expected a spacious cell, given the monstrous size of the aircraft—in her head, she had started calling it the *Behemoth*. Something stark, bleak, and black certainly, but roomy. Instead, Pike and his guards had taken her to an empty room with nothing but a surgeon's operating table in the center and a bronze-and-iron crate on the floor, the sort of thing one might stick a dog in for traveling. A small dog.

Without anything so friendly as a, "Welcome to your new home" or "Step in please, ma'am," the guards had forced Amaranthe into the crate, their strength and numbers defeating her attempts to fight the entombing. The inside lacked windows, grates, or even pinholes for light. What if she ran out of air? Her body tensed at the thought. In the cramped blackness, with her knees to her chest and her back, shoulders, and feet smashed against the walls, she couldn't do anything to release that tension, that fear. Relax, she ordered herself, and inhaled deep breaths, trying to find calm. It worked—sort of—but she found a new emotion too: disgust. The scent of lye soap clinging to the interior failed to hide the underlying odor of urine and feces. Pike must not be the sort to let his captives out for latrine breaks.

With no room to turn around or switch positions, Amaranthe almost dislocated a few joints when she probed the door and seams to search for weaknesses. A few minutes convinced her that there were none. There wasn't any noise either. If anyone remained in the room outside her crate, she couldn't hear signs of it.

After exploring her prison, there was little to do but sit and think. Especially about what would happen on that operating table. To distract herself, Amaranthe made a list of things she wanted to ask Pike. Perhaps it was overly optimistic, but she figured as long as she was in the enemy stronghold, she ought to gather what intelligence she could. And keep the conversation away from Sicarius.

The idea of betraying him worried her as much as thoughts of Pike and that table. It had happened before, when that shaman, Tarok, had used the Science to delve into her mind. She'd been powerless to stop him. Sicarius had killed Tarok before he could spread any secrets, but Sicarius wasn't here. If the information escaped through her lips, there'd be no one to silence Pike.

She dropped her chin onto her chest. In the first few months she'd known Sicarius, before they'd developed a... friendship—yes, she felt confident in calling it that—Amaranthe had wondered if he might ponder the benefits of her death. With his dearest secret in her head, she represented a threat to him. Anyone who learned that Sespian was his

son could use Sespian to strike at him. After a lifetime as an assassin, Sicarius had a long list of enemies who'd like to do just that. Amaranthe also represented a threat to the stability of the empire, or at least Sespian's right to rule. Sicarius had to have thought of that from time to time, that if he got rid of her, this very scenario could never play out. But he hadn't, and here she was. She could *not* betray him.

When hours passed and nobody came to question her, Amaranthe drifted back to less useful thoughts, like what would happen on that table. Logically, she knew she had to keep her mind busy lest self-pity, defeat, and fear start to gnaw at her, and she knew also that being stuffed in that tiny crate was meant as some marinade to tenderize the meat before roasting it. But the discomfort of growing thirst, hunger, and muscle cramps from being unable to shift positions intruded upon her thoughts, making it difficult to send her mind elsewhere. Most of all, she noticed the silence, the utter lack of anyone with whom to talk. Sicarius would probably find the solitude restful, but Amaranthe *liked* being around people. A few days with no one to talk to and she'd be in the right state of mind to babble every secret to Pike.

"Easy, girl," Amaranthe whispered. "Don't let him break you before he's so much as plucked an arm hair out."

A soft clank sounded, the first noise to penetrate the metal walls of her crate. Someone had entered the room. Amaranthe wished she could maneuver her feet beneath her, to prepare to spring out and attack—or flee—if she saw the opportunity, but the tight space denied that much movement. Several moments passed, and nobody opened her door. Ear pressed to the wall of her prison, she listened for voices or footfalls. Maybe there were people out there, but the crate possessed a sound-dampening quality that kept her from hearing them.

When the door swung open, Amaranthe spilled out. Light blinded her, and she squinted her eyes shut. Her legs were numb after being locked in one position for so long, and she couldn't feel her feet, much less get them beneath her. Several hands grabbed her and hoisted her from the floor. No, not hands. Something harder, colder.

Amaranthe forced her eyes open and urged them to adjust to light as harsh and as brilliant as the sun. It emanated from all directions, the walls, the ceiling, and even the floor, though there were no lanterns or obvious sources.

Whatever held her was moving her through the air. It halted with a jolt.

"No, not that one, *that* one. Yes." Odd. It was a woman's voice.

Amaranthe's eyes finally adjusted to the light. She hung horizontally in the air, face toward the ceiling. The first things she made out were six black bars, or maybe arms, around her. They articulated and had six-pronged pincers at the ends, pincers that gripped her as effectively as human hands. She tried to squirm out of their grasp and decided they were *more* effective than human hands. The arms were attached to a vertical bar that attached to a blocky device—some machine, she sup-posed—mounted on the ceiling. The claw-like device carried her away from the crate and swung her toward the operating table. It appeared depressingly secure with a sturdy metal body and legs somehow sunken into the floor.

The gripping machine slid her onto the table, almost. She wasn't high enough, and her head clunked against the edge.

"Oops," came the woman's voice again, followed by a few words in another language. Curses, Amaranthe would guess. She tried to see the speaker, but the claw blocked her view. It bumped her against the table again before rising a couple of inches and laying her flat on her back.

"So this is how it's to go?" Amaranthe asked. "I'm to be beaten against things with strange alien technology until I talk?"

"It's generally not a good sign when the prisoners are mocking you," came Pike's voice from somewhere behind Amaranthe's head. The dry amusement in his tone surprised her. He hadn't struck her as someone human enough to have a sense of humor.

"I'm sure you'll put an end to that shortly," came a new female voice. "The girl needs practice with the equipment. It took too long to shoot down that dirigible."

Amaranthe's mouth sagged open. The voice was familiar. Her thoughts flashed back to her school days. One of… her teachers? Yes, that sounded like—

"I translated everything in the navigation chamber, Ms. Worgavic," the owner of the first voice said, "but even a year of study couldn't prepare me to understand and operate the *Ortarh Ortak* fully."

"Ms. *Worgavic*?" Amaranthe twisted her neck, trying again to see the speakers.

Ms. Worgavic had taught economics at the private business school Amaranthe had attended as a girl. It shouldn't be a shock that one of her old teachers had been drawn in by Forge—Larocka Myll had been providing scholarships for the school, after all—but Ms. Worgavic? She'd *liked* Ms. Worgavic. She still quoted the woman on occasion.

The claw pincers held Amaranthe fast, keeping her from seeing much, but the two female speakers walked over to stand beside the table. Yes, that was definitely Ms. Worgavic, a short, buxom woman with a few strands of gray in wavy black hair pulled back from her face with a clip. Dressed in a long wool skirt and short jacket that accentuated but didn't flaunt her curves, she was the epitome of professionalism, or so Amaranthe had always thought. Her teacher had changed little in the last ten years, though the spectacles perched on her nose were a new addition.

It took Amaranthe longer to identify the younger woman. She was even shorter than Ms. Worgavic and more chubby than curvy beneath her wrinkled clothing. A pencil perched above one ear, and, beneath it, a gold chain clipped to her collar held a monocle with a thick magnifying lens. She clutched a couple of books and had a finger stuck in one, acting as a bookmark. She was about Amaranthe's age, no, a year younger. That was right. She'd been in the class behind Amaranthe. Retta Curlev. That was it. A frumpy girl, who'd avoided eye contact with everyone, read constantly in class, and been teased often. Amaranthe might not have remembered her at all, except that Retta had an older sister who'd been a legend at school, holding all of the academic records, and reputedly never missing an answer on a test. The last Amaranthe had heard, the older sister had gone on to be some world-traveling entrepreneur. The younger sister had become… well, Amaranthe was about to find out.

A slight sneer twisted Retta's lips as she gazed down at the table. Amaranthe didn't think she'd ever participated in teasing the girl, but she doubted she'd offered her any kindnesses either. Their paths hadn't crossed often. Unfortunately, Retta had the look of an angry young woman out to take revenge on the world for the collective wrongs received as a youth. Still, talking to her and Ms. Worgavic *had* to be better than dealing with Pike.

"Afternoon, ladies," Amaranthe said. "It's nice of you to come visit. I've been lonely in my crate. Is this your flying vehicle? It's quite the technological marvel. Find it at an archaeological dig, did you?"

Retta's eyebrows flew up. Had she been wearing the monocle, it would have dropped away. She turned toward Ms. Worgavic, a question on her lips, but the older woman lifted a hand to silence her. One correct guess, anyway.

"Amaranthe Lokdon." Ms. Worgavic clasped her hands behind her back and shook her head slowly. "You were a promising student until you dropped out of school to become an enforcer... What a waste."

Amaranthe should have offered a witty comeback, or at least a good sneer, but she found herself blurting an excuse. "My father was dying. I had to take care of him, and, after he was gone, I couldn't afford to finish school."

Ms. Worgavic kept shaking her head. Given how often her team had thwarted Forge schemes of late, Amaranthe found it strange that her enforcer background seemed to disappoint Worgavic more than anything else.

"Your... ingenuity over the last year shows that you can find a way when you want something badly enough," Worgavic said. "You could have stayed in school, if you'd truly wished it. If nothing else, you had friends and were well-liked by your teachers."

Retta frowned at the last statement, perhaps remembering lonelier school years.

"Why didn't you simply ask someone for help?" Ms. Worgavic asked.

"I..." Erg, her old teacher had Amaranthe more on the defensive than Pike had. She had to figure out a way to cast old feelings aside; she was no longer a student yearning for the praise of a respected mentor. This woman was plotting against the throne and, for all Amaranthe knew, may have hurt or killed the men on her team.

"You used your father's death as an excuse to walk away from your education and the future he worked very hard to ensure you had. Why? Did you fear failure?" Worgavic shook her head again, a hint of disgust underlying her disappointment.

Amaranthe closed her eyes and took a deep breath. Worgavic was stirring up old doubts that Amaranthe didn't want to deal with, certainly

not then and there. Nobody had a knife to her throat—yet. It was time to ask questions of her own. "What I chose to do was stay loyal to the empire and the emperor. My father would not fault me for that." Even if he might fault her for spending time with assassins and taking the law into her own hands. "Why are you plotting against the throne? Why did you align with Forge?"

"Align with it, dear? I'm one of the founders."

If not for the mechanical arms holding her down, Amaranthe would have fallen off the table. As it was, the blatant admission knocked her other questions off the tip of her tongue.

Somewhere behind Amaranthe, a soft rasping started up. The sound of a blade being sharpened.

Worgavic spread her fingers, laid her hands on the table, and leaned as close as she could without bumping into the metal arms pinning Amaranthe. "You do remember your history? Yes? Good. Name a powerful imperial woman for me, will you? One who was powerful in her own right, not because she married or birthed someone important."

"Uhm, Lady Taloncrest supposedly ran twenty miles while eight months pregnant to warn Fort Darkling Spire of a Nurian invasion in 433." A fact Amaranthe only knew because she'd competed in running events as a youth, and one of the distance races was named after the woman. "She was given an advisory position on the emperor's staff."

"An honorary seat with no real power. And, as you said, she was *given* the position. Power is taken or created from within. Try again. Someone important, someone of whom Major Pike over there would have heard."

The rasp of the sharpening stone continued without pause.

"I'm unaware of the depths of his education. Was history a part of his Advanced Torture Techniques class?" As Amaranthe expected, that didn't draw a laugh from anyone in the room. Given time, and less ominous background noise, she might have come up with more examples of relevant women from the past, but she doubted Worgavic truly wanted them. She wanted Amaranthe to admit that women had had little influence throughout the empire's history. "Why don't you let me go, and I'll work on becoming someone important? I have plans, you know."

Amaranthe wriggled her eyebrows and offered a conspiratorial wink, not at Worgavic—if she truly was one of the Forge founders, there was no way Amaranthe would be able to sway her—but at Retta. Despite the sneer, she seemed the most likely person in the room to be won over. Retta blinked in surprise, but the surprise turned into a scowl, one that deepened when Worgavic looked her way.

"Don't include me in your plans," Retta rushed to say, probably worried Worgavic would find that wink suspicious. "I don't even like you."

"Why not?" Amaranthe asked, wondering if she'd offended the girl irreparably at some point.

Retta only scowled.

Worgavic tapped a nail on the table. "Whatever your plans were, they've failed, child. Emperor Sespian is dead. We incinerated your dirigible and everyone on it. Whatever it is you hoped to gain from opposing us matters little now."

Amaranthe's stomach clenched, but she kept her face neutral. She had no reason to trust Worgavic's words. "You wouldn't be asking me about Sicarius if you thought everyone had died on that dirigible."

Worgavic lifted a hand in acknowledgment. "It's true. We're not certain we got him. He's tougher to exterminate than termites, and he's ten times as annoying. Especially now that he has some vendetta against us." She lifted her eyebrows, as if inviting Amaranthe to explain.

"Huh," Amaranthe said, imitating one of Sicarius's unhelpful grunts.

"I will retrieve the information from her," Pike said.

"Yes, I imagine you'll be most efficient." For the first time, Worgavic's gaze softened as she regarded Amaranthe. "You needn't suffer through this. Just tell me why Sicarius has been protecting the emperor and if he'll continue to be a pebble in our shoes once Sespian has been replaced."

A pebble, right. A pebble that had killed thirty of her colleagues in a twenty-four-hour span. The rest of Forge had to be terrified that he'd come after them next. No matter how much security they'd set up, they must fear they couldn't hide from him forever.

"And then what? I tell you what you want to know, and you'll let me go?" After all the grief Amaranthe had given Forge, she couldn't believe anybody in the coalition would do anything except kill her.

Worgavic nodded. "You may have your freedom."

Amaranthe decided it might not be in her best interest to scoff openly, but Worgavic must have guessed at her skepticism. She leaned forward again, lowering her voice. "We aren't evil, Amaranthe. We're simply assuring our futures and the futures of our children. If Sespian had been amenable to working with us, he could have lived a long, healthy, and wealthy life. But since he was not, we've chosen another who's willing to grant our modest requests."

Maldynado's brother. How much had he agreed to give away in exchange for the throne?

"What *are* your modest requests?" Amaranthe asked.

"You see," Worgavic went on without acknowledging the question, "it matters little what man is in charge of the empire, so long as he works with us. Giving Sespian, or any other warrior-caste snob, your loyalty is pointless. And if it puts you on the wrong side, it's worse than pointless. It's to your detriment." Worgavic waved to encompass the operating table. "You must put your emotions aside and weigh, with dispassionate calculation, each opportunity that comes your way. Everyone in Forge understands that you can either make the future or be subject to its whims. What I do today ensures a legacy for my children and their children, and for the descendants of all who ally with us." Some vision only she could see filled her eyes. She and her Forge colleagues. "We have become a formidable force. Opposing us would be just as pointless as staying loyal to those who are destined to fall. Give me the information I seek, and you may walk away unharmed. I have no wish to see one of my former students, however misguided she may be, tortured."

Those vision-filled eyes never wavered, and Amaranthe started to believe the offer might be sincere. It didn't matter.

"You're wrong, Ms. Worgavic." Amaranthe turned her head away from the woman and stared up at the claw entrapping her. "Loyalty doesn't begin to have a point *until* it puts you on the wrong side."

Major Pike stepped into view, a three-bladed trench knife with a brass knuckle-guard in one hand and a rolled up canvas kit full of tools in the other. "Time to begin, eh?"

"Get the information," Worgavic said, "nothing more."

"Of course." Pike's smile was tight, his dark eyes gleaming. "Of course."

Ms. Worgavic strode out of sight, disappearing through a door that opened automatically and closed behind her. Surprisingly, Retta didn't follow her. Amaranthe wouldn't have thought her the type of person who'd want to watch a torture session.

Pike nodded toward her.

Retta hesitated, but only for a heartbeat beneath Pike's hard stare. She propped her monocle over her left eye and opened her book to the page she'd been holding. Her lips moved as she mouthed a few lines. After a moment, she closed the book, moved to the end of the table, and touched something on the side.

A click sounded, and pain slammed into Amaranthe from six directions. Her back arched, and she tried to buck off the table, but the claw held her fast. Something sharp—like swords being driven through her body—had sprung from the pincers, piercing her body at the thighs, wrists, and shoulders. Moving, what little she could budge, only increased the pain. Those blades had pierced straight through her body in each place, all the way to the table beneath her. She took short, quick breaths, trying to control the pain. It didn't work.

"I better go now," Retta whispered and hustled toward the door. Not before Amaranthe glimpsed distress in her eyes.

Little good that did. Pike, a smile on his lips, remained at Amaranthe's side, stroking his wicked knife.

# CHAPTER 4

TWILIGHT DARKENED THE BANKS OF THE GOLDAR River by the time Maldynado and Yara neared Crow Landing, an old mill yard that had been turned into a park after the timber industry waned. Lights burned in nearby cottages, but this quiet part of town lacked the gas lamps and multi-story tenements of the busier city across the water. No lamps at all burned in the park, though Maldynado could make out old donkey engines and cutting blades taller than men that had been turned into sculptures. In the fading light, they cast strange, dark shadows across the fields and trails.

Maldynado expected the emperor and the rest of the team to be waiting near the park entrance, but nobody called out when he and Yara arrived.

"Nobody's eager to try on their new clothing?" Maldynado asked, voice loud enough to carry.

Maybe the others were simply being cautious and staying out of sight. Not a bad idea. Maldynado had seen more soldiers patrolling the streets on the way out of the city core. It'd been so nice of Sicarius to run around assassinating people so that all of the authorities were on edge. One of the guards on the bridge had questioned why Maldynado and Yara were leaving the city so soon, and at night. Fortunately, Maldynado had annoyed the men into waving them through by overzealously handing out business cards and touting the clothing at Madame Mimi's Evenglory Boutique.

"Perhaps they're worried your outfits will accentuate their curves," Yara grumbled.

Maldynado shouldn't have mentioned her outfit. She hadn't seen the clothes yet, but she'd commented several times already that they'd be too frilly to be practical.

"The only thing curving on Basilard are his dagger blades. I have, on occasion, accused Books of having womanly attributes, but I don't think breasts are among them." Maldynado sniffed. "I smell a fire. Maybe they found a camp spot by the river."

"It's cold. Most of the houses around here have stoves going." Yara waved toward the homes abutting the park.

"Coal stoves, yes." Maldynado started down an unlit trail that seemed to head toward the shore. "I smell a wood fire. And is that the scent of cooking fish? Basilard must be making something for the emperor."

"I hope it's an improvement over those meat bars."

Though the gravel trail wasn't wide, Yara insisted on walking beside Maldynado on it. Perhaps she relished the idea of bumping arms and hips with him. He didn't mind, but figured it more likely that she simply refused to acknowledge him as her leader.

"Basilard's a fine chef. You'd be amazed at what he can do with roots and herbs scavenged from the middle of the woods." Maldynado patted his belly, intentionally bumping Yara's arm with his elbow. She scowled at him, and he smiled. "He'll fill our bellies with palatable victuals. A good thing too. Meals have been infrequent this week, and my pants are fitting too loosely. Women like to run their hands along your chiseled muscles; they're less enamored by the touch of boney ribs. I'm sure you'd agree."

"I don't let women touch my chiseled anything. I—what's that?" Yara pointed to the trail ahead.

Maldynado stopped. A shadowy form lay across the path, dark against the pale gravel. He sighed. "Given how things go for this crew, I'd guess a body."

"One of your people?" Yara's hand dropped to the short sword belted at her waist.

"I'd be terribly disappointed in their training if that were the case." Maldynado kept his tone light, but a tendril of concern wormed its way into his stomach. He set down his shopping bags, so they wouldn't encumber him in a fight.

"Someone one of your people *killed*?" Yara's tone grew harder.

While they spoke, Maldynado eyed their surroundings. The sculptures and hedges lining the park, along with the darkness itself, provided countless hiding places. Frogs croaked by the river. An owl hooted from the direction of an old mill, a two-story timber building a hundred meters away. Maldynado seemed to remember that it had been refurbished and turned into a dance hall at some point in the past. Right now, darkness blanketed it, and his imagination conjured not dancers but snipers crouched in the loft, observing the park through the open windows.

"Watch my back," Maldynado murmured and continued down the trail.

This time Yara let him go ahead. Hand on the hilt of his rapier, Maldynado crept closer to the still form. It was definitely a person, though low foliage on either side of the trail blocked the view of the head and legs. Black clothing covered the body. Good. Nobody on their team had been wearing black, unless Sicarius had come back for the purpose of dying on a random park path. That was about as likely as the man developing a sense of humor.

Maldynado drew his rapier and prodded the body. It didn't move. He crouched for a closer inspection and wished he'd thought to pick up lanterns while he'd been shopping.

Blood stained the gravel and saturated the person's shirt. Maldynado rolled over the body, revealing a man with short-cropped hair and a clean-shaven face. A soldier, perhaps, though the tight-fitting black outfit was more suited to an assassin's trade than the battlefield. A crumpled hood lay next to the head. Someone else had been there, trying to identify the man.

Soft crunches sounded behind him—Yara edging closer.

"Knife fight, I think," Maldynado whispered.

"You *think*?"

"Sorry, identifying killing techniques by starlight isn't something my boyhood tutors covered."

"If you hadn't spent so much time selecting curve-enhancing outfits, we could have stumbled across it in daylight."

Maldynado wasn't sure if that was a criticism or a joke. Maybe some of both. "I don't think it would have been here then. His skin is still warm."

Down by the river, the frogs stopped croaking.

Maldynado lifted his head.

"Your colleagues?" Yara murmured.

"Let's find out."

Though only a smear of twilight remained, Maldynado didn't want to stroll straight down the path where his silhouette might be visible against the distant backdrop of houselights. The gravel wasn't conducive to sneaking either. He veered into the knee-deep grass and wildflowers alongside the path and angled toward an old log-hauling wagon. Behind it, a row of hedges defined one of the park's boundaries. He and Yara could follow the shrubbery to the river, hiding in the shadows.

Dew drops dangling from the vegetation hadn't yet turned to frost, and water soon soaked the cuffs of Maldynado's new trousers. The mercenary life was *not* conducive to maintaining a fine wardrobe. He wondered what Cousin Lita and the rest of his family would think if they knew what he did for a living. Or maybe the family *did* know. Could that be why they wanted him back? If Ravido had learned that Maldynado had been training with the infamous Sicarius and had more combat experience than anyone else in the family, maybe he wanted Maldynado for help with the coup.

"Right," Maldynado muttered. Father was, more likely, embarrassed by having to explain that his youngest son was roaming around with outlaws and assassins. He probably wanted to bring Maldynado back and put him to work on one of the family's remote wineries, so he couldn't continue to make a spectacle of himself in the capital.

Distracted by the thoughts, Maldynado almost missed the soft *clack, clack* that whispered across the park.

"What was that?" Yara asked. She'd been doing an admirable job of walking silently behind him.

"It sounded like it came from the old mill."

Maldynado wondered if they should have searched in that direction first. The grounds around it were open, though, and, if someone waited in there, odds weren't in favor of being able to sneak up without being noticed.

"Let's check the river first," Maldynado said.

A dozen paces ahead, water lapped at the banks. The frogs remained silent.

The hedge ended at a pebbly beach. Downstream, a hint of orange came into view—burning embers in a campfire. Maldynado didn't see anyone, but reeds strangled the shoreline in places, and driftwood large enough to hide behind littered the beach.

Staying low, he headed for the fire. The grasses and vegetation weren't high enough to provide much camouflage, and Maldynado felt vulnerable as they approached, but nobody jumped out at them, nor did snipers start shooting from the mill. He and Yara reached the remains of the campfire. *Cook* fire, Maldynado amended, after almost stepping in a refuse hole filled with fish heads and bones. A flat rock by the fire held the oily remnants of a fried meal. Hints of green drew him closer. Yes, those were the remains of herbs—most people in the empire would call them weeds—that someone had chopped to add to the fish. Only Basilard would scavenge up seasonings for a meal cooked on a rock.

"They were here," Maldynado said.

Foliage rustled. That was the only warning Maldynado received.

He spun toward the brush in time to see a dark figure leaping out of the night at him. The outline of a knife was visible against the night sky, a knife meant to pierce Maldynado's back, but he dropped to his belly before his attacker reached him.

"Visitors," Maldynado barked for Yara's sake as he rolled away from the fire pit.

A *twang* cut through the air—a crossbow firing. The quarrel bit into the pebbles inches from Maldynado's face, spraying sand. He leaped to his feet, his rapier in hand, his back to the river. Two hooded men charged him. Two more men were already trading blows with Yara on the other side of the campfire.

Before Maldynado's attackers crashed into him, he leaped to the side of one. As Sicarius had so often demonstrated in group sparring practice, the way to fight multiple opponents was *not* to fight multiple opponents. If he kept one in the way of the other, he'd only have to face the nearest man.

As the closest figure spun toward him, Maldynado launched a feint-stab combination to test his opponent. With multiple foes to worry about, the temptation was to rush and try to finish one first, but a man in a hurry could make mistakes. Especially in such poor lighting.

Maldynado's feint didn't fool his attacker. Steel clashed against steel and the jolt of a hard parry from a heavier weapon ran up his arm. The follow-up came by way of a combination of slashes, alternating toward his chest and thighs. His foe wielded a saber, and Maldynado recognized the style. Pure army. The sort of combinations that were drilled into young soldiers during their early years of training. The attacks were competent, but lacked the lightning speed of something from Sicarius or even Basilard. Maldynado kept his feet moving, so the second man couldn't circle around his comrade, and parried blows while waiting for his foe to repeat a familiar pattern. Further, he used the man's body to block any snipers aiming at him from the brush.

The second man made a wide circle in a new attempt to reach his side, so Maldynado decided to take care of him first. Without slowing his parries, or looking at the encroaching foe, he dipped his left hand to his belt and drew the utility knife there. Using his swordplay to hide the movement, he readied the shorter blade to throw.

"What's the story with the hoods?" Maldynado asked, hoping to further distract the men. "The executioner look isn't in fashion this season, you know."

The hooded figure in front of him said nothing, though, as the saber blows failed to hit more than steel, his movements grew faster and choppier, a sign of growing frustration. Good. Maldynado would turn defense to offense in a moment, but he wanted the second man out of the ring first. He continued to defend, his sword gliding from side to side, eyes ostensibly focused on the opponent to his front, until the other fellow committed himself to a charge.

Without missing a parry, Maldynado hurled the knife. The blade took the man in the chest with enough force to stop him mid-run. He pitched sideways, hands clutching his chest as he thudded to the pebbles.

The attack startled the first man, and he stumbled on a rock. Maldynado knew he had the man off-balance and didn't bother with a feint. He batted his foe's blade to the side and lunged in, leading with his rapier. Under other circumstances, he might have tried to subdue his foe instead of stabbing him, but Yara, enmeshed in a battle of her own, might need help. His rapier slid between ribs, and the man screamed. His saber clattered onto the pebbles.

Maldynado pulled his blade free and raced around the campfire. One of Yara's attackers lay prone a couple feet away from her, but she was on the ground, entangled with the other. Even as Maldynado ran toward them, Yara yelped with pain, and the dark figure found his way on top. He straddled Yara, holding her down with one hand while the other raised a knife, ready to plunge it deep.

Maldynado leaped, kicking the blade as he came down beside them.

Yara's attacker snarled and reached for another weapon on his belt, but Maldynado launched a second kick, this time into the person's shoulder. The man tumbled sideways, helped aside by an angry thrust from Yara. She jumped to her feet, landing in a crouch, hands balled into fists. She snatched her sword up from the rocks and looked like she was going to ram it down the man's throat.

Not certain any of the other three would live, and figuring information would be helpful, Maldynado lifted an arm to block her at the same time as he stepped on the fallen man's shoulder to keep him from going anywhere. Yara snarled, and Maldynado wasn't entirely sure she wouldn't ram her sword down *his* throat. Saving a woman didn't count for as much as it once had.

Maldynado grabbed the man by the shirt and pinned him to the beach. His prisoner snatched a handful of pebbles and hurled them at him. They plunked off his chest. After what Maldynado had endured in the recent train battle, the pebbles were laughable. Using both hands, he hauled the man to his feet. More than his feet. The man lacked Maldynado's height, so his toes dragged across the pebbles. It wasn't necessary, but Maldynado hefted him a couple more inches into the air, in case such power might impress Yara.

She said nothing, merely yanking the figure's hood off. A young, short-haired man sneered at them.

"Who are you?" Maldynado asked. "Why'd you attack us?"

The prisoner growled.

"That's not an acceptable answer." Maldynado lowered one arm and curled his fingers into a ball. He wasn't much for torturing folks, but a fist to the belly often softened a man's resistance—or caused him to throw up on one's shoes.

*Twang!*

A crossbow quarrel sped out of the darkness and sliced into the outside of Maldynado's arm. He cursed and released his prisoner. The man sprinted for the river. During the split second Maldynado was debating whether to chase him or hurl himself to the ground and find cover—*idiot*, how had he forgotten the crossbowman?—Yara raced into the brush. Afraid she'd be shot, Maldynado charged after her.

Before he reached the undergrowth, foliage thrashed ahead of him, followed by a loud thunk.

"Awk!" came a man's pained cry.

Leaves rattled, and the crossbow wielder darted onto the beach, dropping his weapon when it caught on a bush. He leaped over the campfire and dove into the river. His comrade had already disappeared into the water. Splashes announced enthusiastic swimming, and Maldynado couldn't muster the desire to hurl himself into the river on a cold night to give chase.

"Brave men." Yara picked up the discarded crossbow and waved it in the air.

"Well, you *did* hit him," Maldynado guessed. "And you're an intimidating figure. He probably lost the urge to fight after he wet himself."

Yara snorted.

Maldynado headed for her, but paused, his gaze drawn by a light across the park.

"Thanks for helping," Yara half-mumbled. "Not that I couldn't have handled those two on my own, but, if I hadn't been able to, it's good you were there to—Maldynado, are you listening?"

"Uhm." Maldynado pointed at the mill building where soft green light glowed behind the windows and seeped out through cracks between the timbers. "This night is getting stranger and stranger."

\* \* \* \* \*

Maldynado and Yara crouched beside a rusty donkey engine ten meters from the mill. The stout machine, with its broad base and vertical boiler, offered the last bit of cover before one had to cross the gravel paths and short-cropped grass surrounding the old building. A pair of tall, split-log doors marked the front of the structure. One stood ajar, allowing a slash of sickly green light to flow out.

"What's the plan?" Yara whispered.

"I was hoping the rest of the team would show up and tell us," Maldynado said. They'd passed two more bodies on their way to the mill, but encountered no sign of their comrades.

"Do you always wait for others to take charge?"

"Surely, as an enforcer, you're familiar with the chain-of-command concept. And with being one of the lower links."

"Surely *you're* familiar with the concept of the lower links being capable enough to step up and take charge when the upper links aren't around."

A snippy comment came to Maldynado's lips, about how she wasn't taking charge or offering ideas either, but he merely said, "Not really. If Amaranthe is missing, Sicarius bosses people around. If they're both gone, Books lectures us until we submit to him. If those three are all gone… it's usually time to go find a drink and a woman." He rubbed his head. Maybe it was the arguing, but a headache had taken up residence behind his eyes.

"Your devotion to your duty is impressive," Yara said.

"You should be impressed that, in the absence of my teammates, I haven't dragged you off into the bushes to engage in carnal relations yet."

Yara bared her teeth. "You could try."

Maldynado wouldn't admit it, but he found the idea of facing rogue soldiers and creepy magic less intimidating. "I'll look in the mill. Watch my back, will you?" He flicked a finger at the crossbow Yara had claimed for herself.

"Acceptable."

At least she was willing to take orders if he gave them. Yara must believe that, as a newer member of the team, she held a lower rank than he did. Or maybe she just wanted him to be the one to wander in and get fried by some strange, light-emitting doodad.

After eyeing each window and door for signs of people—snipers, more specifically—Maldynado crept toward the closest wall. Full darkness had fallen, but the green light leaking between the timbers cast its glow onto the grass. His skin appeared sallow under the influence. His headache grew in intensity, and he thought of the device Shaman Tarok had deposited in the lake the spring before, and how its power had contaminated water over a hundred miles away, not to mention filling the forest with deranged glowing-eyed animals. Maldynado hoped this light lacked similar properties.

He paused a few steps from a window with a shattered pane. A crossbow quarrel protruded from the frame, and a second one had probably been responsible for the breakage.

Careful not to make a sound, Maldynado eased closer. Scratched and dulled by time, the window offered a poor view. He wiped away a circle of grime and spattered grass clippings from the last mowing. A single, large room with worn wooden floorboards stretched before him. Old mill machinery, the cutting blades removed, had been pushed into corners, leaving a large open area in the center. A squat cylindrical device sat on the floor, emitting the light from four holes in a dome-shaped top.

Two men lay crumpled on the floor on either side of it.

"Emperor's balls," Maldynado whispered. It was Books and Akstyr, neither of them moving. Maldynado wasn't even sure if they were breathing.

For a second, he thought about running inside and dragging them out, but the dull ache behind his eyes had turned to stabbing pain. He had to escape that light for a minute. He and Yara could figure out what to do from across the field.

Before Maldynado could step away from the window, cold, sharp steel touched his neck. Curse Yara, she was supposed to be watching his back.

His first notion was to hurl an elbow backward and try to catch his attacker off balance, but the dagger pressed deeper. Another hair, and it'd slice into his flesh.

Maldynado eased his hands out to the sides, palms open. "Mind if we step away from the light?" he murmured, careful not to let his emperor's apple dance about—and get cut. "I think it's melting my brain."

"Tell me what you know about it."

Maldynado's jaw dropped, a movement he promptly regretted, because it made the knife cut into his skin. But the speaker—the person with the blade to his throat—was the emperor.

"Sire?" Maldynado squeaked.

"Did you arrange for this trap when you were in town?"

"No! We were *shopping*. Look, I'll show you our bags. We left them on the path—"

"Sire," came Yara's voice. "He didn't arrange this. There was a conversation I should tell you about, but I heard enough to know it wasn't about sending men to your hiding place."

Maldynado bit his lip to keep from snapping at Yara for not warning him about Sespian's approach. Best to stand still and not dig himself into a hole—a deeper hole.

A long moment passed before the blade disappeared from Maldynado's neck. He touched his skin and grimaced when blood came away on his fingers.

Arms wide, Maldynado turned, intending to impress upon Sespian just how innocent he was, but the emperor was already stalking away. Basilard had joined Yara by the steam donkey. His approach must have kept her from noticing Sespian as he sneaked up on Maldynado. That Sespian *could* sneak so well was surprising. Maldynado might have to reassess his image of the young emperor as a harmless, bookish sort.

Basilard waved for attention as soon as everyone stood in the shadow of the donkey engine. Maldynado realized he was the only one there who could understand his hand signs.

*We routed the men in black, but we must figure out a way to retrieve Books and Akstyr.* Basilard pointed to the building. *That device didn't start glowing and affecting us*—he paused to touch his temple—*until they were inside. The men with the crossbows tried to ambush us while we ate. I noticed them coming, and we took to the field, but there were a lot of them firing rapidly. We decided to take cover in the mill. As soon as we approached, Akstyr said he sensed magic inside. We were being shot at, so he and Books volunteered to go in and investigate. I don't know if they turned the device on or if it fired up of its own accord, but they fell unconscious before they could run back out. It's been at least twenty minutes, and they haven't moved.*

"What's he saying?" Yara asked.

Maldynado translated.

When he finished, Sespian added, "It was a trap. I think we were all meant to be in there when the device turned on. I don't know how these men knew we were here—" the look Sespian gave Maldynado dripped with significance, "—but they did."

"Sire," Yara said, "it's possible the soldiers identified you when the group stopped on the road to discuss crossing the bridge. Just because we didn't have spyglasses doesn't mean *they* lacked them."

It felt strange to have Yara come to his defense, but Maldynado was relieved she was doing so. "How many of these blokes in black did you cut down?" he asked. "Any idea whose stray cubs they are?"

Basilard considered the park while he tallied numbers on his fingers. *Fourteen.*

"Fourteen?" Yara asked. "Just the two of you?"

Though he knew Basilard possessed a great deal of competence, not to mention the stealthy feet of a cat, even Maldynado found the number surprising.

*The emperor is a capable fighter*, Basilard signed.

Sespian watched his fingers, trying to learn the hand code perhaps.

"He says you're a capable fighter," Maldynado said when Sespian looked to him for a translation. "That's moderate to high praise from Basilard. If Sicarius ever says that, it'll mean you can thump ninety-nine out of a hundred men. Possibly all at the same time."

Yara snorted.

Sespian seemed less amused by the attempt at humor. "We must find a way to retrieve your comrades. The men who originally attempted to ensnare us in the mill are... gone—*dead.*" Sespian winced, apparently not pleased that he'd been forced to such action. "But it's possible they have allies around, allies who might have been alerted when the device went off. Practitioners can do things with their minds and create links to objects they made that are beyond our ken."

So, the emperor knew a thing or two about magic. That was good since their expert, insomuch as Akstyr could be considered one, was unconscious. Or worse.

"Any idea how to get them without passing out? I'll go in and do whatever needs to be done." Given how suspicious everyone was of him lately, Maldynado figured he'd better volunteer for heroics at every chance.

"I've been musing over that." Sespian squatted down, draping his elbows over his knees. "You've noticed how getting closer to the light causes pain behind your eyes?"

"Looking in the window made my head feel like someone had chained me down and forced me to listen to Books's lectures all day." Maldynado glanced about, expecting Books to glare at him or come up with a vocabulary-heavy rejoinder, before remembering that Books was in trouble. "Yes, I noticed," he said more seriously. "I didn't know if it was the light or something else."

*It's the light*, Basilard signed. *The pain intensifies when you look at it.*

"So, we ought to be able to close our eyes, stroll in, and collect our people?" Maldynado asked.

"You can still feel it through your lids." Yara had closed her eyes and turned toward the beam slanting through the open door. Her brow wrinkled. "Pain." She turned her back on the mill. "No pain."

Maldynado lifted a finger, then trotted back to the riverbank. He grabbed one of the discarded hoods the men had been wearing. He'd assumed his attackers were trying not to be identified, but maybe they had another reason for donning the headwear. After a quick poke around the interior, he found a band that could be pulled down over the eye slits.

"Maybe this'll do it," Maldynado said when he rejoined the others.

Sespian, Yara, and Basilard were facing the park entrance, and nobody responded.

"What is it?" Maldynado asked.

*Machinery*, Basilard signed and touched his ear.

A faint rumble floated across the park from the street leading toward the entrance.

"Steam carriages or lorries," Yara said.

"More than one," Sespian said.

"They might not have anything to do with us," Maldynado said.

The others looked at him as if he'd told them Sicarius's next training session would be easy.

"Where's the optimism?" Maldynado waved the hood. "I'll get our lads. Someone yell at me if I'm about to trip or crash into the wall."

"Wait." Yara touched his arm. "We don't know if…" She nodded toward the mill. "There's no way to know if they're still alive, is there?"

Basilard and Sespian exchanged looks.

"We couldn't tell without going inside," Sespian said. "They haven't moved."

"I'm sure they're alive," Maldynado said. "Captured prisoners are more useful than dead ones, right?"

"I... am not certain I'd risk my life on that assumption," Sespian said.

"That's what I'm here for." Maldynado flung an arm around Yara's shoulders. "Don't look so concerned, my lady. I'll not die before I've fulfilled your most concupiscent fantasies."

Yara shoved his arm away. "We've discussed you not touching me numerous times now."

"Does this mean no good-luck kiss?"

The rumbling machinery grew louder, and lights brightened the street leading to the park entrance. Enough trading endearments with Yara. Maldynado had best get going.

Before he could think wiser of it, he tugged on the hood and, arms outstretched, headed for the mill. The soft, black fabric had multiple layers and blocked out the green glow, but he clamped his eyelids shut anyway.

Probing the ground with his toes as he went, Maldynado reached the building without mishap. He mashed his knuckles against the door, but at least his head didn't hurt.

The noise from the vehicles drifted across the park. They sounded like they'd pulled to a stop. He hoped they were in a spot where they couldn't see him.

A thud sounded—someone getting out and a door being shut?

"Hurry, Maldynado," came Yara's whisper.

Maldynado slipped through the front door of the mill and felt his way inside. He slid his boots along the floorboards, hoping he wouldn't get turned around and crash into some ancient piece of machinery with sharp protuberances. His foot came down on a bump, and it took him a second to realize it was someone's hand.

"Oops. Sorry, fellows."

He bent, found the hand, and used it to hoist the prone person over his shoulder. Akstyr, he guessed, as Books was taller and heavier. He didn't take the time to check for a pulse, but the skin felt warm to the touch.

Maldynado patted around with his feet, trying to find Books. In picking up Akstyr, he'd lost his sense of direction. When he thought he

must be close to the second body, he clunked into the magical device instead. With his knee. He cursed and thought about trying to kick the thing over, but it might have defensive capabilities.

A soft bang came from outside. It didn't sound like a musket or pistol, but Maldynado had a feeling he shouldn't linger.

He probed about, faster now, not worrying if he kicked Books. He could apologize later. His toe caught on clothing. There.

Balancing Akstyr on his shoulder, Maldynado grabbed Books by the arm. He debated trying to hoist him over his other shoulder versus dragging him out.

A clack sounded at one of the windows. Someone throwing a rock in warning?

A long squeal came from the park entrance.

"Time to go," Maldynado muttered.

He dragged Books toward the exit as fast as he could. He smacked face-first into the wall and loosed another string of curses before managing to find the door. He kicked it open, no longer worrying about being seen.

He'd gone no more than two steps when something slammed into the mill behind him. Wood cracked and the ground shuddered.

If Maldynado had a hand free, he would have yanked the hood off, but he couldn't let go of his comrades. Still dragging Books, he staggered in the direction he thought he'd left the others. Another crack sounded inside the mill, followed by the patters of dozens of objects hitting the walls and the ceiling. Shrapnel? From an exploding cannon ball or something similar?

Maldynado had no sooner had the thought when an explosion roared behind him. The force hurled him to his stomach. Instead of turning the fall into an efficient roll that would prevent injuries, he grew tangled with Books and Akstyr and sprawled flat. He lost the grip on one man— Akstyr?—and the other landed on top of him. Still unconscious, they were dead weight.

Maldynado pushed them away long enough to tear off his hood.

Half of the mill had collapsed, the roof and two walls tumbling inward, and flames leapt from the remains. The orange glow of the fire brightened the sky in every direction. The green glow had been dulled— beams falling on the device perhaps—but it still leaked into the night,

and Maldynado's headache returned. But not enough to slow him down. He leaped to his feet.

"This way," Yara barked from somewhere ahead.

Basilard appeared by Maldynado's side and hoisted Books over his shoulder. Maldynado maneuvered Akstyr into position over his own shoulder. They hustled to reach the others.

Shouts came from the park entrance. Dark figures poured out of two lorries and ran toward the mill. They carried rifles and pistols, not crossbows, and they were closing ground quickly. Books and Akstyr hadn't stirred yet. As fit as Maldynado and Basilard were, it was unlikely they could outrun trained soldiers while carrying the weight of full grown men over their shoulders. They needed…

"I have an idea for a distraction," Maldynado whispered just loud enough to be heard over the crackling fire that had engulfed the mill. "Yara or, uhm, Sire…" Was it unseemly to ask the Turgonian emperor to tote one's comrade on his back? No time to worry about it. "Can you carry Akstyr? I'll—"

As one, Sespian and Yara grabbed Akstyr. Maldynado waved toward the neighborhood on the far side of the park. "Head that way. I'll catch up with you."

Gravel crunched. The newcomers, at least a dozen of them, were surrounding the burning mill. They didn't seem to realize that Maldynado had made it out of the building. With all the light the fire threw off, they would soon.

After Basilard and the others moved a ways into the darkness, Maldynado sprinted toward the river. He thrashed through the foliage, making as much noise as he could. A rifle fired, and he dove to the earth, rolling to gain ground as he went. More shots fired over his head, but the branches stabbing him as he careened past were more painful. As soon as his momentum faded, he found his belly and low-crawled toward the river at top speed.

Though damp leaves slapped at Maldynado's face, and roots sought to entangle his arms and legs, he made it to the beach without slowing—or being shot. The rifles had stopped, but snaps and rustlings in the brush behind him promised pursuit. That was good… so long as he had time to put his plan into action before they caught up with him. Unfortunately, the men, running instead of crawling, were gaining ground

quickly. Lanterns rattled and banged as people tore down the trail to the beach.

Maldynado veered toward the campfire. Only a couple of dull red embers still glowed, not enough to illuminate the beach. Good.

Maldynado found the body of the man he'd stopped with the knife throw. He dragged it to the edge of the water, then risked rising to his knees to gain leverage. Careful not to grunt or make a sound himself, he hefted the body with both arms and hurled it as far as he could.

It landed with a noisy splash that ought to be audible for dozens of meters in each direction. Maldynado grabbed a few sizable branches from the woodpile by the fire pit and tossed those in too.

"There!" one of his pursuers shouted. "They're trying to swim away."

Yes, keep believing that, Maldynado thought as he crawled back toward the foliage. Doing his best to emulate a snake, he shimmied into the weeds even as the riflemen stormed onto the beach. Pebbles clattered and flew under the barrage of boots.

Maldynado's first instinct was to crawl straight toward the far side of the park, in the direction he'd sent the others, but he remembered his shopping bags. They lay discarded by the path where he and Yara had come across the first body. He stifled a groan. To leave empty-handed, without the emperor's disguise or any of the clothes he'd bargained for, clothes he'd desperately need when dawn showed him just how many new grass- and dirt-stains plagued his current attire…

Maldynado kept crawling away from the river, but lifted his head, trying to gauge where he'd left those bags. It wasn't far from the park entrance and the lorries. The darkness made it difficult to tell for certain, but he didn't think that more than one or two people stood guard over there. The rest were stomping around the beach, calling, "Can you see them?" and "Are you sure they went in?"

A new plan formed in Maldynado's mind, one of which he believed Amaranthe would approve. Still crawling, except where the foliage rose high enough to hide him as he darted forward in a running crouch, he angled toward the bags and the lorries. This wasn't an unnecessary risk, he told himself. It wasn't *just* for clothing. The others might need more time to escape. They were carrying two inert bodies, after all.

"Yes, give that excuse to Books when he's bailing you out of jail," Maldynado whispered to himself. "Or, more likely, lighting your funeral pyre." The sobering thoughts couldn't quite squelch the grin on his lips at the idea of his plan.

Maldynado reached his shopping bags. They'd been kicked into the foliage with a footprint mashing one.

"No respect for fashion around here," he whispered and, taking the bags with him, continued onward.

As Maldynado drew close to the lorries, he stayed lower than ever to avoid the notice of a guard stationed between them. When he circled around the back, he noticed the newness of the vehicles. He would have recognized military vehicles, but these were civilian models. Forge-owned toys?

Maldynado set his bags down and slipped between the two vehicles, hoping to sneak up behind the guard.

The shouts by the river had stilled. He hoped the men hadn't figured out his ruse.

Knowing he might not have much time, Maldynado lunged straight for the guard without checking to see if he had a friend in one of the cabs or on the far side. He took the fellow by surprise, wrapping an arm lock around his neck. Even as he cut off the man's airway, Maldynado forced him to the ground to steal his leverage.

A click sounded—a door opening.

"Emperor's *balls*," Maldynado cursed.

His plan to subtly take down the man by denying him air turned into slamming the bloke's head into the nearest lorry door. It clunked with satisfying solidity. He duplicated the move to ensure its effectiveness, then spun as a second dark figure launched a kick at his head.

Maldynado dropped into a butt-scraping squat in front of the man, just evading the attack. With both hands, he caught the fellow's calf before the foot could return to the ground. He leaped up, hoisting the leg over his head. The man pitched over backward.

Maldynado scrambled onto his foe and pummeled him into the ground. Amaranthe would choose tying people over beating them into a stupor, he admitted, but he didn't have time. So long as they were too battered to move for a few minutes…

When Maldynado stood, neither man did more than moan and curl into a ball. Good.

After a quick glance toward the river—lanterns still moved about on the beach—Maldynado climbed into the cab of the far lorry. He yanked open the furnace door for light and located the safety valve. He grabbed the coal shovel, flipped it, and used the handle to break the gauge. The loudness of the cracking glass made him wince, but he doubted he had time for a quieter tactic. He shoveled heaps of coal into the furnace.

"Oskat, what're you doing?" came a shout from the beach.

Uh oh. Maldynado hustled out of the cab of the sabotaged lorry, grabbed his bags, and climbed into the other vehicle. Whistling a little tune, he threw a control lever into reverse. The lorry belched smoke and rumbled backward.

"Oskat!"

"Hurry, they're stealing our lorries!"

By the time the men were racing back up the trail, Maldynado had the vehicle turned around and was rolling into the street beyond the park. Houses lined the curving avenues, so he resisted the urge to thrust the control lever to maximum speed. Besides, he didn't think he'd need to worry about pursuit. That second lorry shouldn't go far before the overburdened boiler became inoperable. Or airborne. One of the two.

Though Maldynado had only a vague recollection of the neighborhood, he took a few turns and found a route around the park. The shouts faded from hearing. As the lorry rumbled down a broad avenue lined with cedar-shingled houses, he was wondering how he would find the others when he spotted a shadow near the side of a corner market that had closed for the day. Yara?

He clucked to himself, slowed down the vehicle, and stuck his head out the window. Sicarius never would have let the team be so easily spotted. Yara was waving, though, so maybe she'd spotted him first. In the shadows of the building, Basilard supported a groggy Books while Sespian stood with Akstyr's arm slung around his shoulders. Maldynado's lip twitched as he recalled an imperial law about commoners not touching emperors.

"Say," Maldynado called, "do any of you gents, or ladies, need a ride?"

A boom sounded in the distance. Maldynado leaned out and craned his neck to look behind him. A plume of smoke rose from a street somewhere near the park.

"I guess they didn't notice that safety issue," he said blandly, then waved out the window. "You chaps coming? I don't know that it's wise to linger."

"Sire," Books said weakly.

Maldynado rolled his eyes. Barely conscious and Books was correcting him.

"You chaps and *Sires* coming?"

Books shook his head at this disgraceful use of language, but allowed Basilard to guide him into the vehicle. Akstyr, strung between Yara and Sespian, looked less cogent, though he did cast a longing glance back toward the park. He probably wished he'd had a better look at that magical gewgaw before passing out. Maldynado tossed them a couple of shopping bags.

"Don't worry, I didn't lose your new ensembles."

"Joy," Books said.

Sespian climbed into the cab beside Maldynado while the others piled into the cargo area in the back.

"Am I any closer to getting a statue?" Maldynado wriggled his eyebrows at the emperor. It was probably silly, given how the day had gone thus far, but he felt proud of his rescue.

Sespian stared at him as if a fine set of elk antlers had sprouted from his temples. Ah, well.

Maldynado, not certain they had completely eluded their pursuers yet, nudged the lorry into motion. "Enjoying your time with our group thus far, Sire?" he asked in an amiable way, wanting Sespian to know that he didn't hold a grudge for that knife-to-neck moment. Maldynado wished he could think of a way to convince Sespian he'd had nothing to do with that trap. Maybe it was good that they'd have to spend time alone in the cab. Maldynado could work on endearing himself to the emperor, or at least being likable. Amaranthe had often pointed out that people tended to trust those they liked.

"I haven't enjoyed much about the last five years," Sespian said after a thoughtful moment. He pointed behind them. "I still need to get across the bridge."

"Want to see if there's a map in that lockbox? There must be other bridges along the river, and now that we have a ride, it doesn't matter if it's twenty, thirty miles out of our path. We can still get into the city tonight."

Sespian unsuccessfully tried to open the lid of the indicated box. "I don't suppose you've seen a key to this anywhere?"

"Nah," Maldynado said. "Might have been in one of the men's pockets that I was bash—, er, subduing, but I didn't have a chance to search them."

It seemed unlikely that an emperor would have come equipped for lock-picking endeavors, so Maldynado withdrew his sturdy utility knife, leaned over, and slammed the tip into the metal box's thin lid. The blade punctured it and mutilated the lock. When he pulled the blade out, the lid lifted too, hinges squealing. Papers and envelopes fell out.

"You're welcome," Maldynado said when Sespian gave him a strange look.

Maldynado had a feeling the young emperor didn't know what to think of him. It was making him feel self-conscious, but he had to be himself, or he'd seem more suspicious, wouldn't he?

"Not that you needed my help," Maldynado said. "I'm sure you would have come up with a similar solution."

"Perhaps," Sespian murmured and picked up the papers.

"You seem handy with a knife. I reckon emperors get a lot of good training from master duelists and the like."

"Weaponsmaster Orik would be pleased that you found my knife skills adequate." Sespian flipped through the papers. "He found me an inattentive pupil and often lamented that I devoted the majority of my energy to thinking of ways to get out of his practice sessions."

"Huh."

Sespian opened a sealed envelope and frowned.

"Problem?" Maldynado asked.

"These look like orders, but they're encrypted." Sespian patted through the boxes again and sighed. "Nothing. I suppose it wouldn't make sense to ship the decryption key alongside the secret orders."

"You should let Books have a look. Give him some time, and I bet he can figure out what it says. He likes puzzles like that."

"Ah, good idea."

Before Maldynado could slow down the lorry, so Sespian could get out, walk around, and hand the orders to Books in the cargo bed, Sespian crawled out the window.

"Uhm," Maldynado said.

He couldn't see out that window from his position, but, a moment later, thumps sounded in the back.

"Odd lad," Maldynado mused and decided it was unlikely they'd get to spend that time alone together after all.

# CHAPTER 5

"**W**HAT," PIKE ASKED FOR THE FIFTIETH TIME, "is the emperor to Sicarius?"

"I… dunno," Amaranthe mumbled around cracked and swollen lips that hadn't touched water in… she had no idea how much time had passed. Anyway, a lack of water was the least of her problems. Strange that it should even enter her thoughts. Pain. That was the foremost concern.

Darkness ringed her vision, throbbing and undulating, teasing her with the promise of unconsciousness. A part of her wanted to invite it in, to let it swallow her world and steal her pain, but a larger part of her feared it might signify the end. She'd made a point not to look at Pike's work, when he hadn't forced her to, and she wasn't sure what all he'd done, but she knew she'd lost a lot of blood. Would he let her die? Before he received his answer?

Pike set down his knife, and a tiny flame of hope lit within Amaranthe. He leaned against the table and withdrew a pocket watch. Maybe he'd had enough for the day. Or maybe he had a sexy dinner date waiting him, some Forge woman who found a killer with blood on his hands attractive. "Like you?" she thought, an image of Sicarius flashing through her mind. No, Sicarius was different. He wouldn't… *enjoy* his work. That mattered. Didn't it? Either way, after her sanctimonious comments on loyalty, she wasn't going to betray him. She thought of their stolen moment in the dirigible, his hug and promise of "later," and that brief hint of a smile. She knew he hadn't known much happiness in his life, and she wanted to be the person to give him that, not someone who put his son at risk. If Sicarius lost Sespian without Sespian ever knowing the truth…

"Hm." Pike strolled out of sight, then returned again, this time with a fat book in his hands. "How's the vision? Blurry? Or can you still read?"

Being lippy would only get her in trouble—he'd proven that a number of times already—but it seemed important to let him know he hadn't cowed her, not yet. So Amaranthe summoned enough strength to say, "I'm always… up for a good book… Don't suppose… you've got the… latest… Lady Dourcrest novel?"

"I don't read that drivel." Pike hefted the thick tome, slipping it into view between the claw pincers that pinned Amaranthe's left wrist and shoulder to the table. *The Imperial Army Torture and Interrogation Methods Technical Manual.* Lovely.

"Should you be conscious when Ms. Worgavic returns, I'd like for you to verify that I've been operating by the book, as she requested, and not taking too many liberties. She specifically asked, for instance, that you not be raped."

Gee. How thoughtful. Horrible maiming and permanent disfigurement were fine, but no cavity penetration, please. "And here I just thought you preferred boys."

Pike's jaw clenched. Bringing up the man's past might not have been the best idea. He laid his three-edged blade across her collarbone. The cold steel chilled her bare skin. Rape might be off the table, but he had cut off her clothing first thing, spouting a lecture about people feeling armored and secure beneath their layers of garb but vulnerable when naked. Being nude bothered her less than being peeled like an orange. She kept waiting—hoping—to reach a point of numbness, where the pain blurred into one horrible experience and she no longer cared about particulars, but it didn't happen. Every touch, whether with flesh or blade, stirred agony afresh.

"Why this loyalty to Sicarius?" Pike murmured. His gaze roved from her toes to lips, as if her battered and bleeding body might hold the answer.

Amaranthe hadn't been saying anything in response to his questions—unless one counted the involuntary gasps that came out when injury accompanied inquiry—but this was the first time he'd asked this one. The other fifty times, he'd simply wanted to know what the emperor meant to Sicarius.

"I know the boy," Pike went on. "He's attractive enough, I suppose, but I can't imagine he's a passionate lover or one to cater to your whims."

Hearing someone call Sicarius a boy was strange, but Pike had to be close to sixty, and if he'd known Sicarius as a youth, it made sense that he'd remember him that way. Thinking of a young Sicarius spending time with this man, learning his trade, made Amaranthe's insides clench. She supposed it was horrible of her, wishing someone had shared the fate she was experiencing now, but she hoped he'd been more of a victim to Pike than a student. Especially a willing student. The main reason she could, at least somewhat, accept Sicarius's occupation was the machine-like way he pursued it, treating everything from training to killing like a necessary task to be completed, not something he relished.

The point of Pike's knife dug into her flesh, finding a sensitive spot and shattering her thoughts.

"Why the loyalty?" he repeated.

After mulling over whether giving an answer would matter, Amaranthe decided this one probably wouldn't. Pike already knew she was loyal, as attested by the suffering she continued to endure. "He's saved my life," she said. "Many times."

"Ah, so it's a soldiers' bond." Pike nodded. "That makes more sense, though it's still surprising. He always worked solo. You've never screwed him then?"

What an idiot. "No, have you?"

The question seemed to surprise Pike. Amaranthe had asked it reflexively, not out of any real desire to know, but when the surprise faded into a smile, she got her answer. And promptly wished she hadn't.

"Commander of the Armies Hollowcrest insisted that his pupil endure every likely torture he might expect to suffer should he be captured by enemy troops. He had to learn not to give any information away. Hollowcrest didn't even want him to flinch. We began by making him hold burning brands when he was six or seven and, as he grew adept at handling that pain, progressed to—" Pike's smile broadened, "—more advanced techniques."

Amaranthe closed her eyes. A vision crashed into her mind of Sicarius as a sandy-haired boy, locked in a dungeon with this monster, helpless to escape, knowing worse punishment would come if he fought. Hollowcrest and Raumesys watched on, making sure their pupil learned

his lessons well, probably enjoying the show, the perverted bastards. Amaranthe choked, anger surging through her body, her own pain forgotten. She wanted nothing more than to grab Pike's knife and ram it into his heart. No, not his heart. His gut. So he'd die slowly and suffer for a long time first. But, trapped by the table and those all-too-efficient pins, she couldn't do anything more than clench her fists and glare.

Pike, curse the twisted ancestors that had spawned such a bastard, smirked. "Did you think he would have become such a skilled assassin, with such an impressive record, not only of kills but of acquiring necessary information from people, had I not taught him well? To truly understand agony one must experience it oneself. You can guess at the pain of a technique based on another's reaction, but only when it's used on you do you truly understand what is effective and what is not. His training was necessary."

The bastard's smirk deepened. He had to have loved what the emperor and Hollowcrest had deemed "necessary."

A realization popped into Amaranthe's head. Maybe Pike was lying. Maybe he knew this would hurt her in a way his knives couldn't. Especially considering… "He didn't have any scars when I met him," Amaranthe said.

"No," Pike said without hesitation, "and you won't have scars either. Aside from the ones you came in with." He waved to her bare abdomen, forever marked after her encounter with the makarovi. "Despite his distaste for the mental sciences, Hollowcrest knew it would be useful to employ a shaman to educate Sicarius on matters of magic and also to heal him after I worked him over. We could train day after day that way."

The prompt answer, the matter-of-fact way he spoke… Pike wasn't lying. As much as Amaranthe wanted to believe otherwise, she couldn't. With no outlet, her rage faded, replaced by the prick of tears as she thought of the never-ending cycle of pain Sicarius must have endured. To be tortured to within an inch of death, brought back to good health, and then tormented again.

Focus on yourself, girl, spoke a practical voice in the back of her head, on the here and now. On escape. That's what Sicarius would want you to do.

"When do I get to meet my healer?" Amaranthe asked. Pike had showed no sign of melting beneath her charms, but maybe another would prove more pliable. Afraid he might guess her thoughts, she added, "I don't suppose he'll supply water and a steak in addition to doctoring? I'd dearly love some baked apple pudding, too, if you're taking requests."

Pike dug his fingers into an open wound on her inner thigh, and Amaranthe gasped as fresh agony shot through her.

"No one else will be intruding upon us, my dear," Pike said. "When last I was in Kendor, I had a shaman make me a powerful salve with healing capabilities, so there'd be no need to bring an assistant along on... sessions."

Amaranthe gritted her teeth against his intrusions and hoped he brought out the salve soon.

Pike chuckled. "Oh, the relief that sprang to your eyes. It's premature though. In truth, all the salve means is that I can torment you for longer since I needn't worrying about losing you. I can take you to the brink of death again and again. And again."

"As you did with Sicarius?" Amaranthe asked.

"As we did," Pike agreed. "You're fortunate though. He had to be tempered for the life he would lead, so there was no chance of an early reprieve. You, on the other hand, need only tell me one thing. Why is he protecting the emperor?"

Amaranthe turned her face away, weariness plastering her body to the table. "I don't know."

"Ah." Pike's blade burrowed beneath flesh again. "Then we've more work to do."

\* \* \* \* \*

Maldynado, sitting on an upturned crate, tossed his twentieth or thirtieth pebble into a rusty tin can. Had anyone been around, he might have had something to brag over, but, under the circumstances, the demonstration of his rock-throwing prowess failed to alleviate the glum attitude that had settled around his shoulders.

After driving all night, the team had found a way into the city and parked in a large junkyard on the outskirts. Nobody had been manning

the gate, and the lorry had rolled inside before dawn. After dressing in his new clothes, Sespian had left, announcing that he'd return later with the team's funds. He'd refused to take anyone with him. Soon he'd leave the group permanently, and, short of tying the youth up, Maldynado didn't know how to change his mind. He didn't know who to ask for advice either. Books, Basilard, and Yara were snoring in the back of the lorry, as if they didn't have a concern on their minds. Because Sicarius hadn't threatened *them*.

Those parting words echoed in Maldynado's thoughts. *Don't lose him*. He didn't know why the emperor mattered to Sicarius, but, since that moment, it had been clear that he did. Maldynado eyed the broken logging machinery, metal scrap, rusted and warped beams, and demolished military trampers and wagons piled all about. The junk hid the lorry from anyone who might wander past the yard, but all the debris in the empire wouldn't be enough of an obstacle to keep Sicarius from finding him if he lost the emperor.

A scrape sounded behind him. Maldynado rested a hand on his rapier, but it was merely Books. His unwashed hair hung in limp strands around his unshaven face, and smudges beneath his eyes did little to improve his haggard appearance. He hadn't changed into the clothes Maldynado had risked much to retrieve, though Maldynado silently admitted that such a dirty body shouldn't sully fine garments anyway. The entire team needed a stay at a decent hotel with heated baths.

Books squinted at the afternoon sun and sat on the end of a rusty beam.

"I think we're going to have to tie him up and force him to stay with us," Maldynado said.

"The emperor? There's a law against that. Eight actually." Books yawned and dug crud out of his eye. In a quieter tone, he said, "I dreamed about Amaranthe. That she was being tortured by that deviant interrogator, Major Pike."

Maldynado's dreams had revolved around Sicarius strangling him, which probably meant he was more self-centered than Books, but he worried about Amaranthe too. "I wanted to go along to get her. I don't… *not* care about the emperor, but if I had to choose who to help…"

"I know. I'm trying to console myself with the knowledge that nobody is better qualified to find and retrieve her than Sicarius."

"But Sicarius might give up when we wouldn't. Tracking that aircraft, if he can do it at all, isn't going to be easy. He seemed conflicted about who to go after, too, like picking between Amaranthe and the emperor wasn't an easy choice."

Books gave him a sharp look. "Is that so?"

"Yes. What if he only hunts for her for a while, then comes back to help Sespian?"

"I don't think he'll give up on her."

"You don't? Why?"

Books lifted his eyes skyward. "How can a self-professed romance expert fail to see evidence of a relationship between people he's around every day?"

Maldynado sat back so quickly he fell off his crate, upending it and sending a cloud of dust into the air. "What are you talking about? *Romance*? A *relationship*? With *Sicarius*?"

"You're a self-absorbed idiot, Maldynado."

"An idiot who saved your life last night. You could show a little gratitude." Maldynado rearranged his crate and sat on it again.

Though Books didn't apologize, a slightly admonished expression crossed his face. That was something anyway.

"You're wrong," Maldynado said. "I pay attention to those things. They never touch or share any of those little looks that lovers do." He almost choked at linking the word "lover" with Sicarius. A mechanical reaper would be more likely to develop feelings for someone. "They never come back from their outings with their clothes disheveled or a speck of dirt on them. I know they're both fastidious, but you can't catch *every* smudge of evidence."

"Maldynado," Books said in the tone of one dealing with a slow child, "not all relationships revolve around coitus."

"Yeah… but those that don't are called friendships. Like you might find between two mercenaries who respect each other, but don't dream of cavorting between the sheets. I'll allow that *may*be they're friends."

"You didn't see Sicarius's face when he thought Amaranthe was dying last spring," Books said. "After the makarovi got her. I don't know if the man is capable of love, but he cares about her. He won't give up on finding her, not as long as there's hope that she's still alive."

The reminder that Amaranthe might even now be under some torturer's knife sobered Maldynado and dashed worries of who was romancing whom from his mind. He picked up a few more pebbles to throw at the tin can.

"Maldynado," Books said quietly, "Basilard told us what happened last night. I do appreciate that you risked yourself to come for Akstyr and me."

Instead of saying good or making fun of Books for being ensnared in the first place, Maldynado tossed a pebble. The fact that his teammates were suspicious of him of late left him feeling subdued, that he had to be careful about what he said. At the same time, he knew he needed Books on his side if he was going to talk the emperor into sticking with them. Sespian seemed to, if not value Books's council, at least find his knowledge useful. They'd spent a lot of that drive trying to decode that message and blathering about monetary systems from around the world.

"I wouldn't do anything to endanger anyone on the team," Maldynado said. "Amaranthe knows that. I thought… I thought you did too."

Books's lips pursed, and he studied the ground.

"I know we've always argued and called each other names," Maldynado went on, "but have I ever *not* been there when you needed me?"

Books remained silent. Maldynado thought about pressing him, but maybe it was best to stop there. At least Books seemed to be thinking things over.

"Why were you so insistent on meeting with Buckingcrest the night before we left?" Books asked. "Amaranthe clearly wanted you to go along to negotiate with the smoke-grenade lady, but you finagled your way out of that so you could get us that dirigible. The dirigible that came with stowaways who tried to kill Akstyr and me."

Maldynado picked at the corner of his crate. "Books, I'm sorry about that, but I didn't know Lady Buckingcrest had ties to Forge, if that's what it turns out to be. She's just someone I've known for a long time, and I knew she had the flying vehicles. That's what came to mind when Sicarius mentioned snow blocking the access to the pass. And, to be honest, I didn't want to go off with Amaranthe that night because I knew she would dig for information on Ravido. You all know my family's a sore subject with me." Maldynado realized he was talking

rapidly. Lately, every time he opened his mouth, it seemed like he was defending himself.

"Why *is* it a sore subject?" Books asked.

"Because I'm—"

"Disowned, yes, but *why*? For all we know, you're dying for a chance to prove yourself to your family and get invited back into the clan. If I recall my recent history, your kin control copious resources. They're not one of those wealthy-in-land-only warrior-caste families. Should you be welcomed back, you'd be able to return to leading an indolent lifestyle. How do we know you wouldn't betray the emperor if it meant putting your brother on the throne? Maybe said brother would reward you handsomely for your loyalty."

"And maybe I'd be an utter ass if I betrayed the team, and the boss, and set Sespian up to get killed," Maldynado said. "Besides, if you have a face this pretty, you can lead an indolent lifestyle wherever you go. I don't need my brother's help for that."

Though Books snorted, a hint of a smile softened his face. Maybe he *wanted* to believe Maldynado, but couldn't get past his assumptions about the warrior caste and those born into it.

"It may be as you say," Books said, "but I'm not the one you need to convince. From my talk with the emperor, I understood you were ambivalent about sharing details on your family members. You need to choose whether to help him fully… or not. I don't necessarily approve of unthinking obeisance, but that *is* in the warrior-caste code, isn't it? That you must be first and foremost loyal to the emperor? Family comes second, at least according to the various historical precedents. In the fifth century, Lady Dalecrest, upon learning that her husband had sold military secrets to the Nurians, risked her and her children's lives to inform the emperor."

"Great example," Maldynado said dryly. "Yes, Lady Dalecrest warned the emperor, but, after the forces had left to thwart the Nurian incursion, her husband found her and strangled her."

"Unfortunate, but the Nurians were stopped. This story is told to warrior-caste children to explain what's expected of them, is it not?"

Maldynado couldn't believe Books, of all people, was saying he should embrace the warrior-caste, honor-in-death mentality. "I don't want to get *strangled*, Books." Nor did he want to further disappoint his family. When had his life grown so complicated?

"I'm sure that won't happen if you assist Sespian," Books said. Maldynado was on the verge of feeling better when Books added, "Your neck is very thick and muscular. They'd simply shoot you."

"That's much better, thanks."

At least Books smiled. Maybe joking was his way of saying he believed the story about the dirigible. Or maybe Maldynado was being wistful.

"I'm back," came Sespian's voice from a couple of scrap piles away.

He eased into sight, a hand lifted, as if he expected overly vigilant mercenaries to accidentally shoot him. As if Maldynado would shoot anyone wearing such a handsome azure tunic and stylish gray breeches, both with the perfect touch of golden accent embroidery. The wig, beard, and mustache, all dark black and bushy, were a new addition. Maldynado decided not to tell Sespian that he looked far too young to have that much facial hair. Maybe people wouldn't look too closely.

"I've retrieved the agreed upon reward money." Sespian pulled a heavy strongbox out of a satchel, gave it to Books, and clasped his hands behind his back. "I thank you for your assistance thus far, and, in particular for removing that device in my neck." A shudder ran through him. He nodded to Books. "I also thank you for the information you gave me. I will be continuing on my own now."

"Wait, Sire. I…" Maldynado glanced at Books. "I have information for you. About my family."

Sespian's eyebrows twitched upward. "And you are offering it in trade for…?"

Maldynado opened his mouth, wanting to say that he'd share everything if Sespian would agree to keep the team onboard and let them help, but Books spoke first. "Nothing, Sire," he said. "He—*we*—want you to have every advantage going forward."

"I see," Sespian said, and Maldynado wasn't sure if he believed the line.

Maldynado only shrugged. "I found out yesterday that Mari, Ravido's wife is on her way downriver on the *Glacial Empress* and will be staying on Rabbit Island. She'll arrive tomorrow night."

"Rabbit Island?" Sespian asked.

"Yes." Though they couldn't see the river from this side of the city, Maldynado waved to the northeast, indicating that the island was upstream. Maybe Sespian wasn't familiar with the area. "It seems she's been collecting strange black artifacts. She has an entrepreneurial streak as well, so it's possible she's behind Ravido's interest in dealing with Forge. She may even be the one driving him toward this coup attempt. *Rust*, it might be my father too. As I said before, I don't know Ravido well, but I don't think this is a scheme that would have come to him without outside urging."

"I see," Sespian said again, doing an annoyingly good job of hiding his thoughts.

"I just thought you should know." Maldynado lifted a hand, palm up. "She'd be worth talking to if you're looking for information on the family, especially Ravido."

Sespian listened to everything, then turned and, hands still clasped behind his back, started walking. At first, Maldynado thought he was fed up with them and meant to walk away from the team forever. But the emperor chose a circular route. He wasn't walking away; he was pacing.

Maldynado shared a hopeful shrug with Books.

"You say you *just* learned this information?" Sespian asked, a suspicious note in his tone.

Ugh, couldn't Maldynado find respite? Why did things keep happening in a way that made him look disreputable?

"We ran into his cousin on the waterfront shopping street yesterday, Sire." Yara stepped out from behind the lorry, her short hair sticking out in half a dozen directions. "I believe the meeting was unplanned. Maldynado appeared to be getting the information for the first time."

Maldynado crossed his arms over his chest and kept himself from saying, "Good watchdog, good girl." Barely.

"Thank you, Sergeant." Sespian gave Yara a single nod, which she returned.

Hm. Maybe it was good that Maldynado had kept the snide comment to himself. This wasn't the first time Sespian had shown that he valued Yara's council. Amaranthe had said they'd met before, hadn't she? She must have planned this, for Yara to act as a neutral third party, one that Sespian knew he could trust to be impartial, or perhaps even more loyal to him than to the team. It was helping Maldynado now, so he sent a silent thank-you to Amaranthe, wherever she was at the moment.

Several long moments passed with Sespian standing still, his chin on his fist as he gazed at the dirt. "Mari Marblecrest is whom I seek," he finally said.

Maldynado blinked.

"Do you mean that, all along, you planned to speak to Mari Marblecrest, Sire?" Books asked.

"Spy on, not speak to, but yes."

"Truly? You think my sister-in-law is important somehow?" Maldynado almost choked on the word important, given that he was applying it to a salacious, self-absorbed woman who had, at more than one family get-together, chased him around the kitchen island and through the servants' quarters, trying to tear off his clothes.

"Her importance in the organization is questionable," Sespian said, "but I've learned that, of all the Forge members traveling downstream to their meeting spot, she's the only one unlikely to hide her passing."

Maldynado snorted. "If by that you mean that she travels with ten servants and twenty suitcases, then I agree."

"That, and I understand she's stopping to shop on the way." Sespian raised his eyebrows.

Maldynado thought of the black sphere. Shopping indeed.

"Is this secret meeting where they'll be discussing their plans for the fiscal future of the empire?" Books asked.

Fiscal, what? Oh, right, the emperor had volunteered for a lecture on economics.

"I believe so, yes," Sespian said. "This may also be the first opportunity to spy on the leaders all together. Heretofore they've been clandestine with their correspondences."

"You don't have to tell me," Books said. "I've been trying to get the names of everyone, or at least the key people, in the organization for months. Despite my considerable research skill, I've been unable to pinpoint the founders."

"Considerable research skill," Maldynado said. "Nice modesty, Booksie."

"I know *you* aren't disparaging *me* on a lack of humility. When was the last time you managed to get through a conversation without stroking your chest and touting your physical attributes?"

"Are they always like this?" Sespian asked.

At first, Maldynado didn't know whom he'd addressed, but Basilard had hopped out of the lorry. Only Akstyr remained inside, snores reverberating through the junkyard.

Basilard nodded firmly in response to the emperor's question. *Amaranthe keeps them from killing each other.*

Maldynado translated for the emperor.

Sespian frowned and repeated one of the gestures. "That's your symbol for Corporal Lokdon? Someone sweeping? Why? Because she's a woman and you think that's woman's work?"

*No*, Basilard signed, *because she…* He must have realized the emperor couldn't understand him, because he started doing an imitation of Amaranthe, first sweeping, then straightening Yara's sweater and brushing away lint, and finally taking out a knife and tidying the stubble on Books's jaw—too bad he didn't actually scrape some of the grunge away.

The acting show made Yara smirk, but Sespian didn't seem appeased.

"She tends to clean, organize, and tidy when she's concocting a scheme," Maldynado said. "Or worrying about a scheme that she's set into motion."

"Hm," Sespian said.

"She likes to do those things. We don't *make* her do them."

"You simply reap the benefits of her voluntary labor?" Sespian asked.

"Yes. I mean, er…" Arms spread wide, Maldynado beseeched Books for help. How in the empire had he ended up defending himself when *Basilard* was the one who'd made up the sign?

"You said the secret meeting was downstream, is that correct, Sire?" Books said. "But you don't know the final destination yet? You're hoping to find out where from this Mari? Or one of her servants?"

Relieved to have the topic changed, Maldynado threw Books a grateful nod.

"I'm hoping not to be seen by her *or* her servants," Sespian said. "I want to follow her to the destination without Mari or anyone from

Forge finding out. They'll speak freely if they have no reason to believe anyone outside of the organization is listening. I wasn't sure how I'd manage to get close when I had that tracking device in my neck, but now… Ah, actually, I'm still not sure how I'm going to get close." He shrugged sheepishly.

Maldynado relaxed an iota. He liked Sespian better when he appeared uncertain. Given his age, that was normal. When he was trying to hold back his thoughts, he reminded Maldynado of Sicarius. That struck him as odd—*nobody* was like Sicarius—but his mind kept coming back to the idea, regardless.

"Perhaps I can visit my dear sister-in-law and extract information on her destination for you." Maldynado dreaded the idea of speaking with Mari, especially without a kitchen table between them, but if it kept Sespian working with the team… he judged it an improvement over the tie-up-the-emperor-and-hope-he-didn't-hold-it-against-them option he'd been considering before. "She might not think it odd that I'd come to see her, not after what Cousin Lita said."

Sespian tilted his head. "What else did she say?"

"Something about my father. Did I… not mention that?"

"No, you didn't," Books said.

Er, maybe Maldynado shouldn't have voiced his addendum. "It seems Father has extended an offer to, er, *re*-own me if I come help with family business."

Everyone stared at him. Huh, Yara must not have heard that part.

"Business such as overthrowing the throne?" Sespian asked.

"I don't know, but I wasn't planning on accepting the offer. Though I could tell Mari I'm contemplating it as a reason for visiting her."

The slit-eyed suspiciousness had returned to Sespian's face. Even Books was regarding him with speculation again. Maldynado sighed. Why couldn't everyone just trust him? If they knew his family, they'd understand why he'd rather run around with outlaws, but he wouldn't inflict his relatives on anyone.

"Look," Maldynado said, "you don't have to go onto Rabbit Island with me. Mari's arriving on the *Glacial Empress*, so I imagine she'll be continuing downriver, at least for a while, on the steamboat. I can be your distraction while you sneak aboard."

"According to my research," Sespian said, "sneaking aboard may not be easy. Rabbit Island is a private, warrior-caste-only resort with a guarded boat dock, and, if rumors are to be believed, there are domesticated alligators in the water to deter anyone from swimming over."

Maldynado hadn't been there, but he supposed that was all possible.

"Assuming your former warrior-caste status gets you in," Books said, with an eyebrow raise that suggested he doubted the guards would let Maldynado pass, "how do you propose to divert the guards so we can slip by without being shot? Or even get close to the island, for that matter?"

"How do *I* propose…?"

"It's your plan."

"Uhm."

"Careful," Books said, "you'll overwhelm us with such a profuse outpouring of details."

"I'd appreciate it if you'd turn your sarcasm toward someone else. I'm busy thinking." Maldynado stalked away. Just when he'd been feeling grateful to Books for helping him with Sespian, he had to go back to being a stuffy, sourpuss.

Though Maldynado was of a mind to keep walking, and leave the junkyard, he didn't know where he'd go. How did Amaranthe manage to come up with plans while dancing barefoot on a frying pan?

Someone tapped Maldynado on the shoulder. He spun around, prepared to unleash a stream of vitriol—or perhaps a fist—if Books had followed him to give him a hard time. It was only Basilard.

He signed, *Do you need help?*

"Probably. Bas, up until a few days ago, I felt like we were all brothers, family if you will, a family I actually liked, most of the time. But now I'm the outcast all over again."

*Sometimes, friendships are tested. You will survive and all will be well again.*

"I appreciate the faith, especially since you're the only one giving it right now, but I don't know what to do with all of these expectations." Maldynado scraped his fingers through his curly hair. "I don't know if I'm made from enough steel to handle them. My mother used to call me the family weed. Maybe she was right. I wasn't born with leadership qualities. I don't know how to walk in front. Not like Amaranthe. Not

like Sicarius. Rust, even Books would be able to get everyone going in the same direction without sarcastic quips from the troops."

Basilard regarded him for a long moment, no judgment in his pale blue eyes. Somehow, despite the scars, the bulky muscles, and the morose downturn to his lips, Basilard managed to convey much more compassion than most people. *My grandpa used to say that the only difference between a weed and a plant is that one has proved itself useful while the other's properties are still in question.*

"All right," Maldynado said, "I'll come up with something."

# CHAPTER 6

MALDYNADO STROLLED INTO THE JUNKYARD before sunset with a new set of shopping bags dangling from his arms. More business cards stuffed his pockets as well. He vowed to slide some under the doors of suites in the Rabbit Island resort. Maybe he'd foisted a few onto Mari too. The woman dearly loved her shopping.

Maldynado weaved past the towering piles of wreckage and debris until he found the purloined lorry. Several hours had passed since he'd left to come up with his big plan, and he wasn't sure everyone would be around for his return, but Books, Sespian, Basilard, and Yara were all present, their heads bent in some conference. Akstyr sat against a tire at the rear of the vehicle, a book the size of an infantryman's shield propped open in his lap. How he'd managed to keep from losing that amidst all the train explosions and dirigible crashes, Maldynado couldn't guess, though singe marks *did* decorate the corners. More concerned about what the rest of the team was doing—or planning—he hustled toward them, rattling his bags for attention.

"Shopping again?" Yara scowled at him from where she sat cross-legged on the lorry's covered engine compartment. She still wore her dirt-stained sweater and trousers, even though he'd bargained for those clean, curve-enhancing garments for her the day before. Well, if the team accepted his plan, she'd have to wear his more recent acquisition. It would enhance a lot more than curves.

"Indeed so." Maldynado set one of the bags beside her. "I've come up with a plan to get us all to the docks without being shot."

"We wondered if you'd decided to back out," Sespian said. He was seated on a rusty beam across from Basilard, who was cutting the roots off a stack of weeds—knowing him, they were for the stew pot.

"Of course, not," Maldynado said. "I simply needed time to refine—"

"*Silk*?" Yara held up a midnight blue dress. "And, and, what is *this*? *Jewelry*? Have you gone mad?"

Basilard smirked. *Perhaps the garments aren't for Sergeant Yara. They don't seem her style.*

"Who else would a dress be for?" Akstyr asked.

*The emperor?* Basilard's smirk widened. *That might be an effective way to disguise him.*

"I'm glad you fellows have refreshed your senses of humor in my absence." Maldynado pointed to the dress. "That garment, and the jewelry, is for my fiancée."

"Your *what*?" Yara demanded.

"Fiancée?" Books mused. "Definitely not the emperor, then."

Sespian's eyebrows flew up. He hadn't understood Basilard's comments, of course. Perhaps that was for the best.

"Allow me to explain," Maldynado said. "As I mentioned earlier, I believe *I* can get into Rabbit Island. Even if the guards have heard that I'm disowned, Mari should be willing to vouch for me." He hoped he wouldn't have to perform any *favors* to earn that vouching. "And I imagine it won't surprise anyone if I have a bodyguard and a lady friend."

"A fiancée?" Akstyr asked.

"Just so," Maldynado said. "And I believe Basilard would be a very convincing bodyguard. As for Akstyr, Books, and the emperor, someone will have to row the boat I've reserved for our use."

Books made a choking noise. "You want the *emperor* to row your hirsute haunches across the river?"

"He can steer if rowing is a problem," Maldynado said.

Fortunately, Sespian responded with an amused snort.

"Once we dock," Maldynado said, "I'll loudly give orders for my crew to stay and keep the vessel ready for my departure. On the way to the resort, Yara, Basilard, and I will arrange a distraction of some sort, the type of thing a few dock guards might be dispatched to investigate. Then you three can sneak aboard the steamboat."

"Why do I have a feeling it won't be that easy?" Books asked.

"Amaranthe's schemes never go as planned either," Maldynado pointed out. "You're smart. You can compensate."

"Somehow that sounds more convincing when she says it," Books said. "Sire, what do you think?"

Sespian dropped his chin on his fist—he liked to do that when he was pondering, Maldynado had noticed—and gazed at the rusty nuts and bolts scattered on the dusty ground.

"You'll do fine if you have to subdue a few thugs, Sire," Maldynado said. "I can attest to the fact that you're decent at sneaking up and putting a knife to a man's throat." Sespian hadn't shown any appreciation for flattery thus far, and didn't acknowledge it now. Maldynado pressed on. "You'll have Books and Akstyr with you too. Akstyr's got his magics, and Books… He's tall and spindly, but he's gotten decent with his fists."

"Such a magnanimous accolade," Books murmured.

"Shouldn't *my* vote matter here?" Yara asked. "You haven't explained *why* you need a fiancée. I'd, quite frankly, rather play the role of oarsman."

"My lady, you wound me with your distain." Maldynado started to lay a hand on his chest, but remembered Books poking fun at his tendency to do that and offered Yara puppy-dog eyes instead. She glared, and he switched tactics. "To answer your question, I plan to get information by pretending I wish to return to the warrior-caste lifestyle and by agreeing to do whatever's necessary to get back into my father's good graces." His stomach turned at the thought. A pretense only, he told it. "Given my previous disinterest in being in anyone's good graces, I thought my turnaround would be more believable if it were because I'd found the woman of my dreams and decided to marry her."

Yara's lips reared back from her teeth like those of a trained attack dog ready to crush a man's jewels.

Maldynado continued speaking, though he knew his next words might truly endanger those jewels. "And if she's expecting, my change of heart will be even *more* believable. What kind of warrior-caste father would want his child growing up as a commoner?"

"Child!" Yara blurted.

Books rubbed the back of his head. "This *is* starting to sound like an Amaranthe plan."

Maldynado stood straighter. "Do you think so? Would she be proud?"

"I'd like to say she'd be appalled by your entire last forty-eight hours, which included crashing a dirigible and blowing up a steam lorry, but… I can't."

"Nope." Maldynado smiled. "Crashes and explosions have become her hallmarks of late."

Basilard signed, *She'll be proud if your antics get the emperor the information he needs.*

"Ah, yes, always back to business. What do you think, Yara? Will you play the part of adoring fiancée if it'll help the emperor?"

"*Adoring?*"

"That part isn't required. You just have to make it believable."

Yara sighed and dropped her arms. "Will there be touching?"

"No," Sespian said with a warning look to Maldynado.

"Wait a moment," Maldynado said, "it wouldn't be convincing if we kept a distance. Mari *knows* me, after all."

Sespian *and* Yara glared at him.

"You don't have to go," Sespian told her. "You can be on the boat crew."

"No, no, Sire, I *have* to take her. My sister-in-law will find it suspicious if I have a change of heart for no obvious reason. Yara and a pretend-baby-on-the-way make a good reason." And, he had to admit, he wanted to see her in that dress, but he'd best not admit that aloud, not if he didn't want her to throw a knife at him. "Besides, I'm hoping her presence will keep Mari from wanting to be entertained."

That drew a round of blank looks from everyone.

"By me," Maldynado clarified.

The blank looks did not turn into expressions of enlightenment. Would he have to draw pictures?

"By my man parts," Maldynado said.

More than one set of eyebrows lifted.

Yara's lip curled again—it was good at that. "That's disgusting."

"Oh, no, they're quite fine." Maldynado waved to his lower regions. "You're welcome to see them anytime if you don't believe me. Perhaps it'd even be wise, in case someone questions you about my manhood while we're perpetrating this ruse. You wouldn't want to say anything in err, would you?"

Yara's lip curled up further until it was in danger of swallowing her nose. "I meant that it's disgusting that your sister-in-law would proposition you!"

"Oh, yes," Maldynado said. "She's done so during more than one family gathering. For whatever reason—well, we all *know* the reason—she finds me quite irresistible."

"Maldynado…" Books managed a pronounced sigh as he said the name.

"Have you ever returned her… ardor?" Sespian asked.

"Of course not. With my brother's wife? I have some scruples, you know."

"It wouldn't be the first time you've slept with someone's wife," Books said. "Isn't Lady Buckingcrest married?"

Maldynado folded his arms across his chest. "Not to any of my brothers."

*Yes, come now*, Basilard signed to Books. *Maldynado has standards.*

*Of course,* Books signed back. *What was I thinking?*

"I wish I understood that hand language," Yara said.

"They're mocking me," Maldynado said.

"Then I *really* wish I understood it." Yara's eyes glinted.

Maldynado thought to scowl at her, but he'd best not do anything to squash improvements in her mood, slight though they may be.

"Enough of this foolishness," Yara said. "Let's visit your lecherous relative and get this information as swiftly as possible."

"Does that mean you're agreeing to become my fiancée?" Maldynado went down on a knee and opened his arms, inviting her to run into his embrace.

"Let's just say that I believe your family would be highly skeptical that you'd agree to settle down and take on responsibility unless you'd been suitably whipped into submission by a woman." A thoughtful expression came over Yara's face. "Yes, actually, a good overbearing woman who bosses you around and takes none of your frivolity is just what you need. I do believe I can play that role."

If Yara meant that to concern him, she'd be disappointed. Maldynado offered his best lazy smile. "Whatever you say, dear, so long as you do the whipping while wearing that dress."

A perplexed wrinkle furrowed Sespian's brow. "It's hard to imagine you're the group's charm specialist."

"Actually, that's Amaranthe," Maldynado said. "I just get all the women."

"Not all of them," Yara said.

Maldynado kept his response, one of *we'll see*, to himself.

\* \* \* \* \*

Pike's salve hadn't healed Amaranthe entirely, only "enough so you won't die overnight." Locked back in the crate, she hunkered in a ball, face buried in her knees, the walls pressing in from all sides and denying a change of position. Moving wouldn't have been wise anyway. Any time she so much as twitched, a scab opened up and fresh blood or pus dripped down her arm or leg and splashed onto the waste-stained floor.

Early on, Amaranthe had wished to swab the crate with a mop, sterilizing it—and herself—with copious amounts of alcohol. She'd grown too weary to think of such things now. She longed for sleep—oblivion—but it rarely came. Chances to escape were even rarer. The one time she'd tried to sprint for the exit as soon as her crate door opened, the claw had swept down from the ceiling, plucking her into the air before she'd gone more than three steps. Pike had punished her attempt with an extra hour of "work," as he called it, before starting in on question-asking. She'd tried lying to him, hoping to end the torment, but he had, with a knack that reminded her far too much of the one Sicarius possessed, seen through her attempts at mendacity. However many years had passed, Pike *had* known Sicarius well at one time and must have a good idea of what would and what *wouldn't* motivate him to protect someone.

It bothered her that more than once while she was wadded up in the crate, Amaranthe had wondered if protecting Sicarius's secret was worth the continued pain. After all the people he'd killed, did he deserve such loyalty? She loved him, but he'd offered so little in return. Did he *truly* care about her? Did he think about a life together with her when this was all over? Would the suffering she was enduring matter to him? She resented herself for her doubts; more, she resented Pike for causing her to have them.

On the third night, or maybe it was the fourth—the only thing she had to judge time by was the number of torture sessions that had gone by—a soft scrape roused Amaranthe from her latest attempt at sleep. A beam of light slashed into the crate. Accustomed to the blackness inside, she groaned at the pain it elicited and turned her head away.

"Amaranthe?" came a whisper from outside. Retta.

Hope stirred behind Amaranthe's breast. After that first day, Pike had worked the controls for the claw and the table himself, and she hadn't seen Retta again.

Fighting pain, Amaranthe forced her face toward the light. Retta had opened a horizontal rectangle in the door. It wasn't big enough to slip a hand through—even if Amaranthe could maneuver an arm up to it—but she could see Retta's hazel eyes through the gap.

"I didn't know this flat came with a view," Amaranthe rasped. Speaking hurt. During the last session, Pike had experimented with ways to induce panic in her, perhaps believing she'd blurt out the answers he craved, and he'd alternated between choking her and pouring water down her throat.

Retta's eyebrows drew together, creating a tiny furrow above her nose. "How can you make jokes in your situation?"

"Inappropriate jocularity is one of my hallmarks. Just ask Sicarius." Amaranthe decided it would take too much effort to explain that it was better to make jokes to distract oneself from the gravity of one's predicament than to dwell upon it.

Retta leaned in closer, blocking the light with her face. "Why *are* you protecting that assassin? You could be free if you simply answered our question."

*Our.* Amaranthe had wondered how closely Retta was associated with Forge, whether she was one of them or simply someone who'd been pressed into working for them. That "our" was telling.

"I could be free?" Amaranthe whispered. "Doubtful. I was responsible for Larocka Myll's death, and my team has thwarted other Forge schemes this past year. We..." It occurred to her pain-befuddled mind that she shouldn't be volunteering information about what she had and hadn't thwarted. Forge might not know all the details. "I'm sure I'm slated for execution once Pike has the information he seeks," she finished.

"Don't be foolish, Lokdon. Ms. Worgavic *likes* you. You would have been invited to join Forge years ago if you'd gone to work for an alumnus or started your own business. Nobody was going to approach an enforcer though. But now that you're rogue…" The narrow window slit didn't offer a view of Retta's shoulders, but clothing rustled, hinting at a shrug. "When Ms. Worgavic learned that you were leading those mercenaries and not simply tagging along with the assassin, she suggested to more than one person that you should be converted to our side instead of eliminated. As one of the six founders, she has the sway to make that happen."

Amaranthe didn't know what to think of Retta's statement. She supposed it might be true, but Worgavic might have also sent Retta to try and extract information using a slyer method than Pike's. She did tuck the tidbit about Forge having six founders away in the back of her mind. Worgavic hadn't been on Books's list; maybe he hadn't discovered any of the founders yet.

"Why did you come?" Amaranthe asked. She might earn more useful information if she asked questions instead of answering them. Then she'd just have to figure out how to escape so she could put that information to good use. Retta seemed the most likely prospect to help with both goals. "The scowls you gave me that first day didn't seem all that friendly."

"Of course, I was scowling. You think I *like* hearing about what a boon it'd be for Forge if you could be converted? When I'm already here? I've been working for Ms. Worgavic for years and she barely acknowledges…" Retta thumped a hand on the side of the crate. "They wouldn't have any idea how to control the *Ortarh Ortak* if not for me."

Was that the name of the craft? Amaranthe preferred her name, the *Behemoth*.

"*I've* been instrumental to their success of late," Retta continued. "*You've* been a pest gnawing at their toes."

How flattering. Amaranthe kept the thought to herself and grunted encouragingly instead. This was her chance. If she could keep Retta talking and establish a rapport…

"You were one of Ms. Worgavic's favorite students, did you know that?" Retta asked. "*All* the teachers liked you. And our peers too. It

wasn't fair. You weren't warrior-caste, and you weren't even from a good family. Isn't your father some dirty logger, or something?"

"He *was* a coal miner," Amaranthe said.

"Oh." A note of apology came with that *oh*. Retta seemed to realize she'd been more insulting than she intended.

"I apologize because I don't remember, but did I ever... wrong you?" Amaranthe asked.

"No, you never wronged anyone. That's why everyone liked you. It was cursed annoying."

Despite her discomfort, Amaranthe laughed. A short laugh, and the pain in her abdomen immediately made her regret it, but maybe it was worth it, for Retta's blinked in surprise. Amusement was not the reaction she'd expected apparently.

"As I recall," Amaranthe said, "you spent every free moment in the library, and, even in class, kept your face buried in those archaeology books. The teachers might have appreciated you more if you'd paid attention, or at least raised your hand to ask a question once in a while. People like to know others are listening when they talk. Teachers and students too." Amaranthe kept her tone amiable, trying not to make her comments sound like a lecture, but she hoped to show Retta that whatever differences there might have been between them, they weren't Amaranthe's fault. No need to hold a grudge now...

"They *were* archaeology books. How'd you... I mean, I didn't think you even knew who I was."

Amaranthe decided not to mention that the fact had only stuck out for its oddness. All the other girls had carried their textbooks or, if they enjoyed reading, the latest romance or adventure stories. "While I don't mind chatting, you haven't answered my original question. Why are you here?"

Retta glanced toward the door and lowered her voice. "Nobody deserves this fate."

"So, you've come to unlock me? Excellent."

Retta grimaced. "I can't. I owe Ms. Worgavic too much. She was the one who realized I was never going to be like my sister, that I was interested in history and archaeology instead of business, and that I didn't belong at Mildawn. She talked to my family and had me sent to Kyatt to finish my education. After that, she elicited a lot of favors so I could go

to the field to study artifacts with a woman who used to be on Professor Komitopis's team. Do you know who she is?"

Yes, thanks to Sicarius's recent explanation. Komitopis was the one who had translated the language from the race who had crafted the *Behemoth* and ancestors only knew what else. If Worgavic had sent Retta off to study the ancient language, she must have been aware of this craft, and the need to learn how to work it, long ago. She must have seen in Retta not only a girl with an archaeology interest but also one with few friends, one who'd be loyal to anyone who treated her decently. Amaranthe decided not to dwell on the fact that she sometimes pursued similar tactics. What mattered now was figuring out a way to break that loyalty, or at least work around it.

"Amaranthe?" Retta pressed her eyes to the slit, peering into the blackness. "Are you still…?"

"I am, yes." Amaranthe groaned. Eliciting sympathy couldn't hurt her cause. "Do you truly think the other founders would listen to Ms. Worgavic?" Playing along and sounding like she could be swayed might help too. "That they'd let me live? After what I've done? And who I'm… associated with?"

"They want your assassin friend dead, there's no denying that. But if you disassociated yourself from him, and helped us to determine how much of a threat he'll be going forward, then I don't see why you couldn't join Forge. They're smart people. They know it'd be more of a coup to turn an enemy into an ally than to simply get rid of her." The last sentence had a stilted, or maybe rehearsed, cadence. Had Ms. Worgavic had Retta memorize it?

"You think the other founders are that open-minded? Who are they anyway? Anyone I've heard of?"

Retta shook her head. "I'm not going to give you any free information, Lokdon. You'd have to give *us* a lot of information before we'd start to think you might be on our side and trustworthy."

"Then it seems we're at an impasse," Amaranthe murmured.

"It's better to be with them than against them. Trust me. I know what it's like to be on the outside. Not only is this a chance to end your suffering, but you heard Ms. Worgavic. This is a chance to ensure you have a part in creating the future."

"Why do you care if I join or not?" Amaranthe asked.

"Back in school, you didn't look at me with soul-shriveling contempt. And you held the door open once when you saw that I was carrying a bunch of books. Human kindness was rare at Mildawn." Again, the words sounded rehearsed, and they didn't mesh with Retta's earlier bitterness over their different school experiences. She had to be here, fishing for information, at Worgavic's behest.

Amaranthe sighed and tried not to feel like she'd wasted her limited energy talking with the girl.

Retta leaned back from the slit. "Think about what I said. I'm sure you'd make friends easily in Forge, and it wouldn't take long for you to go from suspicious stranger to trusted ally. Winning those people over, it'd just be a new kind of challenge for you."

"I'll... consider it," Amaranthe said.

Retta nodded, apparently accepting that as a small victory. Amaranthe wished she felt like she'd won some victories.

A faint tremor pulsed through the floor.

"I have to go. It's time to land."

"Land? Land where?" Amaranthe hadn't even known for certain that they'd been flying. She wondered how far they had gone. More precisely, she wondered how many miles separated her from Sicarius and the others. Escaping might only be Step 1 in reuniting with them. She sagged under the weight of the idea of a thousand-mile trek.

"The closest unpopulated area to our meeting spot." Retta lifted a hand to close the slit to the crate.

"Wait," Amaranthe blurted.

Retta paused, her hand hovering. "What?"

Yes, what indeed?

Amaranthe rifled through her thoughts, trying to think of something she could say to convince Retta to help her. Something to instill guilt? Would that work? "If I... don't make it, and if Forge wins... whatever you do with this new future you and Worgavic are crafting, please ask yourself if you're truly making the world better or if you're simply replacing one group of ruling elite for another. And, if you're the one responsible for making this aircraft accessible to Forge, please don't let them use it to hurt people. With this much power in one's hands, it'd be easy not to bother with governments at all and simply create dictators."

Retta frowned, disappointment entering her eyes. Yes, she'd thought Amaranthe would give in and divulge Sicarius's secret. She hadn't expected a lecture, and she probably didn't appreciate it.

The window covering slid shut, plunging Amaranthe into darkness again. She sighed. Hadn't she been better at this once?

# CHAPTER 7

TWILIGHT DEEPENED AS THE BOAT GLIDED UPRIV-er, angling toward Rabbit Island where an ancient castle perched at the top of a tree-cloaked pinnacle, its grounds ablaze with gas lamps. Nice scenery, but Maldynado barely noticed it. He kept sneaking peeks at Yara, who sat on the bench beside him, her athletic form quite striking in the sleeveless blue velvet dress. A cape warmed her shoulders on the chilly night, but, from time to time, it drooped, revealing sleek, smooth skin, skin he'd seen for the first time when she had been changing back in the junkyard. Not that he was puerile enough to sneak behind a heaping debris pile to peep, but sometimes a man happened to be passing by on some other errand and accidentally glimpsed feminine flesh.

"When I volunteered for this duty," Books said from behind Maldynado, where he hunched over bicycle pedals, powering the boat's paddlewheel, "I didn't realize this island was *up*stream."

Maldynado, who lounged on the padded passenger bench, his arms draped across the backrest, said, "I assumed that your big brain had a map of the entire empire stored in there."

"As a resort for the indolent wealthy, Rabbit Island isn't worth a mention on many maps."

"I think that means there are holes in his memory," Maldynado told Basilard.

Basilard and Sespian manned the oars on either side of the boat. Akstyr sat behind Books, somehow having wrangled the non-physical position of tiller-man.

"Ssh," Sespian whispered. "We're getting close. There are guards up there."

Even as he spoke, someone moved on the dock, and metal—the barrel of a rifle—glinted in the lamplight. Maldynado picked out six guards pacing near the gangway of a wood-paneled, brass-bejeweled, three-story steamboat. The *Glacial Empress*. Twilight's deepening made it hard to tell, but some of that brass might have been gold.

"There are more guards on the steamboat too," Sespian whispered.

"Guess I'd better make a bigger distraction than I'd planned." Maldynado patted the bulging side of a satchel slung over his shoulder.

"Just don't light the entire island on fire," Books murmured.

The men rowed the boat into the cove with the dock. A few yachts and private water taxis shared moorage with the steamboat. Akstyr aimed their craft toward an open spot alongside the main pier.

"Ready to meet the family?" Maldynado let his arm drop from the backrest to drape around Yara's shoulders.

"Touching," she said, though she kept her voice low.

"Yes, I imagine we should do quite a lot of that tonight," Maldynado whispered, "though with lips instead of hands, don't you think? To make our relationship look realistic."

Maldynado hadn't had many women growl at him, at least not outside of the bedroom, but the noise that escaped Yara's throat sounded like it qualified.

"Now, now, my lady," Maldynado said, aware that the guards could probably hear by now. "You know it's only proper to save the growling for… later."

Two men in crimson-and-black uniforms, those of some private guard service, stepped up to Akstyr's chosen docking spot and turned up gas lamps perched on the poles. The brighter light nicely illuminated the rifles cradled in their arms. Maldynado did a double-glance. They were repeating firearms. It seemed Forge had been busy supplying its allies with the latest models from their secret weapons manufacturing plants.

Sespian lowered his face. The beard and new clothes disguised him well, but avoiding scrutiny was a good idea. He ought to loosen those white knuckles too; he was gripping the oar like he might turn it into a cudgel at any moment. He must hate having his fate in a Marblecrest's hands. Maldynado would show Sespian that he was trustworthy.

"Good evening, gentlemen," he drawled to the guards.

"This is a private island, comrades," one man said. "Unless you have an invitation, you won't be permitted to get out of your boat."

"I'm here on family business." Maldynado waved toward the castle-turned-resort. From this lowly angle, trees blocked the view of most of the structure, but a couple of lit towers stood out against the night sky. A wide, well-lit cobblestone road wound its way up the hillside. "My sister-in-law, Mari Marblecrest, was supposed to arrive today. Did she make it safely? I would be remiss if I didn't come to see her."

The guards exchanged looks. One fingered the trigger of his rifle.

Maldynado stood, so he could take action if he needed to, but also so they could see his fine garments and the arrogant chin tilt he assumed. He hoped they'd believe him warrior-caste based on looks alone. By law, commoners who weren't soldiers or enforcers with orders to do so were forbidden from lifting a hand, even in defense, against aristocrats.

"What's your name? My lord." The guard tacked the latter on, no doubt covering himself should it prove to be true.

"Maldynado Montichelu Marblecrest," he said in his most pompous tone, then removed his hat and offered a slight bow, not the deep one a man might issue to a colleague or a lady, but the type that was considered a gesture of respect when given to commoners.

"Aren't you disowned? My lord?" the man in charge of talking said after another exchange of looks with his colleague.

"He runs with mercenaries and outlaws, doesn't he?" the other one whispered and eyed the rest of the "boat crew."

Ugh, not good. "Ah, you've heard about my exploits down in the capital? I hadn't realized that my tales had traveled this far downriver. I'm done with that life though." Maldynado waved toward Yara, hoping to get the guards looking at her, and that oh-so-lovely bosom, instead of at the men. "I've been told that my father has invited me to rejoin the family and that Mari has the details. Do be a good lad and run along to let her know I've come, won't you? My fiancée is eager to meet her." He kept his hand extended toward Yara, and the guards' eyes were indeed lingering on her, and not her face either. Fortunately Yara's growl was too low for them to hear.

After another shared glance—Maldynado was beginning to think those two might share a brain as well—one of the guards said, "Go check," and the other scampered off the dock.

Maldynado took this as an invitation to climb out of the boat. This drew a frown from the remaining guard, especially since Maldynado stood a half a foot taller than the man, but he stepped back without a word. Still trying to figure out if Maldynado deserved warrior-caste respect perhaps. Or maybe he knew that other guards stood at the base of the pier and would have plenty of time to shoot if anyone tried something. And then there were those additional men on the steamboat.

"My lady?" Maldynado offered a hand, inviting Yara to join him on the dock.

She stood, frowned at the hand, and proceeded to climb out herself. She tried to, anyway. The brass-tipped slippers Maldynado had chosen to match the dress lacked the sturdy soles of enforcer boots, and one of her feet slipped in a damp spot on the dock. Though she probably would have recovered her balance before she pitched sideways and fell into the river, Maldynado caught her about the waist and kept her upright. He needn't have pulled her against his chest to achieve that goal, but opportunities to have a woman feel one's pectoral muscles couldn't be ignored.

Alas, Yara shoved him away before she had a chance to feel much of anything. "Men," she said in a tone that made it clear it was a curse. "Not only do they buy you clothes designed for the benefit of their eyes, but they consider it a coup if those clothes also make it more likely that you'll need their help." She glared at the guard, as if he had colluded with Maldynado to bring about the moment.

The guard skittered back, apparently more alarmed at risking her ire than that of Maldynado, warrior caste or not. He decided it wasn't bad walking beside a woman who could quell men with a glare. If she'd just stop sending that glare his way so often…

"It's a nice dress, ma'am," the guard finally managed.

"Do you like it?" Maldynado withdrew the stacks of business cards the shopkeepers had pressed onto him. "Save up and visit Madame Mimi's Fashion Boutique. I'm sure you'll find something nice for your lady."

The guard gaped at the card in his hand, a perplexed wrinkle to his nose. So long as the man didn't find them suspicious.

A soft clatter arose from the direction of the road. None of the guards reacted, and, a moment later, a bronze-and-wood sphere on a tiny cart

rolled out of the darkness and onto the dock. The knee-high contraption hissed and spat smoke from a tiny vent pipe on the top. Maldynado's hand drifted to his rapier hilt. He'd suffered enough at the hands of magical devices of late.

In the back of the boat, Akstyr's head perked in interest for the first time. When Maldynado met his eyes, he used Basilard's hand code to sign, *Magic.*

Lovely complication.

The guards didn't blink at the sphere's appearance. Given how scarce—and utterly forbidden—magic was in the empire, that must mean they thought it some steam-powered automata.

The closest guard bent, opened a door in the sphere, and pulled out a scroll tied with silk. Maldynado tried not to be obvious about peeking over his shoulder as the man read. Most of the writing was too small to make out, but he spotted Mari's flowing signature.

"You can go up," the guard said, "my lord."

Huh.

"Naturally." Maldynado snapped his fingers at Basilard. "Gather our bags, boy."

Basilard's eyes widened, and his hands moved together, as if to sign a few choice imprecations, but Sespian cleared his throat softly. After a quick glare at Maldynado, Basilard fetched a trunk. Maldynado had found it in the junkyard and done his best to refurbish it, figuring Mari and her cronies would think it odd if he arrived without any luggage, especially when he was traveling with a woman.

Basilard plopped the trunk onto the dock, nearly catching Maldynado's toe beneath the corner. Maldynado moved his foot in time.

*I thought I was going to be the bodyguard*, Basilard signed.

*Bodyguard, lackey, it's all the same to someone in the warrior caste*, Maldynado signed back when the guard wasn't paying attention.

*One wonders how hard bodyguards try to save their clients from harm.*

"You boys, tie the boat up and mind these security fellows. We'll be back later tonight or in the morning." Maldynado flipped the emperor a coin, hoping Sespian wasn't the type to order public floggings for impudence.

Sespian kept his head down, but he caught the coin with a quick snatch and pocketed it. "Yes, my lord."

"He's the best actor among us," Maldynado muttered to himself, then raised his voice for the guard's benefit. "Do we have to walk up? Or are there carriages?" He waved at the message-delivery sphere still hissing where it idled. "It seems there's some technology on this remote rock."

"Sorry, my lord," the guard said. "No steam carriages, but there are porters available if your lady is disinclined toward walking."

"The lady can walk just fine." Yara strode off the dock at a brisk pace, wobbling only slightly in the slippers.

"Come, boy," Maldynado said and hurried to catch up to her.

Had Basilard the ability to mutter under his breath, he surely would have been doing so. But, in silence, he hefted the trunk over his shoulder and followed after Maldynado and Yara.

As soon as Maldynado passed the trio of guards waiting on the road, he pretended to trip on the cobblestones.

"Blast, this is a rough road," he said. "Poorly lit too. Torches would be brighter than these twenty-year-old gas lamps." Two of the guards carried lanterns, and, without asking, Maldynado plucked one from the hands of a fellow who didn't appear particularly alert. "I'll see this is returned to you, lad."

"What? I—"

One of his comrades elbowed him. "Yes, my lord."

Maldynado jogged and caught up to Yara. She said nothing about his delay. The woman wasn't much of a conversationalist.

Bumps and clanks followed them up the hill. At first, Maldynado thought it was something in the trunk, but Basilard wasn't the one making the noise. The message-delivery device, trembling and hissing from the strain of rolling up the bumpy road, had decided to trail after them. That could prove problematic, as Maldynado had planned to create his distraction as soon as they rounded a bend and trees hid them from sight.

"You two see Akstyr's warning?" Maldynado asked, keeping his voice low in case the device could somehow report their goings on to its master. He wagered it did more than deliver messages. When Yara gave him a blank look, Maldynado remembered she wouldn't have under-

stood the sign if she'd seen it. He tilted his head backward. "We seem to have picked up a spy."

"Does it matter?" Yara asked.

Not sure she understood the device's magical significance, Maldynado said, "If it's here to observe us, probably."

She gave him a sharp look. Yes, she understood now.

Maldynado supposed he could leave Books and the others to figure their own way onto the steamboat, but he *had* promised a diversion.

Basilard stopped and set the trunk down with a thump. He shook out his arms and rubbed his lower back. It wasn't that heavy, so Maldynado knew it was a show.

He signed, *Idea?*

Basilard considered their surroundings. They were winding their way up the hill and had left the trees to walk across the open face of a cliff on the back side of the island. Its steep walls rose above and dropped below them. The guards couldn't see them anymore, thanks to the topography, but the steam device clanked to a stop behind Basilard.

He finished his rubbing and stretching and bent to pick up the trunk again. He pretended to stagger under its weight, and stumbled a couple of steps to the rear. The wheeled sphere started to roll backward, but not quickly enough. Basilard stumbled again and *accidentally* punted the thing off the road and over the cliff. Never mind that a star brindle-ball player would have struggled to launch a projectile so far.

The device clunked on a boulder at the base of the cliff and bounced into the river.

*Oops*, Basilard signed with a wink.

"Nice," Maldynado purred.

He opened the trunk and pulled out the tattered, grimy clothes people had been wearing before he resupplied the group with more suitable attire. After dousing them in lamp oil from his satchel, he wadded them up. He tied the bundle into a nice knot, lit it with the lantern, and tossed it onto a promontory below. It landed in the branches of a tree. Perfect. The rocks separating the promontory from the mainland ought to keep the rest of the island from catching on fire, though he supposed that'd make an even more engaging diversion.

He dusted off his hands. "Just enough of a problem that a few guards will need to check it out."

Yara regarded Maldynado and Basilard with pursed lips. "When I first met you people, I thought Corporal Lokdon was the crazy lunatic who'd used her charisma to talk you men into haplessly following her. I see now I was mistaken; you're all crazy lunatics, and you deserve each other."

Basilard asked, *Should we be offended?*

"Careful," Maldynado told Yara. "Basilard says he can do that with people too." He pointed over the cliff at the spot where the device had disappeared into the river.

Basilard punched Maldynado in the arm.

Yara snorted and continued up the road, again striding ahead, showing no interest in waiting for her "fiancé."

"Whoever marries that woman is going to have his hands full." Maldynado lifted the trunk and helped Basilard hoist it back onto his shoulder.

*Or* her *hands*, Basilard signed with his free fingers.

Maldynado scratched his jaw as they started up the hill again. "You suppose that's the case? I *have* been perplexed by how resistant she is to my charms."

Basilard did an impressive job of balancing the trunk without his hands, so that he could sign, *I did catch her giving Amaranthe a speculative look when we were on the dirigible.*

Maldynado stumbled. It was a good thing *he* wasn't carrying anything. "You *did*?"

Normally, he wouldn't mind the notion of two women running off together—indeed, in the past, he'd been known to encourage such activities so long as he could be involved in some way—but the idea of Yara being permanently unavailable chagrined him for reasons he had a hard time identifying. Before his chagrin set in too deeply, he noticed the mischievous glint in Basilard's pale eyes.

"Oh, you're just kicking me in the shin, aren't you?"

Basilard flattened his hand against his chest in an unconvincing "who me?" gesture.

"That's what I get for mistranslating your signs for people, I suppose."

Basilard nodded once, then, as they strolled around another bend, he signed, *I caught her peeking at you when you were sleeping.*

"You did? When I had my shirt off to use as a pillow?" It'd been a bit chilly for shirtless napping, but one had to make sacrifices when trying to impress a woman.

*Yes, it's amazing how often you've been unclothed since she showed up.*

"Pure coincidence." Maldynado smiled, his self-esteem bolstered by Basilard's revelation.

Beside him, Basilard slowed to a stop, his eyes toward the road ahead, or rather what was at the end of the road. *It* is *a castle*, he signed.

Yes, the massive structure possessed all the requirements, everything from massive stone walls cloaked with creeping ivy to a moat winding its way around the base of the structure. Lampposts with intricate wrought iron and glass frames lined the ground inside the moat, ensuring nobody would climb up those ivy-bedecked walls without being noticed. Further, Maldynado thought he spotted caltrops or something similar dotting the ground around those lamps. Above, guards in chainmail clanked as they strolled along walkways protected by crenelated parapets. Towers rose at each of the corners, complete with arrow slits, though modern breech-loading guns had replaced cannons and were perched on the roofs, poised to fire upon vessels coming up or down the river.

"It's a castle," Maldynado agreed, "but a lot of that pomp is for show. I've heard it's a nice resort inside. There are heated mineral baths and massage stations all over the bottom floor. Each suite upstairs has its own dedicated butler."

*Does the structure predate the empire?*

"You'd have to ask Books for the boring details, but I think the first Turgonian conquistadors set it up as a guard post to protect the route inland. Once they found gold and diamonds in the mountains around the Chain Lakes, they weren't looking to have the Nurians or anyone else coming a-visiting." Maldynado waved at double oak doors on the other side of a bridge stretched across the moat. "We better knock before someone starts to wonder where their mechanical spy went."

Though Maldynado wasn't intimidated by the castle itself, uneasy twinges assailed his gut as he approached the drawbridge. He dreaded a chat with Mari. He might not have volunteered to be disowned, but he

hadn't fought it either. No longer having to attend family gatherings had been a relief.

Basilard pointed at the moat. Two crimson eyes stared at them from the surface of the water. *It seems the alligator stories are true.*

*The stories didn't mention glowing eyes*, Maldynado signed, thinking of the tainted creatures the team had encountered while seeking the makarovi-infested dam.

*More magic. We had better pay close attention inside.*

*Because you're the help supposedly, my sister-in-law will ignore you. You might be able to slip away and snoop.*

Yara stood by the door, her hands on her hips as she waited for Maldynado and Basilard to catch up. They'd barely stepped off the drawbridge when she grabbed an iron knocker wrought into the broad ursine head of a grimbal and clanked it three times.

A *clink-clunk* emanated from behind the walls, followed by a faint hiss. The doors groaned open, revealing a brighter entryway than one would have expected from the grim stone exterior. Though the inner walls were also stone, they had been whitewashed. Gas pipes, also painted white, ran along the walls, powering countless lanterns and an elaborate chandelier dangling from a high, arched ceiling. Landscape and portrait paintings mounted between the light fixtures displayed a mixture of the straightforward unimaginative styles of the empire and more exotic and fanciful images from faraway lands. The signatures were all from historically significant artists, meaning the paintings had cost someone a fortune to purchase.

"Pretty," Yara grunted in a tone that suggested she preferred the utilitarian decor of an enforcer office.

"Yes, but not so pretty as you, my lady." Maldynado swept into a bow, figuring people would be observing them by now.

Yara looked like she might throw up, but refrained from telling him to stuff his compliments up his—

"Lord Marblecrest?" a man asked, stepping down from one of four stairways that tunneled into the walls, leading upward from the stone foyer. The slim, mustached butler wore an ornate blue suit choked with gold and silver trim and adorned with coattails one would have to be careful not to trip over. If he didn't feel ridiculous in the outfit... he should. But he likely had no choice. With pale skin and straight blond

hair tied back in a braid, he appeared Kendorian or Mangdorian. Maldynado wondered if he had been hired because he'd work cheaply or if he might be an illegal slave, as Basilard had been. Either way, if foreigners comprised most of the help, Basilard might have an easier time wandering about and spying.

"Yes, good fellow." Maldynado stepped forward. That the man had called him "lord" was a good sign; it meant Mari hadn't squashed his story of having a right to the family name again. He'd best lay on the warrior-caste arrogance thickly. "I insist on rooms for the night and to be taken to see Mari Marblecrest at once."

"Er, rooms?" The butler had been walking toward them, but he halted, almost stepping on one of those flowing tails. "I hadn't realized you'd been invited to spend the night."

Maldynado adjusted his hat, giving it a jaunty tilt. "This *is* a resort, is it not? You *do* have rooms available, do you not?"

"Yes, of course, my lord," the butler said in the soothing tones of one who had mastered the art of placating self-important aristocrats. "They are generally by invitation only, but I can add you to Lady Marblecrest's party. Yes, I'll tend to the accommodations promptly." The butler stepped backward a few paces, avoiding the dangling coattails with subconscious skill that could only come with practice, and extended his arm toward an arched doorway. "You and your party may wait in the Relaxation Grotto."

The double doors at the entrance groaned shut, and Maldynado tried not to find their resounding thud ominous. The butler paused and frowned, his gaze darting about as if he were looking for something. Oh, right. The ambulatory artifact Basilard had booted over the cliff.

"Wait?" Maldynado sniffed, drawing the man's attention to him. "The service here is terribly slow and antiquated for an exclusive resort. I can't imagine what drew Mari to the place. Did she *also* have to hike up a mountain simply to knock on the door?"

"Maldynado, do you *never* stop whining?" Yara asked. "The longer you stand there and complain, the longer we'll be kept from the steam baths and our *private* room." She gave her hips a suggestive wiggle. Though it wasn't as practiced and comfortable a wiggle as Maldynado usually saw from women, it did draw one's eyes to her curvy parts, and he found himself forgetting what he was doing and why he was doing it.

"Er, yes," he managed. "The Relaxation Grove, was it?" Maldynado waved for her to enter first.

"Grotto." Yara brushed past him, their bodies touching for an all-too-brief moment. "Do pay attention, Mal."

Yara gave the servant a wink before she disappeared through the doorway. Despite her admirable acting job—so admirable that Maldynado had to take a deep breath to re-gather his thoughts—the servant's frown remained. As much as Maldynado would love to spend the night entertaining Yara in their "private suite," he had a feeling they should get what information they could and skedaddle off the island as soon as possible. He hoped Sespian and the others had already found an opportunity to slip aboard the steamboat.

Warmth and humidity wrapped about Maldynado as he entered the so-called grotto. The dimness and a return of the gray stone walls, albeit ones carpeted with numerous species of flowering vines, brought a cave to mind, if a luxurious one. Furs muffled the team's footfalls as he, Basilard, and Yara walked around padded benches and lounge chairs, gurgling fountains, potted palm trees, and coal-burning braziers with dancing flames.

Once they were all inside, the door thudded shut behind them.

"I guess we're not supposed to wander," Maldynado said.

Yara skirted a steaming pool with meandering curves and stopped before an oak door on the far side. When she tried the latch, it didn't budge. "It seems not."

Maldynado didn't see any other doors, though the foliage growing from pots and wandering up the walls obscured the view. He walked to the front of the room where a long, cushion-covered bench ran below a window that stretched from side to side and almost to the twenty-foot ceiling. During the day, it must let in ample light and offer an impressive view of the river, but all Maldynado noticed in the darkness was the moat. Two sets of red eyes floated past.

Numerous black iron bars made up the window frame, holding the hundreds of square panes in place. Basilard ticked the metal. *Sturdy.*

Indeed. Nobody could jump out that window.

"Relax," Maldynado said, as much for himself as for the others. "This is a resort, not a dungeon."

"A resort in a very functional-looking castle." Yara strode over to Basilard and extended her hand, palm up. "Do you still have it?"

Basilard lifted a pant leg and fished something out of his boot—a sheathed knife with a leather strap wrapped around it.

"Thank you." Yara propped her foot on a planter, hiked the calf-length hem of her dress up to her waist, displaying a view of a muscular yet shapely leg, and strapped the sheath to her thigh.

A tap on the shoulder drew Maldynado's attention.

"What?" he asked Basilard.

*Do you believe we are likely to be attacked?* Basilard's firm signs emphasized the fact that he was repeating himself.

*Sorry*, Maldynado signed back while Yara finished with the knife. *I was... somewhere else.*

I noticed.

Maldynado cleared his throat and told himself to focus. "I don't know."

*Is it possible we've walked into a trap?*

"It's a little soon to assume that, don't you think?" Maldynado had been proud of himself for taking charge and scheming up a plan to get the team onto the island. He'd hate to think that he'd been ensnared somehow, and that someone had all along wanted to get him here, with the emperor in tow. It *had* been quite a coincidence that he'd happened to run into Cousin Lita in a city with a population of fifty thousand. And it *had* been rather easy for him to snob his way into an invitation to step foot on the island. Not to mention how quickly the servant had agreed to overnight accommodations.

Maldynado moaned.

"What's the problem?" Yara asked.

"Nothing. Just, ah, practicing my moans for the bedroom exploits we'll need to have tonight. In order to convince people that we're truly engaged. Mari knows me. She'll expect audible proof of our joining to emanate through the walls."

The narrowness of Yara's eyes implied she hadn't bought a second of that. "That was a moan of distress, not a moan of passion."

"Well, I did see you strap that knife to your inner thigh. I don't know how rough you like it."

"You're an idiot."

Maldynado wanted to riposte with a retort as sharp and biting as the tip of his rapier, but if he had walked them into a trap, he *was* an idiot.

A soft clank emanated from a corner of the grotto. Maldynado moaned again. Now what? Some giant, steam-powered contraption that would stomp out of a secret chamber and trample them to death? Basilard and Yara dropped into crouches, back to back, knives drawn. Maldynado felt a twinge of jealousy over the fact that Yara chose *Basilard* as her fighting buddy, but reminded himself that they likely had more important things to deal with.

Two more clanks followed. With the last one, Maldynado glimpsed motion high up on one of the walls. Before he could think better of it, he ran across the room, jumped onto a fountain, and vaulted into the air. He landed on the wall, his hands wrapping about clusters of vines. Belatedly, he hoped they would hold his weight. Several vines pulled away from the wall, stolons torn from the mortar and dirt between the rocks, and Maldynado readied himself to be dumped onto the floor, but the tangled mass of greenery held.

"*What* are you doing?" Yara didn't say idiot this time, but Maldynado could hear the word hanging on the end of the sentence.

"Climbing." Maldynado picked his way up the wall toward a metal grid near the ceiling. He felt foolish when he reached it, though, for it was nothing but a grate. No, a vent. And maybe he hadn't been foolish after all. He must have seen the slats opening, and they wouldn't have opened for no reason…

"Is there something flowing out?" Yara asked. "Gas?"

Balanced precariously on the vines, Maldynado waved his hand before the vent. He didn't feel anything drafts, nor did he see anything coloring the air. Thinking he heard something, he leaned closer, ear tilted toward the vent. Yes, it sounded like air blowing out. Not out, he realized when he placed his hand on the grate and felt suction drawing at his fingers. In.

"Are those doors airtight?" Maldynado hopped down.

"What?" Yara asked. "What kind of castle is airtight? They're drafty by nature. That's why nobody lives in them anymore."

Basilard left her side to check the door they'd entered. After probing with his fingers, he turned back and signed, *Possibly. There are no obvi-*

*ous gaps. If they're not airtight by design, a Science practitioner could make them so.*

For the third time, Maldynado moaned. This night was getting worse by the minute. "I was afraid they wanted to trap us. It seems they just want to kill us."

"By removing all the air in the room?" Yara scowled. "That's a cowardly way to kill someone."

"We'll be sure to register a complaint with the city tourism board." Maldynado jogged to the other door, checked it for air cracks, and, when he didn't find any, tried ramming it open. Unfortunately, the oak proved stouter than his shoulder. He tried the latch again, just to be sure, but it still wasn't budging. On a whim, he knocked.

Yara snorted.

"You never know," Maldynado said. "Maybe some towel boy who isn't in on the ensnare-the-newcomers plan will hear me and open it out of curiosity."

Alas, no towel boys poked their heads into the room.

"Let's try the window," Maldynado said. "That's glass, right? Nice, *breakable* glass?"

The tiny panes were too small for anyone to climb out, but a hole would solve the air problem. Maldynado and Basilard grabbed a heavy earth-filled pot with a moss garden fuzzing the top. They dragged it toward the window.

"That seems too obvious," Yara said.

"Maybe they overlooked the window. I don't think my sister-in-law is that practiced at planning murders."

Maldynado gave Basilard a nod to indicate he was ready. As one, they lifted the planter and hurled it into the glass. The heavy pot clunked off the window and dropped to the bench and then the floor, dirt and moss spilling onto the stones.

"Come to think of it," Maldynado said, "it's been a while since I've been to a family get-together. Maybe Mari's new hobby *is* planning murders."

"Your relatives sound delightful."

"Any ideas, Bas?" Maldynado spun in a slow circle, seeking inspiration. "Maybe if we ram the door with one of the stone benches…"

Basilard shrugged—not exactly a glowing endorsement of the idea—and followed Maldynado to a seating area near the door. Even with two people, lifting the granite bench seemed like a Sicarius-inspired exercise. They manhandled it to the door and were panting by the fifth thump against the oak. None of their thumps resulted in more than dents in the sturdy wood.

"You two are wasting our air with all that panting," Yara said.

"So sorry, my lady. I thought it worth the risk if it might mean escaping." Maldynado touched the oak planks. The wood hadn't seemed that thick. "Magic?" Maldynado sat on the bench, not bothering to shove it away from the doorway. "Some sort of enhancement?"

Basilard merely shrugged again. *You should have recruited Akstyr to tote your trunk.*

"I doubt he would have agreed."

*I didn't agree either.*

"No, but you're a more amenable sort, and I knew you'd play along without entertaining thoughts of killing me later."

"How about more ideas and less pointless banter?" Yara snapped. She stood in a crouch by the fountain, her knife clenched in her hand, as if she hoped people would come in and attack her.

"You're welcome to share your ideas," Maldynado said, refraining from snapping back. He figured she hadn't faced death as often as he had—not that he'd learned to relish the notion—and fear spurred her short temper.

The knife in Yara's hand drooped. "I'm sorry. I'm just… concerned."

"Me too." Maldynado knocked on the door again. "Hello, we're not finding the Relaxation Grotto very relaxing. Mind if we try another room in the spa?"

Basilard signed, *Are you actually expecting an answer?*

"A maniacal cackle, perhaps."

Maldynado noticed himself drawing in longer breaths, as if he were tramping about on top of a mountain. Yara stalked to the window and tried smashing the tip of her knife into one of the panes. Whatever that clear stuff was, it wasn't glass, for her blade didn't leave so much as a scratch. All that happened was that her knife flew out of her hand.

She picked it up, the movement not as smooth as usual, thanks to the confines of her garment. "I can't believe this idiotic dress is going to be what I die in."

"You could always take it off." Despite the thin air, Maldynado managed a convincing leer. "I'll strip, too, and we can die entangled in each other's arms, thrashing about on the floor like deer in the rutting season."

"You make sex sound so appealing."

"I'm open to gentle, unhurried methods as well."

"Does he ever think about anything else?" Yara asked Basilard.

*Rarely.*

Maldynado sank down onto the cold stone bench. In truth, he'd have a hard time working up the energy for a good rut. Already his limbs had grown weak. His lungs inflated deeply, but couldn't find sustenance in the air.

Basilard placed a dagger between his teeth and scaled the vines to one of the vents. He tried to pry the grate open.

"In case I don't get another chance to say this," Maldynado said, pausing to inhale between words, "I apologize for dragging you two up here. I should have known my family wouldn't truly be interested in exonerating me. If I hadn't been thinking to fool them myself, I would have realized this was a trap." He slumped. "Cursed ancestors, I hope we didn't set the others up to get caught too. Or worse."

The scrapes on the wall ceased. Basilard hadn't managed to pry the grate open, not that it would have done any good anyway. That duct was too small to crawl through. Basilard hung now from one hand, his eyes half-closed, his chest rising and falling in deep, strained breaths.

"You better come down before you fall down," Maldynado said.

Without any of his usual agility, Basilard climbed down the wall, his grip slipping several times. He landed hard and sank straight to the floor. He leaned his head and shoulder against the bench and stared at Maldynado with defeat in his bleary eyes.

*Sorry*, Maldynado signed.

*I forgive you.*

*Thank you.*

Maldynado wished he could get something similar from Yara, but she appeared too irked to consider tender parting words. He lifted a hand, inviting her to come sit on the bench beside him. Jaw set, she remained standing, her arms crossed over her chest.

Maldynado sighed and closed his eyes.

\* \* \* \* \*

In the dark confines of the crate, after a long, gruesome day of torture, Amaranthe allowed tears to roll down her cheeks. She wouldn't show those tears to Pike, but there, in utter solitude, she saw little reason to maintain a façade. In the beginning, she'd thought she could somehow rescue herself by talking someone over to her side, but she'd made little progress on that front. Perhaps if she had a month, she might find a way to chisel through Retta's barriers, but her body told her she didn't have that month. Healing salves or not, she couldn't imagine surviving three more days of Pike's torture, much less thirty. A hundred times, she'd fantasized about Sicarius appearing behind Pike, slashing his throat, freeing her from that terrible table, and carrying her off to safety. But, in her heart, she knew he'd gone with Sespian. Even if he hadn't, if Retta was to be believed, the *Behemoth* had landed days ago. If Sicarius had been able to follow the craft somehow, he would have found a way on board by now. And he hadn't.

The slit on the crate door slid open. Amaranthe hurried to wipe away her tears, though it couldn't be Pike. He always had the machine yank her out of her prison; he didn't crouch down to chat through the door.

"Amaranthe?" Retta asked hesitantly, as if fearing she might have passed on.

"I'm still here," Amaranthe croaked, wondering if she dared hope her last words to Retta had somehow meant something.

"I have a question for you."

"Unless it's a new one, I decline to answer."

Retta knelt beside the crate and leaned close, tilting her head as if to hear better. Amaranthe knew her voice was weak but couldn't manage a stronger one.

"Why did you leave school to become an enforcer?" Retta asked.

A new question after all. One that surprised Amaranthe because it didn't have anything to do with… anything. At least it didn't seem to.

It must though. Random curiosity wouldn't have brought Retta here to voice questions.

"Why do you ask?"

"I just need to know."

"My father—"

"I *know* that's what you tell everyone," Retta interrupted, "but Ms. Worgavic was right. If you'd wanted to finish school and continue on in the world of business, you could have found a way. Why didn't you? Why choose the enforcers over a chance to craft your own destiny?"

Hm. For whatever reason, Amaranthe had been in Retta's thoughts. That last talk had seemed scripted, as if Retta were only there because Ms. Worgavic told her to question Amaranthe. Now, though, perhaps Ms. Worgavic was gone, off to that meeting, and Retta could ask her own questions.

Amaranthe considered her answer carefully. The truth, the one she had once told Hollowcrest when he'd asked a similar question, probably wouldn't win her Retta's favor. Had she known what exactly the girl wanted to hear, she would have been tempted to provide the appropriate answer, even if it were a lie. Unfortunately, she didn't *know* what Retta wanted to hear.

"I'm not… against the notion of capitalism," Amaranthe said, "and I believe it's possible to do good, both by providing a useful product or service and by putting the money one acquires along the way toward a noble purpose, but as we entered our latter years of study, I came to realize business wasn't for me. I'd always competed at the races, and I preferred a more physical lifestyle. More than that, I wanted to help people. I wanted the *satisfaction* that comes from helping people. I like knowing that I matter, that the work I'm doing matters. I also wanted… to be someone history remembers. I thought I could earn that by becoming the first female enforcer chief in the empire. I didn't want money, or business success, just immortality of a sort."

Amaranthe waited for Retta to laugh or belittle her—no immortality for you now, girl, just a slow death at the end of Pike's knife. Instead, she said, "It's interesting that you didn't start to gain any fame until you broke away from the enforcers and became an outlaw."

"That is true," Amaranthe said, still wondering what Retta wanted.

"My parents forced me to go to that school, to follow in my sister's path, even though I had no interest in business myself. I wanted to study history and archaeology and explore the world, to see what the past could teach us."

Amaranthe grunted encouragingly.

"When Ms. Worgavic offered me the chance to do all I wished to do, if only I worked on her behalf, I saw my opportunity. I could study as I wished and see the world, and the apprenticeship would please my parents as well. It seemed ideal." Retta settled onto the floor, only her shoulder in view as she leaned against the crate door, her gaze toward a distant wall. "But when you tie your dreams to someone else's wagon, and you agree to be bound by their rules, you're never truly free. All the success you achieve is ultimately the result of someone else doing you a favor. And if that wagon starts down a course you wouldn't choose, it may be too late to untie yourself. I wish… I'd been more patient and found a way to do it all on my own."

"There's still time," Amaranthe said. "You're young. Start now."

Retta turned sad eyes in her direction. "I know too many of their secrets. They wouldn't let me walk away."

Amaranthe remembered worrying the same thing about Sicarius once, that he'd never let her walk away because she knew *his* secrets. How fortunate she was that she hadn't wanted to leave him.

"If you let *me* walk away," Amaranthe said, knowing full well that it was too early in this newfound kinship to make requests, but knowing too that she didn't have the luxury of time, "perhaps my team and I can rock the wagon enough that the drovers wouldn't notice someone slipping away."

Retta shook her head slowly. The sadness in her eyes deepened, and that disturbed Amaranthe more than a snort or a "nice try" would have.

"Even if I didn't fear reprisal, I can't betray Ms. Worgavic. She's done everything for me that she said she would, and, wishes for the future aside, I've benefited handsomely from the association." Retta placed her hand on the crate door. "The only way I can release you is if you tell me what everyone wants to know. Ms. Worgavic said she'd let you go if you did, so I wouldn't be betraying anyone. I could do it now, in the middle of the night, when nobody would be around who might… override Ms. Worgavic's wishes for your continued existence."

Amaranthe laid her head on her knees, the tears threatening to swallow her eyes again. She was tired of the fight and of the pain, and was more tempted than she would admit by the offer. "I can't," she whispered and was glad when Retta left without pressing further.

# CHAPTER 8

THEY DON'T MAKE STATUES OF PEOPLE WHO WALK behind others. You have to walk out in front.

The words floated through Maldynado's head, though he wasn't sure where they came from. An indignant snort came to mind—he'd *tried* to lead the way, to walk out front, and what had happened? He'd gotten himself and his comrades captured. Maybe killed. Nothing but darkness surrounded him. Was this death?

Something prodded Maldynado in the ribs. Hard.

In the distance, a woman said, "Now, now, no need for that. Don't leave him with any more scars. He already looks battered for my tastes."

Mari? Maldynado couldn't tell. His ears seemed to have water in them.

"Not mine," said a second woman, practically purring as she spoke. "Kill the others if you wish, but let's bring him along. We'll be on the river for several days, and I wouldn't mind a cabin boy to entertain me."

Maldynado managed to get his eyelids working. Not that the view was exciting. The corner of something stone filled his vision. The bench, he realized. He lay flat on his stomach, apparently where he'd fallen. He tried to roll over, to get a look at the speakers, but ropes bound his hands behind his back. When he attempted to move a leg, he found his lower limbs also immobilized with his ankles crossed, pulled up into the air, and tied to the ropes constraining his wrists. Thick moist cotton filled his mouth. A gag. How fun. A quick glance down his body assured him that they'd taken his rapier and knife.

"That *is* tempting. Ravido needn't know whether he died here or at the end of our trip downriver. The boy's not very bright, so I doubt we'd

have to worry about him masterminding any escapes." The woman cackled.

Yes, it was definitely a cackle, a high-pitched one that ended with a snort. Maldynado remembered it well. Mari. The other voice didn't nudge his memory with a sense of familiarity.

"We can keep him tied up to make sure," the second woman said. "Though I've heard he's skilled in the bedroom, so it'd be a shame not to give him free use of his hands."

Yes, it would, Maldynado thought. He remained still while the women spoke, since they seemed to be working themselves up to the idea of taking him with them on the *Glacial Empress.* He'd be happy to play along as lover-slave until an opportunity to escape arose. Yes, *escape.* He dearly wanted to tell them to slag off and that he was bright enough to plan such a thing, though it was hard to boast of one's intelligence when one was trussed up like a hog on a spit.

Mari's high-pitched laugh sounded again. "I'll let you try the hands-free option, Brynia. You're young and sexy, so you'll have no trouble seducing him. He's alas not been quick to acquiesce to my advances in the past."

"You wish him stowed in your cabin, my lady?" a man asked. It sounded like that butler. He was tending to Maldynado's accommodations after all. How thoughtful.

"Yes, but I want to question him first," Mari said.

"Do you need *assistance*?" another man, this one with a deep, rumbly voice, asked.

"I doubt it. The boy has never been one to put a clamp on his lips."

"Yes, my lady. What do you want us to do with the other two?"

"They're nothing to me. Feed them to the alligators, so there's no evidence that they were here."

At that statement, Maldynado made a more vigorous attempt to turn over. The lover-slave ruse would only be acceptable if Yara and Basilard were safe, or at least not *dead.*

"Ah, he's awake," the second lady, Brynia, said. "Roll him over, will you, Dorff?"

At first, that sounded like a good idea—Maldynado wanted to see more than the bench—but as soon as meaty hands flipped him onto his side, he regretted it. With his arms and legs locked behind him, the new position threatened to rip the bottom shoulder out of its socket.

A woman's face lowered to regard him, and Maldynado stopped squirming. He'd expected Mari, but this was a stranger, a sexy stranger. Clear blue eyes framed by long dark lashes gazed down at him. Shoulder-length blonde hair fell in a curtain about a striking face with a small mole placed artfully on the chin.

"Hello, darling," she said. "Care to answer a few questions?"

The only thing that came to mind was, "Uhm." The gag muffled it, but Maldynado feared they got the gist.

"I told you he's not the swiftest," Mari said.

She had changed little since Maldynado had last seen her. She sat on a nearby bench, legs crossed, hands braced behind her in a way that thrust her chest outward. A pair of onyx clips kept her brown hair pulled away from her face, but couldn't hide its unruly frizziness. Her face itself wasn't entirely unpleasant to look upon, but her dark eyes never failed to have a calculating, predatory gleam that would make any sane man uneasy. Maldynado had been a boy when she and Ravido had married, but he'd always suspected that family connections, and perhaps some manipulation on her part, had been behind the pairing.

"That's all right." Brynia offered Maldynado a sympathetic smile, though he knew it couldn't be sincere. "Not everybody's ancestors favor them in all matters."

Maldynado craned his neck until he located Yara and Basilard. They were also tied and lay where they'd fallen, Yara by a fountain in the middle of the room, and Basilard by the wall on the other side of the bench. Neither had their eyes open, and Maldynado worried that they'd already been killed. No, they wouldn't be tied if they were dead. He just had to figure out a way to keep them from a trip to the moat. As skilled a fighter as Basilard was, he wouldn't be able to defend himself with his arms and legs bound behind his back.

Several burly men loomed about the room, sabers and pistols hanging at their waists. The firearms had revolving chambers to hold multiple bullets. Some carried rifles as well.

Brynia knelt beside Maldynado and untied his gag, her crimson fingernails flashing. As she removed it, she stroked those fingernails along his jaw.

"Where is the assassin, Maldynado?" Mari asked.

"The who?" Maldynado asked.

"Sicarius. My comrades very much want his life to end. The family knows you've been working with him. For the longest time, your father hoped he'd grow weary of your wit and kill you so that your criminal exploits—and the embarrassment to the family—would end, but my business colleagues say that the woman leads the group. We know she's no longer an issue—"

Maldynado's heart almost stopped. Amaranthe was *no longer an issue*?

"—but he's still on the loose," Mari said. "We thought a trap set for you might ensnare him at the same time." She waved around the room. "We wouldn't have gone to such elaborate lengths if we'd known it'd just be you, a thug, and a girl."

Worried about Amaranthe, Maldynado barely heard the part about a trap.

"Who is she, anyway?" Mari sniffed in Yara's direction. "A woman with muscles and knives isn't quite to your tastes. You prefer those vapid, buxom girls who haven't a thought in their heads beyond rubbing against you and rousing your interest."

"Now, now, Mari," Maldynado said, having a notion that he should stand up for himself so they wouldn't know how deflated his foolish choices had left him, "there's no need to be bitter just because I've rejected you. Often."

Mari clenched her jaw.

"Ah, the pretty man has teeth." Brynia, still kneeling beside Maldynado, patted him on the arm and smiled. "Good."

"But," Maldynado said, keeping his eyes toward Mari, "the past needn't set the pattern of the future. If you let my friends walk away from here, I'll go along with you on your trip and perform for you in whatever capacity you desire."

"You'll do that anyway," Mari said. "If you *perform* well, your death at the end can be painless. If not…" Her gaze shifted toward the burly thugs.

Please. After what Maldynado had been through in the last year, threats of pummeling weren't that terrifying. And she was probably bluffing about the death part anyway. Or maybe not. They'd been dis-

cussing that before they knew he was conscious, hadn't they? When they'd had no idea he was listening? Or maybe they'd known he was listening and had been playing a part.

"You're not going to kill me," Maldynado said. "You're not a murderer, Mari. You're a warrior-caste woman, bound by law and honor."

"Don't be naive. Even if I had a reason to feel honor-bound to you—which I don't, because you're a criminal as far as the empire is concerned—your father wants you dead, and I wouldn't be foolish enough to defy him."

"My father wants…?" Maldynado bit his lip. He shouldn't show them that he believed her.

"He was satisfied with disowning you at first, but then you horrified him by turning from dandy to whore, pleasuring old women for coin. And then this outlaw thing. Running around with an assassin who kills honest businesswomen on a whim. Your whole life is an embarrassment to the family."

"Father can't possibly care about Forge." It was the only thing Maldynado could latch onto, because the rest was true. And, with the truth pointed out, he didn't have much trouble imagining his father's displeasure. "He's old-blood warrior caste, through and through."

Mara laughed, the shrill cackle grating on Maldynado almost as much as the discomfort of his position. "You *are* naive. While other warrior-caste families have grown weak over the last century, seeing their lands usurped by the changing times, the Marblecrests have thrived. Your family has done what's needed to maintain its power, and it will continue to do so."

"Mother can't want me dead," Maldynado said, worried that it sounded like a last attempt at defense.

"Your mother never forgave you for Tia's death. Her youngest, her only daughter, gone because of your neglect. I can't tell you how many times I've heard her say it should have been you instead. From what I've gathered, your siblings will also be satisfied to learn of your demise. A death for a death. There's a universal fairness to it, don't you think?"

Maldynado closed his eyes. *It should have been you.* Yes, he'd heard his mother say that often enough to know Mari's words were a direct quote. He couldn't summon the will to argue further on the topic. It didn't matter anymore anyway. What mattered was making sure Yara

and Basilard didn't end up in the moat. But how, by his dead grand-mother's biggest, ugliest wart, was he going to do that?

A knock came at the door nearest to the foyer. Mari and Brynia walked over to open it.

While the women were distracted, Maldynado opened his eyes for another scan of the room. Basilard and Yara hadn't moved, though Basilard's eyes were open. When he saw Maldynado looking his way, he widened them with significance. He flexed his arm slightly, and Maldynado tried to guess what message the movement was meant to relay. Basilard seemed to have shifted a few inches when nobody was paying attention, so he lay on his side with his back to a corner of the granite bench. Maybe he was using the sharp edge to saw at his bonds? As if he could guess Maldynado's thoughts, Basilard nodded slightly.

Maldynado wished he'd been working at his own bonds while the women were talking to him. If Basilard freed himself, he'd have to handle six men with repeating firearms, along with whoever had come to the door.

A potted tree blocked Maldynado's view of the entrance. He squirmed to the side, trying to see the door. A guard standing a few feet away patted the stock of his rifle. Maldynado gave him an I'm-harmless-and-not-doing-anything-besides-being-curious look. The man snorted. Maldynado decided not to push things with further movement. Besides, he could see enough.

Mari had opened the door, and a tattooed man wearing buckskins had come in. Brynia watched from a few steps back as Mari questioned the newcomer—a shaman, Maldynado assumed. He tried to eavesdrop, though the gurgling fountains made it difficult.

"…get him?" Mari asked.

A pang of unease struck Maldynado's gut. *Him?* Him, who?

Maldynado didn't hear the shaman's response, but a nod accompanied it.

"You're certain?" Mari asked. "For a bookish boy who mastered the art of escaping weapons practice as a child, he's proven surprisingly adept at eluding us in the field."

The unease in Maldynado's gut turned to dread. The emperor.

The shaman's chin came up. "Thanks to my abilities—" he lifted his hand and flexed his fingers, "—their boat was incontrovertibly destroyed. Three bodies floated away from the wreckage, and the men you sent with me shot them full of holes. Your emperor is fish food on the bottom of the river now."

No. Books was too smart to let some brute blow him up. And Akstyr would have sensed a shaman coming. It had to be a ruse. Because if it wasn't… their deaths would be Maldynado's fault. *Everything* that had happened tonight was his fault. He closed his eyes and wished he could melt into the floor, never to be seen again. But that wasn't going to happen. And he wasn't going to give up on Books and the others until he'd seen the dead bodies himself. He gritted his teeth and, while most people were focused on the conversation at the door, wriggled back to the bench. If Basilard could scrape his ropes off, maybe Maldynado could too.

"The captain says the steamboat is ready for departure if you wish to leave tonight," the shaman said. "He is concerned tonight's activities will draw enforcer interest to the island."

"This is a private island," Mari said. "Enforcers have little power here. We're not leaving until I know who's dead at the bottom of the river. Did you retrieve the bodies and verify their identities?"

Maldynado didn't hear the answer, but he sure hoped it was no.

"Brynia," Mari said, "can you tell where the knife is?"

Maldynado had been rubbing his ropes against the bench edge, but the question made him pause. The knife? Sicarius's knife? It was the only one he could imagine being referred to as *the* knife. Maldynado assumed Sespian still had it. Rust-for-luck, had Forge figured some way to track the weird metal?

"Give me a moment." Brynia withdrew a black oval from her pocket.

Maldynado couldn't make out the details, but it appeared to be made from the foreign material he'd been seeing far too much of lately.

He rubbed his ropes harder. If he managed to free himself, he'd want a weapon. His were missing, so he'd have to borrow one. He eyed the guards, seeking one with the attentiveness of a sock. Nobody quite that likely presented himself, but one thick fellow with more fat than muscle might make a good shield while Maldynado wrestled his rifle and sword away.

After a long moment spent staring at the black egg, Brynia lifted her head. "It hasn't moved much. It's still near the docks."

She *was* tracking the knife. How long had she been in town? Since the attack in the park? That would explain how those thugs had known where to find the emperor. Maybe she'd been the one to send Cousin Lita to that antique shop. Brynia was probably roaming around the satrapy, collecting all sorts of handy heirlooms with secret powers. Ah, maybe that was how they'd found themselves the monstrous aircraft as well. Though, where, he wondered, had they found the tracking artifact to start with?

"Near the docks?" Mari asked. "Is it in a boat or at the bottom of the river?"

"I can't determine location with that kind of accuracy," Brynia said. "Retta was busy learning how to fly the *Ortarh Ortak* and couldn't spare much time to explain how to use this."

Mari pointed to the shaman. "Take some men and dredge the river. I want to know for certain that Sespian is gone."

The shaman stood straighter and flicked a long braid of auburn hair over his shoulder. "I am not your lackey. When I agreed to work with you, it was because you said she'd lead me to the assassin." He pointed at Brynia, more specifically the oval device she still held. "The boy emperor has never wronged my people. *Sicarius* has."

"I don't care about your revenge dreams," Mari said, not backing down from the shaman's glower. You're being paid for your assistance, and you'll continue to give it. Besides, we thought the knife belonged to Sicarius and that he'd be with the emperor." She tilted her head, as if some new thought had popped into it. "Perhaps this signifies that Sicarius died in the crash and that the emperor grabbed the knife, simply because he did not want to leave a valuable tool behind." As she spoke those last words, she faced Maldynado. "What happened to the assassin?"

Maldynado ceased his manipulations of the rope. "No idea. He was too busy hunting down Forge people to come along with us."

Brynia waved the oval device. "His knife was on that train and then on the dirigible."

Mari tapped her chin. "Perhaps he *is* dead, and we've been worrying for nothing."

"Think whatever you like," Maldynado said. "Just know that your actions have condemned the Marblecrests as well as Forge. Sicarius never stopped working for the Savarsin family, and he'll kill anyone who opposes Sespian." Probably not, but it sounded like a good threat.

With a quick wave, Mari dismissed the shaman. She and Brynia started toward Maldynado. He grimaced. So far all his scraping at the bench had done nothing more than rub his skin raw. He needed more time. He needed—

Basilard sprang to his feet. He sprinted ten feet and bowled into an armed man before anyone reacted. The startled stillness from the guards didn't last. A shot rang out from someone stationed by the window. Two guards by the door pushed the women behind potted trees for protection.

Maldynado flexed his arms, trying to muscle his bonds apart, but he hadn't made enough headway on the cutting.

The guard closest to Maldynado raised his rifle, but by then his comrade was on the floor, entangled with Basilard. Instead of shooting, the man yanked a knife from his belt and sprinted toward the fray.

Maldynado judged his path, then hurled himself into a clumsy sideways roll. The guard saw him and tried to adjust, but it was too late. His foot caught on Maldynado's hip, and he tumbled. The guard turned the fall into the roll of a practiced warrior, but his shoulder clipped one of the big, heavy pots, and his knife flew out of his grasp.

The blade clattered to the floor and skidded toward the bench. Before it stopped moving, Maldynado was rolling back toward it. He managed to grasp it, but, with his hands still behind his back, maneuvering it proved more awkward than sex in a closet. Nearly dislocating his shoulder, he slashed the rope securing his ankles to his wrists, but his limbs were still bound to each other, and cutting his hands free proved a tougher task. At least most of the guards were busy with Basilard who'd freed Yara as well.

Gunshots rang out, and Maldynado didn't have time to feel indignant that he'd helped her first. He started to go for his ankles, but the guard who'd inadvertently provided the blade leaped to his feet. Though he'd lost his rifle in the fall, too, it only took him a split second to spot it. Maldynado saw it too. He hurled himself into another clumsy roll, angling toward the weapon. The knife blade sliced into his forearm, but he couldn't slow down or worry about it. The guard sprang for the rifle. Maldynado reached it first and smothered it with his body. The guard pounced, landing on top of him.

With his wrists and ankles still bound, Maldynado couldn't kick or punch. He did manage to get his knees up defensively. More by luck than design, he caught the fellow in the groin. Shock and pain contorted the guard's face. Before he recovered, Maldynado whipped his head off the ground, smashing it into his assailant's nose. With a buck that would have impressed an irate mule, Maldynado heaved the man off him.

Frustrated at being tied, and determined to get his hands in front of him where he could use the knife more effectively, Maldynado flung his bound wrists over his head. Something popped in his shoulder, and a wave of agony coursed down his arm. Too bad. Forcing the numb arm to move, he hacked at the rope tying his ankles together. Before he could flip the knife to cut his hands free, the guard leaped onto Maldynado from behind. An arm snaked around his neck. Maldynado ducked his chin, partially thwarting the lock before it started. A punch jabbed at his kidneys. Flexing his core to tighten his muscles and protect his insides, he doggedly kept at his ropes. The guard gave up on punches and used his free hand to try and gouge Maldynado in the eye.

"Go down, you fat-headed lizard," the guard snarled.

Maldynado buried his chin deeper and squinted his eyes shut against the probing fingers. Finally, the last strand of rope snapped beneath the knife and his bonds fell free, leaving him the use of his hands. He dipped his shoulder and went down on one knee to throw the guard off his back. The man tried to stay on, but the weight shift tipped him to the side. It was enough. Maldynado had dropped the knife during the throw, but it didn't matter. He grabbed his opponent with both hands and, with a roar of rage and pain, hurled him toward the wall. The guard smashed. Hard.

Maldynado snatched the knife and rifle from the ground, ready to shoot the eye-clawing bastard if he came back for more, but he didn't move.

Gunfire boomed near the door. Maldynado darted around a large fountain, crouching behind its holding pool while he surveyed the situation.

Basilard had disarmed and downed the first man, but Maldynado didn't see him amongst the proliferation of plants, trees, and water features. The sounds of a scuffle drifted from behind a potted hedge near the window though. Yara was kneeling behind a square planter hosting a lemon tree. She'd acquired a rifle and had it balanced on the pot's lip, her finger on the trigger. Even as Maldynado watched, she fired at someone near the door.

A cry of pain rose over the sounds of running water and scuffling men.

"Retreat?" someone asked.

"Get the women out of here!"

Maldynado started to stand, thinking his comrades had the enemy on the run, but he spotted a guard creeping toward Yara, a pistol in his hand. Using the planters for cover, the man slipped from one to the next, creeping toward her. He stopped behind a pedestal sporting a bust of Emperor Raumesys and aimed the pistol at Yara's back.

Maldynado fired his own purloined rifle without hesitation. He'd never shot one of the new weapons, but he couldn't fault its accuracy. The bullet took the man in the side of the head, its force flinging him to the floor beside a fountain several feet away.

Yara's head swiveled, and she gaped at the fallen man. When she met Maldynado's eyes, he gave her a nod that was meant to imply that making the shot had been simple for someone as adept and capable as he. Unfortunately, he'd never advanced the rounds in one of the multi-cartridge guns before, and he fumbled the effort, dropping two bullets on the floor. So much for adept and capable. Yara had gone back to covering the door, so maybe she hadn't noticed.

When Maldynado didn't see any other guards near them, he darted from his fountain to her pot, sliding in beside her. She crouched bare-foot, her brass-tipped slippers stuffed under the mulch of the lemon tree. Really! Maldynado was tempted to lecture her on the appropriate treatment of footwear, but she spoke first.

"Thanks for the help," Yara said.

Pleased with the rare display of gratitude, Maldynado snuffed out his shoe concerns.

"You're welcome, my lady." From his new spot, Maldynado could see the door. One of the uniformed guards ran outside. A quick body count suggested he might have been the last enemy in the room. "We better get over there—"

"—before someone locks us in again, right."

Yara led the way, rifle in hand as she stayed low and used the planters for cover. Maldynado took a second to smile, appreciating not only that

she was finishing his sentences, but that she appeared quite competent as she advanced.

"Not now," he told himself and crept after her.

Before they reached the doorway, Basilard stepped into view, a knife in each hand and two pistols jammed into his belt. Two unmoving men lay alongside the wall behind him.

"Good job, Bas," Maldynado said and jogged through the doorway, ensuring he couldn't be trapped in the Un-Relaxation Grotto again. He anticipated another round of opposition in the foyer, but the oak doors leading out of the castle stood open, letting a nippy breeze flow inside. "Did everyone flee?" Maldynado wondered.

Slaps sounded on the stone floor of an inner courtyard that opened up beyond the foyer. Since Maldynado hadn't had a chance to see any of that area, he didn't know what to expect, and he kept his rifle ready.

A white-haired, pot-bellied man with a towel wrapped around his waist padded into view, his wet sandals slapping against the floor as he walked. He spotted Maldynado, squealed, and dropped the towel. As naked as a newborn babe, he gaped at the group. Almost as surprised, Maldynado gaped back. For a startled moment, the man stood there, his arms and hands in the strange tableau of someone torn between grabbing a towel to cover himself up and simply running away from view. He chose the latter, and sprinted up a set of stairs faster than someone that age typically ran.

"I should have given him a card," Maldynado muttered, touching a breast pocket and finding the business cards still tucked within. Apparently the guards hadn't deemed them as dangerous as his rapier—or his *hat*, which was also missing.

"It looks like nobody bothered to inform the guests that there was a kidnapping going on," Maldynado said when Basilard and Yara joined him.

"You'd think the gunfire would have implied something was amiss," Yara said.

*Perhaps the grotto is soundproof,* Basilard signed.

"So nobody will hear the screaming of the innocent outlaws the establishment is luring to their deaths?"

"Innocent?" Yara asked. "You're about as innocent as a cat with cream smeared all over its whiskers."

"Say, Basilard." Maldynado gave him a thump. "Why'd you rescue her first and leave me tied up? Don't tell me her insults have endeared her to you." Or that you think she's a more able fighter than I, Maldynado thought. That would sting.

*I thought you could free yourself,* Basilard signed. *You've spoken often of exploits involving being tied up.*

"There's a difference between being tied to a bedpost by a hundred-pound woman and having one of those two-hundred-pound brutes trussing you up like the chicken going in the oven," Maldynado said, waving at one of the fallen guards in view in the Grotto.

"I'm not sure what he said—" Yara pointed a thumb at Basilard, "—but, from your half of the conversation, it *sounds* like you're whining again."

Maldynado started to sigh—was this woman never going to recognize any of his finer qualities?—but he caught a slight smile on her lips. Hm. That was promising.

Basilard pointed at the doors leading outside. *We must go after the others.*

Maldynado hadn't seen his rapier, or his hat, anywhere and was tempted to run around the resort to find it, but Books and the others might need reinforcements sooner rather than later. He started for the castle exit, but halted a few feet from the threshold, one foot in the air. Four gleaming metal creatures had slithered out of the moat and shambled onto the other end of the bridge. The alligators they'd seen before.

"That could be a problem." Maldynado put his foot down.

"We'll see." Yara raised her rifle to her shoulder.

"I don't know if bullets will work." Maldynado waved toward the bronze-and-iron hides. He'd seen real alligators on a trip to the Gulf, and they had been green and distinctly non-metallic.

Two of the creatures moseyed across the bridge, their red eyes locked onto Maldynado. He glimpsed an engraving on the top of one of the heads. Tar-Mech. He groaned. That cursed shaman was dead. When were they going to stop running into his creations?

"You see that, Basilard?" Maldynado eased backward a few steps. "Those are like the things we fought in that mine. The things that took explosives to kill."

Basilard nodded grimly. He fired at the lead alligator as it stepped off the bridge. As suspected, the bullet bounced uselessly off the metal hide. The mechanical creatures didn't move quickly, but the two in front would be in the foyer in a few more steps, regardless. Maldynado wouldn't count on those jaws being plagued with the same slowness as the legs.

"All right," Maldynado said, backing farther. "Explosives. Any idea where we can find explosives in a warrior-caste resort?" Books would probably be able to mix something up in the kitchen, but he wasn't—"What are you doing?" Maldynado barked, his thoughts interrupted by Yara running toward the alligators.

She stopped at the threshold and grabbed one of the heavy oak doors.

"Oh, good idea." Maldynado darted for the other door.

He expected it to be heavy, but not so heavy it wouldn't move when he pulled. The shoulder he'd nearly dislocated earlier stabbed him with pain, and he gasped. He gritted his teeth and tugged harder. The door inched away from the wall. Too slow.

Maldynado was about to suggest running into the castle and letting the nude bathers deal with the alligators when the door gave way. Both doors did, snapping shut so quickly Maldynado almost lost his nose. Yara tumbled onto her backside. The doors slammed closed with a thump as one smashed into the lead alligator's snout.

Basilard waved to a spot on the wall and signed, *Switch*.

"Steam-powered doors, right," Maldynado said.

Thuds nearly drowned out his voice. The alligators ramming against the oak. At first, Maldynado didn't think they'd have a chance at breaking in, but the wood planks shuddered under the assault. It sounded like all four constructs had started banging away.

"Who's up for finding a back door?" Maldynado asked. "Maybe we'll stumble across our gear on the way."

"I just hope you don't find that hat with the ludicrous feather." Yara jogged into the courtyard before Maldynado could respond.

Bare feet slapping on the stone floor, Yara veered around benches and potted plants only slightly less densely placed than in the Grotto. Maldynado and Basilard raced after her. She headed for a back wall where a hallway, sets of stairs, and closed doors offered numerous options. She chose the hall, something that might lead to the kitchen

perhaps. Kitchens had back doors, didn't they? For throwing scraps out to dogs or man-eating mechanical alligators?

They found a swinging door at the end. Maldynado peeked inside. A trio of chefs and bakers gaped back at him.

"How do you get out?" Maldynado figured it couldn't hurt to ask. Meanwhile his comrades checked other doors, only to find them locked.

"You don't," a man in a flour-dusted apron said. "You use the garbage chute. Otherwise the gators will—"

An older man shushed him and gave Maldynado a suspicious squint. "Who are you? You don't look like guests." He grabbed a butcher knife.

"Just visitors." Maldynado smiled and shut the door. He looked at the others, hoping they'd found a way out, but Yara and Basilard merely shrugged. "We'll try another way. I don't want a fight with the kitchen staff."

Someone thrust the door open behind him. A glimpse of that butcher knife convinced Maldynado to thrust the door back with enough force to send the chef staggering.

"This way," Maldynado barked and ran back toward the courtyard. Those stairs ought to take them up to the parapets. If nothing else they could climb down an outside wall.

He lunged out of the hallway, ready to race for stairs to the right, but a man stood there, a forty-year-old flintlock musket pointed at Maldynado's chest. It was the old fellow they'd seen in the towel. He was wearing clothes now, and an officer's saber hung from his waist.

"Watch out," Maldynado said, throwing an arm out to stop the others, even as he skittered back, intending to duck into the hallway.

Someone grabbed Maldynado's shoulder. The musket fired, but he was too busy being pulled to the floor to worry about it. Basilard leaped over him and barreled into the old man. Maldynado rolled over and jumped to his feet. Basilard had already knocked the fellow down and taken his musket. He stopped at that. Good. They didn't need to leave a pile of dead resort-goers behind.

"Thanks for the help," Maldynado said, realizing Basilard had been the one to yank him down before the musket ball found his chest.

Basilard nodded once. *What do we do with him?*

The white-haired man wasn't done *doing* things himself. After a moment of lying quiescent, he tried to hook one of his own legs around

Basilard's to throw him off. In his younger days, he might have managed the move, but Basilard reacted quickly. He used the man's momentum against him, flipping the old officer over and pinning him to the floor.

Maldynado pointed for Yara to lead the way up the stairs. "Let's just—"

A bevy of footfalls pounded the hallway floor behind him. The chef with the butcher knife burst around the corner. He'd added a heavy copper skillet to his arsenal. The rest of the kitchen staff—no less than six men—crowded after him.

"There they are!" the chef cried.

"Run," Maldynado blurted, finishing his sentence.

He used his rifle like a staff to block a surprisingly adroit skillet-knife combination attack. Maldynado stood his ground for a moment, giving Yara and Basilard time to race up the stairs without anyone throwing sharp kitchen utensils at their backs.

After blocking another attack, Maldynado teased out an opening and jammed his rifle butt into the chef's stomach. As the man doubled over, Maldynado kicked a young dish boy trying to get at his side. Both attackers stumbled back, hindering the rest of the staff.

Maldynado wheeled about and sprinted up the stairs.

"Duck!" Yara yelled when he was halfway up.

No sooner had he obeyed than the butcher knife cracked against flagstones a few steps above him. Basilard fired from up top. Not to kill, Maldynado hoped, but he dared not pause to check. As soon as he burst onto the top, he, Basilard, and Yara took off, racing down a long landing that was—unfortunately—open to the courtyard below. More knives and sharp utensils clanged off the railing and the walls all about them.

"Unbelievable," Maldynado muttered, pausing to try a door, one of many along the landing. "Only in the empire would the kitchen staff rally to chase off intruders instead of hiding in the pantry."

Basilard ducked a hurled pan and gave Maldynado a quick nod as he tried another door. Both were locked.

"Here!" Yara flung open the last door.

Maldynado and Basilard ran to join her. The kitchen staff had taken to the stairs and the fastest were surging onto the landing.

Just as Maldynado reached the door and grabbed the jamb, intending to propel himself around the edge, something with the heft of a wrecking ball slammed into his back. He staggered forward, and his face smashed against the doorjamb.

"Cursed ancestors," he growled.

A marble rolling pin clunked to the floor at his feet.

"Unbelievable," Maldynado repeated as he darted through the doorway. "Why me? Nobody would throw rolling pins at *Sicarius*." He was starting to rethink his decision not to shoot anyone on the kitchen staff.

The door lacked a security bar or a nearby armoire he could shove in front of it, but it did have a lock, albeit the flimsy type made only to keep an honest man honest, not deter a serious intruder. Or determined chefs. Maldynado thunked it into place, hoping it would slow the mob.

"Move! I see security coming!" someone yelled from the direction of the stairs. "They'll have guns."

Erg, repeating firearms would make short work of that lock. Maldynado spun, hoping Yara hadn't led them into a walk-in closet.

A short hallway led away from the door. At first, all Maldynado could see was a chest of drawers against a wall, but a few steps took him into a bedroom brightened by candles. A man and woman were entangled amongst sheets. The candlelight was bright enough to give Maldynado a view of bare breasts; under normal circumstances, he would have stopped to gaze in admiration. As it was, he only noted that the naked couple had no weapons nearby, though with the night he'd had thus far, he wouldn't be surprised if one of them yanked a dagger out from beneath a pillow. Or a rolling pin. At the moment, they were too busy staring at Basilard and Yara who had burst across the room to a window. Yara's frustrated grunts and pulling motions suggested the wrought iron vines and leaves snaking across the panes were more than decorations.

Bangs sounded at the door.

"How do you unlock this slagging thing?" Yara thumped a fist against the window, sounding like a woman with her patience balanced on the edge of a precipice. She mustn't have expected quite so much adventure when Amaranthe had recruited her to join them in Forkingrust.

"Easy, Yara, we'll get out, and we'll do it in time to help… people." Maldynado glanced at the pair on the bed. The woman had yanked the sheet over her chest, and the man was eyeing a sword belt dangling on a chair near Basilard.

Yara glowered over her shoulder at Maldynado. "How can you be optimistic? Your plan has been a disaster."

The thumps at the door intensified.

"That's true," Maldynado said. "When I imagined spending the night on Rabbit Island with my fiancée—" he winked at her, drawing a fresh lip curl, "—I was picturing us in something similar to *that* position."

"You *were*?" Yara's lip curl vanished, replaced by a gawk.

"Naturally," Maldynado said, surprised by *her* surprise.

*Focus*, Basilard signed. *We must open the window or find another way out.*

A boom roared in the hallway. The door shuddered, though the thumps that followed didn't hurl it open. Someone had bad aim, or the lock was stronger than it looked.

Maldynado stepped further into the room, wondering if there might be a secret passage—this *was* a castle after all. The pair in the bed were probably only guests, but maybe they'd know.

Maldynado smiled, pretended to remove a hat and press it to his chest, and bowed deeply toward the woman. "Pardon our intrusion, but are there any other exits from this room?"

The woman pointed toward a tapestry featuring a pair of randy elk. "There's a—"

"Ssh, don't help them." Her partner covered her mouth with his hand and glanced toward his weapons belt again. "Who *are* you people?"

"Innocent guests who couldn't quite cover the bill." Maldynado jogged to the tapestry and lifted the edge, revealing a door. Excellent. "The prices are a little higher than listed in the brochure."

Maldynado unlatched the door and waved for his comrades to join him. A dark, narrow stairwell led upward to another door. The last words he heard, as he headed up, came from the man. "Brochure? There's no brochure for this place, is there? I thought it was *exclusive*."

Someone shut the door, pitching the stairway into blackness. Maldynado fumbled his way to the top.

"That door better not be locked too," Yara said.

"If it is, it's not my fault," Maldynado said. "You chose this room."

"*You* chose this situation. Besides, someone had to get us off that landing. You were seconds away from being pummeled to death by flying rolling pins."

Maldynado groaned as he groped for a latch. Why'd she have to witness all his embarrassing moments? At least the door was unlocked. Freedom at last. He opened the door to the crisp, cold air of late autumn—and a very small, round tower top that on one side overlooked the courtyard, on the other the castle wall and the cliff on the back side of the island. Basilard and Yara joined him, crowding the tiny space. There wouldn't be anywhere to hide if someone started firing at them from the looming towers at the castle corners.

"If the brochure promised this room came with a balcony, those folks better ask for their money back. You'd be hard-pressed to fit a single lounge chair up here." Maldynado searched for a ladder or way off. There wasn't one. The three-story drop on the wall side led straight into the moat. Or, if one were terribly athletic and could leap past enough rocks, to the river, some seventy or eighty feet below.

"I see I can count on you to think of the important things in dire situations," Yara said.

Basilard pointed at the head of the island. From the elevated perch, the docks and the steamboat were visible. The dinghy they'd arrived on was gone, and there was no sign of Books, Akstyr, or the emperor. The steamboat was belching smoke out of its stack and maneuvering away from the docks, the giant rear paddle turning slowly. In a minute or two, the *Glacial Empress* would be heading downriver at full speed.

"We going after that boat?" Maldynado asked. "Or staying here to look for the emperor?"

"Neither if we get shot." Yara pointed to the courtyard at the same time as someone yelled, "Up there!"

"Fire!" came another cry.

Basilard dropped to a crouch. Maldynado, having already been hit by projectiles that night, took it further and flattened himself to his belly. It was perhaps a bit rude to take up so much of the limited floor space, for Yara tripped over him when she tried to crouch herself. Maldynado caught her as she fell, using his body to keep her from slamming into the unyielding stones.

"So," he said, "we end up entangled after all."

Yara was too busy elbowing him for Maldynado to savor the moment. She climbed past him to peer over the edge on the moat side. Basilard hunkered there too.

*The women must have fled to the boat,* he signed. *The emperor wanted to follow them. If he and the others avoided capture, they will be there.*

"We'll never climb down and reach the docks in time." Maldynado eyed the rocks and the moat. Maybe it was his imagination, but he thought he spotted a pair of crimson eyes floating by below.

*If we jump, we might be able to swim around the island fast enough to catch up. They're still maneuvering out of the docks.*

"What are we discussing?" Yara asked.

"The plan."

"Which is?"

Basilard made a jumping motion and pointed at the river.

"*Jump?*" Yara stared at Basilard and then at the meters of moat and rock between the edge of their perch and the start of the water. And the depth of the drop, too, perhaps. "Did someone kick your ore cart over?"

"If the emperor is alive, he'll likely be on that boat," Maldynado said. "We can't abandon him." Not if there was any chance Sicarius would learn about it anyway.

Basilard nodded firmly. Doubt filled Yara's eyes as she studied the drop.

"If you don't think you can make it," Maldynado said, pushing thoughts of Sicarius's threats out of his head, "I'll stay here with you and fight."

"I didn't say I couldn't *make* it."

A steam whistle blew, its pitch low and eerie as it floated up to the castle. They had to decide quickly if they hoped to catch the boat, but Maldynado didn't want to say anything else that might cause Yara to put pride ahead of wisdom. He wasn't entirely sure *he* could make that leap without landing on the rocks.

Yara cursed, not a choice succinct word or phrase, but an entire stream that impressed him for its ecumenical vulgarity. She hiked up her dress, backed up, and took a running leap, her bare feet launching her from the low wall around the balcony. Maldynado gawked as she arced out over the moat and the rocky drop beyond it. He held his breath, his hands clenched into fists. If she didn't make it…

Yara splashed into the river with a few feet to spare. Maldynado waited for her head to pop up, but it didn't. What if she'd reached the goal only to plunge into water too shallow?

Basilard slapped his arm and pointed. They had to go as well. Maldynado nodded, though he couldn't tear his gaze from the spot where Yara had gone in.

On top of the nearest tower, a rifle cracked. The bullet skipped off the stones at Maldynado's feet.

Basilard backed up for a running start and leaped. Knowing he'd be shot if he delayed further, Maldynado readied himself to do the same. He backed up to the far edge and bent his knees as if he were lining up for the start of a race at the Imperial Games.

His careful preparation was ruined when the door to the balcony flew open so hard it slammed against the wall. Guards surged out of the stairwell and onto the roof, their hands stretching toward him.

Maldynado smacked them away and sprinted for the edge. He jumped onto the low wall and pushed off with all of his strength.

Cold wind whipped hair into his eyes and railed at his clothing. Blood surged to his muscles, and Maldynado wanted to flail his arms, to try and hurl himself through the air by will, but he tucked into a ball instead, hoping it'd carry him farther. He peeped down, trying to judge his path and whether he'd jumped far enough—and trying to see Yara as well. He'd reach the water, but would it be deep enough? Had it been deep enough for her?

Maldynado landed with alarming momentum; the impact from striking the water sent a jaw-rattling jolt through him. As he plunged downward, the cold shocked his body, and he couldn't move, but he was too worried about smashing into the bottom to pay attention to the fact. He must have plummeted twenty feet before slowing. Darkness smothered the depths, and he couldn't see anything in the black water. Praise his dead ancestors, he didn't strike anything. Grateful for the river's depth, he tried to swim for the surface. Glacial numbness clutched his chest, and he couldn't feel his arms or legs. A current tugged at him, and he envisioned himself being swept downstream, trapped beneath the surface by some undertow.

Spurred by panic, Maldynado got his legs working and kicked as if all his ancestors were lined up, watching and mocking his lack of

manliness. His elbow banged against a rock. Startled, he let out his air. Water filled his mouth. He kicked harder, hoping he was going in the right direction.

Maldynado broke the surface and almost smashed face-first into an algae-slick boulder. His first instinct was to push away from it, but the current was tugging at him, and he didn't want to end up miles downstream. He wrapped his arms around the boulder like an enthusiastic lover. He'd lost his rifle at some point during the fall, but he hardly cared. Shivers wracked his body, and he wanted nothing more than to scramble out and find a towel—or, in lieu of that, beat up some guard for his clothes—but concern over Basilard and Yara stayed him. He searched about, trying to find them in the gloom. The lights from the castle didn't brighten the rocky bank, but he could see it above the treetops and used it to guess his position. He'd gone from the back side of the island to the southern tip. He couldn't see the docks, but maybe if he craned his head about—yes, there was the steamboat.

A figure in the water between it and Maldynado waved. Basilard.

Maldynado hesitated before swimming out to him. Where was Yara? What if she needed help? What if she lay smashed on a boulder somewhere? Or what if she'd been swept into the current and had never been able to find the surface?

Basilard splashed the water and pointed at the steamboat. It was on its way to the center of the river, and it'd be cruising downstream, full steam ahead before long. Maldynado wanted to call out to Basilard, to ask if he'd seen Yara, but guards patrolled the boat's deck and the docks would hear. Basilard couldn't respond anyway.

He turned his back on Maldynado and swam toward the boat.

"Emperor's hairy backside," Maldynado growled.

Left with few options, he swam after Basilard. They paddled with the current while angling toward the *Glacial Empress*. At first, Maldynado worried only about being seen. But, as he failed to gain ground quickly, he worried that he wouldn't be able to catch up. Hoping the darkness would hide his approach, and the splashes of the paddlewheel would camouflage his own splashes, Maldynado buried his face and stroked at top speed.

His body forgot the cold, and he caught up with Basilard a few meters from the steamboat. It had reached the channel. Water frothed

and churned as the giant paddlewheel, as broad as the entire back end of the boat, increased the speed of its revolutions.

Legs weary, Maldynado used his last burst of energy to swim along the hull to a dark blob. The anchor. Though it was pulled up, its chain out of sight in a hole, the dangling T-shaped hook offered a handhold. Panting, Maldynado gripped it so he could rest. The deck was lower to the water than on an ocean-going vessel, and it wouldn't take much effort to clamber over the railing, but it might be smart to wait and let security believe they'd escaped the island without unwanted passengers. The guards would be on high alert if Mari's people had sprinted down the hill, shouting of prisoners on the loose.

"Psst," came a whisper from the deck.

Maldynado's heart lurched. He'd been so worried about catching up with the steamboat that he hadn't checked above. For all he knew, three guards were sighting down the barrels of their rifles at him.

"Pssst!"

Maldynado tipped his head backward and made out a single dark figure, though he couldn't identify features. Lights burned on the boat, but mostly on the second and third decks where passenger and crew cabins awaited. The lower deck of the sternwheeler housed the engine and boiler rooms.

"Yara?" Maldynado guessed after a moment of analyzing those pssts. They hadn't sounded very masculine. It was hard for him to believe that she had reached the boat—and climbed onto the deck—before him.

"No, it's the emperor's dead grandmother. Get up here, you twit. Don't they teach warrior-caste brats how to swim decently?"

By then, Basilard had maneuvered around the hull to grab onto the anchor alongside Maldynado. With his mangled throat, he couldn't laugh out loud, but Maldynado had a suspicion the quakes that ran through his body were a result of chortles rather than trembles from the cold.

Maldynado climbed up to the metal railing encircling the deck and, after checking to make sure nobody besides Yara waited nearby, hopped over. He almost landed on an inert body.

"He objected to me coming aboard," Yara explained.

"He's not dead, is he?" Maldynado asked.

"Of course not. But I wasn't sure what to do with him. If we throw him overboard, people might miss him."

"Nah. In the chaos of everyone boarding early and dinghies being blown up in harbor, I'm sure it'll be seen as natural for a few guards to get lost." Maldynado grabbed the man by the back of the shirt, eliciting a sleepy groan—he'd wake up soon enough—and rolled him over the railing. "Like so. Lost."

Basilard had climbed over and joined them. He watched the man splash into the water, then signed something.

"What was that?" Maldynado turned his back to the water, and tried to line Basilard's hands up with a lantern burning near some stairs farther down the deck.

Basilard exaggerated his signs. *Are we going to hide? Or take over the boat?*

"Taking over the boat sounds… ambitious," Maldynado said. Now that he'd stopped swimming and climbing, he noticed the cold wind sweeping down the river, battering at his sodden clothing. All he wanted was to warm up somewhere.

"Take it *over*?" Yara whispered. "There must be two dozen guards, not to mention the passengers and crew."

"Let's just find a place to hide." Maldynado gave her a placating pat on the shoulder. "And get warm. Maybe we can convince the blokes in the boiler room to let us cozy up to their furnaces."

"They probably have orders to throw intruders *into* the furnaces," Yara said.

"If that's the case, they can become just as lost as that first fellow."

"If we keep throwing people overboard, the crew's going to figure out that there are intruders."

"Don't worry. It'll be fine."

The words *sounded* confident. Maldynado hoped they proved true. It'd likely take a lot of days traveling down the river to reach Mari's destination, wherever that was. If Sespian and the others hadn't found a way on board, it might not matter anyway. Only the emperor knew what he hoped to learn from the Forge meeting.

Maldynado gazed back at the lights of Rabbit Island, which were receding as the steamboat picked up speed. He hoped he hadn't, in choosing the steamboat over searching the harbor for his comrades, made yet another poor decision.

# CHAPTER 9

A MARANTHE'S STOMACH GROWLED. HOW STUPID of it to worry about food when there was so much else to worry about. Once again, she lay pinned to the operating table by the claw's black metal spikes. Somehow, when they were piercing her thighs, wrists, and shoulders, they never struck bone or an artery—she chose not to think that someone had designed them with such precision for just this purpose—but they hurt like sword wounds to the gut every time they went in.

Soft crunches sounded a few feet away. Pike had taken a break from his work to munch on an apple and peruse a chapter of his torture book. Meanwhile, tremors coursed through Amaranthe's naked body, and blood dripped down her sides to pool beneath her back and legs.

"Don't you have that book memorized yet?" she hated how weak her voice sounded and, thanks to swollen lips, how muffled the words came out. It was the first she'd spoken that day. She wondered how much longer she'd have the energy for it.

"Nearly so," Pike said around a bite of apple.

It disgusted her that a man could nosh away while a human being lay spread out before him, bleeding and mutilated, but Amaranthe ignored her feelings. She needed to figure him out, to get in his head, and suss out a way to escape before she was too weak to use an opportunity if it arose. She'd hoped Retta might be her way, but the girl hadn't been back since they'd landed. Nor had Ms. Worgavic returned. Pike was the only human being she'd seen of late, and his humanity was questionable. Still, he was the only one with whom she had to work.

"Why do you care?" Amaranthe asked.

Pike strolled to her side, still munching. His black clothing was neat, unstained, and unwrinkled, and, not for the first time, his similarity to Sicarius bothered her.

"Ms. Worgavic set the rules I was to abide by," Pike said. "I will not break them."

"You're from the warrior caste originally, right? Why would you obey a common-born woman?"

"I've been promised the position of Commander of the Armies should we succeed in putting Lord General Marblecrest on the throne."

Amaranthe closed her eyes. She didn't know Maldynado's older brother, but anyone who would employ a torture-aficionado as his right-hand-man couldn't be good for the empire, not the empire Sespian wanted, one where the nation tried to make amends for past evils and pursue diplomacy over war as it went forward. The odd thing was that there could have been a place for strong female entrepreneurs under Sespian's regime. But Forge, perhaps accustomed to negotiating with Hollowcrest and Raumesys, must have chosen to strong-arm Sespian instead of working with him.

"You do not approve." Pike smirked. "You're not good at hiding your thoughts. I'm surprised you've lasted so long without telling me what you know about Sicarius. I'm even more surprised Sicarius inspires such loyalty in you. Or is it fear?" He cocked his head. "Are you worried about what he'll do to you if you betray him?"

Amaranthe had wanted to take charge of the questioning herself, but Pike's words made her pause in consideration. Maybe it was odd, or overly optimistic, but she *wasn't* afraid of what Sicarius would do to her. She was more concerned about disappointing him. She didn't think he'd hurt her physically—she believed they were past that—but he might walk away, never to be seen again. That'd hurt more.

"If that's the case…" Pike leaned closer and stroked a finger along her abdomen. "I'm sure we can arrange protection for you."

Amaranthe wanted to thrust his hand away and punch him in the nose, but the pins through her wrists denied the possibility. The slightest twitch of a finger roused pain. "Forge can't even keep him from killing its own members. You'd best worry about arranging your own protection."

For the briefest moment, Pike paused, his finger frozen where it touched her rib. He recovered and withdrew his hand, then shrugged and took another bite of the apple.

That hesitation inspired Amaranthe to try a new angle. "If you're correct, and the emperor *does* mean something to Sicarius, do you truly want to be on the team that kills Sespian?"

"*I'm* not the one who's been hired to kill the boy."

"Nor, I suspect, were those thirty Forge people that Sicarius slew. It doesn't matter to him. Guilt by association. And you're associated. Also, judging from what you told me about the time you spent with him in his youth, I can't imagine he harbors a great affection for you."

Pike didn't respond. Though he'd chomped the apple down to the core, he'd grown quite interested in it.

"As a boy," Amaranthe continued, "he was indoctrinated to obey Raumesys and Hollowcrest, and I imagine that extended to his... instructors. But, last winter, he killed Hollowcrest, so he must be over any loyalty he once felt."

Pike's gaze sharpened as it fastened onto her face. "Did he? Kill Hollowcrest? From what I've heard, nobody's sure what happened in that mansion."

"Sicarius broke his neck with his bare hands. I was one of the few witnesses."

"Interesting." Pike seemed to have forgotten he was in charge of the interrogation, or that there was even one going on. Good. Amaranthe was about to speak again, but Pike whispered to himself, "So, he's taken out Raumesys *and* Hollowcrest."

Raumesys? Sicarius had killed the old emperor? He'd mentioned secrets that Amaranthe didn't know about, but she hadn't guessed that one. "Nobody from his old life is safe," she said. Better to pretend she knew all of Sicarius's secrets and had an advantage over Pike. "I don't think he appreciated his upbringing."

Pike snorted. "No doubt." Despite the snort, he looked pensive.

"Unless you two became buddies after your years of tormenting him."

"Oddly, he didn't find my company stimulating."

Amaranthe hadn't expected anything else, but she found comfort in the flippant comment. It would have disturbed her to find out Sicarius's

boyhood tormenter had become a friend later on, once they'd been… peers in the emperor's employ. In her heart, she believed Sicarius could have been a good man if he'd been born into another world, another life, but it was hard to maintain that belief at times. The neat checkmarks in Books's journal, denoting those he'd killed, still sent a chill through her.

Thoughts for another time. She had Pike answering questions. Best to press while she could.

"I'm not certain Sicarius knew you were still alive or around the capital," Amaranthe said. "He does now."

Pike tossed the apple core onto the floor.

"We've landed somewhere, haven't we?" Amaranthe asked, ignoring the refuse, though the silly part of her that preferred cleanliness wanted to admonish him for littering. "It's possible Sicarius has followed your craft and is waiting somewhere out there for you. Did you know he's familiar with this technology? He'll be able to find a way in here."

Pike's eyes flickered in surprise, but it only took him a second to regain his poise. "Even if that were true, we've come across hundreds of miles of unpaved wilderness since we picked you up. He couldn't have covered the ground that quickly, assuming he had any idea where we were going. Even Sicarius can't track a bird."

"Perhaps not, but he's relentless. If he's not waiting for you today, he'll be there tomorrow. Or the next day." At that moment, Amaranthe wanted to believe that more than anything.

"Enough." Pike gripped her thigh, fingers digging into a wound where he'd flayed the flesh away earlier.

A fresh wave of agony washed over Amaranthe, and she sucked in a pained breath. It was a warning, and she ought to heed it, but she had to plant a seed in Pike's mind before he went back to his work. As soon as she recovered enough to speak, she panted out, "You needn't live in fear of him. If you… were to release me from this… unpleasant incarceration, I could speak to him… on your behalf. He listens to me. I could get him to spare your life."

"Because I've so obviously left you in the mood to do me favors," Pike said.

"Put yourself in my position. Wouldn't you do anything, *agree* to anything, to escape?"

"Nice try." Pike rested his elbows on the table and leaned in close. "If you want to end this, tell me what the emperor means to Sicarius and why."

"No."

"If you die before you share the answer—and it's a distinct possibility as my salve can only heal the same flesh so many times—it won't matter. The Forge people are smart. They'll figure it out eventually. They'll figure it out and use the knowledge to kill or otherwise unman him. They'll put Ravido on the throne, and I'll have the position I should have had long ago."

Pike strode out the door without applying her salve. Amaranthe had a feeling nobody was coming to put her in her crate—or heal her—that night.

* * * * *

Maldynado eased along the hulking length of one of the steamboat's two boilers. Basilard crept behind him while Yara stood watch near the door. Ahead, the red glow of an open furnace shed light on the back half of the boiler room. Soft scrapes and clanks came from that direction. At least one person worked, stoking the fires. No windows lined the walls in this part of the ship—one wouldn't want upscale clientele to be forced to stroll past something as ugly as boilers or soot-covered attendants—so Maldynado hoped they could overpower the firemen and claim the out-of-the-way spot as their hideout.

The hairs on the back of his neck stirred as he drew close to the end of the boiler. Before Maldynado stepped into the light, he paused to listen. The scrapes continued, someone shoveling coal out of a pile and into the furnace. Nothing to worry about, Maldynado told himself—and those waving neck hairs. The worker might have a comrade or two, but, even without weapons, he and Basilard could surely handle lowly firemen.

Maldynado peeked around the corner of the boiler. Two figures were shoveling coal, their faces, hands, and clothes cloaked in soot. He waited until their backs were to him, then lunged out of hiding, intending to bowl both men to the deck.

Before he'd taken more than a step, something hammered into his back. Whatever it was didn't strike with the force of that cursed rolling pin, but Maldynado dove forward anyway, to put space between him and his attacker. He rolled and jumped to his feet, coming up with his back to a wall and fists cocked.

A tall figure strode toward him, a shovel raised for another blow.

Heat poured from an open furnace door to Maldynado's right. The other two firemen had noticed him and lifted their shovels too. One stopped.

"Maldynado?" a familiar voice asked. Akstyr.

His hair, which was usually spiked artfully about his head, hung damply about his jaw, and so much soot clung to his face that it looked like he'd used his head to swab out a coal bin. Akstyr could have walked past his own mother without stirring recognition, but now that Maldynado knew it was him, he identified Sespian as the other "fireman." Books was the one who'd leaped out of hiding and clubbed him. Naturally.

"Emperor's eyeteeth, professor," Maldynado said, "what was that for?"

Books set the shovel down. "I apologize. I didn't recognize you without your hat."

Maldynado might have tossed out a retort, but he was so relieved to see the others that he let the comment go. Besides, the loss of such a fine hat still upset him.

By then Basilard had slipped in beside Books. With five men crowded between the towering bins of coal and the furnaces, the space had the coziness of a sardine can, but nobody rushed to leave. Basilard gripped Books and Akstyr's arms in greeting.

"Good evening, Maldynado," the emperor said, "and Basilard. Is Yara with you?"

"Yes, Sire, she's standing guard by the door. How did you get on board? We heard..." Maldynado traded glances with Basilard. "Let's just say that you look well for a man who's been incontrovertibly destroyed."

Sespian nodded. "We sensed the trap before they sprang it, or rather, your young wizard did." He extended a hand toward Akstyr.

"Practitioner," Akstyr mumbled.

"Sire," Books hissed.

"*Sire*, they're called practitioners by people who aren't ignorant about such things."

"You really need to stop correcting his lack of honorifics," Sespian told Books. "His words tend to be more insulting when he has a chance to think them over and utter them again."

"Yes, Sire, I apologize." Books glowered at Akstyr. "The youth lacks a proper upbringing."

The dimness of the boiler room didn't hide the rude gesture Akstyr offered Books.

"Yes, you seem to be an eclectic group," Sespian said, then nodded toward Maldynado. "What happened in the castle? There was a commotion and a rather abrupt departure. An officer came in and yelled at us to shovel at double-time to bring the boilers up to full steam. Fortunately, he seemed too fraught to realize we weren't his usual firemen."

"You're rather well camouflaged." Maldynado waved at their sooty skin. "As for the castle… It didn't go well. It seems the rumor that my father wanted me back in the family was incorrect."

"How surprising," Books said dryly.

Sespian eyed the pools of water forming at Maldynado and Basilard's feet. "Were you able to sneak aboard without being detected?"

"Well…" Maldynado exchanged looks with Basilard. "Nobody *currently* on the boat detected us."

"I see."

Maldynado tried to decide if the short statement held censure.

"The plan," Sespian went on, "is to take the role of the stokers, who are also not *currently* on board to object, stay in here for the duration of the trip, and hope nobody cared enough about any of these men to come chat with them and notice that they've been replaced."

"We may have a problem with that plan, Sire. We can tell you the details of our castle trip later—" though Maldynado would rather not, "—but, right now, you need to know that Mari, who is indeed snuggled up to Forge's bosom, can track you."

"Track *me*?" Sespian touched the scab on his neck where the implant had once been. "How?"

"Actually, it's not you so much as Sicarius's knife," Maldynado said. "Mari has recruited a pretty blonde gal who can track that black technology."

Sespian drew the black knife and stared at it. Though the furnace door remained open, the flames inside writhing in a vibrant dance, none of the light reflected on the inky material.

"That would explain the attack at the park," Books said.

"Your assassin set me up?" Sespian asked, still staring at the blade.

"I'm sure that wasn't the case," Books said.

Maldynado propped a fist on his hip and frowned at Books. "How come you're sure Sicarius wasn't setting the emperor up to get captured or killed, but you were so quick to throw me to the alligators?"

"If Sicarius wanted a person dead, he'd stick a knife in his chest." Books grimaced, teeth white against the soot smearing his face. "He wouldn't leave anything to chance. Nor would he worry overmuch about whether you deserved to die or not." Another grimace. He must be thinking of those assassinations.

If the discussion comforted Sespian, he didn't show it. Indeed, the way he glanced at the furnace made Maldynado think he wanted to chuck the knife into the flames.

"I don't think that would melt it," Maldynado said. "But we should figure out something to do with it. As soon as Mari and Brynia get over their scare of having to flee the resort, they'll probably check for it. Mari wasn't convinced you were dead, Sire."

"I can throw it overboard," Sespian said.

Basilard stepped forward, shaking his head. *Not Sicarius's weapon.*

"That'd just make them suspicious anyway," Maldynado said. "We're a few miles downstream by now, so they'd know it had moved."

"*How* is this new woman tracking the artifacts?" Books asked.

"She had a black egg-shaped doodad of her own."

"Small?" Books asked.

"Pocket-sized."

"I wonder how long they've been able to track that knife," Books mused. "Is that how they located the train? For that matter, didn't some assassin jump you in Forkingrust?"

Maldynado touched his temple. "Unfortunately, yes."

Akstyr said, "I thought she was… uhm, something to do with me."

Maldynado hadn't gotten the whole story on Akstyr's situation, but Books had mentioned that the team needed to be on the lookout for bounty hunters sent by gangs.

"Maybe she was freelancing for Forge," Books said. "They have a big reason to want to get rid of Sicarius."

"Who doesn't?" Akstyr muttered.

"That doesn't matter now." Books rubbed his lips thoughtfully. "We need to focus on this new device and the threat it represents to us. What if we set a trap? We place the knife somewhere on the boat where we can easily attack whomever comes to collect it. Then *we* can capture and gain control of this tracking device."

"Oh, I like that idea," Maldynado said. "Then we can hunt down a gigantic dirigible-destroying aircraft for ourselves."

Akstyr brightened at this notion, something that was hard to do with all that soot caking his face.

"Or, we can track *their* craft," Books said, "and whatever else they've unearthed."

"And take it for our own, right?" Maldynado couldn't help it; the idea of controlling that thing made him grin like a boy. Maybe he could learn to *fly* it.

Books sighed. "Haven't you crashed enough types of vehicles already?"

"No, not yet." Maldynado smiled.

Sespian lifted a finger. "While I'm not opposed to depriving Forge of this tracking device, how can we set a trap without alerting them to our presence on the steamboat? If Mari knows I'm onboard, she'll get off and make other arrangements for travel, arrangements I might not be able to track. Or she might simply send all the armed men on the ship down to kill us all."

*She can try*, Basilard signed.

"I fear it'll be difficult to keep our presence masked, regardless," Books said. "Do you have any idea where the final destination is?"

"I don't know if the steamboat is taking her all the way, or only part of the way. She might not be staying on the river." Sespian frowned. "Or in the empire."

"Why do we have to *follow* this Marblecrest lady?" Akstyr asked. "Why can't we tie her up, thump on her a while, and force her to tell us what you want to know?"

Sespian stared at Akstyr. Books winced. Even Maldynado winced. Thumping on women wasn't honorable, even irksome sisters-in-law.

Akstyr scowled back at everyone. "How is that not more practical than hiding down here, risking discovery, and hoping she'll lead us where we want to go?"

*He has a point*, Basilard signed, though he didn't look happy about it.

"Not that I'm partial to Mari," Maldynado said, "but could we explore other options before we start torturing the womenfolk in my family?"

"Yes," Sespian said. "Give me more ideas. Preferably ideas that don't involve violence."

"Wait." Maldynado snapped his fingers. "We *do* know the final destination, don't we? Sicarius drew those lines on the map, right? And Markworth and Deerlick Wood were the only possible spots within five hundred miles."

Books's brow wrinkled. "Even if that craft were flying in a straight line, and those cities represented likely landing spots, Sicarius was hypothesizing about the destination of that aircraft, not the Forge meeting place."

"Wouldn't it be *going* to the meeting place?" Maldynado asked. "Mari's heading south, and that craft was heading south. You don't really think that's a coincidence, do you? What else would they have been heading south for? What with the coup going on and all, I can't imagine they're planning an escape to the Gulf for beach bumper ball."

Books lifted a finger, as if to object, but he lowered it again. He looked around, a faintly perplexed expression on his face. "As unlikely as it seems, I believe Maldynado has a point."

"You needn't sound so surprised," Maldynado said.

"Typically, the only thing pointed about you is your sword."

"Swords." Maldynado winked, never able to resist ribbing Books.

Books rolled his eyes.

"Markworth and Lake Seventy-three are accessible via a river that flows into this waterway," Sespian said without so much as an eyelid flicker at Maldynado's innuendo.

Maybe it went over the kid's head; he probably didn't get out of the Imperial Barracks much. When all this was over, Maldynado ought to take him under his arm and show him how to have a good time.

"There *are* all those islands down there, owned by the wealthy and warrior caste," Sespian added. "Perhaps one of them is the meeting place."

"Sure," Maldynado said, "I've been there. The family has a little island in the middle."

Everyone stared at him.

"What?" Maldynado asked.

"Could it be that obvious?" Sespian mused. "Did your brother invite his Forge allies to enjoy the family manor while they scheme plots that will, among other things, put him on the throne?"

Maldynado shrugged. "I don't know. I didn't get an invitation."

Clangs sounded outside, boots on one of the exterior staircases. Guards on patrol, Maldynado guessed, the noise reminding him that someone might come looking for Sicarius's knife soon.

"Are we going to set a trap?" he asked. "I only bring it up because it might be inconvenient if we're still standing here, chatting about our plans, when a bunch of guards burst in on us."

Sespian sighed. "I am reluctant to abandon my plan to remain in hiding, with Mari unaware of my presence, but I suppose your assassin has taken that option from me." He frowned down at the knife.

Maldynado hoped Sicarius hadn't been planning to ask the emperor for a pardon or any other favors. Trying to be helpful—or at least cheer the kid up—Maldynado patted Sespian on the shoulder and said, "Our plans go awry all the time, Sire. Amaranthe always finds a way, through explosions, scheming, and battles with mechanical monsters, to make things work out in the end."

"She's not here." Sespian eyed the hand on his shoulder.

"Er, that's true." Maldynado lowered his hand. "But you have us. We're excellent at two out of three of those things." He wasn't going to make any claims about scheming, because that hadn't turned out well for him thus far.

Books was shaking his head. Perhaps Maldynado needed to work on his skills at cheering people up.

Sespian said nothing. His eyes were bleak.

# CHAPTER 10

SOMEONE CAME INTO THE ROOM DURING THE middle of one of Pike's torture sessions, and, after they exchanged a few words spoken too softly for Amaranthe to make out, he slathered some salve on her body and walked out. She wasn't sure whether to be thankful for the reprieve or not. The cold, gelatinous paste provided some relief as it permeated her wounds, but she was still stuck on the table with the pins driven through her limbs. Blood trickled from the gouges as well as from other wounds Pike had missed with his rushed application.

This had been his second visit of the day, and he'd seemed agitated, rushing through his "work" and trying harder than ever to pull the answer to that one question from her. The aircraft had been on the ground for days, if Amaranthe guessed right, so she couldn't imagine what fire ants might be crawling over his toes just then.

Sicarius's face floated through her thoughts. What if he *had* left Sespian behind to come for her, and what if he *had* found a way to track the craft? It seemed unlikely, but she dreamed that he'd caught up with them anyway and that Pike was worried because he knew it.

The lighting had winked out when Pike left, pitching Amaranthe into blackness, but a door whispered open and a slash of brightness flowed in from the corridor. A tiny butterfly of hope fluttered in her breast. Sicarius?

Amaranthe craned her neck, trying to see the entrance.

"Amaranthe?" a soft voice whispered. Retta.

The hope-butterfly didn't stop fluttering. People whispered when they didn't want to be discovered, and people didn't want to be discovered when they were doing something of which others would disapprove. Like maybe, just maybe, helping a prisoner escape…

"Still alive," Amaranthe croaked.

Footfalls sounded. The lighting level rose. Retta gasped, and her footsteps faltered. "You look… I can't imagine how you…"

Ah, yes, Retta hadn't seen Amaranthe outside of the crate since the first day.

"You should have seen me before he put on the salve," Amaranthe said.

"I should've told Ms. Worgavic before she left. If she knew—"

"She knows," Amaranthe said. "Any chance my battered state is inspiring you to let me go?"

"I figured out a way to help."

Help. That wasn't the same as letting go, and Amaranthe feared Retta's version of help might not match her own. "Oh?" she asked.

Retta stepped up to the table. She eyed the claw pincers extending their pins into Amaranthe's limbs. "This contraption was created to load cargo."

"How lovely that you've found an alternative use for it."

Retta winced. "I didn't want to… I wasn't thinking of… I mean, I never wanted to torture anyone." She glanced at Amaranthe's body, swallowed, and jerked her gaze back to Amaranthe's face. It must be easier to look at. Pike hadn't done as much work up there.

Amaranthe kept herself from saying anything judgmental. "Why not end it then?" she asked. "You know how to operate it. Let me up. That's all you need to do. I'll find a way out on my own. We're still on the ground, aren't we?"

"We are. The meetings haven't started yet. We arrived early because those attending have to trek over two days' worth of rugged terrain. The area around the lake was too populated to risk coming down closer in the *Ortarh Ortak*. We landed in a swamp. I don't know if it'd be a favor, letting you out there, in your condition…"

"I'll take my chances," Amaranthe said.

"I've already told you that I can't go against Ms. Worgavic unless you share your secrets…"

Amaranthe struggled to keep her patience. "What help *are* you offering then?"

Retta touched her pocket. "In my obsession with this ancient technology, I'd forgotten I had some Kyattese tools." She withdrew a brooch. A bronze backing gripped an opaque, agate fixture that pulsed softly.

Amaranthe had a feeling she wasn't going to appreciate this "help."

"It's a therapy stone," Retta said.

Amaranthe's lips peeled back. Oh, she *knew* she wasn't going to appreciate this.

"I got it on one of the outer Kyatt Islands. They have people who train in psychology and the mental sciences to learn how to help those with emotional issues. In some cases, the therapists use tools to dive into a person's thoughts and to see the world as they see it, the better to help them." Retta tapped something on the back and laid the pulsing brooch on Amaranthe's forehead.

Amaranthe turned her head, hoping to knock it off, but warmth spread through the bronze backing and the device stuck to her skin. Reflexively, she tried to lift a hand, to tear it away, but the pins held her fast. All she earned was a fresh stab of agony for the minute movement she managed.

"Isn't therapy *voluntary* in Kyatt?" Amaranthe asked. "I don't consent to this."

Retta's smile was sad rather than triumphant. "Someone's out there. The ship can sense it. Pike thinks it's the assassin. I think it's some curious native who saw us land, but… I heard him talking. He'll kill you before letting Sicarius see what he's done to you. He's afraid. I need you to live, Amaranthe. You said you'd distract the wagon drover so I can get off."

Not like this, Amaranthe wanted to scream, but Retta laid her hand on top of the brooch, and a strange warmth filled her. She knew she had to save her energy to defend herself.

A glow pulsed between Retta's fingers, washing her face in unearthly light. "I will save your life by getting the information myself."

Between one eye blink and the next, Amaranthe was looking at the world both through her own eyes and through Retta's. She could see Retta hovering above her, but she could also see herself, pinned on the table, naked and bruised, eyes sunken, lips cracked and swollen, flesh peeled bare of her body in multiple spots, hair a knotted tangle. If she

looked that bad *after* the salve, she would have hated to have seen herself before.

*Your minds are one*, came a whisper in her head.

The brooch? That was creepy. How sentient was this—

A flood of memories slammed into her with the force of a tidal wave. Her body stiffened, almost as if she were receiving physical blows. Amaranthe braced herself to block whatever invasive tendrils snaked into her head, trying to tease Sicarius's secrets out of her. Oddly, it wasn't her own memories that assailed her but Retta's.

She was the quiet, pudgy girl in school, walking the halls of Mildawn with her chin down as she avoided eye contact and tried not to bump into anyone. Someone's elbow caught her. She tripped and landed face-first on the waxed wooden floors. Her books sprawled before her. Nobody picked them up or offered her a hand. When she gathered her belongings and hustled away, cruel comments nipped at her heels. "What a klutz." "She's so homely." "She thinks she's so important because of her sister." "Can you imagine her trying to start a business?" The voices dissolved into laughter, and the school halls disappeared, replaced by a rambling mansion on the Ridge. A lecturing woman in spectacles frowned down at her. "Your grades are abysmal. Why can't you be more like your sister?" The mention of a sister came with thoughts of a beautiful woman with auburn hair, sparkling intelligent eyes, and skin bronzed by the sun. She appeared on a ship, then on a camel in the desert, then bartering in some exotic marketplace, and finally in a tent, sending messages back to other Forge founders, details of investments and banking institutions started up overseas. Worgavic. Ravencrest. Omich. Bertvikar. Myll. Founders? Yes, these people were the originals and included the sister, Suan, who corresponded through mail alone and who'd been overseas for more than a decade. She seemed to be a woman that few in the organization had actually met and that nobody had seen in years.

As abruptly as it had started, the sharing of memories ended. Amaranthe could almost hear her separation from Retta, like a piece of paper torn in half, leaving jagged, rough edges. She felt jagged and rough as well. What had happened? Amaranthe had expected to relive her own memories, especially those memories of Sicarius, not go for a trek in someone else's head. Had the device backfired somehow? How much time had passed? Had Retta seen the same thing?

The younger woman pulled the brooch away and stared down at Amaranthe, lips parted in stunned silence. She seemed to realize she was gaping for she drew back and rearranged her face into a neutral expression.

"There." Retta adjusted her clothing and straightened her shoulders. "That's invasive, I'll admit, but surely less deplorable than what Pike's been doing."

"Uhm, all right." Amaranthe was starting to get the impression that Retta hadn't been sharing the same memories as she had. Had she even sensed Amaranthe in there, skimming through her past, learning about the Forge founders? Ravencrest. Omich. Bertvikar. Suan. She repeated the names in her mind, willing them to stick. Other than Worgavic and Myll—that had to be Larocka Myll—they weren't familiar and hadn't been on Books's list. If those were truly original founders, knowing them could be important. If only, she thought grimly, to hand them over to Sicarius. A week ago, she never would have considered it, but after spending time with Pike, she found herself wishing he'd simply succeeded in cutting off all the heads of the hydra.

"And more useful than I would have imagined." Retta turned the brooch over in her hand, gazing at it with a touch of wonder. "I'd only read about it and wasn't sure it'd work. I thought I'd have to fight you all the way, but I simply thought about what I wanted to learn, and it took me straight to your memories on the subject."

Amaranthe grew aware of the icy cold of the table against her back. Or maybe that was her own blood running cold. "Did it?" she whispered.

"Marvelous invention. There's much we could learn from the Kyattese."

Amaranthe kept her mouth shut. Maybe Retta had learned nothing. Maybe she was simply hoping to trick Amaranthe into revealing what she hadn't been able to find.

Retta slipped the brooch into a pocket and withdrew a folded piece of paper. She laid it on the table beside the pincer pinning Amaranthe's thigh. "It's a map to help you get off the ship. I... hope you're able to walk. I don't dare go with you or give you a weapon, not with Pike and his soldiers preparing to search the swamp. If you let him catch you, I won't have any sway over him, not with Ms. Worgavic away. I may not be able to stop..." Retta swallowed. "Just don't get caught. I'll make sure the ship's defenses are shut down so you can escape. Once outside, you'll be in swamp and marshlands. The nearest town is a two-day walk to the north. If you can make it, I'm sure you can talk someone into helping you." She managed a quick smile. "You got me to. I'm sure you don't appreciate it right now, but one day maybe it'll mean something to you that I saved your life."

All Amaranthe could think about during the monologue was whether or not Retta had truly found out about Sespian's parentage. Retta wasn't trying to tease out information or ask for verification. She seemed certain about what she'd discovered.

Retta moved to the foot of the table and fiddled with the controls there. She waved to the claw. "I'm going to delay the release until I'm safely out of the area. I don't think you'd attack me, but your loyalty seems to be such that you might kill to keep that man's secrets. After being in your head, I understand your reasons for doing things, mostly, but Amaranthe, you must see that the son of some common-born assassin doesn't have the right to rule. He never did."

Amaranthe groaned. Retta knew. Cursed ancestors, the last however many days of resisting Pike—all that suffering beneath his knife—had been for nothing. Retta knew, and soon all of Forge would know.

Amaranthe's vision blurred as tears formed. A click sounded, and Retta stepped back from the table. She started toward the door, but paused, then turned back. She grabbed the map, unfolded it, and held it above Amaranthe's eyes.

"I better not leave any evidence that I helped you," Retta said. "Can you memorize this quickly? I seem to remember you were bright and got good grades."

Amaranthe barely heard her. She had the presence of mind to stare at the map, but her thoughts were a jumble, and she wasn't sure how much she would remember. She'd failed. All she could think about was how Sicarius would react when he found out.

* * * * *

Maldynado and Yara crouched in the darkness on one of the two long, cylindrical boilers filling the space. From their perch, they could see two doors, one leading to engineering and the other out to the deck.

They could also jump on anyone who came inside. The black knife lay on the engine room floor, with Basilard, Books, and Sespian hiding in the shadows provided by the towering machinery. The plan was for Maldynado and Yara to wait for Mari's bodyguards—or whomever she sent—to pass, then drop down behind them. Basilard and the others would spring the trap first. Akstyr remained by the furnace, grumbling softly about being stuck shoveling coal. If something went wrong, and muscle and fists weren't enough, he and his Science skills were on backup duty.

Maldynado shifted his weight, careful not to crack his head on the metal ceiling beam between him and Yara. They only had a few feet of clearance above the boiler. Laughter floated down from the dining hall on the deck above. He wondered how many crew and passengers the *Glacial Empress* claimed.

"If they don't come tonight, we're going to be in trouble," Yara said. "An officer will be down in the morning to relieve the night-shift engineer, the night-shift engineer you thumped and dumped into the river."

"I know," Maldynado said. He hadn't *wanted* to thump and dump anyone else, but with the engine room adjacent to the boiler room, it hadn't been particularly surprising that the officer in charge had stumbled across the team making plans for their ambush.

"Covering one of your people in soot isn't going to make him pass as an officer," Yara said.

"I know that too."

They *ought* to have until morning to figure that aspect out. With Akstyr shoveling and Books keeping an eye on the engines, nobody from navigation should find anything amiss until that shift change.

Maldynado adjusted his crouch again. "I hope Mari sends her people soon. My thighs are burning." As soon as the admission slipped out, he wished it hadn't. Yara would accuse him of whining.

All she said was, "I'd laugh if we'd set this all up and they were up there sleeping."

"You do that?" Maldynado asked.

"What?"

"Laugh. I haven't heard it."

The shadows hid her scowl, but Maldynado knew it was there.

"That's because you're not as funny as you think you are," Yara said.

"I haven't seen you laugh at anyone else's jokes either."

"I haven't heard many jokes."

"Ah, that's right," Maldynado said, "you can't understand Basilard. He's hi-*lar*-i-ous."

Yara didn't respond. Maldynado wondered if he'd stunned her to silence or she merely thought the notion ridiculous.

"Really?" Yara finally asked. "He seems glum."

"He is, but he has his moments. He's had a rough past. His people are pacifists, but he was captured, made into a slave, and forced to kill to survive pit-fighting bouts." Maldynado shifted his weight again, trying to find a more comfortable spot on the boiler. He was tempted to straddle the thing, but that'd be a poor position from which to launch an attack. Also, given how much warmth seeped from the metal, he might scorch something important. "All the boys have tough pasts," Maldynado continued, thinking Yara might be more sympathetic to everyone if she knew that misfortune, rather than a puerile urge to irk enforcers, had led them to the outlaw lifestyle. "Books watched his son get killed by Hollowcrest's men. Akstyr grew up on the streets. Sicarius, I don't think, knows what to do with himself now that he's not Emperor Raumesys's personal assassin."

Yara stirred, and Maldynado wondered if that last tidbit was news to her. Sicarius probably wouldn't appreciate him chitchatting about his personal history, but he wasn't there, so too bad.

"I think," Maldynado said, "everyone's hoping that, in helping the emperor, they can rise above their pasts and make a difference in the world. Amaranthe makes a man want to do that."

"You, too?"

"Nah, I just lost a bet."

Yara snorted. It *almost* sounded like a laugh.

Yara stretched her legs out for a moment. Hah, her thighs must be burning too. "Your family sounds awful."

"Uhm," Maldynado said, surprised that she'd bring it up. "I guess."

"My brothers always teased me growing up, and I had to learn to be tough, but I knew they cared for me. Mevlar might have gotten me in trouble after your employer and assassin showed up on my father's doorstep, but only because he thought he was saving the family from

dishonor. And because he's being a whiny loser over the fact that I was promoted first."

Maldynado smiled, both because she was opening up and because he now knew why whining might not sit well with her. He grunted to let her know he was listening. Women always seemed to appreciate that.

"But that's how you expect siblings to be," Yara went on. "You don't expect them to send their wives to throw you to the mechanical alligators."

"To be fair to Ravido, I don't think he was thinking of me at all when he sent, or let Mari go downstream. She saw the opportunity to turn me into alligator fodder of her own volition. Maybe she thought it'd make a nice anniversary present in case the throne-usurping gig didn't work out."

"I never thought I'd feel sympathy for some warrior-caste dandy, but it must be hard knowing your family wants you dead, even your parents."

For a long moment, Maldynado didn't say anything. He had to run her words through his head a few times, because he couldn't believe Yara had implied she felt sympathy for him. Though a few teasing replies came to mind, he thought she might appreciate a serious response. Something about the shadows made it feel safer to be serious. Still, he lowered his voice to make sure the others wouldn't hear from the next room. "They have a reason."

"What happened with your sister?"

Maldynado poked at the riveting on the boiler seam. "I have seven older brothers. My parents kept trying because Mother wanted a girl. Finally, three years after I was born, she had Tia. She was forty and knew it'd be her last child. Somehow, as second youngest, I always got put on babysitting duty while my parents were at their parties and military functions. Mostly, I loved being the big brother and watching out for Tia, not that she needed a guardian. She was real sweet, and everyone loved her. She was good at charming folks, a lot like Amaranthe, and she usually got what she wanted. Like to tag along with me. She—" Maldynado's throat had grown tight, and he paused to clear it. "She always wanted to do what I was doing and to go where I wanted to go. Mother said she could so long as I kept an eye on her. Tia was *my* responsibility, she'd say. By the time I was twelve... Well, I was as dumb as any kid that age and didn't want my little sister hanging around. There was a lot of teasing from the other boys and even my older brothers. Looking back now… it's stupid that I let that bother me, but one summer, when it was hotter than a smelter, we went to the river to swim. We had a great spot with rope swings and platforms to jump off, a whole obstacle course of stuff to play on. Anyway, that day there'd been a storm up in the mountains, and the water was rough and high. I told Tia to stay on the bank and play there. I wasn't watching her though. I was in the water with the boys. I never saw her go in. She was just there, and then the next time I looked, she was gone."

Maldynado blinked and forced himself to focus on the shadowy boiler room and the doors he was supposed to be watching. While he'd been speaking, he'd been back there by the river, playing with his peers. Baking his bare shoulders under the summer sun. Jumping in the cold water to cool off and avoid mosquitos. How vividly he remembered that moment, looking over to the bank by the rope swing and feeling that icy sensation of dread.

"A couple of days later, the neighbors downriver came up to the estate. They'd found…" Maldynado swallowed. "They'd found the body."

Beside him, Yara let out a long, deep exhalation. Maldynado wondered if she was still feeling sympathetic toward him, or if she saw him as more of a careless idiot than ever. The latter most likely. That was the consensus his family had reached.

"Anyway," Maldynado said, finding the silence awkward, or maybe fearing the judgment in it, "it's not my favorite story to tell for obvious reasons. Amaranthe doesn't even know it." Few of his adult friends and acquaintances did. Only those people who had known him all those years ago. Deret Mancrest was one—he'd been among the boys playing on the river that day. Thinking of him made Maldynado wonder what was going on in the capital. Deret's newspaper had reported the emperor missing before anyone *should* have known about the train incident. And the story had given a positive, non-alarming reason for Ravido's troops to be entering the city. Maldynado wondered if Ravido or Father had spoken to him. Deret had always been an honorable fellow, not the sort to kowtow to pressure to publish certain stories, but Deret's father owned the paper and had been friends with Maldynado's father for years. When

Amaranthe reunited with the team, they'd have to visit Deret. Assuming she *did* reunite with the team. Maldynado rubbed his face.

"So, that's why you follow her?" Yara asked.

"Huh?" It took Maldynado a moment to remember that he'd spoken Amaranthe's name aloud. "Oh. Maybe."

"Because in helping her, maybe even protecting her, you're making up for the failure with your sister?"

"I guess. Except I've failed Amaranthe now too. She's probably being tortured in that big black monstrosity. If she's still alive at all."

"What happened with your sister was tragic, and I'm not sure there's anything I, or anyone else, could say that would make you stop blaming yourself for that, but Amaranthe isn't a child. From what I've seen, she's the one who gets herself into these situations. Didn't Books say she was using a homemade slingshot to hurl blasting sticks at the other craft when she was thrown from the dirigible? There's not much you can do to protect someone who takes risks like that."

"I suppose not," Maldynado said, surprised Yara was trying to make him feel better. None of her usual brusque gruffness colored her tone. "But I'm worried about her, and I can't help but wish I'd figured out how to fly the dirigible better. Giant balloons aren't as maneuverable as you'd hope."

A few moments passed without comment, until Yara said, "That explains one thing anyway."

"Oh? What's that?"

"You see Amaranthe as a little sister. I was wondering why you didn't leer lecherously at her like you do at every other woman."

"My leers are *not* lecherous," Maldynado said, relieved to have a lighter topic, one where he could shield himself with his usual flippancy. "I'm far too handsome and charming for anyone to consider my leers offensive or unwanted."

"Please."

"And I don't leer at *every* woman."

"*Please*," Yara said with even more disbelief. "You leer at *me*. And I'm... not someone people leer at."

Something in her voice made Maldynado consider his answer before responding. "Because... you're tall, fierce, and intimidating, so

you figure that deters lecherous leerers? Or because you don't believe you're attractive enough to draw leers?"

"Leerer isn't a word, you twit," Yara snapped.

Maldynado kept himself from asking if Books had recruited her to be a fellow dictionary-enforcer. He recognized that defensive snapping as a way to avoid answering his question.

"If it's the fierce, intimidating thing, that's your own choice, you know," Maldynado said. "You could be a respected enforcer even if you smiled once in a while. If it's the other thing, well, I wasn't positive until I saw you in the dress, but…" He tried to find an innuendo that wouldn't be offensive and yet wouldn't leave room for misinterpretation either. "Any man would be happy to go spelunking in your cave."

Yara made a choking sound. "Dear ancestors, what sort of brain could consider that a flattering comment?"

Drat, misfire. Maldynado shrugged it off. "A male brain, naturally."

Clomps came from a stairwell outside—a lot of clomps.

"About time," Yara whispered.

Though the top of the boiler loomed eight feet above the deck, Maldynado scooted back so his shadow wouldn't be visible if someone coming through the door thought to look up. He missed the comfortable feel of his rapier on his waist, but the emperor had instructed them not to kill anyone anyway. They were to knock everyone out and send them to visit the reeds along the shore. Fists would do for that job. Maldynado flexed his fingers and adjusted his crouch, ready to spring.

Lights appeared through the door window—lanterns dangling from men's arms. Maldynado counted five or six burly guards queued up and ready to enter, more than one face familiar. Yes, these were the men from the Relaxation Grotto. As before, they all carried pistols and short swords or cutlasses. Maldynado craned his neck but didn't see Brynia. She wouldn't have given her important tracking artifact to the security grunts, would she have? Maybe she could tell from her suite where Sicarius's knife was located.

The exterior door opened. A gust of cold air stirred the heat inside. The first two men jumped into the boiler room, pointing their pistols, one toward the engine room and one toward the furnace area. From their position, Akstyr wouldn't be in view yet, but if men charged down that way instead of going straight toward the knife, Maldynado and Yara

would have to jump down early. Or, if anyone looked up with eyes good enough to see through the shadows…

The first two men made all-clear signs and crept inside, one heading toward the engine room and the other toward the furnace. Four more guards filed inside. Most of the group eased toward the engine room, as the team had hoped. One more headed down the aisle toward Akstyr.

Maldynado touched Yara's arm and pointed across her, hoping she understood that he wanted her to help Akstyr. He meant to go with the original plan, assisting the others with the men in the engine room, but, before he jumped down, Mari's buckskin-wearing shaman stepped into view outside the door. He stood, hands spread at his sides, eyes half-lidded.

Before Maldynado had decided what to do, those eyes flew open. The shaman opened his mouth, about to yell some warning.

Maldynado jumped from his perch, landed on the exterior door's threshold, and leaped through it. The first syllable of a yell escaped the shaman's lips, but Maldynado silenced him, catching him about the mid-section and bowling him to the ground.

They rolled across the deck, limbs entangled, their momentum slamming them into the railing. The dark water of the river rushed past a few feet below.

Remembering that practitioners had a hard time hurling magic about when they were distracted, Maldynado reared onto his knees, grabbed the man by his buckskin shirt, and punched him in the belly. His knuckles should have sunk into pliable flesh, but they smacked against something as hard as brick instead. His joints cracked, and pain sprang up his arm.

"What the—"

An invisible force rammed into Maldynado's chest with the force of a sledgehammer wielded by a deflowered woman's father. If his fingers hadn't been wrapped in the shaman's shirt, he might have flown all the way back into the boiler room. As it was, his body took to the air, dragging the shaman with him. Maldynado landed on his back, with his opponent on top of him. Bulging gray eyes stared into his; apparently, the shaman hadn't been expecting a ride.

Taking advantage of the man's surprise, Maldynado gripped his foe's arms and whipped him to the side. Lacking the brawn of a fighter, the shaman flew through the air with satisfying ease, and his head clunked against the deck. Before he could recover, Maldynado hauled him to his feet and lunged for the railing. He heaved the shaman overboard.

"See how your magic-flinging butt likes that," Maldynado growled and shook his hands. His knuckles smarted from whatever chest armor he'd struck. "I hate dealing with—"

Something gripped Maldynado's head on either side, applying crushing force to his temples. He swatted at the air, searching for his attacker, but nobody stood near him. The force intensified, as if someone had clamped a giant vise around his head and was tightening the screws. Maldynado sucked in short, pained breaths and tried to think of a way to free himself, to fight back, but how could he attack a man he'd thrown overboard? His knees buckled, and he dropped to the deck, curling onto his side. He imagined the shaman, floating on his back, laughing as he assaulted Maldynado from a distance.

Akstyr. He had to get Akstyr. Surely he could do something.

Not caring that he was gasping and whimpering, Maldynado crawled toward the doorway to the boiler room. He couldn't hear the scuffles or smacks of a fight. He hoped that meant his comrades had already finished off the guards. Not the other way around.

Something touched Maldynado's head, and it was all he could do not to scream. He did gasp and pull away.

"Don't move, Mal," came Akstyr's voice. "I'm trying to break the…"

Blackness descended upon Maldynado's vision. He expected to pass out, but the light returned in a flash. The pain disappeared so quickly that the cessation made him swoon. He almost threw up.

A pair of shoes came into focus inches away from his nose. Maldynado was looking at the deck, and he sure hoped that was Akstyr standing in front of him and not some guard. He rolled onto his back for a better look. Yes, Akstyr, Basilard, and Books surrounded him, all frowning down at him. Sespian stood in the doorway behind Books, eyeing something farther down the deck.

Yara was kneeling beside Maldynado, a hand on his chest. He thought she might be about to express sympathy, but she stuck to business. "Did you search the shaman for that tracking device before throwing him overboard?"

"Uhm. Oops." Fearing a rebuke, Maldynado rushed to change the subject. "Thanks for helping me with him, Akstyr."

Hands stuffed into his pockets, Akstyr merely shrugged. "I didn't do much, just planted the idea in the shaman's mind that some of those moat alligators might wander out to the river now and then."

"You're developing a subtle streak," Books told Akstyr. "That's good."

Books complimenting Akstyr? That was new. Akstyr only shrugged again, though that might have been a smile tugging at his lips.

"We have a problem." Sespian pointed at something up the deck. "Your cries of pain seem to have drawn attention."

Maldynado rolled to his knees. Two young boys crouched on the stairs leading to the middle deck, their heads tilted toward each other as they shared whispers and pointed. When they noticed the group of adults staring at them, they scampered back up the stairs.

"I hope you're not going to command me to run after those kids and pummel them into silence," Maldynado said as he climbed to his feet, accepting Basilard's hand for support. "The way I feel right now, I don't think I could manage more than a fast hobble."

"I wasn't planning to pummel children," Sespian said, his tone cool.

Before Maldynado could say that he'd been joking—why didn't anyone understand his sense of humor lately?—Sespian spoke again.

"I was merely pointing out that we'll be unable to remain hidden here. Between them and the now-missing engineer, not to mention all of your sister-in-law's minions..." Sespian waved toward the engine room. A man's legs were sticking through the door. "Our presence here can't go unnoticed past morning."

"Or past midnight, I should think," Books rubbed his head as if he'd been struck.

"So, what're we going to do?" Maldynado asked.

"What else can we do?" Sespian was holding Sicarius's knife again, and he gave it a stern frown. "Take over the ship."

"Our small team against the crew of the entire steamboat?" Books asked.

"I thought I'd just tell the captain we're commandeering the steamboat and that he's bound by imperial law to obey me," Sespian said.

Akstyr's nose crinkled. "Does that work?"

"If the captain isn't loyal to Forge and Ravido, it might," Books said.

"I don't know," Maldynado said. "Nothing's ever that easy for us."

*We've never had an emperor along before*, Basilard pointed out.

The small shrug Sespian made implied he wasn't certain it would be "that easy" either. Not exactly confidence inspiring.

A groan came from the engine room.

Akstyr jerked a thumb toward the door. "Are we going to tie those uglies up? Or throw them overboard like the others?"

"The captain may be more willing to consider my requests—my *orders*—if we haven't decimated his crew. On the other hand, Books is correct. It's possible the officers are on Forge's payroll, and that's why Mari chose the *Glacial Empress,* in which case, it may behoove us to remove some of his support staff before approaching him." Sespian considered the shoreline where the scattered lights of farmhouses dotted the night. "We haven't moved into the wilderness yet, so they'll be able to swim to shore and find a way back to town."

"That was a yes, chuck those uglies overboard?" Akstyr asked.

"Sire," Books whispered.

Akstyr rolled his eyes. "Sire, uglies overboard?"

"Yes," Sespian said.

He, Akstyr, Basilard, and Yara went inside to tend to the task. Maldynado touched his back, probing the beginnings of another bruise, and decided he better go in to help, too, lest Yara accuse him of loafing.

Books was standing outside the door, eyeing him.

"What?" Maldynado asked.

"Spelunking in her *cave*?" Books asked. "And you accuse me of saying stupid things to women?"

Maldynado winced. How much of his soul-baring conversation with Yara had Books overheard? Hadn't the others had their heads stuffed behind those pistons? So much for his private conversation. He sighed. This week wasn't going well, not well at all.

# CHAPTER 11

WHEN THE PINS RETRACTED, LEAVING AMA-ranthe's arms and legs free, she melted in relief. Many minutes had passed since Retta left, and Amaranthe had begun to fear that, in addition to failing to keep Sicarius's secret, she would remain at Pike's mercy. She wanted to spring away from the table and sprint for the door, but coercing her body into movement took a lot of effort. The holes left by the pins oozed blood. She scraped some of the salve away from less damaged areas of her body and smeared it into the wounds. Touching them sent a wave of blackness over her, and she groaned, gripping the edge of the table.

"No, we are *not* going to be given freedom, only to pass out on the table," she whispered.

Her first thought as a free woman was that she should find a way to destroy the *Behemoth* on her way out. Her second thought, which came as she was attempting to slide off the table, was that she'd be lucky if she could even stand up. As much as her mind wanted to rebel, to deal Forge a huge destructive blow in exchange for the pain and indignity she'd suffered, her body lacked the strength. Even if she *could* hobble around and avoid recapture long enough to locate an engine room, or the vessel's equivalent, she'd have no idea how to make trouble. Somehow she doubted this ancient craft used something as understandable as steam for power.

When her bare feet hit the floor, Amaranthe flinched. Pike had flayed the skin off the bottoms once. Maybe twice. The hours of torture had blended and grown fuzzy. Unfortunately not in a way that suggested she'd ever forget the experience. Thanks to the healing effects of the salve, she could walk, but each step hurt, like traveling barefoot through a gravel quarry full of particularly prickly pebbles.

"Two days to the nearest town?" she murmured. Against her wishes, her mind tried to calculate how many steps that might be. "It'll hurt less after your muscles warm up," she told herself.

Amaranthe peered about for something she could use as a cane, but the table and her crate—oh, how she'd like to give that thing a vigorous kick—were the only pieces of furniture in the room. After a short eternity, she reached the exit. The tall, narrow door loomed higher than two people and lacked a handle or hinges. Before she could debate overmuch on how to open it, it slid into the wall. Retta must have arranged for locks to be released.

A brighter light illuminated the corridor outside. Amaranthe paused in the doorway to let her eyes adjust and to listen. She didn't hear anything, not even the hum of machinery or reverberations of a distant engine. But then she'd never noticed anything like that, even when the *Behemoth* had been in flight.

Picturing Retta's map in her head, Amaranthe took a right into the corridor. She used the wall for support. Her steps were so slow that she was certain she'd never make it to the next turn, much less get off the ship, before someone came to check on her. Gritting her teeth, she willed her legs to move faster. Fortunately, as she turned right, then left, then, at a five-way intersection, chose the middle route, the corridors remained empty. There didn't seem to be anyone around to hear her stumbles and grunts of pain. Because Retta had arranged to have the way cleared?

"Don't question luck," Amaranthe muttered. "It might get offended by your lack of appreciation and leave you behind."

After turning left and right at least ten more times, not to mention swirling down a ramp she vaguely remembered from the way in, she reached what might have been a cargo bay. The ceiling disappeared into darkness far overhead, and she marveled again at the size of the ship. A pair of crimson lights glowed on the far wall. Retta's map had marked the exit with a couple of red dots. Maybe this was the spot.

Amaranthe left the support of the wall to cross the bay. If the creases or hinges of a door existed in the solid black wall, they were too well camouflaged to detect. She slid her fingers along the wall beside the thumb-sized lights, but didn't find anything like a switch or latch.

Fearing she had the wrong spot, Amaranthe stepped back. "All right, Retta. If this is the door, how do I open it?"

A few seconds passed, and Amaranthe started to move on to check other spots, but a tall, broad rectangle in the wall grew opaque and, a blink later, transparent. Amazed by the technology, she stumbled backward a few steps before pausing, then finding the courage to approach again.

A swamp full of frond-filled trees and lush foliage spread out beneath the feeble light of dawn, or perhaps twilight. A dense green canopy blotted out the sun and the sky. Amaranthe couldn't smell the foliage, feel a breeze, or hear any insects; it was as if she were looking at a painting, an impossibly lifelike painting. A vibrantly colored bird with a six-foot wingspan flapped past.

"Not a painting after all," Amaranthe whispered, alarmed at how different the climate was from that of her home. Her hope that Sicarius might be out there, waiting to help her, dwindled even further.

She edged closer to the… doorway? Window? Scene of the outside? She didn't know what it was, but she stuck a finger out to test it.

The hard, smooth material that comprised the wall had changed into something with give. It was like touching gelatin. Amaranthe pressed harder and her finger broke through. She jumped back, yanking the digit with her. She performed a quick examination of her finger. It appeared normal, though damp on the tip. Upon closer inspection, she noticed plops of water striking the swamp outside. Rain.

Amaranthe pressed her whole hand through the barrier this time and held her palm open toward the sky. Rain drops struck it.

For an uncertain moment, she stood poised there, with only her hand sticking through the doorway. She was naked with no food or gear for surviving in the wilderness, and she was already weak from the days of torment. In her condition, Retta's "two days" to the nearest town might take four. With the canopy blotting out the sky, she couldn't even guess which direction might be north.

"City girl," Amaranthe sighed. She was on the verge of heading back into the corridors to hunt for supplies—and a map—when voices reached her ears.

"…went this way?"

Ugh, no time for supply hunting.

Amaranthe pushed the top half of her body through the barrier. Only when she was leaning out over the swamp did she realize that the door, if one could call it that, was twenty feet above the water. The dome-shape of the *Behemoth* meant the hull sloped outward instead of offering a vertical drop, but the murky water below might have been six inches deep or six feet.

Footfalls—a lot of footfalls—sounded in the corridor behind her.

Amaranthe thrust herself the rest of the way through the doorway and angled herself to fall feet first. Bare butt scraping down the side of the craft, she picked up speed and landed with a splash, a splash that sounded thunderous to her ears. She plunged into chest-deep water. Mud ensnared her feet and squished between her toes.

Careful not to make more noise, Amaranthe half-waded and half-paddled toward the nearest shoreline. Underwater roots and tendrils of vegetation grasped at her shins, denying her efforts to move quickly and get out of view. When she made it to a muddy bank, she rushed for the closest hiding spot, a crooked tree leaning over the water with a snarl of vines dangling from its branches.

A few feet above her, a bird the size of her head flapped its wings and departed. A snake, its body wrapped several times around the trunk, hissed. It must have been making its way toward the bird, hoping for a snack. The snake's head swung down toward Amaranthe, yellow eyes with black slits fixing on her.

She considered the size of the reptile and thought about hunting for a new hiding spot, but two figures appeared at the ship's exit. Pike and a man in army fatigues. Both held rifles, and Amaranthe had a feeling they'd have no trouble shooting through that doorway. Other armed people strode in and out of view behind them.

The two men spoke to each other. Amaranthe couldn't hear what they were saying, but it didn't matter. The quick, choppy gestures told the story. They knew she'd escaped, and they were coming after her.

The snake's head had inched closer, giving Amaranthe another reason to abandon the spot. Using the trees for cover, she hustled into the undergrowth, shunting aside the pain of running on raw feet. She doubted she had more than a few minutes before Pike's men would be after her.

For her first steps, Amaranthe simply ran through the mud and puddles, attempting to put space between herself and the ship. Then she forced herself to slow down and think. Running blindly into the wilderness would only get her lost, especially if Worgavic had chosen this area because it was an uninhabited morass where no one would stumble across the *Behemoth*.

Amaranthe picked a new path, this time circling the ship, hoping she'd come across the footprints of those who had headed off for the meeting. *They* must know which way they were going.

The idea paid off. She came across tracks in the mud and recently cut foliage. Whoever was blazing the path must have used a machete. Even with her limited wilderness-navigation skills, she ought to be able to follow that. Of course, following a path would make it easy for Pike and his men to follow *her*, and her bare feet would slow her down. She had little choice.

Before she'd gone more than a hundred meters, the sounds of voices rose over the chirps of birds and the drone of insects. One clear cry of, "This way!" trailed her.

Amaranthe forced her stiff body into a jog and mulled over her limited options.

* * * * *

Maldynado stared at the door's rich dark whorls, evidence that some exotic, tropical, and expensive wood had been used on the suite. The inside would be luxurious, full of furs and stuffed heads from dangerous predators hunted in distant locales. He expected a full bar and entertaining area in addition to a bedroom and a lavatory complete with flushing washout. No chamber pots behind this door, no, my lord. He didn't think he'd ever been less enthused about going into a room.

"You're sure this is it?" Maldynado asked.

"Yes, Lady Marblecrest is in Suite Number One." Books rattled the passenger manifesto, a multi-page document that Basilard had acquired from the first officer's cabin without waking the man. "We'd best handle this quickly," Books added, glancing down the deck. Numerous other suite doors marked the polished wood wall, with gold-gilded lanterns burning all too brightly at intervals between them. At least a nice fog

was creeping higher as the night progressed, oozing between the metal railings and obscuring the polished wood deck. "If someone wanders out here and sees armed strangers, we'll have more than Mari's people with whom to deal."

Basilard nodded his agreement. He and Books were Maldynado's "backup" for facing Mari and however many guards she had left. Akstyr had been left on coal-shoveling duty again, much to his vocal chagrin. Sespian had taken Yara to accompany him to coerce the captain into helping. Maybe he thought a woman's presence would keep a fight from breaking out. The plan was to gain the captain's assistance, and control over the steamboat, without any of the passengers knowing about it.

The latter might prove difficult. Maldynado eyed the flintlock pistols he and the others carried, the new weapons also courtesy of Basilard's stealthy search of the officers' quarters. The plan was not to use them, but if Mari's people put up a fight...

Too bad Sicarius wasn't there to slip inside the suite with his trusty knife. Of course, that trusty knife had caused all sorts of trouble of late.

*Maybe we could just push a wardrobe in front of the door and lock her in for the duration of the voyage*, Basilard signed, probably wondering if Maldynado was having doubts about apprehending Mari.

"Nah. There'll be another door on the private balcony around the corner." Suite One lay on the starboard side, overlooking the bow of the boat.

Basilard peeked over the railing and around the corner. *Two private balconies.*

"Naturally. Marblecrests prefer to travel in style." Maldynado squared his shoulders. "All right, let's do this quietly."

He lifted a hand but paused, debating whether to knock or barge in and catch them by surprise. They'd be awake and alert, he believed, wondering what was taking their men so long to return with news of the emperor's death. Sespian had left the knife in engineering so that Brynia, if she had the tracking device, wouldn't know that the blade's owner was on the move.

Maldynado tried the knob and found it locked. The sturdy brass hinges, coupled with the stoutness of the wood, suggested it'd be a hard door to bash down. He stood to the side, in case guards flung it open and leaped out, and he knocked.

"It's the captain," Maldynado called, lowering his voice to a gruff octave on the guess that the captain would be an older man. "I'm told you boarded without displaying your ticket. I'll need to see that."

Basilard's eyebrows rose. Books shook his head with the condemnation of a man certain a ruse would not work.

Maldynado shrugged. Given that Mari and company had been fleeing the castle, it seemed plausible.

He knocked again. "Lady Marblecrest?"

A gunshot fired from within. Wood splintered, and a new, bullet-sized hole appeared in the center of the door. Though Books and Basilard hadn't been standing in front of the entrance, they dropped to their bellies on the deck.

Relieved he'd been standing to the side of the door, Maldynado had to gulp before he could offer an unconcerned smile to his comrades. "It's possible she didn't believe I was the captain."

"Or she doesn't like the captain," Books said.

Two more shots fired, and bullets burst through the door. One clanged off the metal railing behind the team. So much for "quietly."

"That's either one repeating weapon," Maldynado said, "or she has multiple armed people in there."

*Balcony?* Basilard signed. *There will be windows.*

"You volunteering?" Maldynado asked.

Basilard twitched a shoulder. *If you provide the diversion.*

Maldynado knocked again, careful not to stand in front of the door. He hoped the walls proved thicker and more bullet-repellent. "Lady Marblecrest," he called, still disguising his voice, "this is unacceptable behavior, especially from a woman of your stature."

Basilard hopped to his feet, climbed into the rail, and disappeared around the corner.

"If you don't surrender your firearms, step out of your cabin, and show me your ticket," Maldynado continued, "I'll be forced to throw you in the brig."

"I'd pay to see a warrior-caste woman locked behind bars." Books rose to a crouch and, after a couple of glances from the door to the corner Basilard had disappeared around, finally decided, with a deep sigh, to follow Basilard.

Another bang came from within. Maldynado wondered how many armed people awaited.

"Make sure to let me in when you get inside," he whispered after Books, then raised his voice for Mari's sake. "Lady Marblecrest, you're going to force me to get the master key and send armed security personnel into your rooms. If you don't want that, I—"

The next door down creaked open, and a man peeked a couple inches of his head out. It wasn't the only door open either. Emperor's warts, everyone on the deck must have heard the gunfire.

"Go back inside." Maldynado waved his pistol to encourage compliance. He knew the lighting wasn't poor enough to convince anyone he was the captain, but maybe if he pretended to be some security guard, the passengers wouldn't feel the need to defend the boat the way the kitchen staff had rallied to protect their castle. "We have the situation controlled."

A shot fired inside the suite. This time glass cracked. A window on the balcony?

"Er, we'll have it controlled soon," Maldynado corrected. Blast, he hoped that wasn't Basilard and Books being shot at.

"…is that man?" a woman asked, her voice floating out from the nearest cabin. "…doesn't look like any of the young officers."

Crashes and thumps sounded within the suite, and Maldynado couldn't spare the other passengers any more thoughts. He pounded on the door. Only gunshots answered him, a *lot* of gunshots. Either Mari had an entire army in there, or Books and Basilard were shooting too. Maldynado hoped Mari had the sense to keep her head down.

A woman screamed. The shooting stopped.

Pounding on the door wasn't getting Maldynado anywhere. He vaulted onto the railing, following Basilard and Books's route. Using the wood trim on the boat's hull for handholds, he crawled around the corner and along the outside of the suite to the balcony several feet away. Fog hid the water churning three decks below him, but he had no trouble hearing the waves slapping at the hull.

By the time Maldynado jumped onto the balcony, a deathly quiet had dropped over the suite.

A hole gaped in the closest window, a spider web of cracks branching out from it. Maldynado grabbed the knob on the door next to it, hoping

this one wasn't locked too. It turned. Flattening his back to the wall beside the door, Maldynado pulled it open without exposing himself.

No shots rang out.

Pistol in hand, he peeked around the jamb. A few lamps burned, revealing the carnage within. Blood spattered white curtains as well as a creamy sofa that had been knocked over and used as a barricade—bullet holes dotted the back side. Ivory Strat Tiles, some also spattered with blood, scattered the floor about a table, upturned chairs, and the bodies of three men in private security uniforms. Maldynado recognized at least one fellow from the resort. Nobody was moving.

"Books?" Maldynado whispered, not seeing him or Basilard.

An interior door stood ajar. After making sure nobody lurked, ready to leap out at him, Maldynado picked his way around the sofa and headed for the room.

Low voices came from within. One was a woman's. Maldynado's gut clenched. Mari and Brynia... They couldn't have taken down Books and Basilard. He shook his head. No chance.

Yet there was a tremor to his hand when he raised the pistol and stepped around the doorjamb.

Relief washed over him at the sight of Books and Basilard standing at the foot of a large bed. A blonde-haired woman—Brynia—knelt in the corner, her back against the wall, her hands up. A second woman's body was sprawled on the carpet in front of Books.

Maldynado must have made some noise, for Books turned toward him. Maldynado got the full view then, one of frizzy brown hair, vacant eyes, and a blood-saturated dress.

"Mari?" A dumb question—of *course*, it was Mari—but it was all Maldynado's stunned mouth could get out.

"We didn't do it," Books said, eyes stark with concern as Maldynado drew closer. "We walked in and—"

"You might not have shot her," Brynia said, "but her death was *your* fault. You crashed in here—our men were defending us, that's what they're paid to do, but in the confusion..." She blinked rapidly and dropped her head, gazing down at Mari. "They were just trying to defend us."

*Convincing tears*, Basilard signed.

"What?" Maldynado asked, not certain he'd interpreted the gestures correctly.

*She had this.* Basilard held up the most feminine pistol Maldynado had ever seen, one with meandering vines etched in the steel and an ivory inlay carved with roses. *And there weren't any guards in the room when we came in.*

Maldynado switched to signs to respond. *You think she shot my sister-in-law?*

"Ma'am, or is it my lady?" Books offered her a hand. "You'll have to come with us. The emperor will want to see you."

Brynia dropped her face into her hands, and her shoulders shook with sobs.

Maldynado waved to Books and Basilard. "Do you want to take her out and see if the emperor is done chatting with the captain? I'll search the room, then check on Akstyr. Left to his own devices he might decide napping is more important than shoveling coal."

"He'll be working, I assure you," Books said.

Maldynado couldn't fathom why Books felt that certainty about Akstyr, but only shrugged as Books and Basilard led Brynia out.

He searched the suite and found the egg-shaped artifact in a bedside table drawer. At least it hadn't gone into the river with the shaman, though as Maldynado gazed at it, with his sister-in-law's dead body on the floor nearby, he could only wonder if their troubles would abate... or if they had simply taken on a pile of new ones.

\* \* \* \* \*

Amaranthe jogged along the muddy path at a speed she'd usually be able to maintain for hours. Now, after ten minutes, the pace was taxing her sorely, thanks to the days of sleepless nights and little food. The torture probably hadn't helped her constitution either. Fronds whipped at her unprotected body, roots snatched at her bare feet, and she found herself wishing for a way to keep certain appendages from bouncing. She wondered if men had as much trouble running nude.

"That's right, girl," Amaranthe huffed to herself. "Concentrate on the important things."

Branches snapped and rattled behind her. Only the copses of cypress trees and the denseness of the undergrowth had kept her pursuers from spotting her thus far. At least, Amaranthe assumed they hadn't spotted her, as no bullets had whizzed through the humid air in her direction. The men didn't seem to be having any trouble following her though. And why would they? Her bare toes left distinct marks in the mud, and there was nothing she could do about it, not if she wanted to keep the path in sight. In the dense, tree-filled marsh, with water forcing numerous turns in the route, she might never find the trail again if she left it.

She longed for night, and the possibilities it offered for hiding, but the sky had grown brighter since she left the *Behemoth*. The start of a new day was upon her. Great.

A crack thundered through the air, silencing birds and insects.

Instinctively, Amaranthe ducked, though the bullet had already pounded into a tree a few steps to her right. Another shot rang out as she sprinted around a bend, hoping the trail ahead would offer copious options for cover. Instead, a pond stretched to the left, and the trees gave way to a field of low vegetation to her right. If she'd possessed the breath for it, she would have cursed. She'd never make it into cover on the far side of the clearing, not with this straight stretch where she'd be in the open.

The pond was about fifty meters across with lilies lining the shallows and thick vegetation crowding the opposite shore. When Amaranthe was in her best shape, she could swim fifty meters under water without coming up for air. She was a long way from her best shape, but she had no other options.

Without breaking stride, she leaped into the shallows. She pointed her toes to slip into the water as quietly as she could and waded out, trying not to make a splash. But, knowing her pursuers would round the bend in seconds, she could only be so careful. Fighting mud that sucked at her feet, she pushed through the shallows until the water kissed her thighs, then took a deep breath and dove.

Cloudy brown water closed in from all sides, leaving little visibility. Before she'd swum more than a few meters, Amaranthe ran into an underwater log. Slick, algae-smeared branches thrust out at her, thwarting her attempts to maneuver around the obstacle. Careful to keep her

back from breaching the surface, she finally bypassed it, but painful seconds—and stored air—had passed.

Hands outstretched, Amaranthe groped her way farther into the pond. Fish brushed her bare skin. Remembering the snake, she hoped she didn't run into anything more inimical. And she hoped she was swimming in a straight line. And, as long as she was hoping for all that, she added a desire to see Pike and his men run past the pond without noticing that the barefoot prints on the trail had disappeared.

Before long, her lungs burned for air. Amaranthe doubted she'd crossed more than a third of the pond. She bumped into another obstacle, a rock this time, and circled it. On the other side, she paused. Maybe it protruded from the surface and would offer cover. She eased her way to the top, staying close enough to kiss the rock. Though her lungs ached, she kept herself from bursting above the surface and taking a great gasp. Instead, she tilted her head back, lifting only her lips above the water. She drew a couple of long, careful breaths. A lily pad floated across her face. Surprised, she inhaled water, nearly choking. She forced herself to drop back down and return to the submerged swim.

Farther out in the pond, the deeper water made for easier going. When she reached the shallows on the other side, she parted two lilies and came up between them, letting no more than her eyes ease above the surface. She hadn't swum in a straight line, and it took her a few seconds to find the bank she'd left.

The clearing she'd left lay empty. Grateful to those men's unobservant ancestors, Amaranthe lifted her head far enough to take a breath.

Pike stepped out from behind a tree at the end of the clearing, a rifle raised.

Amaranthe tried to dive back under, but it was too late. The gun fired, and pain blasted the side of her head.

The blow spun her around—she was lucky it hadn't taken her head off—and she gave up hiding in favor of sprinting. She lunged out of the water and into the undergrowth hedging the pond. Her foot caught on a root, and she sprawled to the ground. The fall might have saved her life, for another shot cracked. She didn't hear what it hit and didn't care. So long as it wasn't her.

Amaranthe crawled through the foliage, not lifting her head above the fronds. Another shot came. She didn't know if it was Pike, taking

advantage of the rifle's repeating mechanism, or if more soldiers had joined him. She veered to the right, thinking he might expect her to flee straight away from the pond, and scrambled laterally to the bank, trying not to rustle branches, lest he see twitching leaves from across the water.

Blood trickled down the side of her face and dripped from her chin. Pike's shot may not have caught her full-on, but it'd been enough to add another wound to those already plaguing her.

A snap sounded ahead of her. Amaranthe froze. Emperor's warts, Pike must have known where she'd gone from the beginning and ordered his men to circle around the pond.

Nestled between two leafy shrubs, she drew her feet under her. She was tempted to sprint blindly into the trees and hope for the best, but if these were indeed soldiers, they'd know what they were doing. They'd know how to spring a trap. Even now, she had a sense of a noose tightening.

Amaranthe clenched her teeth. She was *not* going back to that table. She might be naked, but that didn't mean she couldn't take down a foe. *Sicarius* wouldn't run from these men. He'd pick them off one at a time. She told herself that she could do the same.

After a few deep breaths with which she tried to will the tension out of her muscles, Amaranthe eased toward the noise she'd heard. She parted a few fronds and found herself staring at a beach overlooking an inlet in the pond. She expected a soldier to be crouched there, or perhaps in the nearby reeds, but she didn't see anyone. Then her eye caught movement next to a log. An alligator ambled out of the undergrowth and slipped into the muddy water. The great beast had to be more than ten feet from nose to tail. Amaranthe gulped at the realization that such creatures lived in the swamp. Did they eat people? She wasn't sure. Either way, she was glad she hadn't encountered one on her swim.

A crunch sounded behind her.

Amaranthe turned in time to spot a man's hat above a nearby bush. He was moving slowly, using his rifle to part the reeds and search for her. She dropped to her belly and wriggled beneath a briar bush comprised of a tangle of dense vines and small white flowers that emitted a putrid scent. Nestled amongst the leaf litter, she waited for the soldier to draw near.

Moments passed. Water—or maybe that was sweat—slithered down her spine. A black boot came into sight. It stepped over a bulging root and came down lightly, toe first. The soldier must suspect his prey hid nearby. Amaranthe resisted the urge to squirm deeper under cover. She dared not shake the briar bush now.

The boot drew even with her spot, and a second one joined it. Amaranthe pressed her palms into the moist earth, summoning what energy she could, hoping to spring as soon as the man passed.

He stopped. Amaranthe's heart thundered against her ribs, trying to batter them into the soil. Maybe her legs were sticking out. Maybe he'd seen her tracks. Maybe—

The man continued past.

Amaranthe let him draw another two paces away, then scrambled from beneath the bush, lunged to her feet, and jumped, all in one motion. She landed on his back, one arm snaking around his neck at the same time as her other darted to his waist, snatching a knife housed on his belt. The man tried to twist and smash the butt of his rifle into her head. Amaranthe whipped the blade up to his throat first. She let it bite into his flesh, so he'd know the threat to his life was serious.

"Drop your rifle," Amaranthe whispered in his ear.

The soldier's head came up, and he didn't obey. Maybe he didn't like taking orders from a woman. Too bad. She pressed the blade in deeper. A rivulet of blood flowed down the steel edge. Under normal circumstances, she *wouldn't* follow through with the threat, but she didn't see how she could hope to escape if she didn't eliminate her pursuers. Though the practical part of her mind thought that, she couldn't bring herself to slice the man's throat.

"Drop it," Amaranthe said, trying to frost the words with iciness that would make Sicarius proud.

This time, the man complied. He tossed his rifle into the foliage where it clattered against a branch and rattled leaves. Amaranthe growled, knowing he'd done that on purpose, hoping noise would alert his comrades. Already, she felt vulnerable with her back to the swamp and no friendly eyes to watch it.

"What are you going to do, girl?" the man asked. "Sit there, with your legs wrapped around me all day? If you'd drop the knife, I wouldn't mind breasts smashed into my back, but—"

The only warning they had was a soft rustle from ahead. A split second later, the alligator reared out of the reeds, twisting its body to snap its maw around the man's thigh. With a powerful yank, the creature tore Amaranthe's prisoner away from her.

She let go and scrambled backward. The soldier screamed as the alligator dragged him along the beach and into the water. It happened so quickly she couldn't have helped him if she'd wanted to. One second, he was twisting and clawing at the ground, trying to find a way to pull himself free, and the next he disappeared beneath the surface. Water churned, then grew still, with only a few air bubbles floating to the surface to mark his passage.

"That answers my question," Amaranthe whispered. "Yes, alligators eat people."

Behind her, men thrashed through the undergrowth, pushing their way toward her location. Amaranthe grabbed the rifle and knife, and ran into the brush. Maybe she'd get lucky, and her pursuers would think the man had simply encountered the alligator without running into her. She doubted it.

# CHAPTER 12

DAWN HAD COME, THOUGH THE FOG SHROUDING the river made it seem like night still. Maldynado hoped the passengers all slept in, though he doubted that likely. Numerous people had heard that gunfight, and he expected that rumors were already flying about the steamboat. The officers had to be alerted. As he headed down to check on Akstyr, Maldynado could only hope Sespian had spoken to the captain and that the meeting had gone well.

On the hurricane deck outside of engineering, Maldynado slowed down, a hand going to his pistol. Someone's legs were sticking out of the boiler room doorway.

Footsteps sounded behind Maldynado. He spun around. A balding man with a nightshirt flapping about his ankles charged toward him, a homemade spear raised above his shoulder. Startled—and weary from being up all night—Maldynado barely managed to jump out of the way. He grabbed the spear and used his foe's momentum to fling him in a circle. The man dropped the weapon and caught himself on the wall. Maldynado snatched the spear and used it to force the man back to the railing. Though he felt bad about attacking someone in a nightshirt, *he* hadn't started the brawl. He curled his lips into a snarl and raised the spear, as if he meant to run the man through. The would-be warrior cursed and flung himself into the river of his own accord.

Maldynado examined the "spear" more closely. It appeared to have been made from the frame of a lounge chair.

"You still have a problem," came Akstyr's strained voice from the doorway. He stood on the threshold, straddling the downed figure while thrusting one of his hands in the direction of a lifeboat.

A second man crouched there, this one wearing more clothing and carrying a better weapon—a pistol. The muzzle pointed in Maldynado's

direction. He gulped, glad that Akstyr was somehow holding the man in place.

"Take care of it, would you?" Akstyr asked. "I'm tired and not as good at this as usual."

"Right." Maldynado eased out of the line of fire before angling toward the frozen figure. He'd gotten used to Akstyr's abilities—sort of—but it was creepy seeing a person stuck in tableau like that, and who knew if the man might throw off whatever shackles held him for long enough to get off a shot?

Gingerly, Maldynado plucked the pistol out of the frozen hand. He tossed it overboard, then hoisted the man after. "Let him go so he can swim."

Akstyr already had. The man sputtered and splashed before the fog swallowed him from view.

"Been having an eventful time on stoker duty?" Maldynado asked.

"You got that right," Akstyr growled. Together they tossed the unconscious man overboard too. He woke when he hit the water, sending a stream of curses across the river. "Two security men came running down to protect the engine room on account of passels of highwaymen over-running the steamboat. Supposedly they're led by an impostor impersonating the emperor and shooting up the passengers because they mean to rob everyone." Akstyr crossed his arms. "You know anything about that?"

"Less than you'd think." Maldynado eyed the nearest stairwell, as if angry hordes of passengers might charge down it at any second. "I guess the emperor's chat with the captain didn't go well."

"No kidding."

"The captain probably assumed the real emperor wouldn't sneak onto his boat in the middle of the night or have only one out-of-uniform enforcer sergeant for his personal guard. We... probably should have foreseen that."

"Whatever. I'm off stoker duty now, right? You'll need me to fight."

Leave it to Akstyr to worry about himself first. Then again, Maldynado couldn't imagine many tasks less appealing than shoveling coal. "Yes, let's find the others before the masses get organized."

"Are you *really* robbing people?" Akstyr sounded hopeful, as if Amaranthe's usual plans were a touch altruistic for his tastes.

Maldynado thought of the tracking device in his pocket. "Not... exactly. But we did have a shootout in a suite upstairs."

"Nice," Akstyr purred.

Maldynado, concerned that there'd be more shootouts before the day ended, couldn't muster as much enthusiasm.

\* \* \* \* \*

Maldynado and Akstyr were jogging up the stairs to the deck where the officers were housed when a body flew over the railing above them. A captain's blue hat fell off, revealing tousled gray hair. Bed-head was the least of the man's problems. He flailed and cursed before disappearing into the foggy blanket covering the river where a splash announced his final fate.

On the deck above, pistols fired and swords clashed.

"Looks like they started without us," Akstyr said.

"Our team's latest hallmark," Maldynado said. "Hurling people from steamboats."

He and Akstyr reached the top deck and almost crashed into the back of a mob gathered around the entrance to the officers' quarters. The attackers wore everything from full uniforms to hand-tailored clothing to nightshirts to, er, that fellow was nude. The group claimed such varied weapons as swords, ceremonial muskets, and kitchen cutlery— no rolling pins, thank the emperor. Two old women on the outskirts were dismantling lounge chairs and throwing cushions. At the center of the throng, Sespian, Yara, Basilard, and Books fought to keep the crowd at bay. Though better armed, it soon became clear from their defensive strokes, that they didn't want to kill anyone, and the mob, perhaps sensing this, was forcing them into a tight knot.

"Thieves!" one of the old women cried as she hurled a chair cushion. "Highwaymen!"

Maldynado would have laughed—especially when the cushion beaned someone on her own side—but there were far deadlier weapons in the mix. Even as he watched, someone in the back jumped onto a chair and pointed an old flintlock pistol over the heads of the crowd. Maldynado charged, grabbed the man by the sides, and lifted him overhead. He took five great steps and hurled his burden over the railing. He

whirled back, expecting people at the rear to notice him and attack, but they were so intent on the targets in front that they hadn't seen Maldynado or Akstyr.

In fact, Akstyr had returned to the stairs where he crouched a few steps down. Hiding?

Maldynado frowned. Akstyr was rarely the first to jump into a fray, but he didn't usually *hide*.

Akstyr lifted a hand and beckoned him over. "I have an idea. Watch my back for a few minutes."

"Magics?"

"The *Science*," Akstyr said.

"Yes, yes, do your thing. We can discuss titles later."

Akstyr let his head droop, his eyes closing. Maldynado danced from foot to foot, alternately watching the mob and the steps to the lower deck. Though he wanted to join in the fray, and help the others, Amaranthe would give him a hard time if he let Akstyr be run through by someone with a makeshift spear. A few shouted questions of "What's going on up there?" convinced him more people would be charging up those stairs soon anyway. He braced himself to defend Akstyr's back.

A scream possessing the vocal power of a cannon—it came from one of the cushion-flinging ladies— threatened to rupture his eardrums. More screams and shouts burst from the crowd. Maldynado spun about in time to see two huge, bulky creatures with shaggy black fur shambling down the deck. The fog and the wan lighting couldn't hide the claws like daggers, the fangs like swords, and the naked hunger in their fierce predatory eyes.

"Makarovi!" someone yelled.

Several men leaped over the railing without looking twice. Others gripped weapons and braced themselves as the towering creatures lumbered closer.

"That's impressive, Akstyr," Maldynado whispered, then added, "That *is* your doing, right?" After all, they'd been near a river the other time they encountered makarovi—*real* makarovi—too.

Akstyr, eyes clenched shut, didn't respond.

A few worldly passengers squinted with suspicion, perhaps suspecting magic. It didn't matter. The distraction gave Sespian, Books, and the others an advantage. With nobody paying attention to them any more, they grabbed people as fast as they could, pushing them toward the railing. Books and Yara worked together. Sespian, though the slightest of the group—even Yara had wider shoulders than he—did an impressive job of wrestling people overboard on his own. Though short, Basilard was built like a steam dozer, and he simply lifted people over his head, as if they weighed no more than sacks of potatoes, hurling them over the railing with several feet of clearance.

The pair of "makarovi" stopped a few feet from the edge of the mob. Maldynado had suspected them illusory and hadn't thought Akstyr would let the monsters reach the crowd, where people would realize they could simply swipe their fingers through the images, but he wasn't prepared for what actually happened. The massive, fanged creatures reared on their hind legs and grabbed each other about the waists. Before Maldynado's gawking eyes, they started dancing.

He couldn't help himself. He broke out in guffaws.

"They're illusions, you idiots," someone in the dwindling crowd shouted. "Don't let the—"

Books's fist silenced the man.

Maldynado tapped Akstyr. "Come on."

He was done guarding backs. It was time to help the team finish swabbing the deck.

It didn't take long. Though a number of the warrior-caste passengers must have been military officers at one time, they were all older men, and most of them were strangers, not people who had spent months training together and learning to work as a team. The only time Maldynado faltered was when one of those old ladies raced up to him wearing a red dress, a ruby necklace, and numerous complementary rings. She snarled and raised a hand, displaying fingernails painted to match her jewelry.

"My lady." Maldynado lifted placating hands of his own. "I don't want to throw you overboard." She had to be close to eighty. "Why don't you just wait over—"

The fingernails flashed. A trained warrior such as Maldynado should have moved out of the way more quickly, but he'd underestimated their potential as a weapon. The nails cut through the fabric of his shirt and drew blood.

"On second thought…" Maldynado dodged a second attack, hoisted the woman, strode to the railing, and dropped her over the side.

Basilard, Yara, and Sespian were handling the remaining attackers, and Maldynado had time to probe his wound. The crazy woman had torn through the shoulder of his shirt, leaving his upper arm and left pectoral muscle exposed. The fabric flap waved in the breeze.

"This job is terrible on wardrobes." Maldynado took off the remains of his shirt and used it to dab at drops of blood welling from the fingernail gash.

"Unbelievable," Yara said.

"I know. She was scarier than any of the men." Maldynado waved at the river. "I pity any alligators that cross her path."

"I meant that you've found a reason to take your shirt off again. How is it that you never catch a cold when you're always running around half-naked?"

"My lady, I have a constitution of steel." Maldynado posed for her, flexing his biceps. "Want to feel it?"

"Unbelievable." Yara stalked away.

Maldynado shrugged and joined the others who were tossing the last few men over the side. These had gone down in the fight and didn't put up much of a struggle. Maldynado, reminded of clothing concerns, remembered to tuck a few business cards into pockets before he hoisted folks over. After hiking back to town without their belongings, some of those people might be inclined to visit Madame Mimi's Evenglory Boutique.

Basilard noticed and signed, *What are you doing?*

"Keeping my word, however inconvenient I find it. That's the kind of man I am." Maldynado spoke loudly enough for Yara to hear, though she pointedly had her back to him.

Maldynado tapped his bare chest and signed. *Is she looking at me at all?*

Basilard heaved the last person over the side. *I have more important things to do than monitor her looks.*

"Oh, come on, Bas. You notice everything."

*At this point, it's a foregone conclusion that we're taking over the ship, right?* Basilard signed to the others, ignoring Maldynado.

By then, the team had gathered in front of the officers' quarters, and Books translated for Sespian.

"Yes," Sespian said, "We'll have to. My plan to win over the captain didn't quite work as I'd hoped." Sespian rubbed his face, perhaps to cover the sheepish expression that came with the admission. Despite the long night, he didn't have any beard growth hugging his jaw. Should he and Akstyr ever have a race to see who could grow a mustache the quickest... it'd be a boring contest to watch.

"Must have been a short discussion with the captain," Akstyr said. "I wasn't in the boiler room long before security barged in, blathering about an impostor emperor leading a band of highwaymen."

Books kicked him in the shin. "*Sire.*"

"*Sire.* I was lucky I was actually shoveling instead of working on—" Akstyr glanced toward the spot where the dancing makarovi had been, "—things."

"Things?" Maldynado asked. "I think the emperor has figured out your secret occupation by now. Him and fifty other witnesses now practicing their swimming skills."

Akstyr grimaced, perhaps remembering that there was a gang with a bounty on his head.

"If we force everyone to... disembark," Sespian asked Books, "do you think we can pilot and power the steamboat with this small team?"

Books rubbed his own jaw—it had no trouble sprouting hair, and he was already bristly enough to scrub dishes with his face. "Two on stoker duty, one or two people in the engine room, and one at navigation. That leaves one person free to guard prisoners, should we find any we wish to take."

"Such as Brynia?" Maldynado asked, noting that she was nowhere around. If the team didn't have her, it wouldn't matter that they controlled the steamboat, because they wouldn't know where to take it.

Books winced. Had he been the one to let her escape? "Yes."

"Your duty roster doesn't factor in time for sleep," Sespian said.

Books spread his arms. "It's a luxury we don't always receive."

"Very well. Let's get rid of any lingering opposition and see what we can do." Sespian looked at each of them. "Does anyone have experience piloting a steamboat?"

Nobody raised a hand.

"I had a wind-up steamboat as a child," Maldynado said. "I could get it racing around the bathtub without clunking against the walls more than once or twice a lap."

That earned him a number of unimpressed stares.

"It was a joke," Maldynado said.

Books lifted a finger. "Whoever you decide on to navigate, Sire, I heartily suggest that Maldynado be placed on stoker duty."

"Understood," Sespian said.

"You crash one dirigible…" Maldynado muttered as the team dispersed.

Before Basilard walked away, he signed, *Your butt.*

*What?* Maldynado checked his backside, thinking he'd sat in something.

*That's what she looks at when you're not facing her.*

"Ah!" *I knew she looked.* So, Yara wasn't a chest-and-biceps gal. She liked tight buns. Maldynado was on the verge of plotting a way to display those buns more fully for her, when Basilard signed again.

*Miraculous that she bothers, considering your spelunking comment.*

Basilard walked away before Maldynado could do more than groan and wonder if *everyone* had heard his earlier exchange with Yara.

# CHAPTER 13

IT WAS HARD TO HIDE FROM A SWAMP FULL OF SOL-
diers when one's stomach was growling louder than a busy saw-
mill blade. Weariness dragged at Amaranthe's battered body, and
each step irritated the cut and bruised bottoms of her feet. Though she'd
obtained a knife and a rifle, fate hadn't been kindly enough to favor her
with a chance to acquire boots or clothing. Everything from her feet to
the bullet gash at her temple ached, and she wanted to crawl into a dark
hole, curl up on her side, and hide until the pain went away.

She had lost track of how many times she'd evaded her hunters by
inches, slipping beneath a pond full of lilies or scrambling between
shrubs just before men passed. Luck wouldn't favor her forever. Even
now, they were herding her. She'd long since lost track of the trail and,
not twenty minutes earlier, she'd glimpsed the massive dome of the
*Behemoth* in the distance. She'd made no progress and was no better
off than she'd been when she started out. Her earlier notion that she
might, Sicarius-style, take down each soldier in the swamp one at a time
seemed foolish now. After the first man had disappeared, the others had
started searching in pairs. She'd thought of sniping from the treetops,
but the alligator had stolen her soldier before she could search him for
ammo, so she only had a few bullets.

For the fiftieth time, Amaranthe glanced toward the canopy, wondering if darkness would ever come and if she'd have more luck slipping
through their net at night.

She stepped around a cypress tree and almost landed on a dead soldier lying face-down in the mud.

Stupefied by her weariness, Amaranthe could only stare at it for a puzzled moment. Another alligator, she thought, but wouldn't an animal have dragged the man away to eat?

She shook away the cobwebs lacing her mind. She put her back to the tree and lifted her rifle as she scanned her surroundings. This might be a trap. Maybe the man wasn't even dead; maybe he was a diversion while someone else crept up on her.

Nothing stirred the foliage around her, not even a breeze. Only mosquitoes buzzed about, flying through the humid air and giving Amaranthe another reason to wish she weren't naked. She eyed the worn shirt and trousers on the still form at her feet. He didn't seem to be breathing; if he was playing dead, he was doing a convincing job of it.

She propped her rifle against the tree, gripped the man's arm and leg, and tugged him onto his back. Her breath caught. His throat had been slit.

Sicarius? No, she wanted to believe that, but he couldn't have come so far in… She'd lost track of the days. Five? Seven? More? Even if he *could* have made it, how would he have found her in this place? Maybe she had some other ally out there. Whatever the case, she couldn't stay in one area to contemplate it.

Knife in one hand, rifle in the other, Amaranthe stood up, ready to slip into the vegetation again. A dark figure stepped out of the brush ahead of her.

Pike. That was her first thought, but her visitor's hair was blond, not white, its arrangement more tousled than usual, littered with cypress needles and moss tufts. The start of a scruffy beard covered his jaw, and his face seemed leaner than she remembered. Road grime coated black clothing plagued with holes and tears. Worn and dusty, his soft boots had little sole left to them. His garments hung more loosely than usual, and she imagined that he'd jogged all the way with little in the way of food and water. Looking for her.

A lump tightened Amaranthe's throat, and tears welled in her eyes. She tamped down an urge to leap across the intervening meters and fling her arms about him. What if it was a trick, something else her enemies could do with that ancient technology, something designed to tease her from hiding?

Sicarius did not move except to look her up and down, his eyes full of concern and… pity. In that second, Amaranthe knew it wasn't a trick. Pike and the Forge people never would have put emotion on his face. Indeed, she must look awful to have elicited it. For the first time, in the presence of someone who mattered, she felt self-conscious about roaming the wilderness stark naked except for a weapon in each hand.

"*Oh,*" Amaranthe said, "are you supposed to wear clothing for skirmishes in an alligator-filled swamp?"

She barely managed to get the words out. Emotion, something bordering on hysteria, threatened to bubble out of her. She was tired of holding herself together.

When Sicarius lifted an inviting arm and said, "They are optional," she nearly tumbled into his embrace.

Despite his worn appearance, the arms he wrapped around her were strong, and his body offered the solid dependability of a boulder. Or a steel slab. She wanted to bury her head against his chest and let him worry about Pike and the others. But the memory of her failure arose in her thoughts, bringing forth the tears that had only threatened before. She'd have to tell him, and as soon as she did…

Maybe Sicarius already sensed that she'd failed him in some way, for his body grew rigid beneath her arms, and tension radiated from him. More than tension. Anger.

Amaranthe wiped her eyes and stepped back. She searched his face, trying to guess what he knew.

"Thank you for coming," Amaranthe said carefully. It occurred to her that his being here instead of with the team might mean that Sespian hadn't made it. Maybe rage, and a desire to avenge his son's death, had driven Sicarius down here as much as a need to find her. "Is Sespian… Did he survive the crash?"

"Yes."

Relief washed over Amaranthe. "Thank his ancestors."

No similar relief expressed itself on Sicarius's face. He looked her over again, more slowly this time, as if he were memorizing every detail. "Stay here. Hide. I will find Pike."

His words were short and clipped. His anger, Amaranthe realized, wasn't directed at her. He was furious with Pike on her behalf.

"Sicarius, I… have to tell you something."

"Later." Face hard and grim, Sicarius looked like a man with murder on his mind.

Amaranthe had no argument for sparing Pike, but the rest of his men might not deserve the wrath of a deadly assassin. "Without the head, the wolf will die," she blurted after him.

Sicarius disappeared into the brush without a comment or backward glance.

"Hide," Amaranthe mumbled to herself.

It seemed like good advice, but she didn't think she could bring herself to cower under a tree while Sicarius faced Pike. The emperor's old master interrogator hadn't moved with Sicarius's sinewy grace, but who knew if he had more of that superior technology with him, ready to use in an emergency? At the least, he had a weapon capable of firing numerous shots without being reloaded, and he wouldn't be alone.

Amaranthe eyed the rifle she'd taken from the dead soldier. It had five shots remaining. Maybe if she climbed a high tree, she could see out over the swamp and watch the confrontation. If Pike gave Sicarius a hard time, she could shoot the bastard.

"For once, I'll have *your* back, Sicarius."

Nodding to herself, Amaranthe headed for a cypress with the girth of a small house. A thorn gouged her thigh. Reminded of her vulnerability, she went back to the dead soldier to remove his clothes. She tucked the knife into a belt sheath, and, a couple of moments later, started up the tree, this time wearing green and gray clothes with the cuffs rolled up. The boots she left at the base of the trunk for later. A number of sizes too large, they would only hinder her on the climb.

Normally, scaling the tree wouldn't have winded her. Now… her muscles quivered before she'd risen five feet. Amaranthe continued up doggedly, digging her fingers into the furrowed bark, and pulling herself from branch to branch with the rifle slung across her back on a strap. If Sicarius had traveled hundreds of miles to help her, she'd darn well figure out a way to climb a tree for him.

Amaranthe kept an eye out below as she pulled herself higher, aware that the foliage wasn't as dense as that of the firs and cedars up north. The surrounding trees and leaves should make it hard for anyone to see her from below, but Sicarius would think her an idiot—rightfully so—if she'd survived all she had only to be shot by someone glancing upward.

The thought gnawed at her mind, and Amaranthe was on the verge of climbing down when something moved on the other side of a muddy inlet. A pair of people were hunting in a field of waist-high grass and cattails. One man gazed out at the water while the other bent to check the earth. The one looking at the water wore black; it wasn't Sicarius this time.

Rage filled Amaranthe as she glowered at Pike. She could argue for sparing the men working for him, but, after what he'd done to her—and to Sicarius all those years ago—she wanted him dead. Not just for her sake, but for the good of the empire. Such a man shouldn't be allowed into a position of power again, a position that would let him continue to torture people.

Amaranthe eased out onto a thick branch and lay belly-down along it. Once horizontal, she eased the rifle off her back, moving slowly so she wouldn't stir the leaves. The two men were conversing and looking in the other direction now, but two more had walked into view on the far side of that field.

Amaranthe tucked the stock of the rifle into her shoulder and lined up her sights, targeting Pike's back. Had she still been alone, she would have fired, but, knowing Sicarius was out there, she hesitated with her finger on the trigger. If she missed, Pike would be extra alert. And missing was a possibility, not necessarily because of the distance, but because her hands had started to sweat, and her heart seemed to be thundering with enough force to send tremors through the branch beneath her.

One of the men on the far side of the field disappeared from view. It happened so quickly that Amaranthe hadn't the reason for it. One second he was there, the next gone. His partner, walking a couple of paces ahead and hacking at tall grass with a machete, hadn't yet noticed.

Sicarius at work, Amaranthe presumed. She eased her finger away from the trigger. She'd let him handle the situation and only back him up if he needed it. Maybe it was small and weak of her to let someone else take out—no, not take out, *kill*—Pike for her, but Sicarius might relish the opportunity to get rid of a man who'd tormented him throughout his youth. He'd suffered more at Pike's hands than she had.

The second man on the far side turned around and called out his partner's name. Pike and his comrade heard.

"You see her?" Pike asked.

"No. I lost Bronc."

Before Pike and his partner had taken more than a step in that direction, something grabbed the lone man's leg and pulled him down. His head disappeared beneath the grass.

Pike and his comrade broke into a sprint. They reached the spot in seconds, but, from the way they turned in circles, it was clear they didn't see Sicarius or their missing man. Pike frowned at the earth and knelt. Tracks in the mud?

When he stood again, his eyes were narrowed. Amaranthe had a feeling Pike knew now who he was dealing with. At the very least, he must suspect that hadn't been her work.

Pike whispered something to his comrade, and the man's eyes nearly popped out of his head. He rotated in place, his rifle clenched in his hands, his gaze darting in every direction. Meanwhile, Pike's head bent for a moment. Amaranthe tensed. She couldn't see his hands but thought he might have pulled something out of his pocket. If Sicarius was keeping his head below the weeds, he wouldn't be able to see that.

Pike pulled out something black and dropped it. He clasped his hands behind his back and strolled—yes, it was definitely a stroll—a few paces.

"What is he doing?" Amaranthe wondered. She also wondered if she ought to simply shoot him. At this point, Pike knew someone was out there, killing his men, so even if she missed, it wouldn't matter. It might even distract him for a moment so Sicarius could swoop in and take him down. "Not that he needs my help for that," she muttered.

But she wasn't that sure. Pike dropped something else several feet away from the first thing. Yes, he was definitely up to something devious. The other man kept spinning about, jerking his weapon in one direction and then another. Pike seemed as calm as a panther sunning itself on a rock.

Amaranthe rested her cheek against the stock of the rifle and lined up the pair of sights, centering the crosshairs on Pike's chest. Her finger found the sleek, cool metal of the trigger. And she hesitated. She wiped a bead of sweat out of her eye. For all the evils he'd done to her, and countless others, Sicarius included, she had to wrestle with her instincts to nurture instead of kill. In her heart, she knew the man was beyond reform, and yet…

"Stop it," she whispered to herself.

Pike wasn't worth the self-doubt. If she and Sicarius failed to kill him, and he went on to become Ravido's Commander of the Armies, with power over thousands, his ancestors only knew what harm he might do.

Amaranthe took a deep breath and found the trigger again.

An instant before she flexed her finger, something cold brushed her bare foot. She almost fell out of the tree in surprise. A startled squawk arose in her throat, but she clamped her mouth shut before her vocal cords could betray her.

Barely managing to keep the rife—and her perch on the branch—Amaranthe craned her neck about. A black-and-tan snake with a body as thick as her thigh was slithering across her foot on its way to…

She swallowed. It was coming out on the branch with her.

Its yellow irises stared into her soul, and she knew without a doubt that it wanted her for lunch. With a head that large and a maw that fang-filled, the snake could swallow her whole. She tried to pull her leg away, but it had already coiled halfway around her calf, pinning it to the branch. Its weight surprised her.

Amaranthe thought to maneuver the rifle about and shoot the beast between the eyes. But that would give away her position more surely than a scream. She glanced toward the clearing. Pike's partner had disappeared. In the second she watched, Pike dropped a final item and then stepped to the left. The air shimmered, defining the walls of a cylinder with him inside, then winked out, the view returning to normal. Not good. While Sicarius had been picking off his men, Pike had been creating some sort of protective cage around himself. One Sicarius wouldn't be able to see unless he'd happened to poke his head above the weeds during that second when the "walls" had been visible.

The snake moved up to Amaranthe's thigh. She shifted about as best she could—she needed to leave one hand gripping the branch, lest she plummet thirty feet—and lifted the rifle above her head. She angled the butt, intending to smash the snake between the eyes. It wouldn't harm such a massive creature, but maybe it'd deter it.

The snake saw the blow coming. Its head whipped to the side, evading the attack easily. An angry hiss pierced the air. Its mouth opened and saliva—or was that poison?—glistened on its fangs.

Amaranthe swung the rifle, using it like a club. She connected this time, but the snake didn't budge under the blow. It hissed again, the sound dripping with ire. Its head reared several feet in the air, then it darted for Amaranthe's throat, quicker than lightning.

She swung the rifle back again, abandoning her grip on the branch to throw all her weight into the blow. It deflected the attack—barely. The snake's fangs bit into the branch, inches from Amaranthe's ear. Already off balance from the defensive move, she shifted too far to get away from those fangs, and she slipped from her perch.

Amaranthe would have fallen all the way to the ground, but the snake still had its body coiled around her calf. A jolt of pain lanced through her knee as all her weight came to hang from that leg. Her face smacked into a lower branch, and she lost her grip on the rifle. It fell several feet, landing in the crook of another branch. That left only the knife. Great.

As she yanked it from its sheath, the snake slithered down her body, its head angling for her neck again. Hanging upside down, Amaranthe gripped the knife like a lifeline, knowing she'd only get one chance.

The beast's massive maw gaped open, again displaying that row of fangs. Amaranthe plunged the knife upward, stabbing at the flesh on the roof of the snake's mouth, angling the blade toward its brain. The jaw snapped shut. She yanked her hand out before teeth closed about her wrist. The knife remained, wedged in the snake's mouth.

Heart pounding in her ears, she stared at the creature. Had the knife done enough? Had she reached the brain?

For a long moment, the snake didn't move. Then it slumped, head thumping against Amaranthe's chest. Seeing that massive maw so close to her neck almost made her pee on herself—and wouldn't that have wonderful implications when she was hanging upside down?—but a dullness had come over those vibrant yellow eyes, and she knew she could relax. Sort of. She still had to retrieve her rifle and check on Sicarius.

Amaranthe expected that, with death, the snake's grip on her leg would loosen, but its muscles remained tight, and it held her fast. She swung her arms below her head and managed to reach the rifle. Then, with lack of a better idea, she used the snake's body like a rope, climbing back up to her perch. It took precious time to pry her leg free. With its grip finally broken, the snake fell out of the tree, landing with a thud

that sent birds flying. Bloody ancestors, she might as well have shot the thing if it was going to end up causing that much of a stir.

Amaranthe wriggled back onto her belly and was horrified but not surprised when she found Pike gazing straight at her. His knowing stare sent a chill through her, but, after surviving the advances of a woman-eating snake, she refused to act cowed. She didn't know how many details he could make out over the intervening distance, but she gave him an insouciant smile and a cheery wave. Rude gestures might have been more appropriate, but she thought a bright attitude from a former captive might bother him more.

Pike lifted a long-barreled pistol, and Amaranthe dropped her hand, ready to scurry backward and use the tree trunk for cover if he aimed it at her. He bent his elbow and let the barrel rest against his shoulder, the muzzle pointing skyward. A man ready to fire, not at her but at whomever approached him. He gazed out at the clearing.

Amaranthe eyed the area as well. Even from her lofty perch, she couldn't see through the grass and cattails to spot Sicarius on the ground. She searched farther about, in all the directions she could monitor from the tree. She'd best not forget that there were dozens of men out there hunting for her.

A dark spot behind a tree drew her eye. Sicarius. He wasn't in the clearing after all, but some fifty meters away from Pike. He seemed to be… tying a shoe? No, when he stood, she spotted Pike's partner. The man wasn't dead but tied to the base of the tree with a gag in his mouth. The two other men Amaranthe had assumed Sicarius killed shared the spot. Huh. She hadn't been certain Sicarius had heard her comment about only needing to take care of the wolf's head, but he must have. This time he was going to do as she wished and not kill every enemy he crossed.

However inappropriate the timing, emotion swelled in Amaranthe's throat. He was doing his best to please her when she'd utterly failed him.

Sicarius stood, using the tree for cover, and gazed toward Pike. Amaranthe wagered he hadn't seen that protective cylinder flash into existence, not if he'd been busy dragging men away to tie to trees. She had to warn him.

Amaranthe scooted out farther on the branch and propped the rifle in a crook. She lined up the shot and, this time, had no trouble firing. A

small burst of orange flashed a few feet in front of Pike's head. He didn't so much as flinch. It took Amaranthe a second to realize what the orange represented. Flame. Her bullet had been incinerated.

She glanced at Sicarius, hoping he'd seen. Still behind the tree, he lifted a hand in acknowledgment. Amaranthe jerked her gaze away, realizing she risked giving away his hiding spot. Indeed, she caught Pike glancing in that direction. Sicarius had already disappeared, though, back into the grass.

Perhaps Amaranthe shouldn't have been watching him, for, as she refocused on Pike, he fired the pistol. At her.

A bullet tore off a branch above, and leaves and twigs pelted her. The pistol cracked again. Amaranthe scooted back and buried her face, one arm slung over her head for protection. If she let go with the other, she'd end up on the ground next to the dead snake. Of course, with someone shooting at her, maybe that'd be a better place to be.

Four more cracks sounded, somewhat muted by distance and the heavy swamp air, and bullets peppered the tree all around her. Fortunately, only leaves and broken twigs hit her. Given the hundred and some meters separating them, she ought not be surprised by the pistol's lack of accuracy, but she thanked her ancestors for it nonetheless.

After the sixth shot, silence returned to the swamp. Absolute silence. Not so much as a mosquito whined.

Amaranthe lifted her head. Pike was reloading, his hands steady as he methodically slipped bullets into the revolving mechanism that held them. He wasn't worried about Sicarius getting to him, and why should he be with that shield? If Sicarius even touched it, he might be incinerated. A quelling thought, that one. She was glad he'd seen her warning.

If she hadn't been busy holding branches and weapons, she would have nibbled on a fingernail. Pike's cylindrical barrier had flashed so briefly that she had a hard time remembering the dimensions. Six feet wide or so and perhaps fifteen feet tall. She didn't know if it was open on top or closed. If it was closed, there'd be no way to get at Pike, unless Sicarius burrowed under like a gopher. And for all they knew, the barrier might extend underground as well.

Out in the field, not a blade of grass rustled, but Amaranthe knew Sicarius was somewhere nearby, studying Pike, figuring out a way to reach him.

Pike knew it too. His pistol again rested on his shoulder and he gazed around calmly. "I'm not the one you want, Sicarius. I'm not trying to kill Sespian. I don't care if he lives, so long as he abdicates the throne."

A new concern stampeded into Amaranthe's mind. Had Retta volunteered what she'd learned? Or had Pike encountered her and, angered that his prisoner had disappeared, forced the information from her? Either way, Pike might be about to share his new knowledge with the whole world—or at least the one person that Amaranthe didn't want to hear it. She would have told Sicarius that she'd let the information escape, but having an enemy tell him first… Her shoulders slumped and all the fight drained from her. She stared at her rifle, at the finger that had hesitated, giving the snake time to divert her. If she'd fired at that moment, Pike wouldn't have gotten his shield in place, and he wouldn't be talking now.

"I don't care about Forge," Pike called. "I just want my old job back and, all right, maybe a little more. Ravido has promised me Hollowcrest's position along with the reinstatement of my title and lands. I'll be Commander of the Armies, and the Marblecrests will be back on the throne. It was never meant for Sespian. You know that. You've *always* known that." Pike cocked his ear, as if listening for a response. Even protected by his shield, Pike had to be worried. He couldn't stand there forever. He'd run out of food and water eventually, and he must know Sicarius had the patience to wait. "You could take Sespian and disappear," Pike said. "I have enough sway over Ravido to make sure neither of you are hunted. So long as Sespian can be publicly declared dead, he need not truly die. I'm the only one who can make you that offer. Now that Forge is ready to move, they want the boy dead."

Amaranthe shot at Pike again. The shield ate the bullet, but the attack surprised him to silence, at least for a moment. She told herself she'd fired to distract Pike, in case Sicarius had thought up a way to attack him, but in truth she wanted to shut him up. She didn't want him talking about how she'd blabbed. The bastard would probably take credit for getting the information out of her.

Pike faced her, a weary sneer twisting his mouth. But there was no fear or concern in his eyes. It was the type of sneer one gave to a mosquito. A mosquito might be annoying, but it had no power to kill.

"Eat street," Amaranthe muttered and fired again, this time with more thought guiding her hand. She aimed for a spot about six feet above his head, trying to find the vertical boundary of the shield.

Another orange flash ate her bullet. For a moment, Pike looked like he might fire at her, but he returned his attention to the field.

Amaranthe fired again, higher this time. The bullet passed through without being incinerated, but a slight shimmer disturbed the air before it disappeared. Odd, that had been on the other side of Pike. Had she fired over the top of the barrier, but, because of her elevated position, caused the bullet to zip downward at an angle and catch the shield on only one side? Pike could obviously fire from inside. She tried to remember if the shield had shimmered when he'd been shooting at her, but she'd been too busy ducking to notice. No matter. She suspected she'd just proved that the cylinder was open on the top. Unfortunately, at fifteen feet or so, even Sicarius wouldn't be able to leap that high, not when he'd have to throw his entire body over it without touching the barrier. Still, it was a starting point. If they could make an explosive of some kind and hurl it inside....

Lest Pike notice her silence and attribute it to scheming that he should worry about, Amaranthe fired another shot, aiming for his nether regions this time, for amusement's sake.

Pike stuck a fist on his hip and faced her, leveling his pistol at her again. Unlike with the earlier rapid-fire shots, he took his time in lining up his aim. Amaranthe scooted backward on the branch, thinking it might be a good time to find Sicarius and explain what she'd learned.

Before Pike fired, a dark figure rose from the cattails several meters behind him. Sicarius. He sprinted for Pike, a long stick—a sapling?—in his hands. Before Amaranthe could guess what he intended, Sicarius planted the flexible pole in the ground and used the leverage to vault himself into the air. Amaranthe's heart surged into her throat as he released the stick at the apex and soared toward Pike's cylinder.

She gulped and held her breath. If he misjudged the spot by an inch...

Sicarius dropped out of the air without bursting into flame or disturbing the shield. At the last second Pike, perhaps watching Amaranthe's expression, looked up. But he was too late. Sicarius landed on him like

a boulder falling out of the sky. Both men disappeared beneath the tall grass and cattails.

Amaranthe tried to stand on her branch, to better see what was happening, but her foot slipped, and she almost fell again. She caught the trunk and steadied herself.

A scream tore through the swamp, only to end abruptly, cut off with a gurgle that left little doubt as to what had happened. Amaranthe was surprised, and, she admitted, disappointed at how brief that scream had been. For what he'd done to her—and to Sicarius—Pike had deserved to suffer, to have his own medicine forced down his throat.

An uneasy thought slithered into her mind. What if that scream hadn't belonged to Pike? What if he'd been waiting for Sicarius with another trick in hand. She held her breath, waiting for the victor to rise.

Time trickled past, and nobody appeared. Amaranthe shook her head. What was going on? They hadn't killed each other off, had they? They couldn't have....

She had reconciled herself to the idea of climbing down and going over there to look for herself when a familiar voice called up from below.

"Hiding is generally done from the ground, under or behind an object that can serve as cover as well as camouflage." Sicarius stood beside the dead snake, at the base of her tree, gazing up at her. "Leaves provide camouflage but not cover. We have discussed the difference."

Amaranthe grinned so hard it hurt her cheeks. "I was afraid to hide on the ground because of the snakes."

Sicarius regarded the dead creature in the mud. "This appears to have fallen from a great height."

"How odd." Still grinning, Amaranthe tossed the rifle to him and shimmied down the cypress.

In her haste, she missed a branch and tumbled the last ten feet. Sicarius caught her and drew her into a hug that was far gentler than she would have preferred. Though her wounds protested, she snaked her arms around him and demonstrated how fierce a hug should be. She buried her face in his neck. His hug was a relief—maybe he hadn't realized, from Pike's words, that she'd betrayed him. She'd have to tell him eventually—soon—but she needed to feel safe for a while first. The words "cathartic collapse" floated through her mind. No, it was more than that. She needed to be held by someone who cared.

Sicarius laid his chin on the top of her head. He was being careful not to disturb her injuries, so it was hard to tell, but she thought the hug might mean as much to him as to her.

Too soon for her tastes, he drew back, though he didn't let her go. Amaranthe braced herself, expecting him to question her about Pike's speech, to demand an explanation.

"You were following a fresh trail through the swamp," Sicarius said. "Are its makers the priority? Or is it the craft?"

"The craft?"

"Do you wish to destroy it so Forge cannot continue to use it against us? Or is it more important to follow those who left the trail?"

"Oh. I… think destroying the *Behemoth* may be beyond us. Remember that submerged laboratory? This thing makes that look like something a clumsy child assembled on the playground."

Sicarius's eyebrows twitched. "The *Behemoth*?"

"My name, not theirs." Amaranthe supposed it was possible that she and Sicarius could do something to disable the craft, *if* they could figure out how to get inside, and *if* they could find Retta and question her. Amaranthe didn't even know if Retta was still alive. She might have crossed paths with Pike when she shouldn't have. Amaranthe shied away from the thought. Even if Retta had stolen secrets, she'd saved Amaranthe's life. "I think the meeting is the priority," she said, hoping she wouldn't regret the choice later. "Ms. Worgavic and other Forge founders will be there. I heard a few things, but no details. Somehow they intend to control the future of the empire. To hear Ms. Worgavic talk, maybe the future of the world. We might want to put a stop to that."

"Ms. Worgavic?" Sicarius asked.

He must find it strange to hear Amaranthe add the title to the name; she was probably even saying it with a tinge of that old student-teacher respect.

"She's one of the Forge founders. I only knew her as my economics instructor at the Mildawn Business School for Women."

"I see." Sicarius's gaze shifted to something beyond her, reminding Amaranthe that there were still soldiers on the hunt. The wolf's limbs might not yet know that the head was missing.

"We should—" Amaranthe started.

"Go, yes. The trail is already cold." Sicarius stepped away from her and gave her another look up and down.

Amaranthe attempted to appear sturdy enough for the road, even if her knees wanted to buckle and her body craved nothing more than a hot bath followed by a bed smothered with feather-filled comforters. Alas, both were hard to find in swamps.

"Your pride would object to your body being carried?" Sicarius asked.

Amaranthe cringed at the idea of him burdened by her weight when he'd so obviously traveled a long, arduous road to find her. "How about we walk side by side and lean on each other for support?"

The barest hint of a smile ghosted across Sicarius's face, and he offered her his arm. Amaranthe accepted it, and, if she was leaning more heavily on him than he was on her as they set out, he didn't mention it.

# CHAPTER 14

FTER TWO DAYS OF SHOVELING COAL, MALDY-
nado's back and shoulders ached so badly he was starting
to envy his granny her cane. When Sespian had popped into
the boiler room to ask for volunteers to do another search for Brynia,
Maldynado had nearly fallen over in his haste to raise his hand first.
Akstyr, who'd also been assigned stoker duty, had been equally quick to
offer his services, though he'd spent more of the day "meditating on the
Science" than he had shoveling, so he shouldn't have needed a break.
Ah, well. He might prove useful.

Maldynado and Akstyr left Basilard in the boiler room and spent an
hour searching cabins and common areas. Maldynado wished he could
invite Yara to join the hunt; he hadn't seen much of her in the last couple
of days. She'd been alternating shifts with Sespian in the wheelhouse,
and since said wheelhouse perched by itself on the roof, it was hard to
"happen to pass by" on the way to another destination.

Maldynado yawned so widely that his jaw cracked. He'd lost track
of how many miles the steamboat had covered, but another night had
come, this one dark, thanks to gloomy low-hanging clouds that smelled
of rain. Lights dotted the farmlands on either side of the river, but only
the ship's running lamps pushed back the darkness on the waterway.

"I heard that," Akstyr said from a few meters away. He and Maldynado were on the upper deck now. They'd started their searches on
opposite ends and were working their ways toward each other.

"What?" Maldynado responded.

"You yawning. You should sleep more when you're supposed to be
on duty. You wouldn't be so tired."

"Thanks for the tip. I'll keep that in mind." Maldynado checked a suite. Empty. They had forced everybody overboard on the first day—the antagonistic sorts had gone feet first while more amenable passengers had been shuttled into lifeboats—and, though there'd been a few holdouts, he hadn't seen anyone who wasn't on the team for some time.

Akstyr stuck his head into a cabin a few doors down. "Nothing in any of them. She's probably long gone."

"I don't think so. If she wants to get to this meeting, I bet this boat's the fastest way there."

"She's doing a good job of hiding then."

"On that point, I'll agree." Maldynado opened another suite door, this time pausing to regard the bed, specifically to share with it the yearning gaze of lovers kept apart for too long. "We've searched every cranny at least twice. She must be moving around, changing hiding spots often."

Akstyr leaned against one of the doors, stuck his hands in his pockets, and turned toward the river. Maldynado finished checking the suites on his half of the deck and stopped a couple of steps away. From one of the waterside homesteads, a dog barked at the steamboat's passage.

"Think Am'ranthe is still alive?" Akstyr asked.

"Yes," Maldynado said.

Akstyr gave him a sidelong look. "Really?"

"Yes." Maldynado wasn't prepared to accept any other possibility.

"If she's not…"

"Don't worry about it. Books knows about your deal with her, that you get some of that money the emperor brought so you can go to school."

"That's not why I was asking."

Now Maldynado was the one to give Akstyr a sidelong look. "Really?"

Though the boy had a few unique skills and had proven useful to the group at times, Maldynado had never seen evidence suggesting he cared for anyone except himself. The team watched his back, so he did what Amaranthe asked. That seemed to be the extent of anyone's relationship with him.

"Yes, *really*, all right?" Akstyr jammed his hands deeper into his pockets. "I don't want some ugly Sicarius-type torturing her. She's like…" He scuffed the deck with his boot.

"A sister?" Maldynado suggested.

"I guess. I never had one. I never had anyone. You know my mother is trying to have me killed?"

"Someone mentioned that, yes. Because some hoodlums put a bounty on your head, right? And she's trying to get a piece of the reward."

Akstyr nodded. "When I was little, I wished I had a real family. Where people didn't yell at you and hit you and... Well, that doesn't matter now. It's just that Am'ranthe was the first person to..."

"Care?"

"Yeah. I don't get why she would, but I wish I'd told her... that it mattered, you know? If not for her, you and the others would've never..." Akstyr shifted his weight and scuffed the deck with his other boot. "She's sort of like a big hunk of chewed up chicle. Things stick to her, things that wouldn't normally stick together otherwise."

"Chicle?" Maldynado couldn't help himself. The comparison of Amaranthe to chewing gum made him throw back his head and laugh. "It's a good thing you've got talent as a wizard because you'd never make it as a poet."

"Aw, eat street, Maldynado." Akstyr scowled and stepped away from the door. "And they're practitioners not wizards."

Maldynado grabbed his shoulder. "Sorry. I know what you mean. I do. Truly."

Akstyr's scowled faded slightly, though his eyes remained suspicious.

"You'll get a chance to tell her that you appreciate her... gum-like nature," Maldynado said. "She's alive, and Sicarius will find her, and we'll all meet up again." Where and when, he didn't know, but Akstyr seemed to find some reassurance in the words, for he leaned against the door again, the tension seeping out of his shoulders.

"I can't wait to finish up this stuff with the emperor," Akstyr said. "I want to go study, and none of the gangs will be able to find me if I'm on the Kyatt Islands. That bounty isn't big enough that anybody would go halfway across the world to get to me."

"Probably not," Maldynado said.

"You should visit me over there sometime when I'm studying. All of you. Well, maybe not Sicarius, but Am'ranthe and the others for sure. It'd be like a vacation. I heard some of the women go topless on the beach too."

Maldynado probably shouldn't poke fun at Akstyr, not twice in five minutes, but this uncharacteristic rambling tickled his sense of humor. "Aw, I see what this is about. We might be on our final mission together and you'll get to leave soon, and you're realizing you'll miss us." He slung an arm around Akstyr's shoulders.

"I will *not*." Akstyr shoved the arm away. "I just thought you might like the Kyatt Islands. That's all."

"Topless women, you say?" Maldynado decided not to tease the boy any more, at least not for expressing his feelings. His ancestors knew that opening up and making overtures of friendship to people wasn't Akstyr's strength. "You reckon you'd know what to do with one?" There, normal manly teasing, that shouldn't bother him.

Akstyr crossed his arms. "I know what all the parts are for, yes."

More jokes popped into Maldynado's mind, but he restrained himself. He didn't want Akstyr to feel overly punished for sharing his feelings. All he said was, "When we *do* reunite with Amaranthe, make sure you tell her the gum thing. Women can usually figure out that you appreciate them, but they like to hear it too."

Akstyr's eyebrow twitched. "Have you told Sergeant Yara that you appreciate her?"

"What? No. I mean, why would I?" Maldynado groaned inwardly. Why did that subject make his tongue fumble so?

"Uh, because you like her?"

"I barely know her. She's only been with us… Emperor's warts, has it even been two weeks since we started on this crazy adventure?"

"I've seen you talk a lot of women into beds, usually without paying—" Akstyr's lip curled in envy or perhaps disgust, "—and you're usually so smooth and confident that they don't gag on your dumb lines, but you can't talk to Yara without saying something stupid."

"I hardly think that's true. I—"

"Spelunking," Akstyr said.

This time, Maldynado's groan wasn't inward. Seriously, had *everyone* heard that? Or had it simply gotten around? "Fine, fine, I'll tell her I appreciate her next time she's not insulting me." He yawned. He needed to find some sleep. "You check that one?"

Akstyr turned around and tried to open the door he'd been leaning against. "It's locked."

"Oh? It wasn't locked when we searched yesterday."

At first, they'd encountered numerous secured doors with passengers hiding on the other side, unwilling to exit the steamboat prematurely. Maldynado and the others had evicted all of those folks, though, and he remembered all of the suites being unlocked on his last search.

Maldynado gave it a harder tug and, when it didn't budge, knocked.

"Do you actually expect a stowaway to answer the door?" Akstyr asked.

"No, but it seems polite to knock before barging into someone's room. Can you use your magics to tell if someone's inside?"

"Magics," Akstyr muttered, clearly disgusted at Maldynado's ongoing irreverence for words related to his studies.

Maldynado made a note to continue using the term.

Disgusted or not, Akstyr placed a hand on the door and closed his eyes. "Yes, I think so. One person."

"A woman?"

Akstyr tilted his head, brow furrowing. "Yea. She doesn't have, uhm, yea."

Curiosity piqued, Maldynado asked, "What exactly do you *see* when you do that?"

"Stuff." The boy had mastered the art of being vague and unhelpful.

"*What* stuff? Can you see me through my clothes?"

"Ew, no, why would I want to?"

"I'm just wondering…" Maldynado sighed. "Never mind. I don't suppose you'd like to bash down the door? I've done a bunch of them over the last couple of days, and my shoulder's bruised and sore."

"Can I use the Science?"

"Sure," Maldynado said, envisioning him picking the lock somehow.

"Really?" Akstyr's eyebrows flew up, and Maldynado realized they might not share the same vision.

"Wait, how would you do it?"

"Well, the door's made of wood, and wood burns…"

"Never mind," Maldynado said and applied his shoulder. Three jaw-rattling thumps later, the door flew open, crashing against the inside wall.

Maldynado expected darkness inside, but a couple of lamps burned at low levels, creating two soft bubbles of light in the seating area.

The suite appeared identical to the one Mari had occupied, though no thoughtless intruders had shot up the furniture in this one.

Akstyr stepped past him, halted, and grunted in surprise. Expecting an enemy, Maldynado pulled out his knife while missing his rapier anew. Akstyr wasn't staring at an enemy poised to attack, though; he was ogling a woman's undergarments that were draped across a chair beside a door leading to the sleeping area. As if drawn by a string, Akstyr stumbled forward. He held a dagger, but it drooped, forgotten, by his waist. Maldynado hung back. While he found the notion of a naked woman as intriguing as the next man, he doubted Brynia would be lying on the bed, waiting for them.

Akstyr stopped at the doorway, his posture rigid. Maldynado started to ask if there was a problem, but Akstyr waved for him to come closer. Maldynado checked behind the furnishings in the outer room and inside a large clothes trunk before joining Akstyr. If Brynia had shot Mari, she was a dangerous woman.

Still standing in the doorway, Akstyr hadn't moved an inch. He was staring past the bed at an opaque screen set up between a wardrobe and the lavatory door. A lamp burned behind it, illuminating the silhouette of a woman's body, a woman's naked body, one with voluptuous curves that tantalized even the thoughts of such a seasoned bedroom warrior as Maldynado.

Akstyr crept forward. Only his ancestors knew what he thought he'd do when he reached the screen, but he was stalking over there as silently as a cat.

Again, Maldynado hung back. This had to be a trap, a trap designed to capture horny male outlaws. Without advancing an iota, he looked about, checking the room's nooks, shadowy corners, and even eyeing the dark recesses of the ceiling.

A premonition flicked at the back of his neck. Maldynado spun around as a slender figure dressed in black slipped through the outer doorway. Though she'd changed clothing, and added a sleek black hat to her ensemble, the fitted garments didn't disguise feminine curves. Brynia.

She saw him at the same second he saw her. Her arm lurched up, a pistol in her hand. Maldynado threw his knife at her even as he flung himself behind the sofa. She lunged to the side, evading the weapon, but

the movement threw off her shot. The bullet struck a lantern on the wall, almost knocking it onto Maldynado's head. He caught it before it hit him, doused the flame, and threw it to distract Brynia while he slipped around the other end of the sofa. With only one light left in the room, the shadows hid him. He crept forward three steps, sprang over a cider table, and leaped at her.

The movement drew Brynia's attention away from the sofa, and she lifted the pistol for another shot. It was too late. Maldynado crashed into her, bearing her to the deck. Despite her willingness to shoot people, she lacked combat experience, and he soon had her disarmed and face down on the floor.

"It's a stupid doll," came Akstyr's voice from the doorway.

"What?" Maldynado looked up.

Akstyr held up a shapely doll. "It was propped in front of a candle, making the shape look big on the divider."

"Don't you think the fact that the silhouette wasn't moving should have been a clue?" Maldynado pulled Brynia to her feet. "Congratulations, my lady. You're our prisoner again. The emperor still wishes to see you."

Brynia lifted her head. The hat had fallen off and her straight blonde locks tumbled about her face. She smiled up at Maldynado and leaned back, pressing her body into his. "What's the hurry? It's a long trip downriver." She spared a smile for Akstyr too. "The doll is based on the real thing, my handsome young fellow. Perhaps you'd like to see?"

Akstyr stared at her, then at the doll, then at her. "Uh, really?"

"We need to get you a woman, Akstyr," Maldynado said.

"That can be arranged," Brynia said.

Maldynado gave her a warning shake and, without relinquishing his grip, readjusted her so a couple of inches of air separated their bodies. A flash of irritation crossed her face, but she molded it into an interested smile and kept beaming it in Akstyr's direction.

Maldynado turned Brynia around, intending to march her out the door. Something pink on the deck made him pause. A feather. He gawked. "That's my hat. You stole my hat?"

"Not at all," Brynia said. "I claimed it after its owner abandoned it."

"Abandoned it? I was knocked unconscious."

"The truth is elusive, depending on who speaks it, isn't it?"

Maldynado shoved the woman outside. She was slipperier than wet soap. They'd have to watch her closely for the rest of the trip, maybe have Sergeant Yara guard her. He hoped Sespian was brighter than Akstyr and wouldn't fall for those batting eyelashes.

\* \* \* \* \*

Amaranthe had no memory of collapsing on the trail or falling asleep, but when she woke up cradled in Sicarius's arms, she knew it must have happened. Cicadas droned from the trees, and twilight had finally come to the swamp. At least, she *hoped* it was twilight and that she hadn't been asleep for hours, forcing him to carry her all night. But, no, he was following the muddy prints and cleared foliage that the *Behemoth* team had left. He wouldn't have been able to do that in the dark. Probably. It *was* Sicarius, after all.

His long, sure strides covered the ground efficiently. Amaranthe wondered how many miles had passed beneath his feet in the last week. His arms supported her knees and her shoulders, bearing her weight easily, as if she were a toddler. She had no memory of wrapping her own arms around his neck and laying her head against his shoulder, but she had to admit, despite the aches pulsing through her body with each step, it was a nice place to be. Bandages made from torn strips of clothing wrapped her wrists where those pins had pierced. She sensed the support of other bandages around her shoulders and thighs. Thinking of the intimacy those bandages implied made her flush.

Amaranthe lifted her head. The slight movement brought fresh pain, something reminiscent of the blasting headache one might suffer after a night carousing with Maldynado. Not that she'd been foolish enough to do that. More than once anyway.

"We will stop soon. It has been some time since I heard sign of pursuit." Sicarius's dark eyes lowered to meet hers, and a little flutter teased Amaranthe's gut. Given what she'd endured, she probably shouldn't be in the mood to melt over looks from men, but they hadn't spent a lot of time with their heads close together, and his eyes held a gentleness she'd never seen in them before. It seemed impossible to believe, but he must not have pieced together the fact that she'd betrayed him. Maybe he'd been too busy figuring out how to thwart Pike.

Amaranthe broke eye contact and cleared her throat. "They probably stumbled across Pike. I assume from that scream that he's dead."

Sicarius's focus returned to the trail. "Yes."

"Thank you for not... eliminating anyone else."

"As you said, they were not a threat once their leader was gone."

A perfectly logical way to say it, one that meshed with his philosophy of not leaving enemies alive behind him, but Amaranthe preferred to think that he'd made the decision because he knew it would please her. Some men brought women flowers. Sicarius chose not to kill people. The latter seemed a tad more momentous. Of course, his solicitude might all be in her head.

He didn't come all this way because of *logic*, girl, she told herself. He *cares*.

Unless he'd come because he was worried that she would, under the pressure of torture, betray his secrets. Even now he might be waiting for the moment to ask if she'd blabbed.

Amaranthe grimaced. Why couldn't she just enjoy the fact that she was snuggled in the man's arms?

"You are thinking," Sicarius said. A hint of censure laced the words.

Amaranthe forced her thoughts away from treasured secrets cast upon the wind like dandelion seeds. "Yes. Is that not allowed?"

"Your body and mind need rest."

"We're following the trail of enemies we'll have to confront. I think the rest portion of the exercise comes after we deal with them."

"The trail is cold. We will not likely encounter them until we reach their destination." He flicked his gaze toward the twilight darkness of the sulfurous, alligator-and-snake-filled, strangled-by-vegetation swamp, no doubt implying it unlikely that the Forge meeting place was anywhere nearby.

"So, I should simply lie snuggled against your chest without thinking for a while?" If only she could.

"Yes."

Amaranthe laid her head against his shoulder. She managed to keep her brain—and her mouth—still for almost thirty seconds. "How did you find me?"

Tired and aching though she may be, she couldn't help but smile at the hint of disapproval that flattened his lips. Someone else wouldn't see

it at all, or would take it as a sinister glower. She knew he was simply irked at her inability to obey an order to rest.

"They flew in a straight line." Sicarius stepped over a creek and left the trail, turning to follow the gravely bed upstream.

"I'd forgotten your knack for answering questions with terseness bordering on obscurity." Amaranthe touched his jaw fondly to let him know she was teasing. Her fingers brushed against the short hair of his fledgling beard. "If you'd let me use that sharp black knife of yours, I could clean this up for you."

"Sespian has the knife."

"Ah. Another blade then. I'm sure they're all sharp. Of course, you don't have to opt for a clean shave. The scruffy look has merit. The growth just needs a little tidying." Amaranthe supposed, by babbling on inane topics, she could avoid the one that awaited sharing.

"I'm more concerned with tending *you*."

Amaranthe's breath caught at the simple statement, and at the way he gazed straight into her eyes as he said it. No, she wasn't imagining his solicitude. His words warmed her, but they filled her with bleak guilt as well. First, because she'd doubted he truly cared. And second… because she'd failed him.

The ride grew bumpier as Sicarius climbed higher off the trail. Amaranthe was on the verge of asking where he was going when he pushed aside a few ropy bundles of moss dangling from exposed tree roots and peered into a dark opening. He found a flat spot and set Amaranthe down. Thanks to her inactivity, her muscles had stiffened terribly, and she could scarcely move without sucking in a pained breath—or spouting out a stream of curses. She was relieved to play spectator as Sicarius investigated a small cave, gathered fronds and boughs for bedding and a fire, and finally struck flint to one of his knives. He dragged in an unfamiliar satchel Amaranthe hadn't realized he'd been wearing. It must have belonged to one of the soldiers, or perhaps he'd traded his heavier rucksack for it at some point on his journey.

"Any chance there's food in that sack?" Amaranthe crawled into the low cave and propped herself against the dirt wall behind the fire. Roots dangled from the ceiling, and the husks of dead bugs littered the earthen floor. After that crate, it felt like a luxurious warrior-caste resort. She didn't even have the urge to fashion a broom from a branch and sweep.

"The sort of energy-high but nutrient-deficient travel rations soldiers carry, yes. I saved something better for you." Sicarius dug into the satchel and pulled out a canteen for her and two of *his* travel bars, the ones made of dried meats and fat. Smashed from his days on the road, they looked even less appealing than usual. When he held them out, like someone making a gift of a cherished possession, Amaranthe managed to hold back a groan—barely. Those "energy-high" snacks the soldiers had been carrying sounded far more promising, like they might be full of sugar or dried fruit.

Sicarius's eyes narrowed. He'd probably gone hungry a few days to reserve them for her.

"Thank you, very considerate of you to save them," Amaranthe said, seeking a compromise that might let her dig into the soldier rations, if only as a dessert. "But, ah… after your grueling trek, I'm sure you're in as much need of nutrients as I. How about we each have one?"

He hesitated before nodding. "Acceptable."

Sicarius handed her a bar, then built up the fire. He went in and out of the cave, bringing in enough wood to supply an army stuck in a frozen outpost on the Northern Frontier. Amaranthe wished he'd join her against the wall, shoulder to shoulder, so that she could lean on him and sleep until dawn, knowing she didn't have to worry about anyone hurting her. But perhaps, for the conversation they needed to have, distance was better. While she debated how to broach the subject, she chewed on the corner of her bar, grimacing at the fact that her teeth felt loose in their sockets. Was that from a week's worth of malnutrition? Or was her body simply that much of a mess? Relieved the cave lacked a mirror, she resolved to avoid clear pools of water for a while.

"Do you want a bath?" Sicarius asked.

Surprised out of her musings, Amaranthe gaped at him. Her first thoughts bounced back and forth between tantalized speculation and outright disbelief—had he *truly* offered to bathe her?—but they all crashed to the ground under the weight of reality. How could she accept the spa experience when she was wondering how to tell him she'd betrayed him? Remembering the last time he'd assisted her with a bath—and the ice cubes floating about on the surface—*spa* might not be the best word, but still.

Sicarius was waiting for an answer. Amaranthe groped for something.

"Are you saying I don't smell good these days?" Ugh, that was a horrible thank-you for his sweet offer.

Sicarius held up a canteen and a damp rag that had probably been a soldier's shirt. "You look like you could use…" He was too tactful to tell her she was a wreck.

"Tender ministrations?" Amaranthe raised her brows. "Are you offering?"

Sicarius gazed into her eyes. "Whatever you wish, Amaranthe."

He'd never voiced those words before, and, in another situation, they would have flooded her with warmth, but she suspected they were born out of pity, or maybe guilt. She wasn't sure why that word came to mind. What did he have to feel guilty about? Maybe it bothered him that it'd taken days to catch up with her and that she'd been tortured in the meantime. If so, that wasn't *his* fault. *She* was the fool who'd gotten herself thrown out of the dirigible and washed up onto the beach where Pike and his men happened to be loitering.

"It's not that bad now," Amaranthe said.

Sicarius eyed her, and she remembered that he'd seen her sans clothes.

"Did Pike have a shaman?" he asked.

"A concoction that a shaman had made."

Sicarius grunted. "Advances in Science."

Amaranthe tried to decide if there was bitterness in his tone. Did he know about her newfound knowledge of his past? He must suspect. Would he be concerned that she'd think less of him? Or had he long since put the experiences behind him? A selfish part of her wanted to remind him of the indignity, if only so he'd be more understanding when she admitted her failure. Before she could think better of it, she said, "I… understand you were as much his victim as his student."

Sicarius's jaw tightened, but he said nothing.

"Not that you're worried about it, but I wouldn't… judge you for anything that happened back then." Amaranthe paused. When she didn't receive a response, she lightened her tone and said, "Your own personal shaman, eh? I often wondered how you'd gotten so far in your career without gaining any scars. Until you met me, anyway." She waved toward his back and the soul-construct claw marks that lay beneath his shirt.

"Yes. The wounds were healed by an expert." His tone had grown unreadable.

Fearing she was angering him, she finished with a soft, "The ones on the outside, anyway, eh?" and resolved to leave it there.

Sicarius nodded and turned dark eyes that had grown somber in her direction. He came around the fire to sit on the boughs beside her. Amaranthe realized that, while she was talking about him and his internal scars, he must think she referred to herself and what she'd suffered. She closed her eyes and drew in a shaky breath. For so long, she'd dreamed of him lowering his defenses and letting her see what lay beneath that flinty exterior. Now, he was finally doing it when she least deserved it. She wanted to bury her face in her knees and cry.

"Before you take up the hobby of offering ministrations—" Amaranthe's voice cracked, so she pointed to the canteen and rag, giving herself a second to recover, "—you should know I... may not be deserving of your care."

His eyebrows dove for his hairline. It was the greatest indication of surprise she'd seen from him. She tucked it away, along with the image of his eyes full of concern, to remember later, in case his icy, expressionless demeanor returned soon.

"I... did my best," Amaranthe said. "I don't mean to make excuses, but I want you to know I *am* disappointed in myself. You always think you're tough before you've been tested and that you're too smart to be tricked."

"Of what do you speak?"

Right, Amaranthe thought, get to the point. As Basilard said, cleaning a fish didn't get any more pleasant for having put the task off.

"I resisted Pike, but Ms. Worgavic's assistant had some Kyattese device that got into my head and..." Amaranthe poked at some of the needles on the boughs beneath her. "I didn't know how to thwart it. By now, Ms. Worgavic may know and perhaps all of Forge does. Pike certainly did." She risked a glance at Sicarius.

He wasn't giving much away, but she got the feeling that he wasn't certain what she was talking about. He'd heard Pike, hadn't he? The suggestion that Sespian had never been meant for the throne?

"They know Sespian is your son and not the rightful ruler of Turgonia," Amaranthe said.

"Yes, I gathered that."

"You *did*? I mean, I thought you should have, but you didn't react. You didn't…" Amaranthe swallowed. "Aren't you… angry with me?"

The long look Sicarius gave her reminded her of those she'd often received from the men upon announcing her crazy schemes, the ones where they wondered if her brain existed in the same world as theirs. "You are the one with the right to anger," he said.

"Uhm?"

"You were captured because of me. You endured *torture* because you held my secrets. All along, your difficulties in achieving your goals—in earning your exoneration—have come because you've chosen to associate with me, because you've been trying to help me achieve my goal." Sicarius picked up a branch and prodded at the fire. "In the beginning, I stayed because I thought you could help me with Sespian. Later, when you ceased to simply be a means to an end for me, I thought to leave because I knew I was making your journey more arduous, but I found myself unable to walk away. I…"

Amaranthe had so rarely seen him uncertain about anything. She found herself holding her breath, waiting for his next words as he nudged one half-burned log closer to another.

"Though I have studied psychology and am familiar with the notion of love, it has always been an academic familiarity, not a personal experience. Perhaps because of this, your loyalty has perplexed me at times. I have not always… appreciated it as I should have. Or, more correctly, I have not always… demonstrated my appreciation of it. But I *have* appreciated it."

Sicarius captured her gaze with his, and Amaranthe had to fight not to melt into a puddle in his lap. Easy, girl, she thought, he's not declaring his love. In fact, she was pretty sure he'd just said he didn't know how to feel love. But from him, appreciation was something, wasn't it? Especially if he'd never *appreciated* anyone else….

Sicarius seemed to notice he was fidgeting with the logs and laid down his poker. "I have on occasion admonished you for impulsive actions."

"I've noticed," Amaranthe said dryly, then wished she hadn't said anything. He was speaking of feelings, for the first time *ever*, and she

was rewarding him with irreverence. "I've deserved it," she added in a more serious tone.

"My reaction, upon finding out that Forge was responsible for implanting Sespian with that device..." Sicarius's expression remained neutral, but he took a deep breath, as if struggling to calm himself in the face of the memory. "I had the impulsive thought that I could forgo playing Tiles with Forge in favor of destroying the organization all at once. Or, if that wasn't possible, I wished to hurt them badly enough that they would consider going after Sespian too much of a risk."

"I know. I don't have any children, but I'm sure I would feel similar frustrations if I did. Perhaps not to the extent of, er, *slaying* people, but I can understand impatience and..." Why couldn't words ever come out in an intelligent, flowing manner when she spoke to him on important topics? Amaranthe sighed and scooted closer to lay a hand on his forearm. "I might be... distressed by some of your choices, and I don't expect I'll ever stop trying to convince you to use more humanitarian means, but I'm not angry with you, nor have these events changed how I feel about you." There, that sounded halfway decent. Didn't it?

Sicarius exhaled a long, slow breath, and Amaranthe wondered if he'd actually been concerned about that, about what she would think in the aftermath of Pike's attention. She patted his arm and leaned against him.

"I may never understand why you value the lives of those who have declared themselves your enemies, but..." Sicarius slipped an arm around her back and pulled her closer. "I *am* sorry that my choice resulted in pain for you."

Amaranthe felt her eyes widen so far they were in danger of plopping out of her head and into his lap. He had *never* apologized to her. She'd never heard him apologize to *anyone*. From him, it was almost... better than a proclamation of love.

"Thank you." Amaranthe leaned her head against Sicarius's chest. "I'm sorry you had to endure Pike's... cruelty as a boy. No one should have to deal with something like that, much less a child. He's one enemy I'm relieved to see dead."

Sicarius did not respond. If it had been someone else, she might have wondered if he'd fallen asleep, but she doubted he would relax that completely while out in the wilds. Or anywhere.

"Are you the one who gave him that scar?" Amaranthe asked.

"Yes."

Ah, there he was. "The boy got old enough to decide what he would and would not endure?" she asked.

"Something like that."

Amaranthe tilted her head to gaze up at his face. "You know… when you have a woman snuggled in your arms, that would be an appropriate time to open up and tell stories."

"*Story-telling* is what a man is supposed to do when he has a woman in his arms?" Sicarius's eyes glinted.

Heat scorched her cheeks. "Well, I… Uhm."

Sicarius laid a hand on the side of her face, being careful not to touch any of her bruises. "You have enough horrors of your own in your head now. You don't need to add mine."

Amaranthe swallowed. "I was surprised that, after what you endured, you didn't make Pike suffer more in the end." She knew it was little of her, but she couldn't help but feel that a "master interrogator" not only deserved death, but a painful one at that.

"After seeing what he did to you… it *did* occur to me to prolong his death."

"And?"

"I did not think you would approve."

"Oh." Amaranthe didn't know what else to say. Somehow he thought her a better person than she was. "I wouldn't have begrudged you some degree of… comeuppance to avenge your past."

"Actions taken in the present cannot change those received in the past. Hollowcrest was the master smith, forging my destiny. Pike was merely one of the many tools he employed."

Amaranthe dropped her chin. It seemed strange that an assassin was giving her a morality lesson, but there it was. No, not morality—that had never been a concern for Sicarius—but practicality. A lesson in practicality and moving on with one's life. She hoped she'd be able to put Pike behind her as effectively.

"Was anyone kind to you as a boy?" Amaranthe asked.

"That was not encouraged." Sicarius used his hand to lift her chin again. He brushed his fingers across the skin of her forehead, as if to remove the furrow of disapproval there. "Not everyone was like Pike.

Tutors came and went, so I wouldn't form attachments, but most were tolerable."

Tolerable. What an accolade.

Heaviness weighed upon Amaranthe's eyelids, and keeping them open was a struggle. But she found herself reluctant to sleep, to miss the moment, the fact that Sicarius was stroking her face and, for once, answering her questions. What if his reserve returned in the morning?

"Amaranthe?" Sicarius asked softly.

She opened her eyes, not realizing she'd closed them. Sicarius had lowered his hand, though he was still watching her.

"Yes?"

"I must speak to you of one more matter."

"Oh?"

A twinge of concern ran through her body. Such a preamble could only signal bad news. Indeed, wariness had entered Sicarius's eyes. "It is in regard to Sespian. And you."

Amaranthe sat up, a jolt running through her body. Meddling ancestors, he wasn't going to offer to step aside or some other nonsense, was he? She remembered that he'd seen them together on the dirigible, that brief second when she'd grabbed Sespian's hand. He must think... Emperor's warts, who ever knew *what* he thought? Now that he was finally showing her warmth and affection, she'd be burned at a funeral pyre before letting him disappear over some misunderstanding.

Amaranthe planted her hand on Sicarius's chest, fingers splayed. "If this is about the dirigible, I wasn't holding his hand out of any romantic notion. He'd brought up the fact that he might have a shortened lifespan because of that drug, and I was expressing sympathy, the same way I would if Books or Maldynado had that problem. Let's be clear on the situation here. He's a sweet kid, but nothing would happen between us even if you weren't around." Amaranthe, realizing she'd been rattling words off quickly, forced herself to slow down and take a deep breath before finishing. "I love *you*, Sicarius." Odd how saying things like that to him made her feel more vulnerable than lying naked beneath Pike's knife had. "You're stuck with me," she added doggedly.

"I had already decided that while I was coming to find you."

Amaranthe watched him through her lashes, wary but hopeful as well. "That... you're stuck with me?"

Sicarius's eyes were half-lidded as he gazed back at her. "That I was unwilling to let someone else have you."

The blunt statement sent a little shiver through her. The words, "It's about time," floated through the back of her mind, but the intensity of Sicarius's eyes squashed any inklings of flippancy. "All right," she whispered.

"When you have recovered, and you are ready, come to me. I'll be waiting."

Amaranthe didn't move a muscle, but her heart was beating against her ribs so hard Sicarius must've felt it. She wasn't sure if he'd made a request or issued an order, and she didn't care. She was suddenly hyper aware of his body next to hers, the honed steel of his torso, the fact that she was almost in his lap. Her body had to be crazy to respond this way, after all it had endured. She doubted Sicarius would accept an entreaty then, even if she made one, but it was with the squeaky hoarseness of a titillated teenager that she uttered another, "All right."

Sicarius brushed the backs of his fingers along her jaw, and his gaze drifted to her lips. Amaranthe held her breath. A kiss? Was that what he had in mind? A little promise that there'd be more later? Yes, after the pain of the last week, it'd be nice to experience something pleasant. More than pleasant, she thought, cheeks flushing anew at the memory of the single kiss they'd shared in the Imperial Gardens that summer. She parted her lips, lifted her chin, and closed her eyes.

"You should sleep," Sicarius said abruptly.

"Huh?"

He removed his arm and slid away from her, leaving Amaranthe alone on the hard, poky boughs. He tossed a few branches onto the fire. "I will stand watch."

Before she could object, he disappeared through the cave opening.

"*Sleep?*" Amaranthe said, not caring if he overheard. Though she might have been weary a few minutes ago, sleep was the last thing on her mind now. She swatted at one of the roots dangling from the ceiling. "How am I supposed to *sleep* when you took my pillow? Impossible man."

Only the drone of cicadas answered her. Amaranthe flopped onto her back on the boughs.

At least he'd offered something more definite than the "later" on the dirigible. Once she'd healed and they'd finished the mission—or at least made sure the others were safe—she'd pounce on him. And she'd make sure she kept him too busy to think of fleeing the cave. No, not a cave, she decided. The baths perhaps. A *private* bath overflowing with bubbles. Or maybe the training ring after a particularly sweat-inspiring workout, one that encouraged the removal of shirts. Yes, she liked that idea.

When Amaranthe finally dozed off, she slept well, the nightmares of the previous nights replaced by more pleasant, if rather erotic, scenarios.

# CHAPTER 15

BRYNIA TRIED TO SEDUCE MALDYNADO THREE more times on the way to the wheelhouse. Had it not been for his current interest in Yara, he might have propelled the woman into a closet and given her what she was asking for. She *was* a beauty after all. But what she was asking for probably involved distracting him long enough to yank out his knife and stick it in his belly.

Raindrops splashed onto the damp deck and pattered onto Maldynado's reclaimed hat. Though he should have appreciated the warmer climate, Maldynado found himself homesick for his haunts back in Stumps. He wondered if the first snow had fallen yet and if Yara would find it romantic to stroll along the canal on Third Avenue, listening to music flowing from the numerous waterfront hotels, dance halls, and drinking houses.

"You don't really want to take me to see that boy, do you?" Brynia purred.

Maldynado chastised himself for letting his mind wander. The woman might have wriggled free and escaped again right there. "Why do you say that?"

"You're hesitating."

"I was thinking." Maldynado pushed her toward the stairs leading to the rooftop and the wheelhouse.

"I was given to understand that you didn't do that much."

"Good." He hoped she'd been flummoxed when he hadn't walked into her trap. "Why'd you kill my sister-in-law anyway?" Maldynado threw it out there casually, hoping he might startle a response out of her.

"Why, *I* didn't, my lord. *You* did."

Maldynado halted. "What?"

"That's what your family will assume when the word reaches them."

"You didn't kill her just to frame me," Maldynado said. "My family has enough reasons to hate me already. You want her position in Forge or something?"

"My position is fine. Regardless, *I* did not kill her. Your comrades barged in, causing a guard to accidentally shoot her."

"Uh huh." Maldynado nudged Brynia so she'd resume walking. She wasn't likely to tell Maldynado anything useful, and he lacked the stomach to use force on a woman. Maybe Sespian would have better luck questioning her.

"Are you sure you don't want to duck into one of those cabins for a few moments of enjoyment?" Brynia asked, doing her best to dawdle by insisting on walking around each puddle instead of through it. She stopped and leaned her breasts into him. "I won't even try to kill you afterward."

"How thoughtful," Maldynado said. "I know you're trying to avoid chatting with the emperor though. Up the stairs, my lady."

"I'm not worried about a conversation with that timid boy. I simply thought you might enjoy the embrace of a skilled lady. Besides, after listening to Mari speak longingly of your honed body, I'm curious to know if her distress over your rejections was founded. We won't be able to find out later if your reluctance to dally with married women remains true."

Reluctance to dally? With whom? Mari? What did that have to do with anything now?

"Uh huh," Maldynado said, as if he understood her every nuance, "up the stairs."

"So stuffy." Brynia sighed. "You *look* like you ought to be fun."

"I *am* fun. I'll even give you a ride to prove it." Maldynado adjusted his hat and hoisted her over his shoulder. If she wouldn't walk, he'd carry her.

Brynia's response, whatever it might have been, was muffled by the fact that her mouth was pressed into his back. He strode up the steps, taking them two at a time. He faltered, and almost clunked Brynia's head against the railing, when he found Yara waiting on the catwalk that connected the stairs with the wheelhouse. Inside, Sespian stood before the six-foot-wide wooden wheel, windows on all sides offering him a

three-hundred-and-sixty-degree view of the dark river. Lamps brightened the interior while two lanterns burning on either side of the door
illuminated Yara, highlighting the dampness of her short hair.

"My lady." Maldynado greeted her with a nod and said nothing of
the woman slung over his shoulder.

"The emperor was hoping you'd show up with that." Yara waved at
Brynia as if she were a package from the postal service, then brought
her hand to her mouth to cover a yawn.

Sespian must have recently relieved her from the day shift at the
wheel. Maldynado wondered why she was lingering in the rain instead
of going straight to her bunk. Maybe she'd come outside, heard him
talking to Brynia, and hadn't wanted to interrupt.

"I better deliver it promptly then." Maldynado knocked on the door.

"I see you got your hat back," Yara said.

"Indeed, I did." At the emperor's beckon, Maldynado strode inside
and plopped Brynia onto the floor. "Brought you a gift, Sire." He held
up a finger. "One moment." He patted Brynia down, found a dagger
strapped inside her thigh, and, since she wore trousers, had to have her
drop her drawers to remove it. Even though she'd been offering to drop
them all night, doing it in front of Sespian and in an utterly non-sexual
way seemed to disturb her dignity, if the pink tinge to her cheeks was
anything to go by. Good. Maldynado didn't want her at her most vixen-
ish to talk to the boy. "There we go."

Apparently taking his job as helmsman seriously, Sespian had only
partially turned from the river, and he kept one hand on the wheel.
"Thank you."

Brynia refastened her trousers and stared Sespian in the eyes. "Your
plan won't work."

He might have snorted with indignation or given her a wave of dismissal. Instead, he blinked a few times and looked at Yara. "She thinks
we have a plan at this point? That's encouraging, yes? That our enemies
are ascribing us with more competence than we actually possess?"

"I'd say so, Sire," Yara said.

Maldynado wondered if Sespian was being intentionally disarming,
the better to tease information out of Brynia. He didn't know how much
shrewdness to grant the kid. At least he wasn't leering at Brynia's chest
the way Akstyr had.

"Want me to stay while you chat with her, Sire?" Maldynado asked.

"No, we'll speak alone." Sespian nodded to Yara. "I'll have you step outside, too, Sergeant."

Yara adopted a lemon-sucking expression, but merely said, "Understood, Sire."

When Yara strode past Brynia, she deliberately bumped shoulders. Yara had a good six inches on the other woman, and Brynia nearly fell down. Yara pushed open the door and stalked out without looking back. Her abruptness seemed to startle Sespian.

"We have some unpleasant history with the prisoner," Maldynado told him. "She wanted to feed Yara to mechanical alligators. And, even more egregious, she stole my hat." Maldynado walked outside, closing the door behind him. "Wait there, will you?" he called to Yara.

She stopped at the top of the stairs. "Why?" The word broke under the force of another yawn. She'd probably been dreaming of sleep.

"Never mind," Maldynado said. "I'll stand watch myself."

Yara frowned. "Over them? It sounds like the emperor wants privacy."

"She seems to be an accomplished seductress whereas the emperor seems... naive. Brynia might feel inhibited if someone's standing out here, ogling through the window."

Yara leaned against the railing. "Would that inhibit *you*?"

"Depends on who's doing the ogling." Maldynado leaned on the railing next to Yara. "You can get some sleep. I can ogle by myself."

"I'll bet." Yara gazed down the stairs but didn't leave. "I'm surprised you didn't take advantage of her offer."

"Oh," Maldynado said, disappointed that she'd be "surprised," but he supposed he wasn't known for chastity.

"Maybe not as much as I would have been a week ago," Yara said.

Oh? Progress.

Maldynado stifled a yawn of his own and gazed at the cloudy sky, thinking again of snow and walks along the canal. The rain had tapered off to a mist.

Yara nodded toward the wheelhouse where Brynia stood, her breasts targeting Sespian like guns on a battleship as the young emperor spoke. "So, the future Lady Marblecrest, eh?"

"*What?*"

"You don't think she's eyeing your brother? I thought that line about your reluctance to sleep with married women meant she planned to become your brother's next wife."

Maldynado stared at her, his mind fumbling about as he tried to remember if Brynia had said anything about Ravido.

Yara tilted her head. "You don't think so? I thought she might have shot Mari to rid Ravido of the current wife and that she planned to be the one to deliver the news and console him over the loss. After Ravido becomes emperor, he'll have lots of women courting him, but if Brynia sinks her talons into his shoulder first…"

"Is that… all a hunch?" Maldynado was trying to decide if he was being dumb for not having put that together or not. It did sound plausible, but…

"We enforcers like to call them educated guesses." Yara shrugged, as if to agree there wasn't a lot of evidence to back it up.

Maldynado chuckled. "Well, I hope we don't find out. I'd prefer that Sespian stay on the throne and my brother die a bitter old widower."

"Agreed."

Inside, Sespian was leaning forward, gesturing with one hand while he held the wheel steady with the other. He seemed to be speaking a lot. Maldynado feared he had things backward: wasn't Brynia supposed to be answering questions?

"Though it's sweet that you want to protect him from a wanton woman's charms," Yara said, "I don't think you need to be concerned."

"Why not? When I was his age, I would have been first in line to, ah…"

"Go spelunking in her cave?"

Maldynado groaned and rubbed his face. Why did he have a feeling that ill-advised line would be etched into his urn after his funeral pyre?

"I think his heart is taken," Yara said.

Maldynado's hand dropped from his face so fast it smacked the railing. "What? By whom? He's been out of town for months, and there's nobody out here."

Yara's eyebrows elevated.

"I mean, not *no*body, but, er…" Bloody dead ancestors, had Amaranthe been right? Was Sespian competition for Yara?

"It's Amaranthe, you twit."

Maldynado blinked slowly. "That doesn't make any sense. They've barely spent any time together, and she's… well, she's pretty enough but not exactly trip-over-your-toes-and-fall-in-love-at-first-sight gorgeous. Especially not when she's running around in blood- and grime-spattered military fatigues."

"You're being all kinds of flattering tonight, aren't you?"

Maldynado rubbed his face again. Maybe he should go down to the engine room and find a tool to rivet his lips shut.

"He hasn't confessed having such feelings out loud," Yara said, "but, while we've been up in the wheelhouse, he's mentioned being concerned about her fate often. If you're still trying to get him to bond with you, maybe you could give him tips for attracting older women."

Maldynado thought of Books's insinuation that Amaranthe and Sicarius had some sort of relationship and grimaced, though his thoughts quickly shifted to Yara. "Tips? I wouldn't have thought you'd admit that I have any expertise in that area."

"A week ago, I wouldn't have thought so either." Yara only met his eyes for a moment before looking out over the dark river.

A giddy frog hopped about in Maldynado's stomach. Was that… an admission? That his efforts were working on her? He decided not to push things. He'd ask for the canal walk later and, as Akstyr had suggested, let her know he appreciated her.

The door opened.

"Sergeant Yara," Sespian said, "will you take our guest to the brig?"

"Of course, Sire."

Yara escorted Brynia down the stairs. Meanwhile Sespian stood in the doorway, regarding Maldynado through slitted eyes.

"Did she tell you her destination, Sire?"

"She told me the town of Markworth. I didn't believe her."

"I wouldn't either."

"I *do* believe it is as we guessed and Lake Seventy-three is the correct area. If she hopes to meet her comrades, she'll need us to land nearby."

"So, where are we actually going?" Maldynado asked, noting that Sespian's eyes remained slitted. The kid still didn't seem to trust him overly much. Or perhaps Brynia had said something to implicate Maldynado in Mari's death. That figured.

"Once we reach the lake, you will direct me on how to find Marblec-rest Island."

Sespian stepped into the wheelhouse and closed the door with a definitive the-conversation-is-over thud.

"Can't wait," Maldynado muttered.

\* \* \* \* \*

Soft rain splashed onto a clear pool. While Amaranthe washed up, she avoided looking at her reflection too closely, though she'd already glimpsed more than enough. Her cuts and bruises, though they were healing, had turned her face into a mottled patchwork of sickly blue-yellow that failed to flatter.

She pulled her bare feet out of the water and dried them as well as she could before applying a purplish paste Sicarius had made. City girl that she was, she found herself skeptical that anything that came off a dirty leaf instead of out of an apothecary's jar could truly have medici-nal qualities, but she slathered it on anyway. Given the grimy state of her makeshift bandages, and the even grimier state of the swamp, she needed all the armor she could cobble together to fight off infection.

Aware that Sicarius was waiting, and had to be chafing at their slow pace, Amaranthe finished with her ministrations and eased her feet back into the oversized boots. They'd been on the move since dawn, and she wanted to take a nap, but that wouldn't help them catch up with Forge.

When she returned to the trail, she expected to find Sicarius pacing about or perhaps standing watch from high up in some tree. Instead he stood beneath a branch, using the foliage as shelter from the rain as he wrote on a piece of paper. When she approached, he put his pen away, folded the page into precise thirds, and tucked it into his pack.

"If that's a shopping list, I'd love a stack of flatbread and a jar of apple butter."

"You are hungry?" Sicarius asked.

"No, no, it was a joke." Amaranthe immediately wished she hadn't made it. He'd greeted her with raw fish that morning, insisting that it held superior nutrition in an uncooked state. He'd further treated her by saving the eyes for her consumption. With no other options, she'd eaten his offerings, but she willed her body to recover speedily, if only so he'd

stop procuring such choice "nutritious" specimens for her. "I'm still full from breakfast. Very full."

After a moment of shrewd consideration—Amaranthe hoped her stomach wouldn't growl and betray her—Sicarius extended a hand toward the trail. He'd been insisting that she lead so he could walk behind, steadying her with a hand on the back when she stumbled. Accustomed to being independent, she tried to appreciate the help instead of resenting the fact that she needed it.

"You're not going to tell me what you were working on?" Amaranthe headed down the muddy trail. "Is it a sonnet or poem for me?"

She looked over her shoulder at Sicarius, but he said nothing. That probably meant, "No."

"In case you were wondering, that *is* the sort of thing that warms a woman's heart. Even more than piles of fresh fish eyes." She smiled to take away any sting from her teasing. As much as she loathed his culinary choices, it touched her that he was going out of his way to provide for her.

"It is a letter," Sicarius said.

"To me?"

"You are walking in front of me. For what purpose would I write you a letter?"

"Because it's easier to bare your heart to someone in a letter than it is when you're gazing into their eyes, worried they're judging you or that they'll reject you at any moment." Hm, maybe she should have written *him* a few letters.

Sicarius didn't respond to her comment, nor did he appear particularly enlightened. She supposed that meant no poems or sonnets were coming her way any time soon. She'd have to settle for fish eyes.

"Never mind," Amaranthe said. "If it's not for me, who's it for? Sespian?"

"I would rather not say."

"And here I thought we had reached a new level of trust and sharing in our relationship." Amaranthe said it lightly, but his secretive response did sting a little. Maybe he was afraid he couldn't share anything private with her again, lest some enemy suck the knowledge out of her head. She sighed for more reasons than one.

"I will post it in Markworth. It is unlikely anything will come of it." Sicarius almost sounded apologetic.

That, of course, piqued Amaranthe's curiosity all the more, but she forced herself to admit that Forge was the priority now anyway. "Markworth, I wonder if that's the town Retta spoke of. That's on Lake Seventy-three, isn't it?"

"Yes," Sicarius said.

"That's a resort area full of privately owned islands, isn't it? Maybe someone's having a meeting on their shiny new summer estate. I wish I'd thought to dig around for that information in Retta's head."

"Explain," Sicarius said.

Amaranthe had been half talking to herself and had forgotten he was listening. "Retta, the person who set me free, used a Kyattese device—she called it a therapy stone—to dig out the information about you and Sespian. During the procedure, I also saw some of her memories. I'm not certain she realized it, but I know the names of the Forge founders now."

Sicarius halted and touched her arm so she would do the same. "You did not share this information."

"No, when I was doing my sharing last night, you distracted me with confessions of feelings." Amaranthe smiled.

Sicarius did not.

Amaranthe spoke the truth—she'd been so worried about what his reaction would be to the information she'd given up that she hadn't thought about her paltry discoveries—but now that Sicarius stood before her, expecting the list of names, she found herself reluctant to give it up. What if he pursued the mass-assassination tactic again? She didn't want to have the weight of those deaths upon her shoulders, especially now that she'd learned that she *knew* one of the Forge founders. Ms. Worgavic wasn't some goatee-stroking super villain from the tales of eld; as far as Amaranthe knew, she was someone who'd simply chosen a questionable route to a goal that, while perhaps megalomaniacal, didn't seem to be willfully evil. It didn't escape Amaranthe that someone else might very well apply that description to her and what she'd been doing in the last year.

"You will not tell me?" Sicarius asked.

"I'm... concerned that your response would be to hunt them down as you did the others, perhaps believing that cutting down Forge at the root would destroy the organization before your secret becomes public knowledge."

Sicarius stared at her, his face a mask, his eyes giving away nothing, yet Amaranthe swore she sensed a mulish, "Yeah, so?" attitude beneath the façade.

"First off, I don't think killing the founders *would* destroy Forge," Amaranthe said. "The very fact that this meeting place is down here, close to the Gulf instead of up in the capital, makes me think the organization's reach goes beyond the satrapy and maybe beyond imperial borders. The girl who used the therapy stone and learned to fly the *Behemoth* has a sister who's been abroad for years, perhaps spreading the word about Forge and drawing in international allies. We *can't* simply slay everyone who opposes us. I don't want to create martyrs. The only solution that I can see making sense is a diplomatic one."

Though he kept the muscles in his face from so much as twitching, a flare of intensity fired in Sicarius's eyes at the word diplomatic. "These people have been trying to kill Sespian."

"I know, but this goes beyond Sespian. And beyond you. We need to figure out how to get everyone out in the open for negotiations."

"They will not negotiate with us. Other than the limited ability to threaten their lives, we have no power with which to manipulate them."

Unfortunately, Sicarius was right about that. Unless they succeeded in spying on this meeting and some weakness was revealed that they could exploit.

"Give me time. I'll come up with something." Amaranthe shrugged and waved a hand, implying—she hoped—that she already had ideas and he had no need for concern. Strange, after all they'd been through, that she still felt the need to oversell herself to Sicarius. Or perhaps not. Just because he'd admitted he appreciated her didn't mean he wouldn't attempt to slay every Forge member at this meeting, in an attempt to end it all in the most efficient, if barbaric, way possible.

After staring at her in stony silence for a long moment, Sicarius took out his pen and the letter. He pressed the page against a tree so he could add another line at the bottom. Before Amaranthe could creep

close enough to read the addressee, he finished and returned everything to his pockets.

"It is imperative that we reach Markworth as soon as possible." Sicarius brushed past her, taking the lead this time.

"So that we can catch up with Forge or so that you can post your letter?"

"Yes."

Amaranthe shook her head and forced her sore limbs into a semblance of a jog so she could catch up. It crossed her mind to offer to give him the list of founders in exchange for a chance to read the letter. Her conscience wouldn't forgive her if he used the information to assassinate people, though, so she'd have to keep wondering whom he wanted to turn into a new pen pal.

# CHAPTER 16

AFTER TWO DAYS OF LABORIOUS TRAVEL, THE swamplands finally gave way to sycamore, oak, and sweet gum trees. The Forge trail Amaranthe and Sicarius had been following turned onto a broad road kept clear of foliage and debris. Part of the old imperial transportation system and therefore built in an era that predated steam vehicles, the worn highway featured flat stones set into a cement-and-sand-based mortar. It lacked the smoothness of the vehicle-friendly paved aggregate highways radiating from Stumps to all the borders, but it had the same quality of being too hard to offer signs of passersby.

"We're not going to be able to track them on this, are we?" Amaranthe asked when Sicarius returned from one of his side trips to forage.

"If they leave the road, I'll see it." Sicarius said.

Unless more roads of a similar style crossed this one, allowing one to walk without leaving tracks.

"If their destination is one of the islands on Lake Seventy-three," Sicarius added, "we won't be able to track them into the water, regardless."

"Maybe you should go ahead." The thought had crossed Amaranthe's mind numerous times that day, but this was the first she'd spoken it aloud. She didn't want him to leave her side. Every time a twig snapped in the woods, or something scurried through the undergrowth beside the trail, she flinched like an abused dog anticipating a kick. Though she knew Pike was dead, she kept imagining him lunging out of the brush and dragging her off for another round on that table. If not him, some other sadistic bastard. They were foolish thoughts—she was armed now, after all, and she could take care of herself if she wasn't ridiculously outnumbered—but the imagery persisted nonetheless. "You can travel twice as fast, find them, see what they're doing, and come back to get me if there's time."

"Twice?" Sicarius asked.

"Sorry, was that insulting? I meant to say ten times as fast. Without breaking a sweat or breathing hard. I'd add without mussing your hair as well, but…" Amaranthe eyed his tousled locks. Sometime when she had been sleeping, he'd scraped away the beard and washed off the road grime, but his hair beckoned for attention. "Are you ever going to let me cut that for you? Just a trim. To even out the edges?"

Sicarius laid a bunch of berries in Amaranthe's hand. "You are regaining your humor."

"That's a good thing, isn't it? Proof that all the highly nutritious food you're feeding me is doing its job to rekindle my strength and witty personality?" Amaranthe kept walking as she spoke, knowing he wouldn't appreciate delays for pointless conversations.

Sicarius fell in beside her. "I will remain with you."

Amaranthe supposed she couldn't be offended that he'd chosen to answer the more pertinent of her questions, though she *was* determined to cut that hair someday. "I appreciate your presence—more than you'll ever know, I suspect—but I'd hate for my slowness to cause us to miss this opportunity." She popped one of the purple berries into her mouth, appreciating a hint of sweet beneath the tart.

"Meetings on how to take over the world are not over quickly," Sicarius said.

The light response made Amaranthe pause. "Was that a joke, or are you speaking from experience?"

Sicarius gave her a sidelong look. "Yes."

Someday Amaranthe would learn not to ask him two questions at once. "Even if a meeting between numerous powerful and opinionated people will require many days, you might want to be there ahead of time to scout around. What if the others are making their way down? This has to be the same meeting Sespian wanted to spy on, don't you think?"

"Likely."

"You could muster a little more excitement at the prospect of seeing him again." Amaranthe smiled.

"I have… failed to make inroads with him."

"He's had a certain image of you in his head for almost twenty years. It'll take time to change it, that's all."

Sicarius's grunt of acknowledgment had a dubious tone to it. "I must tell him of our link, lest he hear it from Forge first. I do not know how to speak of it. I have avoided the straightforward, in hopes that he will find it less... deplorable if he's adjusted his vision of me somewhat beforehand. There is no time for that now."

He so rarely shared his concerns with her, and Amaranthe wished she had a good answer for him, one that would allay his fears and prove correct as well. She couldn't lie to him though; she doubted Sespian would respond well. The revelation would be like pulling an arrow out of one's shoulder—it might hurt worse than touching molten lava, but the healing couldn't begin until it'd been done.

Since words failed her, Amaranthe clasped Sicarius's hand. He'd been as chaste and professional as always in his physical interactions with her over the last couple of days, but he accepted the grip and, after a pause, twined his own fingers between hers.

"Perhaps I should try levity again," Sicarius said.

"Er, on Sespian?"

"Yes."

Thinking of how Sespian had misconstrued some of Sicarius's earlier comments, Amaranthe feared that approach might backfire. "We'll talk to him together when we all meet up again. I just hope he's well. Forge..." She stopped. No need to raise concerns that might provoke further worry.

"He *better* be well," Sicarius said. "I tasked Maldynado with protecting him."

"You tasked *Maldynado*?" Amaranthe's mouth dropped. "Are you... attempting levity now?"

"Maldynado was the only one around when I left to pursue you."

"Ah." Not levity, desperation. "I'm sure the others are helping him stay on track." Actually Amaranthe suspected Maldynado had the ability to take charge, if he was so motivated—and Sicarius could certainly motivate people, if not with his charisma then with his knife. "You had to choose, didn't you?" she asked, realizing for the first time how that must have played out. "After the crash, you had to choose whether to come after me or help Sespian."

"Yes."

"Thank you. I... wasn't expecting it. I mean, I understand that Sespian must be your priority." Amaranthe cleared her throat. She hoped she wasn't insulting him, but she hadn't believed he'd trust the group with Sespian's care.

"You are *both* priorities."

Warmed by the simple statement, Amaranthe had to tamp down an urge to kiss him. Given her current condition, it wouldn't be much of a reward. But Sicarius looked down at her, perhaps expecting a reaction, and she changed her mind. She rose on tiptoes to kiss him on the cheek and wrapped her arms around him in a tight hug. Knowing they didn't have time for dawdling, she soon released him, though she retained the grip on his hand, and started walking again. She thought she caught a glint of satisfaction in his eyes.

"I still think you should go ahead and search for Sespian," Amaranthe said. "If they're coming on a boat, they could..." She stopped talking because Sicarius was pointing at something ahead of them. A glint of blue water visible through the trees.

"Lake Seventy-Three," Sicarius said. "This road will lead us through Markworth."

"It's not a populous town, is it?"

"Not this time of year."

Right, if it was a water-based resort area for the upper class, then late fall wouldn't be a popular time for visits. That might explain why they hadn't seen much traffic on the road that morning.

Amaranthe wondered if a group of Forge folks strolling through might constitute worthy small-town gossip. If they'd taken a boat or ferry to their chosen island, someone might have witnessed it. She doubted she and Sicarius would stumble across a roadside sign proclaiming, "Secret Forge meeting held this weekend at the Randy Rooster Hotel and Eating House."

As Amaranthe and Sicarius drew closer to the lake, they started seeing cabins and cottages set back from the road, but, alas, no giant signs.

"These are more modest homes than I expected." Amaranthe nodded toward a one-room cabin with an outhouse perched on a knoll out back.

"Those are the people who cater to the wealthy and warrior caste. Those with means stay on the islands."

"You sound like you've been here before," Amaranthe said. It'd be handy if he knew the area.

"Raumesys came down a couple of times."

"And invited you along to ensure his water-ball team won?"

Before Amaranthe could do more than start to imagine Sicarius in swimming trunks, muscles glistening in the sun as he maneuvered through the water, thrashing and dunking men to get to the ball, he gave her a flat look and said, "To deliver proof of missions completed."

Ah, the severed head thing again. Amaranthe chose not to imagine *that* scenario.

"Do you want to scout around when we get to town?" Amaranthe asked. "See if you can find sign of the party's passing, in your own assassinly way? Meanwhile, I'll look for someone who will chat with me about the weather, the crops, and if they've seen any strangers wander through recently."

"I will stay with you," Sicarius said.

"That's not necessary."

"You find trouble when you *chat*."

"I'm sure I don't know what you're talking about."

His grunt said more than his words ever did.

Again, Amaranthe didn't mind that he wanted to stay with her, but she hoped he wasn't going to develop a permanent over-protective streak. Maybe he simply sensed that she wasn't comfortable in her skin just then.

They reached the shoreline where the road branched to go separate ways around the lake. Signposts proclaimed the right headed north, to Sunders City and Armelion—the name for Stumps that nobody except cartographers and sign-makers used. To the left, Markworth was visible through the trees. Docks of all sizes and a few buildings, none more than two stories tall, lined the bank.

Along the lake, more traffic traversed the road, if one could call old, dented bicycles and mule-pulled wood carts traffic. The passing people wore homespun cotton and wool clothes in utilitarian styles. Amaranthe's purloined military fatigues, with the cuffs rolled up, drew more than a few second glances, or maybe it was the rifle she carried.

Even if it wasn't forbidden for citizens to own firearms in rural areas, the way it was in Stumps, women certainly didn't tote such things about in the empire. Not women who didn't want to be gawked at and forced to answer questions, anyway.

"I may need to acquire a costume to better fit in." Amaranthe handed Sicarius the rifle. The sleek, repeating weapon would draw looks no matter who toted it, but it fit him more. "Right now I look like…" She eyed her oversized, wrinkled, blood- and dirt-stained clothes.

"Someone who fought with a soldier and stole his garments?" Sicarius suggested.

"Someone who fought *poorly* with a soldier and stole his garments. Either way, I'd prefer not to be the topic of the chats I intend to have with folks."

"I will find something." Sicarius took a step toward the woods, no doubt already having someone's clothesline in mind.

"Farmer-ish, I think," Amaranthe said. "Maybe a straw hat too. In fact…"

He stopped, a hint of wariness on his otherwise expressionless face.

"If you're going to stick with me, maybe we should have you reprise your role as Pa, the farm dis-ci-pli-nar-i-an." Amaranthe smiled. "I'll be Ma. Rural accent and everything."

Sicarius stared at her.

"It's not too late to change your mind and scout about from the shadows," she said.

Sicarius sighed. "You want me to acquire two farmer costumes."

"And two hats." Amaranthe winked, but then blurted, "Wait," as a new thought occurred. "Maybe not. I forgot how I look." She pointed at her face and neck to indicate the bruises. "We better not make you my husband. People will think you, uhm, you know."

"Beating your wife is not illegal out here."

That didn't surprise Amaranthe—laws against striking wives and children had only been on the books for twenty years in Stumps, a change lobbied for by one of the early female entrepreneurs—but that wasn't her reason for bringing it up. "Lovely fact, but I don't want people to believe *you'd* do it. They'll think you're an…" She decided not to use any of the epithets that came to mind.

Sicarius's eyebrows rose slightly. "Does it matter?"

Given the number of people he'd killed in his life, being upset over the notion of spousal abuse might be silly, but Amaranthe lifted her chin and said, "It does to me."

"Propose an alternative."

"All right, you can be..." Amaranthe grinned as a new idea came to her. "You can be the handsome stranger who was passing through the rural village where I live with my brutal husband. It was an arranged marriage, of course, thanks to my parents being disillusioned with my adventurous streak and wishing to force me to settle down, for my own good. But *you* came along and saw how poorly... Millic, yes, *Mean Millic* was treating me, and you stepped in, giving him a taste of his own... fist." Amaranthe smacked hers into her open palm for emphasis. "You promised to show me the world if I ran away with you—" she stretched her arm toward the horizon beyond the far side of the lake, "—and I, being left breathless by your ardor, naturally threw myself into your arms and agreed wholeheartedly."

It was amazing that a man could wear such a bland expression in the face of such infectious enthusiasm. Amaranthe thought it was infectious anyway. Sicarius merely looked at her forehead for a moment before meeting her eyes again.

"What?" Amaranthe asked.

"Do you house a mental filing cabinet full of ideas in there, or do you come up with all of them on the spot?"

"Yes." Amaranthe grinned, delighted to use his own question-answering strategy against him. "Now, do you agree to play the role, or not?"

Sicarius lifted a hand in acceptance—or resignation—and resumed his walk toward the woods. He paused before slipping into the trees. "What sort of costume does a 'handsome stranger' require?"

Amaranthe almost told him he was wearing it, but his black was too signature Sicarius. Even down here, they might run into someone who had seen his wanted poster. She ought to give him honest advice, but she couldn't help but smirk and say, "Yellow or orange. Floral, perhaps."

The unwavering—and un-amused—stare he gave her implied he did not find her suggestion helpful.

"Just get something different from what you usually wear," Amaranthe said as he strode into the woods.

\* \* \* \* \*

The wise thing to do would be to wait for Sicarius to return with costumes, but enough people were passing along the road that Amaranthe felt conspicuous standing there in the grimy fatigues. She slipped between a few trees and down to the beach, figuring she could be useful and search for a rowboat they could borrow if necessary. Sicarius would have no trouble following her trail.

A few green islands of various sizes dotted the blue water, though Amaranthe couldn't begin to see all seventy-three. If she remembered her useless trivia correctly, the lake had been given its unimaginative name not only because of the number of islands but because it was a seventy-three mile walk around it. On maps, it appeared long and narrow with more bends than a drunken snake.

Surprised there weren't any fishing boats out on the water or anglers on the shore, Amaranthe tried to remember if some imperial holiday had been looming. The town seemed quiet, too, what she could see of it.

"Off season," she supposed, though, now that her mind had started to ponder oddities, she realized all the people who had passed her on the road had been on the quiet, even glum, side. Sicarius's presence often deterred conversations, but even after he'd disappeared, nobody had stopped to ask who she was and why she wore oversized men's clothing. It had been some time since she'd seen a newspaper. She hoped nothing had happened back in the capital.

"Don't give yourself extra reasons to worry," Amaranthe commanded herself. As usual, herself wasn't good at taking orders.

She followed the shoreline past a couple of cabins, then picked her way down to a sandy beach, intending to fill her canteen and wash up. When she dipped her hand in, she let out a surprised mew. It was warm. Not steaming, like the public baths in the city, but warm enough to invite one in for a dip on a cool day.

"A bath, now there's an appealing thought."

Amaranthe supposed the spot was a tad public for disrobing—she hadn't come *that* far from the road—and, besides, Sicarius would return soon. If she were going to set the stage for him to accidentally wander in on her bath, she'd make sure she was looking vibrantly sensuous rather than wanly bruise-covered.

Still, Amaranthe found herself looking up and down the beach for witnesses, thinking she might get away with a quick dip. The sight of industrial-sized piers and a wooden warehouse perching waterside disavowed her of the thought. Though she didn't see anyone outside, it looked like a place of business, something that would be occupied during mid-morning. What type of something she didn't know. Not a cannery, she thought, and there were no boats tied, though a dark dome nestled in the water between two piers. She couldn't tell what it was.

As long as she was waiting, why not check it out?

Amaranthe had gone less than ten meters down the beach when a "No trespassing" sign came into view. The fine print at the bottom piqued her curiosity. "Barcrest Military Academy Research Center." Disobeying the sign might not be a good idea, but she wanted to know what that dome was. For some odd reason, black objects had developed a tendency to bestir wariness within her.

Amaranthe strolled down the beach, hands clasped behind her back. She kept her face down, as if she were picking a careful way along, oblivious to her surroundings, but she surreptitiously watched her surroundings. Though the sign hadn't promised trespassers would be shot, as other signs she'd encountered had, one never knew with military facilities.

She reached the piers without seeing anyone. Water lapped at the black dome. She still couldn't identify it, though she was close enough to see that it was simply iron that had been painted black, not another piece of ancient technology. Some upturned boat? No, a handle and hinges protruded from the top. Huh.

When Amaranthe reached the base of the first pier, more of the body came into view in the clear, shallow water. An entire sphere lay beneath the surface, supported by caterpillar treads resting on pebbles below. Two sets of varying-length articulating arms stretched out from either side of a glass porthole in the front of the craft. The entire structure was no more than six or eight feet in diameter and might have room for two people to sit inside.

Amaranthe envisioned herself and Sicarius cruising around the lake, checking out the islands. After another glance about to ensure she didn't have company, she hopped onto the curved hull and tugged at the hatch. Locked. She returned to land and headed toward the building, hoping she'd find it abandoned with a set of keys hanging somewhere accessible.

The windows were too high off the ground to peek through unless one happened to climb the firewood conveniently stacked at one end of the structure. Amaranthe scrambled up the log pile and found glass panes so dirty they served as a greater deterrent to spying than the no-trespassing sign.

Copious amounts of spit and sleeve wiping created a peephole. The diffused sunlight struggling to pierce the windows didn't brighten the dim interior much, but she made out piping and pumping equipment in one corner, along with rows and rows of objects in display cases. Each one housed small collections or single specimens of... She squinted. Fish? Eels? Maybe the facility was simply there to research the local flora and fauna. But why would a military academy care about—

The grass rustled with the sound of footsteps.

Amaranthe spun and hopped from the woodpile, hoping she could flee around the corner before anyone saw her.

But *anyone* was already there, standing a few feet away and holding a musket.

"The sign said no trespassing," the man said, his voice rougher than the pockmarked skin on his face. Though young, he already had lines etched at the corners of his mouth, probably from glowering often. The way he was now.

"Did it?" Amaranthe asked, mustering her most innocent expression. "I didn't see it."

"Them."

"Pardon?"

"*Them.* The signs. There are fifteen or twenty around the property."

"Oh." Amaranthe smiled. The fellow didn't look like the type to be impressed by her smile, but at least he hadn't shot her yet. That was something to feel cheerful about. "Do you work here? Doing research?"

His thick eyebrows drew together, forming a V. "What did I say that could possibly be construed as an invitation to ask questions?"

"When you didn't shoot me, it was assumed. I'm the curious sort. Aren't you? You must be if you're collecting all those specimens in there." Amaranthe hoped her chatting—burbling, Sicarius would call

it—made her seem innocent and innocuous. "Is that what the underwater cart is for?"

The man's head drew back. "*Cart?*"

"Yes, that black ball on the treads."

"Woman, that is a UWMTV, a research vessel equipped with the latest imperial technology for underwater maneuverability. A sophisticated wind-up mechanism allows one to turn human energy into ten times the amount of stored energy, sufficient to propel the craft around the lake shallows. It has dual-articulating arms with mechanical hands, suitable for gripping and clipping foliage or scraping samples into bottles. A shock stick holds an electric charge for stunning and collecting ambulatory specimens. It *can* be applied on nosey trespassers as well." The man's glower promised severe repercussions if Amaranthe dared to call it a "cart" again.

"That's impressive," Amaranthe said. "Can you truly power something so big with a clockwork mechanism? No furnaces and boilers?" She decided not to mention magic, as that would truly set this man on a rampage, and, from his pride, she could already tell nothing but imperial technology powered the vessel.

"That's right."

"How do you transfer the energy? Through a crank?"

His eyebrows rose. "I'm not going to give you instructions on how to steal it and crash it. That's happened often enough already. Thrice-cursed kids."

Amaranthe chuckled, though it was a nervous chuckle. After all, she *had* been thinking of stealing, er, borrowing it herself. "Is that the reason for the signs?"

He grumbled an affirmative under his breath. "Emperor knows, these rural clods wouldn't be interested in our research."

"The fish?" Amaranthe asked, still wondering why this facility would be military-funded.

"That's part of it." The man lowered the musket so that it no longer pointed at her. "The electrical charge system I mentioned, that came out of studying the eels. My lieutenant does that research. It's the hot springs and the geothermal system that I work on."

He eyed her, a question on his face. Maybe he wondered if she might be interested in *his* specialty. Given the way he'd gone off about the cart, he must be an engineer or something similar.

"Geothermal? Like using nature to create steam that can be used to heat a building or power an engine?"

For the first time, a smile softened his face. "Yes. Want to see my lab?" He pointed at the building.

His willingness to offer a tour to a stranger surprised Amaranthe. She supposed this remote of an outpost, one manned by only two people, didn't hold itself to the same security standards of a typical army fortification. Perhaps, as well, the rustic townsfolk failed to show interest in his work and he yearned for someone to listen. Realizing he awaited a response, she nodded for him to lead.

"I'm Amaranthe, by the way," she said as they approached the door.

"Sergeant Pabov." He faltered when she stepped out of the building's shadow and into the sunlight. He frowned at her bruises. "What happened to you?"

"I didn't see someone's no-trespassing sign."

Pabov snorted and led the way inside. "That I believe."

Amaranthe hesitated on the threshold. As soon as Pabov had entered, he'd leaned the musket against a wall, but she had to fight down an uneasy premonition that going into a building with an unknown man wasn't a good idea. It was an old type of uncertainty, something she hadn't felt since she'd finished her training as an enforcer and gained the confidence that she could take care of herself in most situations, and she knew she had Pike to blame for it.

Amaranthe clenched her teeth and strode inside. She could *still* take care of herself. Besides, Pabov had stopped exuding menace during their conversation outside, and she trusted her ability to read when people were and weren't a threat. That hadn't changed either, she told herself.

Fortunately, Pabov hadn't noticed her hesitation. He offered a cursory overview of the specimens in the display cases, nodding to a few unusual frogs, eels, and fish that were only found in the tepid waters of Lake Seventy-three—the only time he lingered was to point out, with the pride of a ten-year-old boy showing off a truly disgusting find, the stuffed body of a fifteen-foot-long "mutant" eel—then he led her to what

was obviously his passion. The pipes, tanks, and turbines humming in the back.

Though Amaranthe listened as he explained the technology and what sorts of improvements he'd been working on, she still hoped to spot that key and, every time he looked away, scanned the walls and work benches. A large map tacked above a schematic-filled desk distracted her from the search. It featured the lake and its islands. Amaranthe drifted toward it while making encouraging grunts to keep Pabov talking. She eyed the islands, noting that several had eponymous names such as Deercrest Isle or Dourcrest Cove. She hoped to see one with the name of a Forge founder, or—her spine straightened at the new thought—maybe the Marblecrests had an island, one that might have been loaned out to friends arranging to put certain generals on certain thrones? Unfortunately, only a handful of the seventy-three dots on the map were labeled.

Pabov surprised her by coming up behind her and pointing over her shoulder. Amaranthe jumped. Even though his approach hadn't been as silent as Sicarius's always were, and all he was doing was pointing to some of the islands on the map, she had to fight down a nervous urge to skitter out of reach.

"That one, that one, and that one have impressive geothermal facilities on them." Pabov didn't seem to notice Amaranthe's nervous twitch. "They've been here longer than the academy's facility. In fact, we used to lease the one on Dourcrest Cove for research, until Lady Dourcrest decided that having our soldiers roaming around interrupted her terribly important writing."

"I don't suppose there's a Marblecrest Island?" Amaranthe asked, though she doubted allies of Ravido would choose such an obvious meeting spot.

Pabov frowned fiercely.

"Is that a no?"

"There's one somewhere in the middle, yes, but why are you concerned with the Marblecrests?" His eyes had hardened with suspicion.

"Well, I've heard they're…" Amaranthe spread her hand, hoping Pabov would take the bait and share what was on his mind. It sounded like he might have heard of the coup and that he disapproved. If so, he might make a useful ally for more reasons than his underwater vehicle.

"Trying to declare the eldest son the next emperor?" Pabov asked. "Yes, they are. From what the papers say, General Ravido Marblecrest is already occupying the capital with his troops, making sure there are lots of men around who are loyal to him. With Sespian dead—"

Amaranthe's mind hiccupped, and she didn't hear what Pabov said after that. Sespian *dead*?

No, Sicarius had said Sespian was alive, that he and the rest of the team had walked away from the crash. Unless Sespian had been killed after Sicarius left the area...

No, she thought again. The papers were wrong. Either accidentally or deliberately. After all, Sespian's train had been blown up, thanks largely to her. The rest of the world didn't know he'd survived. Yes, that had to be it.

"You haven't heard about his death?" Incredulity wrinkled Pabov's face.

"I've been... tied up recently."

"Emperor Sespian died in a train crash," Pabov said. "This is the official mourning day. It's why so few are about."

"I see."

"The papers report much chaos going on in Stumps. The Marblecrests are making a bid for the throne, as well as the Moorcrests, the Wolfcrests, and several of the satrapy governors with roots back to the Savarsin line. Then there are the women with babies who have shown up, some fifteen that are supposedly Sespian's bastards."

Amaranthe coughed, almost choking on that idea. He had to be the least libidinous teenage boy she'd met.

"A couple of older boys, too, who are reputedly Raumesys's illegitimate spawn. You really hadn't heard about any of this? Where did you say you were from?" Pabov squinted at her, wearing the expression of a man starting to wonder if he'd made a mistake in confiding in her. He glanced around the facility, a facility he probably had orders not to show to unauthorized personnel.

"I'm from Stumps," Amaranthe said, hurrying to talk before he thought overmuch on her inquisitiveness and the way she'd wheedled information out of him. "I came down on business and made the mistake of wandering off alone and getting attacked by local boys. They took me off and..." Amaranthe closed her eyes, as if she were too pained at

the memory to go into details. It wasn't far from the truth. "There's a distinct lack of civility in parts down here, I noticed."

"Oh." Pabov considered her bruises again, then stuck his hands into his pockets. Sheepishness replaced the suspicion on his face. "Sorry. Do you need any help or a place to stay?"

"No, no." Amaranthe eased toward the door as she spoke. "I shouldn't have bothered you at all. You just seemed nice. And interesting. Your work, I mean." She waved at the snarl of pipes and tanks.

"Oh," he said again, brightening at her compliment. "Thank you. If you're in town for a while, come back and see me. I'll take you on a tour in the UWTMV."

Amaranthe halted. She'd been halfway to the door, but there was an invitation that tempted. A quick trip with him and she could learn how to use the vehicle.

"I have time now," she said, hoping she didn't sound too eager.

A smile returned to Pabov's face. "Great." He opened a drawer—ah, there were those coveted keys. Amaranthe and Sicarius could come back for them after dark. No need for a musty rowboat.

Pabov jangled the keys and jogged out the door, only to halt so quickly that Amaranthe almost crashed into his back. She peeped around him and groaned. Horrible timing.

Sicarius had been walking from the beach to the warehouse. At Pabov's appearance, he'd halted. He wore sable, brushed cotton trousers and a matching vest that complemented his deep brown eyes, and a crisp ivory shirt that drew out the warm olive tones of his skin. The clothing fit well—he must have visited numerous clotheslines—and few women would have trouble fancying him as a "handsome stranger." He wore only one weapon, a dagger belted at his waist, and appeared far more approachable than usual. At least Amaranthe thought so. From the rigid way Pabov stood, he didn't agree.

"Pabov," she said, trying to draw his eyes toward her and hoping his wariness stemmed from the fact that this was a trespasser rather than recognition on his part. "This is my friend... Hansor," she said, plucking out a name she'd used for him before. "He helped me escape the thugs who—"

Pabov ran around her and back into the warehouse.

Remembering the musket, Amaranthe barked, "Pabov, don't!" and spun to follow him.

Sicarius sprinted past her, entering first.

Inside, Pabov snatched the loaded musket from the wall. Sicarius sprinted across the intervening ground so quickly Amaranthe would have missed it if she'd blinked. Pabov whirled toward him, raising the weapon, but Sicarius was already there, tearing it from his hands.

"Don't—" Amaranthe blurted, a hand outstretched as visions of dead enforcers rampaged through her head.

A thump sounded—a head hitting wood. Before she'd taken more than two steps, Pabov lay on the floor, unmoving.

"—kill him," Amaranthe finished weakly.

"He is alive." Sicarius searched through drawers and found a coil of rope. "But he will escape eventually if we leave him here alone."

His over-the-shoulder glance was unreadable, so maybe she only imagined him thinking how much easier things had been when he simply killed everyone.

"We wouldn't have that problem if…" Amaranthe stopped. She couldn't blame him for coming to look for her, especially when she hadn't left a message to explain her absence. As usual, this was her fault. "Never mind. It was unfortunate timing. I was ten seconds away from getting a tour of an underwater craft that might let us sneak up on the secret meeting island. Did you know there's a Marblecrest Island?"

"No."

Pabov groaned as Sicarius kneeled on him to tie his wrists behind his back.

"Don't break him, please," Amaranthe said. "He's been an amenable fellow."

"To you." Sicarius finished tying and stood. "It did not work."

"What?"

"The costume you recommended I obtain." He'd been wearing black for far too many years if he considered *normal* clothing a costume. Perhaps he simply felt crabby without his knife collection within reach.

"It will in town," Amaranthe said. "He's a soldier. I think all soldiers have your face etched in their memories."

Pabov, cheek mashed into the floor, glowered at Amaranthe. "Who are you?"

If they were going to leave Pabov alive, they'd better not tell him anything that might get them in trouble later. Unless there was a chance Amaranthe could talk him into helping. She glanced at Sicarius, wondering if he would be against sharing if it might yield them an ally.

"I *know* who he is," Pabov growled.

"Yes, I gathered that from your mad musket dash." Amaranthe smiled sadly at Sicarius. "Perhaps you should have kept the beard."

"I just want to know… have I betrayed the empire?" Pabov's gaze fell to the floor, and he mumbled, "Should have known better than to talk to some strange woman. Obviously spying. What was I thinking?"

Amaranthe knelt beside him. "You haven't betrayed anything. We're working for the empire, for Sespian. He didn't die in that train wreck. He's still alive."

Sicarius stirred. Amaranthe didn't know if he'd heard of Sespian's reputed death yet. It better only be "reputed," she thought. If Sicarius had gone on a killing bent when he'd learned of the implant in Sespian's neck, his death might send him over a precipice and into a very dark, very deep canyon. And would he blame her? Because he'd chosen to come after her instead of helping Sespian?

"No," Pabov said, "I don't believe you." Despite his words, he stared into Amaranthe's eyes, as if seeking some truth, as if he *wanted* to believe her.

"The Marblecrests have been working with a nefarious business coalition to oust Sespian and put someone new on the throne. If they have their way, General Ravido Marblecrest."

"Who *are* you?" Pabov asked again.

"Amaranthe Lokdon."

The pronouncement earned a blank look. Amaranthe supposed it was too much to wish that her team's fame had spread hundreds of miles. She wasn't certain her name would be recognized in Curi's Bakery, much less remote lakeside towns.

"I—" Amaranthe smiled and spread her hand across her chest, "— am the former enforcer who talked the infamous assassin, Sicarius, into changing his vile, man-slaying ways and working for the good of the empire."

She thought Sicarius might object, or more likely snort, but he only lifted a single eyebrow at her proclamation.

"You're not *that* charming," Pabov grumbled.

"Really." Amaranthe sniffed and resisted the urge to point out that she had charmed *him* effectively enough. "Perhaps it'd be worth telling him the truth," she told Sicarius. "He knows the lake, the locals, and he has that lovely underwater craft that could serve useful if we could get a ride."

"The truth," Sicarius said in a flat tone. He no doubt wondered just what "truth" she had in mind.

"I'm not helping an assassin," Pabov said.

"Not even the emperor's personal assassin?" Amaranthe asked.

"What?"

"Sicarius worked for Emperor Raumesys his whole life," Amaranthe said, "until Raumesys's death five years ago. You know about that, right? I thought everyone did."

Sicarius pinned Amaranthe with a why-are-you-telling-this-stranger-about-me look.

*He seems to be loyal to Sespian*, she signed. *He can help us.*

Pabov didn't respond to her questions right away. Maybe he *had* heard rumors about Sicarius's past. Mitsy, the former owner of The Maze had once told Amaranthe that everyone knew Sicarius was Hollowcrest's man. Of course, she'd been talking about the underworld "everyone," not soldiers.

"I'll believe he's working for the emperor when I see Sespian alive and walking arm-in-arm with him," Pabov finally said.

That… might be possible. If Sespian was on his way down, maybe he'd arrive soon. Or already had.

"If that happens, you'll let us borrow your craft?" Amaranthe asked.

"If Emperor Sespian strolls in here, alive, and wants a tour, I'll drive him around the lake myself."

Sicarius regarded Pabov's back. This time there was nothing harsh about the stare. Amaranthe wondered what people would think if they knew they could soften his razor-sharp edges simply by proclaiming allegiance to Sespian.

"I'll accept that as a promise," Amaranthe said. "In the meantime, we need to gather information about a meeting we believe to be taking place down here. That business coalition I mentioned? They've come

down here to plot. Any idea about where a clandestine gathering might be held?"

"No," Pabov said.

Amaranthe sensed that he'd withdrawn within himself and had no intention of providing helpful answers. She couldn't blame him. With nothing else to go on, her claims had to seem wild to him. "Did you see or hear of any strangers walking through town? Perhaps yesterday or the day before?"

"No."

"Truly?" Amaranthe asked, disappointment creeping into her tone.

Pabov frowned up at her. With his face still mashed into the ground, he couldn't feel that sympathetic toward her plight, but he offered an apologetic, "I don't get into town much."

Amaranthe's gaze returned to the map on the wall. She'd planned to ask after the Forge party in town, but if she could figure out which island they'd gone to, she wouldn't need to wander around, raising people's suspicions as she poked into everyone's business.

"Is there a real estate library in Markworth?" she asked. "Someplace where records are kept of who owns what land and where it lies?"

"I think the records are in the capital," Pabov said.

The capital that was over a week's travel away. Not helpful. "There must be someone local who handles real-estate transactions."

Pabov hesitated, his gaze flicking toward Sicarius.

"We won't harm the person," Amaranthe said.

"The Pickle Lady," Pabov said.

"The *Pickle* Lady?"

"She breeds long-haired rabbits and knits their fur into sweaters too. I don't think the stipend the empire pays for handling real estate is particularly large."

This place was even more rural than Amaranthe had realized. No wonder Forge had chosen it. Nobody who mattered in the grand political or business scene would be down here to chance upon their meeting. "Thank you," she told Pabov. "I'm grateful for your help."

"Grateful enough to untie me?"

"Do you promise not to tell anyone we were here?" Amaranthe had no idea if there was a local military garrison, but Markworth would have enforcers to ensure nothing untoward happened to those wealthy people vacationing on the lake.

A moment passed before Pabov answered, and Amaranthe wasn't surprised when he said, "No."

Sicarius pinned Amaranthe with one of those cool gazes, one she had no problem reading as, "Leaving him alive is going to cause trouble."

She waved her hand. They weren't killing someone when she'd been the one trespassing on *his* property.

After they walked outside, Sicarius stepped in front of Amaranthe. "You told him much."

"I was preparing him to eventually join our side and help us." Amaranthe smiled. "If Sespian shows up, this fellow is ready to be his devoted guide."

"*If* Sespian shows up," Sicarius said, a grimness to his usual monotone.

"You've heard what the newspapers are reporting?" Amaranthe had thought he'd been gone a long time just to furnish his wardrobe.

"I heard."

"I'm sure he's well," Amaranthe said. "Forge knows Ravido can't make a real move until the populace believes Sespian is gone. Since he's not in the capital to refute the reports of his, er, death, they can print whatever they want."

"*The Gazette* is the paper that published the story," Sicarius said, his grimness disappearing, replaced by an iciness that, even after all the time they'd spent together, still sent a chill curling through Amaranthe. She was glad Deret Mancrest was hundreds of miles away.

"If our men are with Sespian," she said, "they'll keep him safe."

"If Sespian dies, I'll kill Maldynado."

"Levity?" Amaranthe asked, though she knew it wasn't.

"No."

"I'm still not clear on how Maldynado came to be in charge."

Sicarius stalked away without a word. That probably meant he wasn't sure either, but now considered his choice a mistake.

Amaranthe followed Sicarius back to the beach where she'd originally intended to wait for him. He moved aside something bright and picked up a stack of folded garments on a log half-hidden by ferns. Wordlessly, he handed her the clothing and a practical pair of canvas

boots. She shook out an ankle-length walking dress, a high-necked blouse, and a long muslin apron. Though Maldynado would perhaps fault the sedate colors, Amaranthe thought Sicarius had a surprising knack for picking out clothing that matched and, more importantly, fit. More than that, the outfit would hide a multitude of bruises. She was on the verge of complimenting and thanking Sicarius when he dropped a woven hat into her arms. The pastel greens, blues, pinks, and yellows crisscrossed each other in a pattern that could only have been imagined by a woman deep in the applejack bottle.

"This *has* to be levity," Amaranthe said.

"Yes," Sicarius said, though no spark of humor glinted in his eyes. He walked away to give her the privacy to change.

He was too worried about Sespian to find amusement in anything at the moment, Amaranthe supposed, but couldn't help but call after him, "I don't know why you'd want to kill Maldynado, when it's clear you'd make fabulous hat-shopping buddies."

# CHAPTER 17

A COUPLE OF DAYS HAD PASSED SINCE CAPTURING Brynia, and Maldynado was headed down to engineering. Basilard had mentioned that Books hadn't been sleeping or eating. Why this was Maldynado's business, he didn't know, but he supposed he should make sure Books hadn't fallen into a funk and started drinking again. Though they were getting by as satisfactorily as could be expected given how many plans had gone awry, the team *did* lack structure without Amaranthe and Sicarius there to demand everyone rise at dawn for training. At least Maldynado had finally caught up on his sleep and recovered from most of his wounds.

He strode into the engine room and almost tripped over a stack of books in front of the door. Books, his chin sporting several days' worth of salt-and-pepper beard growth, was sitting on the floor next to a towering flywheel. Its revolutions ruffled the pages of journals and reference books spread out around him like spokes on a wheel. He must have pillaged the steamboat's library. A few dishes loaded with untouched food sat near the wall. Books held a book open with one hand while he scrawled across the blank page of a journal with the other. His pen, one of several around him, zipped along, creating lines of text faster than a printing press. At least the straightness of those lines suggested he wasn't drunk.

"What are you doing?" Maldynado asked over the clamor of the pumping machinery.

The pen didn't slow, and Books didn't acknowledge him.

"Researching more Forge stuff?" Maldynado asked.

"This facility lacks a desk," Books said without looking up or slowing his scrawling.

Maldynado propped his hip against a railing. "It's good to see that you're alert and ready to jump to a specific piece of machinery, should a call come down from the wheelhouse, demanding quick action."

Books finished his page of writing, blew on the ink to dry it, and promptly started on the next page.

Maldynado wondered if someone shouting a warning of an impending pirate attack would make that pen pause. He stepped closer until Books couldn't possibly miss seeing his boots alarmingly close to his papers and said, "Booksie, Basilard said you've been skipping meals."

When Books finally lifted his head, he seemed surprised to see Maldynado there.

"What?"

"Is that Forge stuff?" Maldynado waved at the mess.

"No."

"Economics stuff the emperor asked for?"

"Also no, and perhaps you can find a more descriptive noun than 'stuff'."

"Would you prefer if I called it junk?" Maldynado asked, knowing it would irk Books.

Books's lips flattened. Yup, pure irk.

"What *are* you working on?"

Books looked at something out the door. "That's not the emperor out there, is it?"

"No, Akstyr. It's his turn shoveling. The emperor... I haven't seen much of him. He avoids me, despite the fact that I've been trying my best to be useful."

"I believe he's still struggling to disassociate you from your family," Books said. "It doesn't help that you came off as a fop the first night he met you."

"Fop? I was fighting to defend him on the train."

"You were telling him how great you'd look as a statue in the Imperial Gardens," Books said.

"In *between* assaults on the locomotive cab, during which I bravely helped protect him."

"I'm working, Maldynado." Books bent over his papers again. "Go away."

"People are concerned that you're overly involved with that work. You're not eating. What *are* you doing anyway?"

"Devising a new governmental paradigm for the empire."

"Uhm. Why?"

Books started writing again.

"Did the emperor ask you to do that?" Maldynado asked.

"No."

"Aren't we helping him so we won't have to *have* a new governmental paradigm?"

"We are helping him to ensure no idiotic relative of yours takes the throne. What happens after that… Let's just say I have a hunch, and I am hoping to anticipate the youth's needs."

Trying not to feel completely perplexed, Maldynado walked out of the engine room. "I don't know why I bother talking to that man."

\* \* \* \* \*

Amaranthe had never seen so many pickled vegetables in one place. Cucumber jars, of course, took up a number of shelves, in spicy, dill, garlic, and—she stopped to gape—chocolate varieties. Sicarius, walking behind her, followed her gaze with his eyes, and she hustled on, certain he'd disapprove of chocolate anything. Besides, though Amaranthe hadn't had a dessert in a while, she wasn't sure she wanted to break her sweets fast with candied pickles.

Other vegetables, from carrots to asparagus to beets were also represented in the tiny shop. Packed jars rose on floor-to-ceiling shelves lining narrow aisles that one had to turn sideways to navigate. Someone like Maldynado probably wouldn't fit through the rows at all.

At the back of the store, Amaranthe and Sicarius found an older woman sitting in a chair, her legs propped on a large desk that was as cluttered as the rest of the store, with cages occupying most of the free space. Inside them, a mixture of long-haired and short-haired—or perhaps long-haired and *shaved*—rabbits munched on carrots. Amaranthe wondered if the half-chewed vegetables were pickled too.

"Help you?" the woman asked without looking up. Knitting needles dove and darted as they formed a sock.

"Are the chocolate pickles good?" Amaranthe asked. Maybe she could find the woman's passion, the way she had with Pabov, and encourage chattiness.

"No, I keep them on my shelf because they're disgusting."

The woman's delivery was so deadpan that it took Amaranthe a moment to recognize the sarcasm. Perhaps pickles were not her passion.

"Are there any you'd recommend?"

"They're all good."

"Do you have any samples?"

"No." The woman still hadn't looked up from her knitting.

*I'm getting a sense of why this woman needs three jobs to make ends meet,* Amaranthe signed to Sicarius.

*Just get the information.*

As always, business first with him.

"This seems like a nice town," Amaranthe said. "I heard you're the one to ask about acquiring property near the lake."

With an exasperated sigh, the woman set her knitting down. "You have money?"

"Yes," Amaranthe said, though she lacked a single ranmya. "Not enough for one of those islands, of course, but I can't imagine any of them are for sale anyway."

"No, they're not." The Pickle Lady dug in her desk and pulled out a thick notebook with corners and edges of pages sticking out on all sides.

Sicarius shifted, perhaps thinking of simply taking it and leaving, but Amaranthe held up a hand behind her back.

"Are they *ever* for sale?" Amaranthe asked. "Do you remember anyone buying one?"

"If you can't afford them, they're not any of your concern, are they?"

"I suppose not, but I get curious. Don't you?"

"No."

Amaranthe was on the verge of waving Sicarius forward to do whatever he had in mind when a bell jangled, announcing another customer's entrance. Several thuds sounded, heavy feet jogging across the threshold. Maybe not customers after all.

Sicarius pushed Amaranthe behind him, a knife appearing in his hand.

"No killing," she whispered.

Feet pounded down the aisle. A jar smashed to the floor, glass shattering.

The Pickle Lady jumped to her feet. "Blast your ancestors," she hollered before anyone came into view, "what're you doing?"

Before the woman finished yelling, Sicarius had pulled Amaranthe into the aisle adjacent the one with the charging intruders. He clenched his knife between his teeth, gripped the shelving unit with both hands, and heaved. It wobbled for a moment, hundreds of pickles quivering, before succumbing to its fate and toppling. Shelves and jars thudded into people and crashed to the floor amidst startled grunts and cries of pain.

One man had reached the end of the aisle before the unit collapsed, a fellow in a gray uniform and carrying a short sword. It wasn't the same uniform as Amaranthe had once worn, but she knew an enforcer when she saw one. Sicarius did too. He pounced on the man like that alligator in the swamp. The enforcer hit the desk, and rabbit cages toppled. The Pickle Lady skittered backward. Amaranthe, hoping the woman wouldn't notice in the chaos, grabbed the notebook.

Sicarius slammed the enforcer's head into the desk. The man's eyes crossed, and he slumped to the floor. The Pickle Lady screamed for the enforcers.

In the collapsed aisle, broken glass and shelves shifted as men tried to climb free.

"Leaving would be good." Amaranthe headed for the door.

Sicarius slipped past her before she could lead the way outside, but she supposed she couldn't fault him for being protective when she was armed only with a notebook. Thanks to the imperial day of mourning, there weren't many passersby on the cobblestone street outside, so she and Sicarius slipped into an alley and out onto the next block without anyone noticing. He lifted a hand to stop her, then climbed a drainpipe to the roof of a two-story warehouse next to the public docks. Scouting the neighborhood and seeing if any other enforcers were about, Amaranthe guessed. She eyed a sternwheeler ferry docked at the last pier, wondering if the Forge people might have passed through the area on the way out to their island. More likely, they had arranged private transportation from a private dock.

"Your new friend is loose," Sicarius said from behind her shoulder.

Amaranthe almost dropped the notebook. "That was fast. I thought you had better tying skills than that."

Sicarius leveled a cool stare at her. Just when she'd thought they were to the point in their relationship where he'd stop doing that.

"Never mind." She patted him on the arm. "He was an engineer. They're crafty." She waved to the rooftop. "No more enforcers coming?"

"That may be the town's entire complement. They're regrouping outside the pickle store."

"Perhaps we should take to the woods." Amaranthe lifted the notebook. "And hope the answers we seek are in here."

"Agreed."

\* \* \* \* \*

Amaranthe yawned and squinted at the real-estate notebook, trying to read by the predawn light. She sat on a boulder perched on the water's edge with gentle waves lapping at the base. From the surrounding trees, birds chirped a variety of songs. The spot would have been peaceful if she weren't straining her eyes, anxious for the sun to come up so she could read what the pages held.

The day before, Sicarius had insisted on putting a few miles between them and Markworth's enforcers, and twilight had fallen over the lake before they reached a suitable—to his vigilant eyes—campsite. They'd have to be doubly careful now that the law knew he was around. Perhaps Amaranthe shouldn't have let her curiosity draw her to that research station. She hoped nobody in the Forge group was paying attention to the goings on in Markworth or keeping tabs on enforcer reports.

Amaranthe held the book up, angling the pages toward the brightest section of the sky.

"Millcrest," she murmured, starting to be able to pick out words and names. Unfortunately, the unorganized notebook contained far more than recent real estate transactions. Rentals, within-family transfers, and boundary adjustments were all recorded, and not simply for the islands but for the numerous properties in Markworth and all around the lake as well. "This'll take forever."

She needn't read every page, she reminded herself. She could simply skim through and look for names she recognized. Thanks to Books's research and rooting around in Retta's head, she knew quite a few Forge members. She could also look for properties purchased in the names of businesses as a way to hide personal ownership. Larocka Myll had done that back in the capital.

Bertvikar. Amaranthe pointed to the name. That was familiar, one of the founders.

"You found something," Sicarius said from behind her.

Startled by his arrival, Amaranthe almost fell off the boulder. Even after she recovered her balance, her heart pounded in her chest. She gripped the cool stone beneath her and silently cursed her body's over-active reflexes. She'd *known* he was about. Was she going to flinch at *everything* now?

Sicarius did not comment, though he must have noted her response.

Amaranthe cleared her throat and lifted the book, holding the pages close to her face. "Maybe. I recognize this name, but it doesn't seem to be for a plot of land. It's a…" She flicked an annoyed glance to the east, wondering why the sun was taking so long to peek over the distant mountains.

"Should I have searched for spectacles to accompany your costume?" Sicarius asked mildly.

"Absolutely. If I were clearly near-sighted, people might assume I'd picked out that hat on accident. I…" Amaranthe lifted her head as something dawned on her. "Did you just tease me?"

"Yes." Sicarius stood beside her boulder, his hands hooked behind his back. "Are you offended?"

"No, no, I approve. I've been teasing you for months."

"I've noticed," he said dryly.

"I've been trying to figure out what might elicit a smile from you."

"Knowing Sespian is safe."

It would be tough to make that happen; as long as he was the emperor, there'd always be people plotting against him. Though she couldn't imagine Sespian continuing to accept his position once he learned the truth about his parentage. Maybe Sicarius would be happy, or at least willing to smile, if he and Sespian could walk off somewhere and spend time together, not as emperor and imperial assassin, but as father and son.

"We better work on making that happen then." Amaranthe handed him the open notebook. "Can you, with your superhuman anatomy, read this page?"

Sicarius accepted the book. "The Bertvikar entry?"

"Yes."

"Bertvikar acquired the mineral rights in a… freehold estate." He lifted his eyes.

"Ownership in perpetuity rather than for a fixed time period," Amaranthe explained while she drummed her fingers on her thigh. Mineral rights? She wasn't sure whether to find that interesting or dismiss it as a dead-end. Buying mineral rights might be what had brought the lake to a Forge person's attention in the first place, but she couldn't imagine all these wealthy people holding their meeting in some dingy mine shaft. "Which island is it, do you know? Those are map coordinates listed in the entry rather than the metes and bounds way of defining things that most of the parcels down here use."

Sicarius gazed out upon the lake, running calculations in his head perhaps, as he considered the mouth of a river and a few dark islands silhouetted against the predawn sky. He flipped to a map at the beginning of the notebook. "It's a trapezoid between Forestcrest, Arrowcrest, Marblecrest, and Duncrest Islands."

"*Between*? As in the land under the lake?"

"Yes."

"I've heard of mining dry lake beds, but how would they pull minerals out from under all that water?" Amaranthe scratched her head. "It must have to do with the hot springs. The same power the military academy is researching could push minerals to the surface."

Sicarius handed her the notebook. "It is unlikely this has anything to do with the meeting."

"I know. I'll keep looking. I—did you say *Marblecrest* Island?"

"Yes."

Amaranthe switched from drumming her fingers on her thigh to drumming them on the open pages of the book. "Pabov said there was a Marblecrest Island, but I'd dismissed it as being too blatant a choice for a secret meeting, given that they're Ravido's allies. Of course, it's not widely *known* that Forge has a link to the Marblecrests." It wasn't even widely known that Forge *existed*, Amaranthe reminded herself.

"We didn't know anything about it until a couple of weeks ago. Maybe it's not such a stretch."

Sicarius grunted noncommittally.

"You don't think it'll be that obvious?"

"No."

"We might as well check," Amaranthe said. "How do you feel about taking a morning row out to Marblecrest Island?"

The second grunt was even less enthused than the first.

# CHAPTER 18

D AWN WASN'T A GOOD TIME TO KNOCK ON SOME-
one's door, especially not when that someone was the Turgonian emperor and not overly fond of the person doing the
knocking. Yet Maldynado stood outside the captain's cabin, with his
fist raised. The steamboat had turned off the Goldar River earlier that
night and would reach Lake Seventy-three before long. This might be
Maldynado's last chance to leave the emperor with a good, or at least
amenable, impression of him. He'd also, after doing some mental wrestling with himself, decided that Sespian would be better for Amaranthe
than Sicarius.

Maldynado knocked.

Not many seconds passed before the door opened. Darkness bathed
the interior, and Maldynado, standing next to a lantern on the exterior of
the cabin, didn't see anyone at first. After a moment, his eyes adjusted
and he picked out a dim shape.

"Sire?" Maldynado said. "I came to see if… uhm, Yara said I should
talk to you." Not exactly, but that might get him an invitation in.

"I see," Sespian said.

That didn't sound inviting. Maldynado was trying to think of something else to say when a match flared to life inside.

Sespian set a dagger down on a table and lit a lamp. It wasn't Sicarius's black dagger, but a more mundane blade.

"Sit," Sespian offered and took a seat of his own, one where he
could reach the weapon.

Maldynado sat on the opposite side of the table, leaning against the
far armrest, so Sespian wouldn't think he wanted anything to do with
the dagger. So few people had ever thought of him as dangerous that it

seemed odd that Sespian considered him a threat. Though maybe he'd simply answered the door holding a dagger to be on the safe side. For all they knew, stowaways remained on board.

"What is it?" Sespian wasn't yawning or rubbing his eyes like a man who'd been sleeping. More likely, he'd been lying awake worrying.

"I heard... Ah, Yara mentioned... Sire, if you'd like any advice on pursuing ladies, and getting them to pursue you back, I'm an expert on—" Maldynado stopped. Sespian wouldn't be impressed by bragging. This might be a time for modesty. "I've won the hearts of a few ladies over the years and could answer questions on the opposite sex if there's anything you want to know. Not that you *need* advice. I mean, I really don't know how much, er, experience you have." Maldynado decided he better stop talking. A red hue colored Sespian's cheeks, but he had no idea if anger or embarrassment caused it. "I thought I'd see if you had any questions. That's all."

"Are you... suggesting I seduce Brynia for information on the meeting?"

"What? No. Yara said you liked the boss."

Sespian stared.

"Amaranthe," Maldynado clarified.

The clarification didn't cause Sespian's gaze to blossom with enlightenment. Yara, he recalled, had been *guessing* that Sespian had an interest in Amaranthe. Some feminine hunch. Perhaps such a hunch shouldn't have driven Maldynado to knock on the emperor's door at dawn.

"I see I'm mistaken." Maldynado stood. Bad idea. This had been a bad idea. "I'll just leave you alone."

He crossed the cabin, and his hand was on the doorknob, when Sespian said, "Wait."

"Sire?"

"Perhaps..." Sespian's hard gaze had faded, replaced with a hint of youthful uncertainty. "Sergeant Yara loathed you a week ago. Now she watches as you leave a room."

"She does? Er, of *course* she does." Curiosity intruded upon Maldynado's ability to leave the last sentence alone. "In what *way* does she watch? Like she's regretting my absence, or...?"

"Like she's trying to figure you out."

"Oh." Maldynado didn't know how much of a victory that was. He often watched Sicarius the same way. Some people were just cursed strange.

"Like she *wants* to figure you out," Sespian said, "because she might find something there worth discovering. She doesn't strike me as a woman to care overmuch about a pretty face. That you're swaying her opinion of you leads me to believe you might truly have some expertise with women. That is something that eludes me."

"Having a pretty face always helps," Maldynado said, heading for the chair again, "but if you're an idiot who says all the wrong things, it won't save you."

Sespian winced.

"Not that you're an id—that thing, Sire. I mean, I haven't heard you speak to the boss much." Now Maldynado winced. Speaking of saying the wrong things…. He leaned back and took a deep breath. "That's not important. Let's establish a starting point. Has she suggested she might be interested in you?" It was, after all, entirely possible that Books was wrong about Amaranthe and Sicarius sharing some sort of attachment. Books certainly didn't have a noteworthy personal record when it came to romance. And if Amaranthe *had* shown interest in Sespian, Maldynado could understand the kid mooning over her. Blood-spattered military fatigues or not, Amaranthe did, when she wanted to, have a way of gazing into one's soul, seemingly without artifice or evasion, and convincing a man that her interests were his interests as well.

Sespian slumped against the backrest of his chair. "No. She said I was too young."

"Ah. That means she's not interested. A few years wouldn't matter if she was attracted to you."

Sespian sank deeper into the chair. "I was afraid of that."

"That doesn't mean there's no hope. You might simply need to make her see a different ore in your vein."

A spark kindled in Sespian's eyes. "How?"

"Well, for one thing, you look *young*. Younger than Akstyr even. Can you get any of those chin hairs to grow out?"

"Not… densely."

"I've heard of apothecary potions that might help. We'll come back to that. Let's talk about the rest of your look. We all thought you were the bookish and artsy type."

Something in the way Sespian lifted his eyebrows told Maldynado that Sespian thought he was the bookish and artsy type too.

"In my experience, women *say* they like men like that, as friends. You do not want her thinking of you as a *friend*. You want her day-dreaming about you when the sun is out and fantasizing about you when she's alone in bed at night, eh?"

A flush crept into Sespian's cheeks. "I suppose."

"It's all right to have a sensitive side—they love finding warm, gooey stuff hidden beneath the crusty outside of an apple tart—but you need to be manly too." Maldynado sat straighter, puffed his chest out, and flexed a biceps to demonstrate. "Virile and powerful. Not power-ful in the I-was-born-an-emperor-so-of-course-I'm-powerful way, but in how you strut about the room and make things happen. If you take your shirt off, there should be muscles there. You may want to start throwing sand balls around. No matter how independent the woman is, she'll have times when the world sends a grimbal after her. When that happens, she needs to lean against someone with strong arms, someone who makes her feel safe and secure."

"I'm not sure—"

"Don't tell me that's not you." Maldynado pointed a finger at his nose. "You sneaked up behind me and put a knife to my throat, and I've seen you prove useful in a few scraps. You just need to invest some time in your physique." Maldynado thumped a fist against one of his pectoral muscles. "It'll make it easier to strut around in a manly way if you *feel* manly."

"So, your advice so far is to grow hair and muscles."

"Any businesswoman will tell you that you have to spruce up the packaging before you put a product on the market. I'll take you clothes shopping when we're back in the capital."

Sespian tilted his head back, watching Maldynado out of the bot-toms of his eyes, like he might have some regrets over having started the conversation. Or perhaps having opened the door at all.

"Enough of the superficial," Maldynado said, sensing his pupil's flagging belief. "There's a bigger issue you have to deal with when it comes to the boss. Her pet guard dog."

"Sicarius."

"They go *everywhere* together. I kid you not, I set her up for a nice dinner date with Deret Mancrest last summer, and she took him along. I'm not sure whose idea it was, but can you imagine trying to share tender moments with a woman while an assassin is standing there, glaring at you over her shoulder?"

"No," Sespian said. "I can't imagine wanting him in the same city as me. I have wondered…"

"Yes?"

"If he's controlling her somehow. He's very powerful and dangerous, and I'm sure it'd be easy for him to exert his influence to… You're shaking your head."

"That's because nobody controls Amaranthe. We've all tried. Not to control her, but to rein her in on some of her crazier ideas. She has a strong will and a thought process slipperier than the contents of an icehouse. She's the one who rounded us all up after all. Sicarius might be harder to wrangle than a Books or an Akstyr, but she's talked him into doing a lot of things I *know* he otherwise wouldn't have."

"So, I have to get rid of him somehow," Sespian said, a hint of calculation in his eyes. "They're not… I suppose I should have asked this first, but I didn't get the impression that Amaranthe was… romantic with anyone in your group."

"Nah, I don't think so," Maldynado said without hesitation. Forget Books's hunch. Even if there were something to it, Maldynado did *not* want to see Amaranthe doomed to a relationship with a man colder than the razor-sharp blades he carried around. "I doubt Sicarius even knows what the word romantic means," he added.

"Good." Sespian nodded to himself. "That's good. Maybe—"

Someone pounded at the door. Sespian hopped to his feet, reacting more quickly than Maldynado, and snatched up his dagger. He reached the window first. Night's grip had relaxed outside, and Basilard stood visible against the rosy sky. Akstyr jogged up behind him.

As soon as the door opened, Akstyr thrust a hand toward the river behind the steamboat. "We've got a problem."

Maldynado and Sespian stepped outside. It didn't take long to find the "problem." Two sleek, black boats were cutting up the river after the steamboat.

Basilard waved a spyglass and signed, *They're enforcers. At least twenty men on each boat. They're well armed and have grappling hooks. There are also guns mounted on the foredecks. Big guns.*

"Uh oh," Maldynado said. "Some of those passengers we tossed overboard must have found their way to town to report the hijacking."

"This vessel doesn't have any weaponry, does it?" Sespian asked.

"No, but it has a swimming pool and netball courts," Maldynado said.

"We're almost to the lake." Sespian fiddled with the dagger. "If we can simply reach it, those enforcers can have their steamboat back."

"How do you suggest we tell them that?" Maldynado asked.

"Just… get ready to defend the ship. You, Basilard, you're a fighter, right? Can you and Maldynado handle the defenses? Akstyr, join me in the wheelhouse. I understand you're good with makarovi."

Akstyr grinned. "Yup."

"We'll relieve Sergeant Yara and send her to the boiler room to help Books," Sespian went on. "We'll need all the power we can get out of those engines. We're already going against the current, so these last few miles will be a push."

A boom sounded, and birds erupted from the trees on either side of the river. A round splashed into the water several meters to the side of the steamboat.

"Warning shot," Maldynado said.

"Go." Sespian waved to the men, then sprinted for the closest stairs.

Akstyr ran after him, leaving Maldynado and Basilard alone.

Basilard signed, *We get to defend this huge boat by ourselves? Against forty trained fighters?*

"Apparently," Maldynado said. "You want the left side or the right side?"

Basilard gave him a grim look. *We need an Amaranthe Plan.*

"I'm going to round up as many rifles as I can find. Let me know if you come up with one."

\* \* \* \* \*

Though the pink glow of dawn lightened the eastern sky, fog shrouded the lake, making it feel as if morning had yet to come. The rowboat Sicarius had purloined glided through the calm waters, surging forward with each powerful stroke of his oars. Across from him, Amaranthe shifted on the hard bench, feeling a tad useless, even if he had, with a wordless pointing of his finger, insisted she assume the passenger role.

"When are you going to stop treating me like a wounded kitten that you've adopted, and go back to insisting that all forms of physical exertion are 'good training'?" Amaranthe asked.

"You wish to row?" Sicarius had abandoned his workman's garments and returned to the humorless black, now clean and wrinkle-free. Perhaps he'd only donned the other clothing because his preferred garb needed time for a wash and dry.

"No." She smiled. "I was just wondering how long I could milk this torture experience to get out of work."

Sicarius rowed onward without comment. He was probably watching the mainland to make sure no enforcers with sniper aspirations lurked there. Amaranthe couldn't fault his dedication to duty, but it was a long trip to Marblecrest Island, and a conversation would be nice. In truth, there were questions on her mind, questions she'd been trying to muster the courage to ask. Once they reunited with the team, private moments might be hard to come by.

She took a deep breath. "A couple of weeks ago… you mentioned that I didn't know all the secrets from your past. Is there… anything you'd like to tell me? To help you with Sespian?"

"No."

Not exactly an invitation to probe further. She chewed on her lip and finally asked what had been lurking in her thoughts. "Pike said you killed Raumesys."

Sicarius's features, masked as usual, betrayed nothing of his thoughts.

"Is it true?" Amaranthe asked, remembering that he didn't always consider statements worth comment.

He didn't respond to the question either.

"Did he find out that Sespian wasn't his son?" Amaranthe guessed. "And you had to… take care of him before he disowned Sespian? Or punished his mother? No, wait, she died a few years before Raumesys,

didn't she? The winter that Nurian flu ravaged the capital. But if Rau-mesys *had* found out, he would have…"

Sicarius was giving her a flat, you're-imagination-is-working-too-hard look. "Soon," he said.

"What?"

"If you are hale enough to burble, you are hale enough to exercise. Your training will resume soon."

Amaranthe didn't quite manage to stifle a groan. "Fine, you don't have to tell me. But how many other people know? If it comes out later and Sespian learns of it, will he be angry with you for killing the man he considered his father?"

"Unlikely."

Amaranthe glowered in response to the one-word answer.

"Raumesys treated him poorly," Sicarius said. "Sespian," he added, his voice softening, "preferred to spend time with his mother."

"Did Raumesys… beat him?" Amaranthe wondered if that might explain the emperor's premature demise. The newspapers had claimed Raumesys had succumbed to a fatal heart condition, but many poisons could simulate such a death.

"Physical abuse was rare," Sicarius said. "Verbal assault, less so. Raumesys was disgruntled that Sespian showed no interest in military and combat studies. He told the boy. Often."

"Mental abuse can be as cruel as physical. And it's difficult to watch when it's happening to someone you care about."

Sicarius grunted.

"Did it bother you?" Amaranthe asked. "Raumesys's treatment of Sespian?"

"Yes."

"But not enough to kill him over it?"

Sicarius glanced over his shoulder. His sure strokes had brought them into the shadow of Marblecrest Island more quickly than Amaranthe would have guessed. She feared their approach meant she wouldn't receive an answer.

Above the fog shrouding the beaches, verdant foliage bathed steep hills with deep draws that might hide numerous secret nooks. Near the island's high point, the roof of a log structure came into sight. Ama-

ranthe would call it a mansion or lodge, but Maldynado's family probably thought of it as a rustic cabin.

Sicarius took a few extra strokes on the right side to angle the rowboat toward a cove with a dock.

"Sicarius," Amaranthe said, taking one last stab at pulling the answer out of him, "Sespian will want to know." All right, *she* wanted to know.

A few more strokes passed in silence as he made adjustments to their approach. Finally, he pulled them in, letting the boat's momentum carry them across the serene, misty water. "Sespian was a catalyst. I had many missions and was rarely in the Imperial Barracks. Had I witnessed more of his interactions with Raumesys, I may have… rethought my allegiance sooner. It wasn't until I stood before Raumesys and refused an assignment that my relationship with the emperor changed. My declination of the mission did not mean I had thoughts of betraying the throne, but he interpreted it that way. I believe he had long feared me. I'd always been Hollowcrest's employee, more than his, and we rarely interacted. Shortly after that day, Raumesys tried to have me poisoned. I learned of it ahead of time and meant to discuss the situation with Hollowcrest, but he was away from the city. Before he returned, I walked in on Raumesys berating Sespian. That was when I decided."

"To kill him?" Amaranthe's voice came out as a whisper.

"At fifteen, Sespian was still too young to rule in his own stead, but I imagined I could stand at his back and protect him from those who sought to connive or ingratiate themselves to him. I did not anticipate him…"

"Firing you?"

"Essentially."

The rowboat glided up to the dock, bumping softly against a wood piling.

"What was the mission you turned down?" Amaranthe asked.

"A story for another time." Sicarius secured the boat and hopped out.

Amaranthe hmphfed, but she supposed she'd gotten more out of him than expected.

Despite his threat that he'd resume her training soon, Sicarius extended a hand. She accepted it and climbed onto the dock. A rat skittered out of a clump of grass at the base and disappeared through a crack in

the boathouse. Sun-faded and peeling, the dock had not seen a maintenance man in many years.

"I guess the Marblecrests have been too busy plotting coups to enjoy their vacation getaway in recent years," Amaranthe said.

Sicarius did not comment, and they were soon pushing through foliage, walking up a gravel road so overgrown a machete was almost required. More of the log home came into view as they climbed, including expansive glass windows that promised no less than fifteen or twenty rooms inside. Halfway up the hillside, the path meandered past a rocky precipice that was bare of grass and trees. Amaranthe diverted from the trail to walk to the edge. It overlooked the lake and offered a view of three nearby islands, all dark and quiet in the early morning light.

"Are those the ones on the map?" Amaranthe asked when Sicarius joined her. "The ones that form a rectangle with this one?"

"A trapezoid," Sicarius said.

"Forgive my imprecision. I wonder if… should we be looking *under* the island instead of on top of it?"

"For entrances to mines?" Sicarius asked.

"Or whatever it is they were doing down there. Let's check the house first though. Just in case."

Amaranthe and Sicarius continued up the main path, which dove into a stand of trees clogged with blackberry brambles. A few minutes into the copse, a hiss sounded to their right. Amaranthe jumped.

"Hot springs." Sicarius pointed to a side path barely visible through the overgrown shrubbery.

"Of course," Amaranthe said, remembering Pabov's tour.

On a whim, she veered onto the path. Wordlessly, Sicarius followed. Thorny vines grasped and scraped at exposed flesh, but it was a short trek. Tiny, steaming pools appeared through the trees, connected by a natural lava rock deck that overlooked a cliff on the north side of the island. Only one of the neighboring islands stood in view along with a river that flowed out of the lake a mile away. After another hiss sounded, a geyser to one side spewed a fountain of water.

Amaranthe bent and dipped a hand in the closest pool. Hot water caressed her fingers. Forget the beach, she thought. *This* was a bathing spot. Too bad they had other priorities; though she flirted with the idea of sending Sicarius to explore the house on his own while she tore off

her clothes, flung herself into the pool, and soaked blissfully in sybaritic indulgence.

Sicarius's hand came to rest on her shoulder. Maybe he was thinking of a soak too. But, no, he was pointing past the lake and toward the river. A three-decked steamboat was barreling up the waterway, gray plumes of smoke flowing from its twin stacks. It looked like one of the vessels that plied the Goldar River, carrying passengers from Stumps and other cities around the Chain Lakes down to the Gulf and back. For some reason, this one had diverted to Lake Seventy-three, something that might be normal during the summer season, but now? It seemed unlikely.

"It's going too fast," Sicarius said.

Now that he mentioned it, the steamboat *did* seem to be exceeding its typical speed. The paddlewheel was churning so quickly that water flung in all directions. Two smaller craft plowed up the river behind the sternwheeler. Painted black with pointed bows and sleek, compact frames designed for speed, they were gaining on the steamboat.

Amaranthe recognized the symbols on the sides. Enforcer boats. If Forge saw the authorities swarming into the area, would they cancel their meeting before it started? "What idiot is leading enforcers down here?"

"Sespian." Sicarius had a spyglass to his eye.

"Er, levity?" As much as Amaranthe wanted to see her men again, she didn't want their arrival to spook Forge.

"He is at the wheel inside the pilothouse. Alive." Uncharacteristic relief had seeped into Sicarius's tone. "Though he looks concerned."

"Understandable if they're being chased by enforcers. It looks like they're coming in our direction. We better get down to the beach." When Amaranthe turned toward the path, she found that Sicarius had already disappeared, leaving only a few leaves rustling in the wake of his abrupt passing.

# CHAPTER 19

M ALDYNADO STOOD AT THE REAR OF THE HUR-
ricane deck, next to the paddlewheel, with a row of loaded
muskets and rifles leaning against the railing. Three pistols protruded from his belt where a cutlass and more knives hung. He
felt like a Sicarius caricature.

A brisk wind tugged at his clothing and swept hair into his eyes.
The steamboat bumped and swayed as it picked up speed, fighting the
river's current. At last glance, the lake hadn't been in sight. The sky had
lightened, and the enforcer boats were close enough that every armed
and armored man waiting on their decks was visible. As Basilard had
promised, several of those men carried grappling hooks. They *all* bore
short swords and repeating crossbows. Maldynado wished his firearm
collection assured victory, but the weapons ranged from old service
muskets that had long since seen their prime to ornate—and probably
ineffective—antiques from the private collections of the *Glacial Empress's* former passengers. None of the firearms could hold more than
one charge at a time. Though the enforcers themselves didn't carry
black-powder weapons, their boats had more than enough guns mounted
on the fore and aft decks to make up for the lack. They hadn't fired since
that first warning shot, but that couldn't last.

Afraid someone might find him an appealing target, Maldynado kept
his body behind machinery used for lifting the lifeboats from the deck
to the water. On the other side of the paddlewheel, Basilard maintained
a similar position as he observed the second enforcer boat. Instead of
lining up firearms, he'd found a longbow to use, though the beadwork
quiver and colorfully fletched arrows made the weapon appear more
decorative than functional.

"Attention river pirates," a voice called through a megaphone on the closest enforcer boat, "you are in violation of Bergonla Satrapy Code, Forty-five-dash-six and Imperial Law Number Three. You will slow down and prepare to be boarded. If you do not comply, we will take offensive measures."

"Law Three? What, by grandmother's hairiest mole, is that?" Maldynado figured it had to be an important one since it didn't have any dashes or extra numbers in it.

"Impersonating the emperor," came Yara's voice from behind him.

"Impersonating!" Maldynado raised his voice to holler over the splashing of the paddlewheel and the churning of the engines. "We're not impersonating anyone! We have the emperor on board, and your ancestral spirits will strangle you if you illiterate louts shoot down his officially commandeered ship." While yelling made him feel better, he doubted the enforcers could hear him over the engines and paddlewheel.

Yara, however, frowned at him. "Illiterate louts? There are written as well as oral portions of the enforcer exam."

"Sorry, I didn't mean… Uhm, illiterate louts, where did that come from anyway? That's more something Books would say. Maybe Akstyr used his foreign magics to put the idea in my head."

"That's pathetic."

Maldynado was glad the emperor wasn't around to hear him irritating Yara. His supposed expertise on women might be questioned.

Yara waved toward the sleek vessels. "They're just doing their jobs. Someone must have reported the steamboat hijacked."

A crossbow bolt skipped off the railing, whizzed past Yara's arm, and slammed into the wall behind her. Maldynado grabbed her and pulled her behind the lifeboat machinery. It seemed the "offensive measures" had begun.

"Still sympathetic because they're just doing their jobs?" Maldynado asked.

A boom rent the morning air, and a flaming projectile slammed into the paddlewheel. Wood splintered and flew into the water, while shards pattered onto the deck around Maldynado and Yara. The flames were quickly extinguished as the paddles rotated into the water, but that wouldn't be the case if one of those projectiles hit the boat itself.

"Yes." Yara picked a shard of wood out of her hair. "But less so now."

Maldynado grabbed the closest musket and leaned around the lifeboat, searching for a likely target.

"Don't shoot to kill," Yara said. "The emperor won't want the blood of his own people on his hands."

"I know. Amaranthe gets huffy when we kill people too. Maybe they'd make a decent couple after all."

"What?"

"Nothing."

On the closest boat, two men were loading the forward gun while a third waited to shoot it, some sort of metal shield protecting him. Maldynado aimed at the leg of one of the unprotected enforcers. He fired, though the musket had the accuracy of a drunken peg-leg sailor launching a wad at a spittoon. The ball clanged off the gunner's shield, ricocheting uselessly into the water.

"That's your idea of not shooting to kill?" Yara picked up one of the ornate muskets in the lineup. "You were two inches from hitting that man in the eye."

"That's not the one I was aiming at. Besides, aren't you supposed to be helping Books in the engine room?"

"He said he could handle it by himself."

Another boom sounded. This time, the shell soared toward Maldynado and Yara. They flattened themselves to the deck. The round smashed through the wooden lifeboat and the wall behind it. A bong reverberated from the engine room, followed by an ominous grinding sound.

"That might be about to change," Maldynado replied.

A second flaming projectile smashed into the wheel; paddles flew off like scales torn from a pine cone and cast upon the wind.

Yara fired, the crack of her musket sounding inches from Maldynado's ear. If her shot hit the boat, he couldn't tell. It certainly didn't make any of the enforcers flinch.

Maldynado cupped a hand over his ear. "Nicely done."

"It seems neither of us is the sharpshooter we'd like to be," Yara admitted. "Enforcers aren't encouraged to learn how to shoot firearms."

She grabbed a powder tin to reload the weapons and pointed for Maldynado to keep firing.

"It's not you. They're not close enough for these old, inaccurate muskets. They're staying back to—"

Another projectile soared over the railing, this time on Basilard's side, and pounded through the wall and into the engine room.

"—incapacitate us," Maldynado finished.

"We need to take out their boats somehow," Yara said. "If we can crash them or sink them, we can make it to the lake before reinforcements come up the river."

"An excellent notion. How do we make it happen?"

Yara shrugged. Maldynado kept firing while she reloaded for him, but the enforcer artillery weapons were destroying the paddlewheel. Without that, the steamboat would be dead in the water. Maldynado would like to return the favor, but, from his position, he couldn't see the engines or boilers of the smaller crafts. Even if the design didn't hide those vulnerable points, he lacked weapons that had a chance of damaging them.

"What would Amaranthe do?" he muttered. "Something inspired. Something crazy."

Maldynado peered about, but the limited items within sight certainly didn't inspire him. The lifeboats dominated the back half of the deck, and the lounge chairs and tables in the middle appeared neither menacing nor useful. He imagined chucking them over the side at the oncoming boats. Those sleek crafts were small compared to the steamboat, but not small enough that hitting a folding deck chair would derail them. Something larger perhaps. He laid a thoughtful hand on the half-destroyed lifeboat they were using for cover.

"I have an idea," Maldynado said. "Keep them busy."

Without waiting for an acknowledgment of his order, Maldynado ran to one of the large cranks used for raising and lowering the lifeboat. The wide handle was meant for two to operate, and he had to throw his entire body into each stroke. Yara grabbed a handful of muskets and moved closer to the paddlewheel, either because she wanted the enforcers focused on her instead of him, or because she was worried Maldynado would drop the lifeboat on her foot.

More flaming rounds pummeled the back of the steamboat. A string of expletives erupted from inside the engine room. Maldynado glanced in that direction, worried that Books had been hit. Flames crackled behind shattered windows, and smoke poured through ragged holes blasted in the walls.

"They're getting closer," Yara said after firing another round. "They must sense that they've got us. Whatever you're going to do—"

"I should do it *before* we sink. I know." Maldynado returned to the crank and gave it a few good heaves.

The lifeboat inched higher, finally clearing the level of the railing. The wind shifted, and smoke billowed into Maldynado's eyes. Hot, sooty air seared his lungs, and a round of coughs sabotaged him. Eyes watering, he grabbed a lever under a brass plaque depicting stick figures dropping a stick lifeboat overboard.

"Wait!" Yara yelled. "There's a partial beaver dam sticking out from the shore ahead. If you time it—"

Maldynado paused, his hands gripping the lever. Tears streamed from his smoke-beleaguered eyes, and he could barely make out the shore. For all he could tell, drunken beavers could be dancing atop the brown smudge that Yara claimed was a dam. He dragged a sleeve across his eyes.

"Now!" Yara barked.

Maldynado threw his weight into pulling the lever. The machinery groaned in protest, and he feared nobody had oiled it for ages, but the lifeboat eventually released. He hoped it wasn't too late.

As soon it splashed down, Maldynado realized he was vulnerable with only the metal railing for protection from snipers. As if to confirm the thought, a crossbow quarrel gouged into the deck at his feet. He sprinted for the protection of the battered paddlewheel, nearly crashing into Yara.

Shouts and curses came from the water behind them. The lifeboat had splashed down in the closest boat's path. The small, maneuverable ship veered to the side in time to avoid a collision, but their new course sent them toward the beaver dam. Water sprayed as the pilot tried to bank so the craft wouldn't crash. He almost managed the maneuver, but struck the logs sideways with enough of a jolt to hurl several men overboard.

Maldynado hoped his sabotage would incapacitate the craft, or at least delay it significantly. The steamboat plowed past the dam, and he gave the enforcers a friendly wave. No less than five men threw their arms up in obscene gestures.

"Enforcers are so crude," Maldynado said.

Yara gripped his arm, and he expected to be abraded for his comment, but she said, "Good work."

Before he could bask under the influence of her rare praise, a great shudder ran through the steamboat. The piston arms powering the paddlewheel were no longer pumping smoothly. One had developed a hitch that made the boat lurch and tremble with each rotation. Each rotation also sent more wood paddles flying from the wheel.

"How much farther is that lake?" Maldynado wondered.

Yara shook her head. "We better help Basilard with the other boat."

Maldynado took a step in that direction only to pause. "Where *is* Basilard?"

A throwing knife lay on the deck where he'd been, but the long bow was gone, as was he. An entire section of the railing was gone, the two ragged ends dangling. Maldynado swallowed. If Basilard had taken one of those giant shells in the chest...

No, Maldynado told himself, there'd be a body. Unless Basilard had been knocked overboard...

Two grappling hooks clung to the railing on either side of the missing section. The paddlewheel blocked Maldynado's view of the ropes and the other boat, but a sick lurch ran through his stomach. Not only was Basilard missing, but enforcers might have come on board while Maldynado had been busy with his sabotage. They could already be advancing on the wheelhouse and the emperor. And if they thought Sespian was an impostor....

"What's the penalty for violating Law Three?" Maldynado asked.

"Death," Yara said grimly.

"Emperor's bunions," Maldynado spat. He started to sprint toward the grappling hooks, to head off any more enforcers trying to board, but a flaming projectile burned through the air ahead of him, smashing into engineering.

"Help!" Books cried, his voice garbled.

Maldynado groaned, not sure in which direction to run.

"I'll check on him," Yara said and sprinted toward the closest door.

Maldynado ran to the end of the paddlewheel, knowing that he'd be an easy target if he popped into view in front of the broken railing. An enforcer's hands gripped the railing, and the man started over. Abandoning cover, Maldynado sprinted over and used the stock of a musket to club him in the face. In the middle of climbing off the rope, the man couldn't defend himself. He let go and fell in the water with a splash, narrowly missing being caught up in the churning paddlewheel.

Four more enforcers were climbing up the twin ropes running from their craft to the steamboat railing. Maldynado whipped his musket up and loosed a shot. It caught the closest man in the shoulder. He screamed and dropped into the river.

"Fire!" came a cry from the boat.

Enforcers were lined up on their foredeck, crossbows aimed in Maldynado's direction. He dropped to his belly faster than a five-hundred-pound weight. Quarrels slammed against the railing and the wall behind him, one skimming so close to his jaw that he wouldn't need to shave that spot for a while.

Maldynado scrambled for the protective cover of the paddlewheel. He made it, but had lost the musket in the fall. For a second, he thought about waiting there and trying to punch men as they came over, but he couldn't do that without exposing himself to the crossbowmen on the boat.

"Some help would be nice," Maldynado growled, racing back to his earlier spot by the lifeboat machinery. Akstyr should have been down here making makarovi illusions.

Three loaded muskets remained near the railing, though they'd fallen to the deck. Maldynado stopped so fast he skidded and almost knocked them overboard. He grabbed one and spun, lifting the weapon as he turned.

Huge clouds of black smoke blew out of the engine room, and he almost missed seeing the first two enforcers sprint across the deck to disappear on the opposite side of the ship. The third one was pulling himself over the railing. No longer caring if he shot to wound or kill, Maldynado aimed at the man's torso.

Before he could squeeze the trigger, the steamboat slammed into something. A massive jolt hurled Maldynado to the deck. He skidded

several feet on his side, the force almost slinging him through the railing and into the river. Up ahead somewhere, wood snapped, the noise ear-splitting as it rolled across the foggy lake like thunder.

Foggy lake? Maldynado sat up. When had they reached the lake?

The waterwheel was still spinning, the engine moaning and groaning worse than Books when forced to train, but forward progress had ground to a halt. Water lapped over the edge of the deck, soaking Maldynado's pants. Shadows stirred on the opposite side of the boat, and he remembered the enforcers. He lurched to his feet, patting around for a sword, musket, or, if nothing else, a hefty piece of wood to use as a club.

More men streaked over the railing, heading toward the front of the steamboat. Half of them didn't even glance in Maldynado's direction. They had to be running toward the wheelhouse—toward the emperor. Only they'd think Sespian *wasn't* the emperor.

Maldynado snarled and found a rifle. It wasn't loaded, and he had no idea where the powder and ammunition had gone. Over the side probably. Well, he'd crack people on the head with the butt.

He started to run toward the enforcers, but wheezing coughs from the nearest doorway distracted him. Yara stumbled out of the smoky boiler room, dragging Books across the deck behind her.

Torn between running to the emperor's defense and helping Books, Maldynado hesitated, frozen for a second. Sicarius's threat rang between his ears.

"Akstyr ought to be up there," he finally muttered and ran to Yara's side.

Books's eyes weren't open.

"Is he...?" Maldynado asked.

"Help me get him off this boat," Yara said.

"Off... where?" Maldynado didn't know if they'd hit land or some sizable boulder protruding from the waters.

Still pulling Books, Yara threw him an exasperated glare. "Anywhere!" She jerked her chin toward the smoking engine room. Inside flames licked their way up the walls. "That boiler could blow up any second!"

"Bloody, dead ancestors," Maldynado said, though the back of his mind found the time to thank those dead ancestors that, for once, *he* hadn't been the one to crash the ship.

He grabbed Books's legs, and he and Yara soon had him draped over the railing. Maldynado patted his cheek. "Wake up, Booksie. This'll be a lot easier if you can swim."

Yara splashed water into his eyes. They moved under the lids, but he didn't open them. He'd either sucked in piles of toxic fumes, or he didn't want to see where Maldynado was about to toss him.

"We're on an island." Yara had leaned out to peer toward the front of the steamboat. "I can swim well enough to get him to shore."

Maldynado nodded. "Good. A ton of enforcers ran past, so I need to check on the emperor."

"Don't stop to fight them. Just get the emperor off before this broken beast blows up." Yara hopped over the railing and into the lake.

"Don't stop to fight them, sure." Maldynado lowered Books down to her. "I'm game to follow those orders, but I'm not sure they'll cooperate."

Yara shifted Books onto his back, wrapped one arm across his chest and pulled him toward the shore. She looked like she knew what she was doing, so Maldynado offered a quick wave and sprinted for the nearest staircase.

As he climbed to the top deck, he finally got a good look at the island, and he nearly tripped when he realized where they were. Marblecrest Island.

"Of all the luck…" He didn't know whether to call it good luck or bad luck. At least he knew where the boathouse was and that there ought to be canoes and dinghies they could use to reach their real destination. Wherever that was.

When he reached the base of the stairs leading to the wheelhouse, Maldynado intended to charge straight up, but two enforcers were guarding the spot. Clangs rang out from up above, the clangs of swords banging against swords.

The enforcers spotted Maldynado immediately and lifted their crossbows to shoot. He hurled the unloaded rifle at them, whipping it sideways in an optimistic notion of disrupting both their shots. As soon as he threw it, he turned his run into a sprint and dove into a roll that, he hoped, would carry him crashing into their legs, causing a massive discombobulation.

Before he hit the deck, a crossbow bolt thudded into his shoulder. Pain ripped down his left arm. Idiot, Maldynado thought, even as his

momentum threw him into that roll, you're probably the only one discombobulated here.

Three rapid revolutions later, he smashed into something hard enough to drive the air out of his lungs. It wasn't the enforcers' legs, as he'd hoped, but the stairs themselves.

A nearby rasp announced a sword being drawn. Maldynado leaped to his feet. The enforcers had parted as he barreled toward them, and both had their swords out. He couldn't fight one without putting his back to the other. Easy fix. He ignored them both and scrambled up the stairs.

A startled shout trailed him.

"Just following my lady's advice," Maldynado called back.

As he reached the top, Maldynado almost took a boot in the face. He jerked his head to the side, just evading heavy, black treads. Enforcers swarmed the catwalk between the stairs and the wheelhouse. More than one set of boots turned toward him, and he feared that his choice to charge up had been unwise.

"What's new?" he grumbled, then ducked again, this time to avoid a sword slicing toward his head.

The stairs were wet from the rain, and his heel slipped off. He managed to keep his feet under him but stumbled down several steps, crashing into one of the enforcers who'd been on his way up. Sword raised, the man had been about to take a swing at Maldynado's legs. To avoid the strike, Maldynado leaped over the railing. He would have landed on the enforcer waiting below, but the man scurried backward. Before his feet hit the ground, Maldynado kicked out, catching him in the chest. As soon as he landed, he sprang after the man. If he could pummel the enforcer into defenselessness before his colleague got turned around on the stairs…

The man went down beneath the assault, but wasn't ready to give up. A knee rammed into Maldynado's gut. He gripped the enforcer's uniform jacket with both hands and slammed the man into the deck. His head clunked against the wood. Before the enforcer could recover, Maldynado jumped to his feet, still gripping the jacket. He dragged his opponent to the railing, gritting his teeth against the pain of having a crossbow bolt in his shoulder, and, with a great grunt, heaved the enforcer over the side. Again, Maldynado almost took a boot to the head as the man flung a kick outward, a last try at stopping him.

"Why do they always aim for my face?" Maldynado asked as he spun back, fists up, ready to defend against an attack from the second man. Given how long he'd had his back to the stairs, he was surprised he hadn't already received that attack.

Oddly, the enforcer was lying on the deck. Face down. Maldynado didn't remember hitting the man on his way over the railing.

A black-clad figure sprinted past, a throwing knife in hand as he vaulted up the stairs.

"Ah," Maldynado said.

Shouts and, a split second later, screams came from above. Unlike Maldynado, Sicarius had no trouble flying off the steps fast enough to avoid attacks.

"I believe," came a familiar voice from farther up the deck, "they aim for your face because of your looks. They're envious and wish to mar your beauty so they'll feel better about their own lesser visages."

Maldynado's throat tightened with emotion. Amaranthe, walking at a much slower pace than Sicarius and with a noticeable limp, smiled as she approached. For a moment, Maldynado forgot the fight. He ran forward and swept her into a bear hug.

Cracking wood and the clangs of steel convinced him it needed to be a short hug, so he reluctantly released her. "I always suspected that was the case," he responded, his voice thick with emotion. She looked like a prisoner of war dragged out of some enemy camp's dungeon, but at least she was smiling, and her brown eyes still held a warm sparkle.

"We should probably help them." Amaranthe waved toward the wheelhouse.

"Right. I'll go first." Maldynado, at first focused on her bruises and the weary way she held herself, almost hadn't noticed the garish pastel hat she wore. Blind ancestors, couldn't he trust anyone in the group to dress themselves appropriately? "Unless you want to see if you can startle the enforcers into falling off the railing with that hat?"

"Not necessary."

No more than a minute could have passed from the time Sicarius raced up the stairs to the time Maldynado and Amaranthe reached the catwalk, but it might as well have been an hour. The enforcers were

gone. Not dead, Maldynado was pleased—for Amaranthe's sake—to see, but thrown overboard. A few soggy souls were wading through the shallows to the beach. When Maldynado leaned over the railing, he spotted Yara and Books standing on a rocky bank. Good, Books was awake and alert, albeit leaning against a tree for support. He and Yara had acquired crossbows, and she was disarming enforcers while Books kept them in his sights.

The wheelhouse door had been half-torn from its hinges, and numerous dents marred the wood. The glass was cracked, too, and laced with bullet holes. The enforcers must have broken in right before Sicarius arrived. Maldynado hoped that his own distraction, however clumsy, had helped in delaying them.

"…could have handled them," Akstyr's voice floated out.

Maldynado stepped up to the doorway. Sicarius stood inside, looking as cold and deadly as ever, though he had lost a couple of pounds since parting ways with the team. Had he *run* all the way to Lake Seventy-three? There weren't even roads out in that wilderness along the base of the mountains.

Two men in enforcer uniforms lay on the deck beneath the wheel. One was groaning, and Maldynado didn't see any broken necks, so he didn't attempt to block Amaranthe from entering when she squeezed past him.

Akstyr had been pushed back to the far corner. Sicarius stood beside Sespian, whose face had taken on a pale cast, whether from the crash or from Sicarius's reappearance—and closeness—Maldynado did not know. He managed a smile, though, when Amaranthe stepped inside. He stepped toward her, his hands lifting, as if he might embrace her, but caught himself and dropped his hands. "It's good to see you alive, Corporal Lokdon."

Maldynado sighed. The hug would have been better.

"It's good to see you alive as well, Sire," Amaranthe said. "The newspapers have been alarming us with their reports of your passing."

Her tone and polite smile were utterly professional. Even Deret Mancrest had earned more feminine interest from Amaranthe. The kid would have a tough time if he wanted to win her heart.

Sespian winced. "Yes, I've heard."

Sicarius was looking out the back window, the only one that hadn't been cracked in the crash. The second enforcer boat hadn't appeared yet, no doubt thanks to its encounter with the beaver dam, but the remaining one was pulling up to a nearby beach. There might still be fighting to do.

"I will take care of them." Sicarius strode out of the wheelhouse without a word of thanks, or even a friendly nod, to acknowledge that Maldynado had fulfilled his duty to keep the emperor safe and close. It figured.

Before he turned away from the window, Maldynado glimpsed a bald-headed figure swimming across the lake toward the island. "I believe Basilard will be joining us soon."

"Good, I was concerned when I didn't see him," Amaranthe said, then stood on her tiptoes to track Maldynado's pointing finger. "But why is he swimming along after the boat instead or riding inside it?"

"Less dangerous out there." Akstyr, still standing in the corner with his hands in his pockets, shifted his weight uncertainly.

Maldynado, remembering that Akstyr supposedly wanted to let Amaranthe know that he appreciated her, gave him a little nod and tilted his head toward her. He needn't get mushy with so many others looking on, but he could at least say he was glad she wasn't dead.

"Hullo, boss," Akstyr said.

Such a spring of emotion. Amaranthe walked over and gave him a hug anyway.

"Staying away from gangs and bounty hunters?" she asked him.

Meanwhile Sespian gave her back a wistful look. Yes, seeing someone like Akstyr get a hug over him had to hurt.

Maldynado peered between the cracks in the front window, admiring the close-up view of a copse of trees, their leaves turning the rich browns and reds of autumn. "So, who was responsible for docking the boat halfway up the mountain?"

Sespian flushed, glanced at Amaranthe, and then studied the floor assiduously.

"I assumed it was you," Amaranthe told Maldynado, "until we encountered you on the way up to the wheelhouse."

"*Me?*" Maldynado flattened a hand on his chest. "I was on the hurricane deck, risking all sorts of bodily harm to keep those enforcers from boarding. I'll have you know that the men who *did* get on didn't come

up on *my* side of the boat." Since Basilard wasn't there, Maldynado decided it wouldn't hurt to leave out the fact that Yara had been helping him, and Basilard had been forced to defend his side alone.

"So… the emperor crashed it?" Amaranthe's eyes twinkled, though Maldynado wasn't sure if Sespian noticed that. The kid's flush had grown deeper. Even his ears were red.

"I lost tiller control," Sespian said. "They were shooting at the paddlewheel and the engine room. They must have smashed the rudder as well." He looked back and forth from Amaranth to Akstyr to Maldynado and added, "It wasn't my fault."

Maldynado laughed. "I've said that many times, and it hasn't worked to shift the blame away from me yet."

Sespian's shoulders slumped. "This isn't at all how I imagined this mission going."

Emperor or not, Maldynado patted the kid on the shoulder. "I think this means you're officially one of us now, Sire."

Though he meant the pat to be reassuring, Sespian grew more glum and mumbled something that might have been, "Bloody bears."

Amaranthe, at least, looked amused. "We better collect the others, tie these enforcers up somewhere, and see if we can find a way to get under the lake."

"Under the lake?" Maldynado gazed out at the deep blue water.

"One of the Forge founders apparently owns the mineral rights to a chunk of land between this and a couple of other islands. We're surmising that there are mines or tunnels or some sort beneath the lake bed. Though it doesn't sound like the posh sort of place that I imagined wealthy business owners and bankers meeting up, it's… my best guess after perusing the real estate records for the area."

"You've been busy." Sespian eyed Amaranthe, his gaze lingering on bandages around her wrists. Maldynado could tell he wanted to ask about what she'd endured. Rust, he was wondering, too, but if it was half as awful as he thought it might have been, she probably wouldn't want to talk about it.

"I was all over the island as a boy, and I never came across any tunnels or secret entrances. Though I suppose now that we have our expert interrogator here—" Maldynado flicked a finger toward Sicarius, "—someone can get more precise answers out of Brynia."

"Who's Brynia?" Amaranthe asked.

"A woman who may have shot Mari, my sister-in-law, who was heading south to be a part of this Forge meeting," Maldynado said. "I guess the emperor had been meaning to follow Mari down here all along."

"Clandestinely," Sespian said, his face still glum.

"They might not have heard us coming," Maldynado told him.

Sespian gave him an incredulous look and waved at their "docking job."

"Uh, right." Maldynado lifted a hand to his mouth and side-whispered to Amaranthe, "How *far* under the lake are these tunnels?"

"We won't know until we find the entrance. Where's this woman? If she knows where the entrance is, it'd be handy. This is one of the larger islands out here."

"Naturally." Maldynado leaned against the back wall and smiled. "Whichever of my ancestors purchased it knew a prodigious piece of land would reflect the Marblecrest family attributes."

"Big heads?" Akstyr asked.

Maldynado gave him a quelling look, though, as usual, Akstyr refused to appear quelled.

"She should be in the brig," Sespian told Amaranthe.

"Let's go for a stroll then, shall we?" Amaranthe said.

Smoke hazed the air toward the stern of the steamboat. Remembering Yara's warning about the boilers, Maldynado said, "Yes, and we may want to stroll quickly."

* * * * *

Down on the hurricane deck, the gate to the tiny cage—a sign above proclaimed it the brig—was open, creaking as it swayed in the breeze.

"I assume this means your prisoner is missing?" Amaranthe asked.

After the team had put out the fire in the engine room, Maldynado had led Amaranthe and Sespian to the brig. Sicarius had joined Books and Yara ashore to deal with the enforcers. Only three had arrived in the boat, but well over a dozen more had made their way to the beach after being thrown overboard. Amaranthe trusted Sicarius to keep them from making trouble.

"She must have figured out a way to escape during the attack." Maldynado prodded the unsecured lock dangling from the wrought-iron door. "We were a tad distracted."

Amaranthe grimaced. She didn't know if this Brynia person could have given them any useful information, but she *did* know the woman could run straight to the Forge meeting and warn them of spies coming. Though maybe she was being delusional to believe Forge didn't already know. The steamboat landing hadn't exactly been quiet.

"It's not my fault." Maldynado must have noticed her frown. "Your old enforcer colleagues were so close on our rears, they could have braided our butt hair."

Though Amaranthe promptly willed her mind to wipe that image away, she smiled and gave Maldynado a hug. She'd missed his irreverence.

"I'm confused," Sespian said. "How does talk of… posterior hair warrant an embrace?"

"I have no idea," Maldynado said over Amaranthe's head, "but remember this, Sire, the next time you're perplexed by a woman. It's not anything wrong with you. It's them. They're unpredictable. And inconsistent. One time, they're scowling at you for making a mess, and the next time, they're finding your mess adorable."

"Adorable isn't *quite* the feeling." Amaranthe stepped back. "I've just missed you all."

"Ah," Maldynado said.

Sespian wore a wistful expression, as if *he'd* wanted a hug, and Amaranthe had to hold back another grimace. Apparently her plan to make him fall in love with Yara hadn't taken root in her absence. Well, she had more important things to worry about.

"It's all right." Amaranthe waved at the empty cage. "Now that we have the emperor, I have an idea about how we can more thoroughly search for this entrance. But, just in case there's a way in from land, Maldynado, I want you to collect Yara, Books, and Akstyr and search the island. You can be their guide. Take them any place where there might be a hidden cave or a trapdoor in your house."

"A trapdoor?" Maldynado scratched his head. "In a log cabin?"

"That *cabin* is bigger than Enforcer Headquarters back home," Amaranthe said. "For all we know, there's a warren of tunnels under it. If they're there, I need you to find them."

"You see, Sire," Maldynado said, "her hugs aren't all that desirable, as they're typically a precursor for an assignment of work."

Sespian acknowledged this with a wiggle of his fingers, then told Amaranthe, "What about me? Are we going somewhere?"

"Yes, I have an acquaintance in Markworth who may be willing to lend us his conveyance if he knows it's at your behest."

"You already have *acquaintances* in Markworth?" Maldynado asked. "How long have you and Sicarius been here?"

Amaranthe glanced at the sky. Though gray rain clouds hid the sun, she figured it was still early morning. "Almost a day."

"Making friends even more quickly than usual," Maldynado said.

"This friend tried to turn us over to the enforcers."

Maldynado winked at Sespian. "Yes, that's usually how things start."

Sespian's arched eyebrow suggested Maldynado hadn't yet succeeded in inducting him into his League of Beset Upon Brethren, but Amaranthe no longer sensed the stony mistrust that Sespian had leveled at him before.

"Didn't I assign you a task?" She waved Maldynado toward the shore.

"Sure, boss, whatever you say." Maldynado started past Sespian, but paused to stage-whisper, "Just don't let her make you drive this 'conveyance.' If you crash it, you'll get blamed, even though you were simply following her directions. It's usually her fault."

"My fault?" Amaranthe propped her hands on her hips. "I wasn't even onboard the steamboat when you two crashed it."

"You *two*?" Maldynado had been on his way to the gangplank, but he halted and turned around so quickly he almost tripped. "How did I get included? I wasn't anywhere near the wheelhouse when the emperor crashed us."

"Wasn't it your failure to defend the boat that resulted in the rudder being destroyed?" Amaranthe didn't truly blame him for any of this, but she hadn't had much amusement in her life of late, and it was fun seeing his flamboyant protests.

Maldynado spread his arms and faced Sespian, clearly expecting the emperor to defend him.

A glint of amusement entered Sespian's eyes. "It *was* the loss of tiller control that resulted in running into the island."

For a long moment, Maldynado gaped at him. Then, shaking his head, he slouched down the deck toward the gangplank. Basilard was climbing onto the steamboat, and, when they passed, Maldynado issued a warning.

"Don't go over there, Bas. They're hurling blame around like artillery rounds on a battlefield."

Basilard gave Maldynado a weary pat and kept walking. Dripping water and wearing a number of new bruises, he appeared as beleaguered as Amaranthe had felt of late. She gave him a hug as soon as he came close.

Sespian also approached Basilard and gripped his shoulder. "Thank you for fighting so hard to defend the steamboat. I know this isn't your battle, and I appreciate your willingness to risk yourself on our behalf."

Fortunately, Maldynado had left the boat, or he would have had a fit over seeing Basilard praised when he'd simply been teased, but Amaranthe was glad Sespian made the effort for Basilard. As far as she knew, Sespian hadn't made him any promises in exchange for his help, so Basilard could only be hoping that his actions would result in someone eventually looking into the slavers who were targeting his people.

"We're paying a visit to the mainland," Amaranthe told Basilard. "Do you want to come with us or stay here with Maldynado and the others? They're going to look for secret entrances to underground tunnels."

Basilard ran a hand over his scarred scalp. After that fight and that swim, he looked like a man who wanted nothing more than a nap.

"Or you could rest," Amaranthe amended.

*Perhaps*, Basilard signed, *I could make a hot meal.*

"That's an option too." One that instantly appealed to Amaranthe after days on the road, relying upon Sicarius's questionable culinary skills. At least they'd run out of those awful travel bars early on. "I imagine the log palace on the hill has a comprehensive kitchen."

Basilard brightened.

"Ready to go, Sire?" Amaranthe asked.

"Just the two of us?"

"Not exactly." Amaranthe looked toward the beach where Sicarius was tying up prisoners. "The enforcers are aware that he's in the area, and this crash might not have gone unnoticed. I'm not at my fighting peak right now, and it may behoove you to have someone along who can protect you." And maybe Sicarius and Sespian could have a chat while rowing across the lake.

"If they're looking for him, that sounds like a good reason not to bring him," Sespian said.

"I'm not positive he'd let me go off without him right now. Actually, I'm not positive he'd let you go off with only me to keep an eye on you." That was saying more than she should, but, now that Forge knew about Sespian's heritage, he'd learn why Sicarius cared one way or another soon anyway.

"Do you realize that he gave me that black dagger of his, and that Forge was able to track me because of it?" Sespian asked. "I was personally attacked twice because of it. They are determined to make their newspaper article a reality."

Chagrin weighted down Amaranthe's shoulders. If Sicarius had given Sespian his knife, he'd surely meant it as a gift, one that might prove useful. He'd be horrified, or as close to it as he came, to learn that it had endangered his son. "He didn't know," Amaranthe said. "He couldn't have. How were they able to track you?"

Sespian dug in a pocket, fished out a black egg-shaped device, and handed it to her. "I haven't been able to ascertain how it works. Brynia knew how to use it to locate other pieces of that ancient technology."

Amaranthe turned the seamless tool over in her hands. "I met the woman who probably taught her how to use it. I wonder if it's how they located the *Behemoth* in the first place."

"The what?"

"Oh, I named their craft before I heard the real name." Amaranthe returned the device. "At least, if we have it now, they can't use it to track the knife anymore. You *do* still have that, don't you?" A jolt of alarm ran through her at the thought of Sicarius's faithful dagger lost forever on the bottom of the river hundreds of miles back.

"It's in one of the cabins." Sespian waved dismissively toward the upper decks.

Amaranthe felt stung on Sicarius's behalf. *He* would probably be too practical to care, but it hurt her to think of Sicarius making a gift of his most valued belonging, only to have the recipient shun it.

"It's a handy blade," Amaranthe said. "If you're not going to use it, I'm sure he'd like it back."

"I'll get it then." It was only in Sespian's eyes that he said "good riddance," but the words hung in the air nonetheless. "I don't know why you worry about him, Am— Corporal Lokdon. About what he thinks. If you knew half of what he'd done, you wouldn't choose to spend time with him. He's heartless and inhuman."

Amaranthe wanted to argue Sicarius's merits, but she doubted Sespian was ready to hear them. Instead she opted for, "Nobody's born inhuman. But some people… the world sculpts with a cruel hand. Perhaps they're the ones who most need us to spend time with them."

Sespian's shoulders sagged, and Amaranthe sensed that she'd made him feel guilty. It wasn't exactly what she wished to do, but perhaps it was a start down the right path.

# CHAPTER 20

THE OARS ROSE AND DIPPED IN AN EASY RHYTHM that belied the tension that had to be lurking behind the rower's mask. Amaranthe tried, every time Sicarius met her eyes, to give him significant now-would-be-a-good-time-for-your-private-conversation looks. She, Sicarius, and Sespian were the only ones in the boat. The craggy forest-shrouded rocks of Marblecrest Island were falling behind, and the beaches near Markworth had yet to come into sight. Soft raindrops splashed onto the lake surface, muting sound. There wasn't a soul around to overhear Sicarius if he chose to broach a certain subject with Sespian.

At the moment, Sespian, sitting on the bench beside Amaranthe, was busy rummaging in his pack. Sicarius observed the movement, and, a couple of times, he opened his mouth. She leaned forward, waiting for his words. Sespian spoke first.

"Here it is." He pulled out the black dagger and extended it, hilt first, toward Sicarius.

"You did not find it useful?" Sicarius asked.

"It almost got me killed."

Sicarius didn't let any surprise show on his face, and continued to row without a hitch in his stroke, but he did glance toward Amaranthe, and she sensed the question there.

"Forge had a device that allowed them to track the ancient material," she said.

"Yes," Sespian said, his tone cold. As the rowboat continued to glide across the lake, he detailed an incident in a park where numerous men had attacked the group and tried to kill him. He gave a terse list of everything else that had happened since Amaranthe had been taken from

the team. It was probably a sign of questionable sanity, but she wished she'd been with them for the adventure. Then again, maybe it was perfectly sane; if she'd been with them, she *wouldn't* have been with Pike.

Sespian finished by looking Sicarius in the eye and saying, "I thought you might have set me up."

For the first time, the oars faltered. A long moment passed—Amaranthe imagined the shock and horror that lay beneath Sicarius's expressionless facade. How else could he feel? After all he'd done to protect Sespian, what he'd intended to be a magnanimous act had almost gotten his son killed.

"No," Sicarius finally said. "Nobody ever tracked me through the blade."

"Well, I'd rather not take a chance that it'll happen again." Sespian leaned forward and, keeping a wary eye on Sicarius, set the dagger on the bench beside him.

"I see."

That was the last thing Sicarius said. He returned to rowing. Faster than before. A couple of times, Sespian turned toward Amaranthe, as if he meant to start a conversation with her, but each time he glanced at Sicarius and ended up not saying anything.

Amaranthe was mulling over ways to start a conversation of her own, one that might entice both men to speak, preferably to each other, when smoke on the shoreline caught her eye. Moving smoke.

"Did you notice any steam vehicles in Markworth when we ran through on our... tour?" Amaranthe asked.

"No." Sicarius took a long look over his shoulder.

"Think the enforcers called in backup?"

Sicarius handed her his collapsible spyglass and adjusted his route, angling for a rocky beach with trees sheltering it. Too bad the rain had chased the fog away. Someone gazing out at the lake now could easily see their rowboat.

With the spyglass to her eye, Amaranthe searched for the source of the smoke. Three black vehicles rolled along the waterfront road, winding in and out of the trees. Enforcer vehicles. After spotting Sicarius, the local headquarters must have called for backup. Or maybe this had something to do with the stolen steamboat.

"This could be a problem," Amaranthe said. "Sire, I don't suppose you'd like to abandon your incognito ways and give a few orders to the lieutenant or captain in charge over there? Something like, 'These aren't the outlaws you're looking for, so you can all go home now.'?"

"I would," Sespian said, "but the enforcers we've encountered lately have been under the impression that I'm an emperor-look-a-like leading a band of riverboat pirates."

Amaranthe lowered the spyglass. "You didn't mention that when you were sharing the week's events, Sire."

"Didn't I?"

"There are numerous people around the research warehouse." Sicarius had his head craned over his shoulder again. His tone held a hint of reproach, as if to say he'd given Amaranthe the spyglass so she could scan the shoreline, not chat with Sespian.

Abashed, she lifted it again. "Enforcers. There's a vehicle parked out front, and there's our friend, Pabov, talking with them."

"*Our* friend?" Sicarius asked.

"Ah, yes, he was more attached to me than you, I think." Amaranthe lowered the spyglass again. "Maybe we should turn around and forget the underwater vehicle. We won't be able to get it anyway, not with all those people around the warehouse."

"Too late." Sespian pointed toward the research facility. The enforcers had stopped their conversation and were running out to the dock. "I think they've already seen us."

\* \* \* \* \*

Rain splattered on the brim of Maldynado's hat with an enthusiasm that would have impressed a faucet. Or a waterfall. He and Akstyr strode down a sandy beach on the east side of the island, eyeing the hillside for cave entrances or anything that might indicate a secret passage. Maldynado had explored the beaches and forest thoroughly as a boy, so any such features would have to be new additions.

"How long do we have to search?" Akstyr shook his head like a dog, flinging water out of his hair. The boy needed a decent hat.

"Until we find something," Maldynado said. "Or someone rings the dinner bell." The rain had grown harder in the last few minutes, and he

caught himself casting longing gazes at the log home. Yara and Basilard were already up there, searching for passages and preparing a meal. Maldynado had yet to escape the drizzle. He and Akstyr had stuffed the captured enforcers into the steamboat's cramped brig, then headed out to circle the island. They'd left Books to guard the prisoners, though he'd shown more interest in salvaging his research materials from the soot-covered engine room.

"There's something." Akstyr pointed to the beach ahead.

An egret standing in the shallows flapped away at Maldynado and Akstyr's approach. They stopped before a set of fresh tracks in the gray sand. This side of the island hadn't seen any action during the steamboat fight—and crash—so the sand ought to have been undisturbed. Maldynado set his own foot next to one of the prints.

"That's either a woman or a child," he said, though he already had an idea as to whom the tracks belonged.

"Brynia?" Akstyr asked.

"That's my guess."

The sand made the prints easy to follow. They started at the waterline and led to a log where it looked like Brynia had sat down. Maldynado expected the tracks to head into the trees above the beach, but they veered back toward the water.

Akstyr scratched his head. "She climbed out of the water, rested, and decided to take another swim?"

"It seems that way."

"It's a long swim back to the mainland. I would have hidden here until I could steal a boat, but women are funny."

Maldynado grunted, but he was busy thinking that Brynia might not have had any intention of returning to the mainland. Maybe she was looking for something beneath Marblecrest Island, like the entrance to her colleagues' secret underwater hideout.

"Should we keep looking?" Akstyr pointed up the beach.

"No, I don't think we're going to find anything *on* the island. We better hope that Amaranthe really does know somebody with an underwater vehicle and that she gets back soon."

\* \* \* \* \*

Shouts echoed through the trees and drifted across the lake. Amaranthe, Sespian, and Sicarius hunkered in a thicket, being stabbed and scraped from all sides by thorny vines, as they waited for a pair of enforcers to jog past. If the enthusiastic shouts were anything to go on, someone had found the recently abandoned rowboat.

"We'll be shot if we try to cross back to the island in anything *but* an underwater vehicle," Amaranthe whispered.

"They might not shoot us," Sespian whispered back. "They might follow us to the island so they can shoot everybody."

"Everybody on our team anyway. They wouldn't bother the Forge people. I doubt they're doing anything that's technically illegal at that meeting. In the law's eyes, those people are stalwart citizens, while we're…"

"Outlaws and steamboat pirates?" Sespian suggested.

"So it seems."

"A plan, Lokdon," Sicarius said, in a tone that implied that if she didn't come up with one, *he* would. "We did not have time to hide our tracks well. They will find us."

Though the closest pair of enforcers had disappeared from sight, snapping foliage promised many more remained in the area.

"I know where Pabov keeps the keys to the vehicle," Amaranthe said. "If you can provide a diversion that lures the enforcers away from the warehouse…"

"Very well." Sicarius parted the leaves.

"No killing," Sespian said.

"And no lighting the entire town on fire," Amaranthe said, remembering the incendiary nature of some of Sicarius's past diversions.

He paused, eyeing each of them in turn, and she could only guess at his thoughts. Maybe that his job would be twice as difficult now that he'd be nagged on two fronts.

"Not even the pickle establishment?" Sicarius asked.

Amaranthe blinked and almost asked him if that had been meant as "levity." Sespian must not have seen it that way, for he scowled.

"While the shopkeeper's manner was almost deplorable enough to warrant such misfortune," Amaranthe said, "I think she's suffered enough, due to the decimation of her shelf system and inventory."

"I will seek alternatives," Sicarius said, then, after checking for enforcers, slipped out of the brambles.

Amaranthe planned to follow promptly, but a belligerent voice bellowed from the nearby shoreline.

"I don't care, just find him!"

Branches broke and leaves shook as enforcers pounded through the woods to try and obey the order. Amaranthe sank lower into the thicket. Two new men ran past, this time heading in the opposite direction.

"I wonder if that 'him' refers to me or the assassin," Sespian murmured.

"It's usually Sicarius. The whole world wants him dead."

"Understandable," Sespian said, then, as if anticipating a frown—or a lecture—from her, lifted an apologetic hand. "If it matters, I have a similar problem."

"You two share something in common then. Perhaps you should chat about it sometime."

Sespian snorted. At least she'd gotten the apologetic wave.

When the uproar died down, Amaranthe whispered, "Let's go."

They eased out of the brambles. She led the way before she realized she was leading the way. Was it presumptuous to take charge when one had an emperor in one's party? Sespian said nothing, though, merely following in her wake as she eased past trees, around boulders, and between bushes. They had to stop several times to avoid searching enforcers, and Amaranthe worried Sicarius would put his diversion into action before she and Sespian reached the warehouse.

Seconds after she had the thought, a boom echoed across the lake. A flurry of wing flaps came from a bush next to Amaranthe, and a flock of birds took to the sky.

"What was *that*?" Sespian asked.

"Our diversion, Sire." Amaranthe tugged on his sleeve. "We need to hurry."

Two more booms and a crash sounded before Amaranthe and Sespian reached the warehouse. They stopped behind trees at the edge of the clearing. The air stank of scorched metal and burning wood. She had a feeling the enforcers would be walking back home. The wagon that had been parked in front of the warehouse was gone, and Amaranthe didn't see anyone, not outside anyway. Good.

"Do you want to wait here while I run in and get the keys?" Amaranthe whispered.

"That seems… cowardly," Sespian said.

"Not if I get captured and you charge in and rescue me."

Sespian considered her for a moment. "Do you truly deem that a possibility, or are you trying to protect me by keeping me out of trouble?"

"Yes," Amaranthe said with a smile.

She made a gesture for Sespian to remain behind the trees and jogged toward the warehouse. She doubted anyone would see her approaching through the dirt-crusted windows, but she stayed low anyway, hugging the building's shadow.

When she reached the front entrance, before her fingers could brush the latch, the door opened. An enforcer on his way out almost tripped over her. A crossbow dangled by his side, but he paused to look at her face, probably not expecting an outlaw to be wearing a hat birthed in the pastel section of a yarn basket. Amaranthe, on the other hand, did not hesitate.

She launched the heel of her palm toward the man's nose. He reacted, pulling his head back, but not quickly enough. Her strike caught him under the chin, which proved equally effective. As he stumbled back, Amaranthe kneed him in the groin and tore the crossbow from his startled grip. She shoved him into the building, using his body as a shield in case more armed men waited within.

Only one other person stood inside though. Pabov. He'd yanked a knife out as soon as the enforcer stumbled backward. Amaranthe pointed the crossbow in his direction to discourage him from using it. She pushed the enforcer, who'd bent over, one hand to his groin, toward Pabov, so she could target either man.

Pabov opened his mouth, but nothing came out. He gaped past Amaranthe's shoulder. Hoping it was Sespian and not a squad of enforcers, she stepped aside so she could check without turning away from the men.

Sespian stood on the threshold. He gave her… hm, she hoped that was an *appreciative* smile, not an adoring one, and said, "Nicely done. You're a very capable woman, Am—, Ms. Lokdon."

Amaranthe couldn't manage a return smile for him. All she'd done was kick a man in the groin whereas Sicarius was out there dodging

enforcers and risking his life blowing up boilers to buy them their requested manslaughter-free diversion.

"Is that...?" the enforcer wondered, lifting the hand that had been gripping his groin toward his chest, as if to give a salute. Confusion crinkled his features, and he turned to Pabov.

"I think so." Pabov had been studying Sespian for several seconds, and he gave a firm nod, then thumped his fist to his chest and bowed. "Sire, we are honored by your presence."

Only Amaranthe was close enough to hear the relieved sigh that Sespian exuded.

"How may we help you?" Pabov asked.

"I understand you have a unique vehicle that we may be able to borrow," Sespian said.

# CHAPTER 21

GUIDED BY SICARIUS'S HANDS, THE UWMTV crunched over the bumpy rocks and swaying seaweed of the lake bottom, scaring up schools of fish that flitted away posthaste. Amaranthe sat next to Sicarius in the only other seat, peering into the gloom beyond the glass shield bulging from the front of the globe-shaped vehicle. During the slow, underwater trek from Markworth back to Marblecrest island, she hadn't spotted anything stranger than an eel with two tails, but they'd picked up the rest of the team and were heading for the boundaries of Forge's "mining rights" territory now. Who knew what they might see? She hoped they had the time they needed to explore. Pabov had sworn not to mention the team's visit to the enforcers when they returned, but the promise of the man Amaranthe had bruised had been less heartfelt.

A soft clunk came from behind her chair.

"This is intolerable," Books said. "Someone's ludicrous pink hat feather keeps jabbing me in the nose."

"This isn't a pleasant experience for me either," Maldynado said. "When was the last time you washed that armpit you have thrust in my face?"

"My armpit wouldn't be so close if you weren't taking up so much room. Did you have to eat *three* servings of Basilard's meal?"

"Yes, those were the most excellent eel filets I've ever had. And I don't know what those dumpling things were, but they were also fabulous."

Though the men had insisted on it, Amaranthe felt guilty sitting in a seat while Yara, Sespian, and the rest of the team crowded the specimen-storage area behind her. Shoulder-to-shoulder and backs bent,

they were constantly clunking body parts against the exposed pipes and the overhead hatch. Weapons and rucksacks full of lanterns, rope, and other gear they'd salvaged from the steamboat further cluttered the space. Only Basilard had arm-room, but he'd had to volunteer for the task of cranking the human-powered engine to receive it. Interestingly, Sergeant Yara, who stood on Maldynado's other side, hadn't voiced any complaints about "touching."

"The dumplings *were* good," Sespian said, speaking for the first time since everyone had crammed into the vessel.

Basilard paused his cranking for long enough to offer a half bow to his peers.

Though he could barely move his arms in the limited space, Sespian hesitantly signed, *You good chef.*

Basilard's eyes widened. That must have been the first time Sespian signed something to him. It tickled Amaranthe to see that he'd been paying attention and trying to learn some of the hand code. After Basilard's surprise wore off, he offered another half-bow, this time to Sespian alone.

"We're entering the trapezoidal area," Sicarius said.

Amaranthe faced front again though she hoped Sicarius had seen the exchange—in particular that Sespian was willing to get to know even the most brutish-looking member of the group. Granted, Basilard had a gentle soul beneath the scars, but the fledging camaraderie ought to give Sicarius hope.

Sicarius nudged the vehicle to the left, toward a wide, dark area in the lake floor.

"How well do you know these waters, Maldynado?" Amaranthe asked.

"I swam and fished out here as a kid, but, as far as I know, nobody in the family has been down since I was twelve or thirteen. More than fifteen years."

"You never explored beneath the surface?" Amaranthe leaned forward as their vehicle's treads rolled closer to the dark area. Fish and eels swam through the light seeping down from above.

"No diving suits in the boathouse," Maldynado said.

"You mean you didn't go spelunking in any caves down here?" Akstyr snickered.

When more snickers answered his, Amaranthe peered over her shoulder at the tightly packed men. Books and Basilard wore identical smirks. Maldynado rolled his eyes upward while a blush colored Yara's cheeks.

"I think we missed a joke," Amaranthe told Sicarius.

Without bothering to glance at the men, Sicarius lifted a hand from the throttle. "We can't go farther in this craft."

They had crawled to the lip of a drop-off. A sharp drop-off. Utter blackness lay below. The bottom might be dozens of feet down or hundreds. It reminded Amaranthe of the area in the lake back home that had hidden that underwater laboratory.

"No chance of exploring down there?" Amaranthe asked.

"This is pure imperial technology," Books said, "with no magical enhancements. It appears to have been designed for operation in the lake's littoral zone. The increased water pressure beyond more than fifty or one hundred feet down could result in leaks."

"It lacks buoyancy," Sicarius said. "We can't drive off a cliff."

"Ah, yes, that too," Books said.

"Given how often we end up cruising around on lake bottoms," Maldynado said, "perhaps diving suits should be part of our regular gear."

"Or we could get a submarine," Akstyr said. "That'd be golden. We could go anywhere there's water and nobody could find us."

"I don't think a submarine is in the budget," Amaranthe said.

"Why not? Don't we have all that money the emperor brought?" Akstyr lifted his head, clunking it on the ceiling. "Who has that money anyway? We didn't leave it on the steamboat, did we?"

Amaranthe twitched a shoulder. She'd never seen it.

"It's safely hidden," Sespian said.

Rocks crunched beneath them as Sicarius turned the craft around.

"That's good," Maldynado said. "We don't want imperial money to be wasted. Extra funds should be set aside to hire a sculptor to immortalize our team in statue form."

"The team or you?" Yara asked.

"I'm thinking of everyone here," Maldynado said. "Don't imply I'm a more selfish lout than I am."

Sespian cleared his throat. "Is that some sort of illumination up ahead? Or simply sunlight from the surface?"

"No," Sicarius said.

Sespian looked at Amaranthe, the way he might if he needed a translation of Basilard's hand signs.

"He's a little selective in which questions he chooses to answer," Amaranthe said.

"I wouldn't mind a return to the surface," Books said. "Did you see that library full of books in the house? I'm certain some of them could help with my current project, a project that was severely derailed by that fire in the engine room. I was fortunate to get most of my paperwork out before the flames spread."

"Books was working on his *project* while we were being fired upon," Maldynado said, "and yet I'm the one who gets blamed for the crash."

Amaranthe had forgotten how much the men talked—and bickered. Part of her was glad to be back with them, but part of her missed the quiet of being alone with Sicarius.

"Maldynado," Amaranthe said, "why don't you give Basilard a break back there?"

Amaranthe thought he might object to being singled out for work, but Maldynado merely rolled up his sleeves and eased past Yara to take Basilard's place. Amaranthe wondered how much of his willingness to accept the task had to do with the way one's forearm muscles tended to flex and ripple while manning the crank. Yara's gaze *did* follow him. Yes, Amaranthe would have to give up on her hope of setting Yara up with Sespian.

"There *is* light over there," Akstyr said. "I see it too."

Though Sicarius had been ambiguous with his answers, he had turned the vessel in the direction Sespian had noticed. A rocky cliff dropped down from the surface before leveling out where it met the lake floor. Amaranthe recognized the cliff; she'd stood on the top when checking out the hot springs above. The water bent and contorted the light, but it seemed to be leaking from a fissure.

The vehicle rumbled closer until Sicarius stopped it at the base of the cliff.

"The light may simply be the sun filtering through from an opening above," Books said.

"What sun?" Akstyr asked. "It was raining harder than a pissing donkey by the time Am'ranthe picked us up."

"Lovely imagery," Books murmured.

"It's wider than it looked from back there." Amaranthe waved toward the fissure. "Think we can drive inside?"

Sicarius slanted her one of his unreadable looks.

"What?" All right, *wider* wasn't the same thing as *wide*, but Amaranthe didn't think the opening was that narrow. Just because it twisted and turned and one couldn't see anything except darkness and rock ahead...

"I was wondering who would get blamed should the vehicle crash," Sicarius said.

A few silent heartbeats skipped past before Akstyr whispered, "Was that a joke? Did he make a joke?"

"Nah," Maldynado whispered back, "he doesn't know how to do that." He raised his voice and said, "It's been my experience that it's never the woman's fault."

"That is my concern." Sicarius nudged the vehicle forward and gripped the control wheel.

Amaranthe smiled as they crept into the fissure, inching across a bottom that had changed from rocks to sand. "It's good to have the team back together."

"Says the woman who has her own seat and isn't wearing Basilard's elbow on her belt," Books said.

Busy watching their progress through the fissure, Amaranthe didn't see if Basilard signed a response, but something prompted a few snickers from the men.

Minutes passed as Sicarius guided the vehicle through a zigzag of turns that made a lightning bolt seem straight. They were climbing slightly, and Amaranthe wondered if this might be a secret passage up the inside of the mountain, one that would take them all the way to some hidden entrance below the house.

"Are you *sure* you didn't know about this?" Amaranthe asked Maldynado.

"Uh uh."

"If this passage comes up beneath your bed, we're going to have trouble believing you."

"The only thing beneath his bed is a stack of smutty Lady Dourcrest books," Yara said.

"That's not true." The crank stopped rasping as Maldynado stood straight, clunking his head on the ceiling. "Actually... that might be true. I was eleven or twelve the last time we came down here. That's about the age I got curious about biological matters."

"*Very* curious if all the dog-eared pages are an indicator," Yara said.

"Lady Dourcrest," Books said. "Such erudite literature."

"They're sure to be classics," Maldynado said, then poked Yara. "What were you doing snooping around in my room anyway? You must find me fascinating if you thought to research my childhood."

Yara sniffed. "I was merely searching for secret passages, as I was instructed."

"Continue cranking." Sicarius's voice cut through the chatter like a knife slicing butter.

Maldynado grumbled something and went back to work. The vehicle continued to climb, the light growing brighter as it advanced. The walls lining the fissure changed from the water-eroded edges of a natural formation to the jagged contours of something carved out by men. The passage straightened as well.

Without warning, Sicarius halted. Though they hadn't been going fast, the abruptness threw Amaranthe forward in her seat, and she had to brace herself with a hand on the controls. An inch of air had appeared at the top of the viewing window. Uh oh. That meant the access hatch and a foot of the vehicle's domed hull would be visible above the water if anyone was out there to see it.

"There are four people on a ledge," Akstyr said, his voice stiff with the concentration he used for applying the mental sciences. "And a bunch of other things with us in the water."

"*Things?*" Amaranthe asked, envisioning giant lake monsters.

"Inanimate objects, I think. Boats maybe. Or—"

"Submarines." Sicarius pointed at something ahead and to the right of them.

The dark shape was hard to make out, but Amaranthe agreed that it might be the hull of a submerged vessel.

"Are the people armed?" Sicarius asked.

"I can't tell," Akstyr said. "Maybe."

"There's four of them and... uh... seven of us," Maldynado said.

"Your counting skills are impressive," Books said. "Are you volunteering to go first? Because we can only pop out of this sardine tin one at a time."

"My job is to turn the crank," Maldynado said. "I can't be spared for target practice."

A thump sounded on the roof. Sicarius leaped from the controls, somehow finding a spot to land where he faced the hatch. His black dagger appeared in his right hand, a loaded pistol in his left. The latter he pointed at the hatch.

Three bangs sounded. Not bangs, Amaranthe realized. Knocks.

"Do we answer that?" Books whispered.

"Uhm." This was so unlike what Amaranthe had expected—not that she'd known what to expect—that she didn't know what to say or do. She met Sespian's eyes, wondering if she should defer to the emperor—or, more specifically, wondering if said emperor had a plan.

Sespian opened his mouth, but whoever was standing on the hatch spoke first.

"Go forward fifteen meters," came a man's muffled voice. "Then turn right after the black submarine and dock at the end of the row."

Sicarius looked to Amaranthe instead of Sespian for instructions.

"Better do as the man says." She waved him back to his seat.

"We're not *supposed* to be expected," Sespian murmured.

"Not cordially expected anyway," Books said.

Sicarius pressed the pistol into Amaranthe's hand and returned to the controls. As he maneuvered their craft, following the directions, other vessels came into view. Akstyr was right. They were all submarines. Or at least, all underwater conveyances of some kind. There was no uniformity amongst the eclectic designs, and Amaranthe had the sense of looking at custom furnishings in a woodworking show. Or perhaps, she mused, custom-designed yachts for the wealthy. What if everyone except Maldynado's sister-in-law and those on the *Behemoth* had come down the river in these underwater crafts to ensure no one would witness their passing?

"Any reason why your sister-in-law wouldn't have one of these?" Amaranthe asked Maldynado.

"She's claustrophobic?"

"Are you asking her or telling her, you dolt?" Books said.

"Either way, I wasn't talking to you." Maldynado nodded to Amaranthe. "She *is* claustrophobic. There's a family rumor about her being unwilling to, ah, service my brother on conjugal visits when he was a young LT staying in the barracks. She found the tiny rooms too constricting."

"Thanks for the details," Amaranthe said. "I think."

"According to my network of trusted spies in the Imperial Barracks," Sespian said, "Mari Marblecrest was the only one likely to be tracked. Perhaps everyone else did have submarines crafted for this meeting."

"You have a trusted spy network, Sire?" Amaranthe asked, surprised he had managed to find allies amongst all the Forge infiltrators. "It's good that you've been able to suss out loyal people and make use of them."

"Actually... I'm the network. I spy by crawling through the old hypocaust ducts in the Barracks. In my socks. So as not to make noise." Sespian studied the floor. "I haven't particularly trusted my ability to choose loyal people since the debacle with Lieutenant Dunn."

Amaranthe didn't know if she'd met that lieutenant, but he might have been the one who'd tricked Sespian into entering Larocka's clutches the winter before.

"We have arrived at the designated docking space," Sicarius said.

Something bumped into their craft, rocking it to the side. If not for a control lever she could grasp, Amaranthe might have ended up in Sicarius's lap.

"What was that?" Maldynado asked.

A dark shadow swam across the front of the craft, blotting out the view for a moment. It was too close to identify features, but the length made Amaranthe think of those eels Basilard had caught and frizzled up. Except this had been far too large to fit into a frying pan.

"The welcoming committee?" Amaranthe suggested.

Three more knocks struck the hatch. Maybe it was her imagination, but they sounded rushed and nervous this time.

"I'll stick my head out first." Amaranthe looked for a place to tuck the pistol, but her dress lacked a belt. She settled for tucking it into an apron pocket and wondered if any other mercenary in history had charged into battle wearing a farmwife's smock. "If they're expecting more people, maybe they'll think I'm a Forge member arriving late."

"Or they'll recognize you and shoot you," Sicarius said.

Amaranthe patted his arm. "Your cheery optimism always bolsters my spirit."

Sespian snorted.

Amaranthe slipped out of the seat and grabbed the wheel that controlled the hatch's locking mechanism. It squeaked as she turned it. A couple of footfalls sounded. Their greeter stepping off the hatch? There wasn't much room for walking around on top of the sphere-shaped vessel.

Amaranthe opened the hatch an inch. "Hello?"

Their vehicle lacked a ladder, so Amaranthe would have to fling the hatch open before she could pull herself out. She didn't want to expose the interior though. Maybe she could—

Hands gripped her waist, hoisting her until her head was level with the hole. That worked.

"Thank you, Basilard," Amaranthe whispered.

"State your name," a man said. A pair of shiny black boots waited to the side of the hatch.

"Retta," Amaranthe said.

"You're not on the list."

"I work for Ms. Worgavic. I'm the one who flies the…" Amaranthe groped through her memories for the official name of the *Behemoth*. "Are you aware of the *Ortarh Ortak?* There's a problem on board. I need to speak with Ms. Worgavic immediately."

The greeter, or whatever he was, did not answer. Beneath her, the men shifted as much as they could in the confined space. More than one pistol had appeared. Sicarius crouched on his seat, one foot on the backrest as he faced the hatch, a throwing knife in hand.

Hoping to see more of the area, Amaranthe eased her head as high as she could without opening the hatch farther. A wide stone ledge rose on the other side of the pool, and it supported four sets of legs wearing shiny black boots and facing in her direction. She couldn't see the men's upper bodies, or what weapons they might hold in their arms, but she had no trouble making out belts laden with ammunition pouches. No powder tins hung on those belts, so she assumed the ammo was for the new multi-shot rifles.

Waves undulated across the surface of the pool. A few feet away, something black broke the surface. Amaranthe glimpsed a fin, a large fin, before it disappeared beneath the water.

"Show yourself," the man above said.

Amaranthe lifted the hatch a few more inches, hoping she could crawl out without revealing everyone inside. Unfortunately, the man had other ideas. Perhaps thinking he was helping her, he pulled the hatch the rest of the way open. Amaranthe grabbed the lip and scrambled out. Maybe if she got her feet under her quickly enough, she could block his view of the interior.

It didn't work. The man raised a shiny new rifle and blurted, "There's a bunch of—"

A hand gripped his ankle and yanked him into the vehicle. A flying elbow caught Amaranthe in the ribs, and she barely avoided tumbling into the water. She scarcely had time to note a floating dock arranged in an X across the pool, with submarines tied up alongside it, before four rifles were being lifted in her direction.

Amaranthe had only a split second to decide what to do. She *should* have jumped back down into their craft to avoid being shot, but, with some deluded notion that she needed to draw fire so the men could climb out, she leaped off the craft and onto the dock. She sprinted several meters and, anticipating a barrage of gunfire, dove off the backside, landing on the square hatch of a long, tube-shaped submarine. She winced when she came down on one of her bruise collections, but managed to yank her pistol out anyway.

The dock hid the men from view—and, Amaranthe hoped, provided an obstacle they couldn't shoot her through. When a couple of heartbeats passed without gunshots, she lifted her eyes over the level of the wood planks. Nobody shot her. Three of the men who had been standing on the ledge were lying on it now. The fourth had fallen into the pool. He paddled one-armed, trying to reach solid ground again, though pain contorted his face. Something silver stuck out of the front of his shoulder. Just as he found a grip on the ledge, the water stirred next to him. Amaranthe blinked, and he was gone, pulled beneath the surface. Bubbles floated up, but nothing except stillness followed. She realized the men on the ledge weren't moving and rose to her knees.

Sicarius stepped into view on the dock. He lowered a hand toward her. Amaranthe accepted it, letting him pull her up beside him. Akstyr was sticking halfway out of their vehicle, staring at the downed men on the ledge.

He turned his stare to Sicarius. "I didn't know you could do that."

Without comment, Sicarius jogged off the dock and circled around to check the men. No, not to "check" them. To verify that they were dead and to pull his throwing knives out of their chests.

"He popped up and threw all four at once," Akstyr said. "Two in each hand. I didn't know that was possible."

Sicarius gave Amaranthe a look, like he might be concerned that she'd chastise him for the deaths, but how could she? He'd likely saved her life—as usual—and he'd even kept the men from firing. She had no idea how far away this meeting place was, but she doubted it was so distant that people there wouldn't hear gunshots fired in the parking pool.

"See if there's anyone else nearby that we need to worry about, please," Amaranthe told Sicarius.

He continued along the ledge toward a pair of tunnels. The under-water cavern had a twelve- or fifteen-foot ceiling, all chipped and hewn by tools rather than by nature. Gold-gilded lamps burned on the walls and in holders on the dock, spreading light about the chamber. At least twenty other submarines, or other types of underwater conveyances, were tied up in the wide pool, a variety of hatch styles and paint jobs on display in the portions that peeped above the water.

Someone jostled Akstyr from below.

"As much as we appreciate the view of your scrawny backside," Maldynado called up, "we'd like to get out."

Akstyr scrambled onto the dock.

"Be careful climbing up here," Amaranthe said. "Whatever that thing in the water is, it finds humans tasty."

"Joy," Books said.

As the men were climbing out, a creak sounded behind Amaranthe. A hatch lifted, and a pair of eyes came into view. She dropped to a knee and aimed the pistol between those eyes.

"Nothing going on out here, friend," she said, guessing this was someone's servant or pilot left behind to watch the craft. "I suggest you lower that hatch and forget you saw us."

The eyes sank out of view. Clanks drifted from within the man's craft, as he not only shut himself in but bolted a lock or two.

"I have to say you're looking particularly grim and serious today, boss," Maldynado said.

He and the others were lined up on the dock behind her. Everyone carried weapons, Sespian included. Her team looked ready for a fight.

"It's been a grim couple of weeks," Amaranthe said. "Sire, any orders? Is there a way you have planned to go about this?"

"Planned?" Sespian pushed a hand through his pale brown hair. "My plans fell over a cliff more than a week ago. I'm still hoping to learn what Forge is up to—besides attempting to kill me and replace me with a warrior-caste puppet—but I don't know how plausible that is at this point."

Amaranthe lifted a shoulder. "They didn't seem to know we were coming. Not these guards anyway. It might be useful to question someone." She pointed toward the open hatch of their vehicle. "Is the first man still...?"

"He's alive," Maldynado said. "Not entirely conscious though. Questioning might be hard."

"Well, there are only two tunnels." As long as those two didn't branch into fifty more, Amaranthe figured they had decent odds of picking one that would lead them to the Forge people. Sicarius had already disappeared into one. "Let's see what we can find."

She led the team off the dock. She was about to ask if anyone had seen which tunnel Sicarius had gone down when he emerged from the closest one.

"Lodging, baths, and kitchens are in that direction," he said.

"Not tents and campfire pits, I'm guessing," Amaranthe said.

"Forty separate domiciles carved into the stone walls, each with room for servants."

"Under *my* family's island?" Maldynado asked.

"Some of it is under the lake," Sicarius said.

"It must have taken them years to hollow all of this out. I can't believe my parents didn't know. Or, if they knew all along… that's hard to believe too. How *long* have these people been scheming?"

"It's been ten years since I studied under Ms. Worgavic," Amaranthe said, "and, if she recruited one of my classmates to learn the ancient technology, she must have known about it for at least that long." At the round of blank looks the men gave her, Amaranthe remembered that she'd spoken of her old teacher only to Sicarius. "I'll explain later. Forge has been a number of years in the making."

"I'll scout ahead," Sicarius said.

He disappeared into the second tunnel without waiting for an acknowledgment.

"Was that a stay-here order or an invitation to follow?" Sespian asked.

Amaranthe eyed the submarine-filled pool. "Either way, we shouldn't linger here. Since the guards didn't shoot us as soon as we popped up, they must have been expecting at least one more party to arrive."

"Good point."

Amaranthe led the team into the tunnel Sicarius had chosen. It angled downward. More gold-gilded lamps lined the chiseled black walls, each one worth more than an enforcer's annual salary. The display of wealth couldn't take away from the fact that the team was walking through a dank, underground—no, under *lake*—passage. Dampness clung to the walls, and a musty smell floated in the air. At least the tunnel was tall and broad with an even floor one could have driven a truck over.

As they rounded a bend, Books touched the porous black stone. "You said they'd acquired the *mining* rights? I haven't noticed any promising veins."

"Or promising anything," Maldynado said. "This place is dreary."

Up ahead, Sicarius glided out from behind another bend.

"The tunnel slopes steeply downward and ends at two closed double doors," he said. "There are forty people waiting in a chamber outside, servants, I believe."

"*Forty?*" Amaranthe asked. How were they supposed to sneak past forty people to spy on the meeting? "Any other tunnels that branch off along the way?"

"Many."

Ugh. *Many* tunnels was as bad as forty people. Unless there was a handy map somewhere that proclaimed, "Spying Balcony this way," Amaranthe feared they'd either get lost or spend so much time wandering that someone would notice the missing dock security men.

Sicarius tilted his head, indicating the team should follow. They soon reached the first of the tunnel branches he'd mentioned, and he paused in front of it. "There are four more before the doors. This is the only one that is unlit."

Amaranthe peered into the darkness. The passage might lead to a secret nobody was meant to explore, or it might lead to a storage closet. Though she didn't care for the idea of splitting up her team, especially when she had no idea how long these side tunnels might extend, all they needed was for one person to make it within earshot of this meeting.

"Let's split up," Amaranthe said. "Maldynado and Yara—"

Sicarius jerked up a hand. Voices drifted down the passage from somewhere ahead, voices that were drawing nearer.

Amaranthe pointed at the tunnel. *Never mind. We'll all check this one.*

She hustled into the passage, but Sicarius, before they'd gone beyond the influence of the light, waved the others onward and drew Amaranthe aside.

*Do you want me to keep them from reaching the dock?*

*By tying and gagging them?* Amaranthe asked, well aware that these might simply be servants with little to do with their employers' schemes.

*Yes. I will find a dark nook in which to store them.*

Only Sicarius would think of a person as something to "store." So long as he didn't kill anyone.

*Do it*, Amaranthe signed.

More aware than ever of the limited time, Amaranthe hurried into the darkness to catch up with the others. After groping around a couple of bends, the walls disappeared on both sides. A draft caressed her cheek. They must have entered a larger space.

A soft scrape sounded, and a match flared to life. Basilard, his pack open at his feet, lit a lantern.

Brass and steel glinted in the shadows. Basilard moved in that direction, lifting the lantern. The small flame revealed a row of sturdy tunnel boring machines. Eight steam lorries with open cargo beds occupied a second row.

"The carriage house?" Amaranthe mused.

Books gazed toward the rocky ceiling. "It was reckless of them to hollow out these big tunnels with the lake right above. A single hole, or any seismic activity in the area, and water would flood the entire complex. It's hard to believe they'd do all this just to create a secret meeting place."

"We can ask them what they were thinking if they capture us," Amaranthe said.

"If that's the only way to find out, I can live with not knowing," Yara said.

"Yes." Maldynado gave Amaranthe a pat on the back. "It doesn't look like they treat their prisoners well."

Everyone turned sympathetic eyes toward Amaranthe. She couldn't fault her team for their sympathy, but she'd rather forget the entire experience, or at least push it to the back of her thoughts and move on.

Perhaps sensing her discomfort, Maldynado added, "If that hat you were wearing earlier is an example of the type of clothing they force their prisoners to wear, I truly couldn't withstand such exquisite torture."

Amaranthe decided not to mention that she'd been nude. She didn't need anyone speculating about that.

A tunnel left the vehicle chamber on the far side, and Amaranthe was of a mind to keep exploring—and put this conversation out of its misery—but Sicarius hadn't rejoined them yet. She walked around the area, searching for more clues as to what Forge had been doing down there. The "carriage house" lacked any sort of symmetry; it didn't seem to have been excavated with any design or purpose in mind. It was more like people had simply been digging, looking for something, and had stopped when they'd found it.

"Oh," Amaranthe said.

Once again, all eyes swiveled in her direction, this time with curiosity.

"Sire," Amaranthe asked, "do you still have that black whatchamacallit? The thing for tracking?"

"Yes." Sespian removed a knapsack and poked through a tangle of socks and shirts.

Amaranthe thought of the meticulous way Sicarius packed his clothing and gear. Fastidiousness must not be hereditary.

"Nobody here knows how to use it, though." Sespian finally found the egg-shaped device and handed it to her.

Amaranthe held it and rotated it, pointing it in different directions. "No noticeable change. Too bad. I thought it might glow or get warm or something. Unless they've removed everything and there's nothing left around."

"Uh, boss," Maldynado said, "did you forget something? Like to explain that yarn ball of musings rolling around in your mind?"

"Sicarius said he first encountered this technology at an archaeological dig site. Maybe someone in Forge found this, figured out how to use it, and—"

"Employed it as a tuning fork that led them here?" Books nodded. "Yes, of course."

"We had better press on," Sespian said. "Time isn't on our side."

Yes, he'd given up much to come down here, so he'd be even more aware of the need to hurry. Sicarius hadn't rejoined them yet, but Amaranthe headed for the tunnel on the far side anyway. She trusted him to find them again.

They'd only gone a few meters when a small alcove opened to one side. An ordinary wooden table sat in it, providing a resting place for five extraordinary black cubes.

"I guess there are artifacts left around, after all," Amaranthe said.

Akstyr stuck a finger out toward one of the cubes.

"Don't touch them!" Sicarius barked, jogging out of the tunnel behind them.

Everyone jumped, both at his abrupt appearance and at the shout. Amaranthe couldn't remember ever hearing him shout, and he'd certainly never let that much urgency seep into his voice, not that she'd heard.

"Back away," Sicarius said, his tone calmer, though it left no doubt that he was giving an order.

Akstyr, who had frozen at his initial shout, lowered his arm and took an exaggerated step in reverse.

"We should go back," Sicarius told Amaranthe.

"Because these are…" She waved toward the table.

"Deadly. And indestructible with the gear we have." His gaze flicked toward the cubes. "They fly. And incinerate you."

"Really?" Akstyr sounded more intrigued than alarmed.

"If they're here to guard the tunnel," Sespian said, "perhaps that's a sign that we're going in the right direction."

"How're they activated?" Amaranthe asked.

"I don't know," Sicarius said, "but if we're standing here when they are, we'll all be dead."

Amaranthe pushed a few stray strands of hair behind her ears. The intensity in Sicarius's eyes made her believe that obeying him would be a good idea, but Sespian stepped past her.

"We'll keep going," he said. "If they're that deadly, it won't matter if we're behind them or in front of them, right? We'll have to hope they don't get activated."

Sicarius's eyes grew grim. Amaranthe supposed it wasn't the time to point out that, if he'd had a certain discussion with Sespian by now, he could legitimately threaten to turn the young man over his knee for a spanking instead of having to succumb to orders he found distasteful.

Despite the emperor's announcement that they'd keep going, Yara and the men looked to Amaranthe before moving. Sespian's lips flattened. Amaranthe didn't want him to feel slighted, so was quick to say, "As you wish, Sire."

Sespian took Basilard's lantern and looked like he meant to lead the way, but Sicarius slipped into the tunnel ahead of him. As they traveled deeper, the passage continued to slope downward. Soft hisses grew audible, and heated currents stirred the air. In spots, cracks emitted tendrils of steam. Openings appeared in the walls, ceiling, and occasionally the floor. Vents? Most of them were fist-sized, but they passed a few holes large enough that one might crawl inside.

"Are we under the lake?" Amaranthe whispered. Thanks to the bends and turns, she'd lost her sense of direction.

"Yes." Sicarius stopped beside one of the largest vents they'd seen and peered inside.

"Does it go anywhere?" If the team crawled into a maze of vents, Amaranthe would lose not only her sense of direction but herself as well. Still, if there was a chance one led to the meeting room…

Without responding, Sicarius shimmied into the vent, his boots soon disappearing from sight.

"We're not supposed to follow him, are we?" Maldynado asked. "I don't think I'd fit. I'm a bigger man than him." He propped a hand on his waist, fingers pointed downward, and added, "In *all* senses of the word."

Yara snorted.

Basilard signed, *Should you say things like that when he might still be in earshot?*

"Er." Maldynado dropped his hand. "Perhaps not."

Sicarius's head popped out of the vent, cobwebs cloaking his short hair. "This way. Do not bring the light." He slithered into the main tunnel long enough to turn around. Before heading back in, he paused to add, "Someone should stand watch, but there's room for everyone," with a dismissive glance toward Maldynado.

After he disappeared again, Maldynado muttered, "I may be in trouble when our training exercises start up again."

Basilard signed, *My grandfather used to say bees are worth braving for their honey, but only fools delve into a hornets' nest.*

Amaranthe, not certain Sicarius would stop to ensure everyone had followed him, didn't wait to see where the conversation would go. "Who wants to stay and stand—"

"Me," Books said.

Amaranthe had figured he wouldn't be enthused about crawling into that tight vent, but she couldn't agree with the choice. "If we do find a way to spy on the Forge people, we may need you to help us figure out what they're talking about."

"Oh." Books's shoulders drooped. "Of course."

"I'll stay," Akstyr said.

"Good," Amaranthe said. "Maldynado, you and your big body back him up, please. If people come, hide. If deadly technology comes… warn us somehow, please."

"And then hide?" Akstyr asked.

"Precisely."

Maldynado smirked. Amaranthe frowned at him to let him know she meant the bit about hiding. She hadn't seen anything worry Sicarius

the way those black cubes had, not even the deadly makarovi or Arbitan Losk's soul construct.

Amaranthe crawled into the vent on her hands and knees. She trusted that Sicarius wouldn't take them somewhere they'd all get stuck, but it was hard not to feel the panic of claustrophobia in the utter darkness of the tight passage. Especially after his warning about those cubes. This would be an awful place to get trapped.

The uneven walls jabbed at her shoulders, and she had to run a hand along the ceiling to locate protuberances before her head smacked against them. At times she had to drop to her belly to avoid them. The incline grew steeper, evoking images of sliding backward and crashing into the men below. Scuffles and grunts floated up from behind her as the rest of the team followed. Sicarius didn't make a sound. He might have been five feet in front of her or fifty.

Whispers of hot air flowed from cracks and heated the rock beneath Amaranthe's hands. Unlike the machine-hewn tunnels below, the vent had the rounded contours of a passage carved by water over thousands of years. She tried not to think about what would happen if a crack opened up in the lake floor, one that would allow water to enter the cavity once again.

"Just keep climbing," she muttered.

\* \* \* \* \*

Maldynado leaned against the wall next to the vent, the lantern dangling from his arm. If *he* were the one crawling into a black shaft of indeterminate length, he would have taken a light with him.

A few feet away, Akstyr sat cross-legged on the floor, eyes closed, doing whatever it was fledgling wizards did when they were supposed to be on watch. Maldynado didn't know how much time had passed since the others had disappeared up the hole, but it had been a while. He thought of Yara's words about statues and who deserved them. Maybe he ought to do more than stand around.

"Stay here, and pay attention," Maldynado said. "I'm going to check ahead, see if there's anything useful."

Akstyr opened an eye. "You mean you're going to look for good hiding places?"

"Ah, sure."

Maldynado dug a second lantern out of someone's pack, lit it for Akstyr, then headed deeper into the tunnel with the other light. More of those vents, appearing at all different levels, dotted the walls. He wondered if they were a result of water passing through or the remnants of lava flows. He seemed to remember some vague trivia about the lake being part of an extinct volcano.

After passing through two excavated chambers with nothing in them, Maldynado came to another vehicle storage area. This one held a steamroller and a couple of haulers. A workstation scattered with boxes and parts lined one rock wall. He perused the latter, though he wasn't sure what he was looking for. Something that might prove useful if some lackey stumbled across the team and sounded an alarm. Nothing in the work area inspired him, but the steamroller did draw his eye more than once. The horizontal rolling tube at its front was taller than he was. He smirked as he imagined barreling through the tunnels, rolling over any Forge minions who dared to stand in the path with guns raised.

Maldynado started to dismiss the thought, but propped a fist on his hip. "Enh, why not?"

Given how long it took to fire up a steam engine, one couldn't simply grab a truck on a whim. Why not start it now, and if the team didn't end up needing it, who cared? Forge could afford to waste a few pounds of coal.

The smirk returned as Maldynado crawled about the machine, checking fuel and water reserves. He decided it wasn't a sign of immaturity that he found himself tickled by the idea of Forge people flinging themselves out of the way to avoid being flattened. They'd tortured Amaranthe after all. He was just returning the favor.

# CHAPTER 22

AMARANTHE WAS UTTERLY AND HOPELESSLY lost. Sweat beaded on her forehead and dripped down the sides of her face. The vent had crossed other vents, widening and then narrowing again, as it continued an upward path. How far upward, she didn't know, but she worried that they'd come out on one of the Marblecrest beaches instead of anywhere useful.

Her knuckles brushed against something that wasn't as hard as the surrounding rock. Sicarius's foot? It moved before she could be certain. Thinking of that giant eel in the pool, she *hoped* it had only been his foot.

Faint voices drifted to Amaranthe's ears. At first, she thought they came from the men behind her, but the sounds were farther away than that. Nervous excitement ran through her body. Maybe they were going to succeed at finding a spy hole after all.

A draft brushed her face, a faint sulfuric scent hanging in the air. Maybe it was her imagination, but it didn't seem as warm as the earlier drafts. As Amaranthe continued forward, the blackness lightened to gray. The vent opened onto a rocky shelf with three or four feet of clearance overhead. A ledge with a drop-off was to the right. She couldn't see what lay at the bottom, but the light came from that direction.

Sicarius, belly-down on the far end of the shelf, faced the open area. He waved for her to join him. The shelf was less than ten feet wide and lacked any other exits. Amaranthe *thought* her team might fit if they lined themselves up with Sicarius and didn't mind temporarily storing their elbows in each other's pockets. Turning around and climbing back out again wouldn't happen quickly. She crawled toward Sicarius, but halted when she glimpsed what lay beyond the drop-off.

The cavernous chamber that opened below them was so large that she felt as if she was perched on the rim of a volcano. The crater sloped inward and downward on all sides, its porous rock shells containing more gaps than Mangdorian bubble cheese. The team's shelf was not unique.

At the bottom of the crater, a polished black-tile floor gleamed beneath dozens of lamps. It held a circle of desks three tiers deep. Most of the men and women occupying the seats possessed the olive to bronze skin of Turgonians, but there were a few foreigners as well, some with features as pale as Basilard's and others with flesh almost as dark as the vent Amaranthe had just left. Each desk held an open binder with a stack of papers and a pen holder. The double doors Sicarius had mentioned stood closed at the end of a short access tunnel recessed into the concave walls. In the center of the desk circle, a man was in the process of leaving the floor to sit down while a woman in a hand-tailored skirt and jacket replaced him.

Someone touched Amaranthe, reminding her that she'd have to scoot to the end so the others could squeeze in. She crawled over to Sicarius and lay down on her stomach beside him. His eyes were toward the floor, his face unreadable, and she imagined him studying each person, gauging the threat.

"Fascinating," Books murmured as he settled in next to Amaranthe. "This must be where they found the aircraft."

"Oh, of course," Amaranthe said. It was obvious once he had said it. If that tracking tool had a way of conveying the magnitude of the artifact it was pointing to, Retta, or whoever had originally mastered the device, must have been giddy at the idea of unearthing something so large. To think, while Amaranthe had been going to the enforcer academy and learning how to put men into joint locks, one of her old schoolmates had been mastering the language and technology of an ancient, alien race and learning how to, among other things, fly. Amaranthe tried not to feel like an underachiever.

Sicarius lifted a finger, directing her attention upward.

Some twenty feet above them, a clear convex ceiling served as a window into the lake. Enough light filtered down from the surface to reveal schools of fish drifting past.

"How is that possible?" Amaranthe whispered. Other than the crater walls themselves, the hundreds-of-feet-wide "window" lacked visible support. It couldn't possibly be made from glass.

Sicarius shook his head once.

"Thank you for allowing me to speak, my colleagues," the woman in the center of the circle said, the acoustics of the chamber making her voice easy to hear. Amaranthe made a note to limit her own words. "And thank you, Thovic, for explaining our plans to move the ranmya from a gold-backed currency into a fiat money system."

Sespian had settled in on the other side of Books, and his head jerked up. Books's eyes, too, sharpened.

"I agree with my colleague that we may need to outlaw the ownership of gold in order to force acceptance by the people. While paper money has become commonplace in the major cities, it's still viewed with suspicion in smaller areas, and the warrior caste are notoriously hard to sway to new ideas."

"New ideas?" Books scoffed. "The Minyar Empire tried a fiat currency centuries ago, and it played a role in their collapse."

"Our proposition will solve the empire's current money shortage problems," the speaker said, waving toward the binders, "without requiring draconian tax increases that might bestir citizens to revolt. The common man will be unaware of how inflation works, so it'll act as a hidden tax that benefits the government, allowing Turgonia to maintain its expansive military and infrastructure."

Amaranthe hadn't realized the empire might be in trouble financially. She supposed the slowdown in colonization and outright usurpation in the last fifty years had meant fewer fresh resources to plunder. Certainly industry was still running strong, but much of that belonged in private hands, and Turgonia *did* have a lot of resources to maintain. She peered past Books to Sespian. He must know all about Turgonia's current state of affairs. Like Books, Sespian was focused on the speaker. No, he didn't appear surprised by the talk of financial difficulties, though a wrinkle of concentration drew his eyebrows together, as if he might not have considered manipulating the money supply as a solution. Not surprising. Historically, Turgonian emperors had solved financial problems by conquering someone new.

"Of course," the speaker said, "the government is only a concern of ours insofar as we can profit from it. Our plan is to control the money-creation system, ensuring that we benefit handsomely."

Sicarius looked at Amaranthe. She wasn't sure if it was a questioning look or not—he often surprised her with his versatility and knowledge, so she wouldn't put it past him to have a handle on economics. The history of currency was fairly esoteric information, however, and she couldn't imagine that Hollowcrest had felt the need to include it in his studies. She had only a basic understanding herself and suspected she'd be asking Books for clarification.

"Right now," Amaranthe whispered, "ranmya notes say they're redeemable for gold or silver, depending on the denomination. If that backing is taken away, the only reason paper money would continue to have value would be because the government said so. Because there'd be no finite resource limiting the amount of money in circulation, the government could, and likely would, print more as it needed more, and that would lead to inflation. Prices would appear to go up year after year, though it'd actually be a case of the value of the existing currency being diluted so that it'd be worth less and less. The average person would suffer because his or her buying power would be eroded." Amaranthe glanced at Books, hoping he'd nod to indicate she was getting her information right—it'd been ten years since her classes with Ms. Worgavic, after all—but his eyes were focused on the speaker below. Figuring she had better wrap up and listen as well, Amaranthe finished her explanation with, "Those who *gain* from the process are those at the source, those who have their hands on the currency first, spending it as it's printed, before the expansion of the money supply dilutes the value of each note."

During Amaranthe's speech, Sicarius's expression never changed. At the end, he looked to Books and asked, "They're not talking about establishing a central bank, correct? They seek to create a private banking cartel that counts the throne as its biggest customer?"

"Yes." Books lifted a finger to his lips and pointed toward the floor.

Amaranthe blushed, realizing Sicarius hadn't needed her explanation. His look had probably meant he'd been wondering if *she* knew what was going on. She hunched down and focused on the woman below.

"As many of you in banking know," the speaker was saying, "our industry hasn't been exceedingly profitable in the past. Business mavens are seeing a time of fantastic profits, however, by getting rid of competition and working together to fix prices at levels acceptable to profit margins."

"At levels more expensive to consumers," Books muttered.

"I propose we do something similar with banking," the speaker said. "By creating a banking system that handles the creation of money in the empire, we can then handle all the loans that are made, including the loaning of money to the government. Currently, businesses are doing well, too well, and the trend is toward private capitalization. They haven't needed our loans, but if we can lower interest rates to make loans more appealing… Well, in the current system, that's not possible, but if money is no longer backed by anything, and we can simply create more when we need it, then we can make interest rates as low as we wish and still earn a handsome profit."

A man in the back lifted a hand. "What makes you think the empire will go for this? The idea of a central bank is nothing new, but what government would give up control to private parties?"

Ms. Worgavic, who had a front row seat near the door, stood and straightened her jacket. Smiling, she said, "That's already been arranged. We're handing Ravido Marblecrest the throne, and, in exchange, he's agreed to this. I doubt he has any idea what the ramifications are, as he seemed quite relieved to be asked for nothing more, but this, my colleagues, is how we ensure our prosperity and the future prosperity of our children."

Amaranthe wondered if there was some Forge mandate about addressing everyone as "my colleague." She'd have to remember that nuance if she ever tried to infiltrate the group.

"Everyone in this room," Ms. Worgavic went on, "who wants to be a part of this is invited. You'll have a position on the board of directors, a hereditary position that guarantees that your descendants will be a part of this organization for decades and centuries to come. Your offspring will not only be very wealthy in this new world, but they will shape how it evolves."

The first speaker was nodding. "It starts with Turgonia, but it doesn't end there. With the ranmya as the world's reserve currency, it will only

be a matter of time before we have a foothold in every nation on the globe."

"Few if any of them appear to be armed," Sicarius whispered. "They left their servants and bodyguards outside."

It took Amaranthe a moment to realize where he was going with the comment. She scowled at him, though he didn't seem to notice. He had crawled closer to the edge and was eyeing the drop-off beneath them. It had to be more than forty feet to the polished floor, but, due to the concave curve, one might be able to slide down it without breaking one's leg. Still…

"You're not going to jump down there and murder fifty people," Amaranthe whispered.

"Forty-one," Sicarius said.

Of course, he would have counted every person. No doubt he'd judged the fitness and athleticism of all those people and also taken note of bulges beneath jackets that might represent concealed weapons.

Amaranthe gripped his arm and tilted her head to indicate they should move away from the edge to discuss. As clearly as she heard the speaker's voice, it was a foregone conclusion that overexcited whispers might float down to the floor as well.

Sespian was scowling at Sicarius, too, and he scooted back with them. "I forbid you to employ your assassination techniques here."

Good. She'd known Sespian wouldn't be interested in mass murder as a solution either, but she hadn't known that he'd stand up to Sicarius.

Two against one odds didn't bother Sicarius. He merely said, "Those people represent the head of Forge. If they don't walk out of this room, their plans die with them. Without their support, General Ravido will be—"

"No." Sespian chopped downward with his hand.

Amaranthe winced, fearing the word would carry.

Sespian caught himself and lowered his voice. "Don't you understand, assassin? If you must become a monster to defeat your enemies, then, even if you win, you lose."

Sicarius's gaze didn't waver under Sespian's criticism. "When leading human beings, virtue must be backed by steel, or someone will take advantage of you." He thrust his hand toward the chamber.

Amaranthe hoped Sicarius wasn't implying that Forge getting this far was due to some failing of Sespian's. He'd had less than a year of truly being in power, and the inception of this plot seemed to be at least a decade old, if not more.

"Or, worse," Sicarius continued, "you'll end up with a dagger in your back. You needn't bloody your own hands, Sire. This is why I was created."

Amaranthe winced at his word choice. Created. As if he were some machine that had been assembled simply to kill.

Sespian unclenched his jaw to say, "I would *never* employ someone like you. Employing someone else to bloody their hands on your behalf is even more deplorable than doing it yourself."

Amaranthe rubbed her face. They were supposed to be bonding, not sniping at each other. And this wasn't the time or place for either act. She lifted her hand, patting the air in a placating gesture, but neither man was looking at her. Books was still listening to the oration below, but Basilard and Yara were eyeing Sicarius and Sespian uneasily. Yara pointed at the two men, met Amaranthe's eyes, and lifted a finger to her lips.

"I know," Amaranthe mouthed.

"We don't need to resort to murder anyway," Sespian said. "Now we know who's involved and what they're planning. We can outmaneuver them at their own game. We can—"

"What I want to know," a man demanded from below, his voice echoing in the chamber, "is what you plan to do if Sespian Savarsin strolls back into the capital. Just because you've had him declared dead doesn't mean that he is. Nobody's found a body yet, have they?"

At the mention of the emperor's name, Sespian and Sicarius released each other from their intense stares. Both men scooted back to the edge in time to hear Ms. Worgavic's response.

"If he is still alive, it won't matter for long. He is *not* the son of Raumesys."

Sespian sucked in a startled breath, and he wasn't the only one. Papers rustled, and murmurs broke out below.

"We have it from a reputable source," Worgavic said, "and our people in the Imperial Barracks are collecting evidence as we speak. If Sespian appears in the capital again, we will publish everything."

Reputable source? It was all Amaranthe could do not to sputter the words. Who would consider a tortured outlaw a reputable source?

Though she was afraid to look at Sicarius, and draw Sespian's attention before facts had been stated, Amaranthe watched him out of the corner of her eye. He had grown corpse still. She flexed her fingers, ready to grab him if he decided to leap off the ledge and streak into the room, slaying people left and right to keep the rest of the secret from coming out.

"Who *is* his father then?" the man who'd brought it up asked.

"Yeah, *who*?" Sespian squeaked, his eyes so wide the whites gleamed around the irises.

Books looked at Amaranthe. Not only did *his* eyes lack surprise, but he glanced toward Sicarius. Numbly, Amaranthe wondered how long Books had known.

"His mother is from the Castlecrest line," the man below continued. "If the father is warrior caste, Sespian might yet have a claim as good as Ravido's."

For whatever reason, Ms. Worgavic was hesitating. She must not know Sicarius's lineage and couldn't say for certain that her colleague's point was moot. Or maybe she worried that Sicarius would somehow find out that she'd spread his secret to the world and come for revenge.

Ms. Worgavic's back was toward the elevated shelf, and Amaranthe saw the moment when her old teacher firmed her spine and decided. Sicarius rose to a crouch. Amaranthe gripped his forearm.

"Don't," she whispered low enough that Sespian wouldn't hear. "Not like this. He'll never understand."

Understand or forgive, she thought.

Ms. Worgavic spoke. "The father is—"

One of the massive double doors flew open. It smashed into the rock wall with so much force that it sounded like a gun being shot.

A blonde-haired woman ran inside with one of her shoes missing and the rest of her clothing saturated and clinging to her body.

"Oh, dear," Books murmured.

Amaranthe winced. "Is that—"

"Our escaped prisoner," Books said, "yes."

\* \* \* \* \*

"Go, go," Amaranthe whispered, hustling the men toward the vent. If a general alarm hadn't been issued yet, it would be soon. She didn't know how many of those servants outside the door had weapons, but she doubted the Forge people had traveled down without numerous well-trained bodyguards.

Thanks to the low ceiling and awkward tightness of their hiding spot, the time it took the team to shuffle one-after-the-other into the vent seemed like hours. It couldn't have been more than a few seconds, but, as she maneuvered closer, Amaranthe heard all too much of Brynia's rapid relaying of events. Before she reached the vent, shouts for guards and warnings of intruders echoed through the tunnels.

"Hurrying would be good," Books whispered to whoever was ahead of him.

In the dim lighting, Amaranthe had lost track of the ordering. When Books's feet disappeared ahead of her, she dove into the vent without hesitation. Going down was much faster than going up, and she slid more often than she crawled, suffering bumps and bruises from the rough rock walls.

Only after dropping ten or twenty feet did Amaranthe, with a sick feeling in her stomach, think to worry that Sicarius might not have followed her. She tried to peek over her shoulder, but she couldn't see anything behind her, not when she was sliding, headfirst down a steep slope. Concerned that he'd chosen to go against her and Sespian's wishes, and taken the other route off the shelf, Amaranthe scarcely noticed when the vent ended. She tumbled out in a pile, crashing into someone's legs.

Basilard hoisted her to her feet. Clangs, like someone striking a massive gong, reverberated through the tunnels.

"Out the way we came?" Akstyr pointed in the direction of the underground pool. No one had raced down their tunnel, weapons waving, yet.

"Yes, be prepared to fight." Amaranthe glanced around. Sicarius hadn't come out of the vent yet.

"Where's Maldynado?" Yara asked.

Akstyr was already running toward the exit with Basilard and Sespian charging after him. Yara, fists planted on her hips, had the stubborn immobility of a statue.

"Akstyr," Amaranthe called, as loudly as she dared—shouting and telling Forge *exactly* where their intruders were probably wasn't a good idea. "Where's—"

"Back here." Maldynado ran down the tunnel toward them from the opposite direction.

"How were you standing guard for us from back there?" Yara demanded.

"Not now." Amaranthe tore her gaze from the vent—if Sicarius hadn't appeared yet, he wasn't going to—and waved for everyone to follow Akstyr.

Maldynado fell in beside Amaranthe and, as they ran, said, "I've got a steamroller running back there."

"Why?" Amaranthe asked.

"In case we need to roll our way out of here. Over a few corpses of Forge people who stand in our way."

"That's macabre."

"I thought you'd appreciate it given your recent experiences with them."

Amaranthe hadn't explained her recent experiences and didn't want to, but she supposed the men could infer much from her bruises and bandages. "Let's hope we don't need—"

"Dead shriveled donkey balls!" came Akstyr's voice from ahead. "Back, back!"

A scream of surprise—and pain—followed the order. Dread filled Amaranthe's heart. Yara and Sespian were in front of her, and she tried to push past them, to get to Akstyr, or at least see what was attacking him. But at the same time, Basilard pushed her backward. He had Akstyr slung over his shoulder, and Amaranthe's feeling of dread increased.

Reading the warning in Basilard's eyes, she scurried backward. On her way by, she grabbed Maldynado's arm and propelled him around. "I think it's time to visit your steamroller."

"It's the cubes," Sespian said, his voice calm despite the chaos. "They shoot out rays of... fire," he said, though his head shake suggested that wasn't the right word. There probably *wasn't* a right word to explain the technology.

Everyone was running now, save for Akstyr, who bumped and flopped on Basilard's shoulder. His eyes were open, but pain contorted his face. His shoulder was smoking.

Tending to his wound would have to wait. Amaranthe urged the men to run faster and hoped they wouldn't end up trapped in a dead-end. Sicarius's terse warning about the black cubes raced through her head, and she feared that a steam-powered rolling machine wouldn't be enough of a tool to harm them.

As the team rounded a bend, a flash of crimson streaked out of the darkness. Fortunately, it struck the rock wall instead of hitting one of the men. Amaranthe hunched her shoulders, expecting a spray of shrapnel. But the beam burned into the wall and, instead of blowing away rock, it melted it somehow. When the crimson ray winked out, a gaping black hole remained.

Someone gave her a not-so-gentle shove from behind. Yes, not a good idea to stand and stare while the floating artillery boxes caught up with them.

Maldynado was leading the way now, and Amaranthe sprinted to catch up with him. When they passed the vent they'd used, she sent a scowl at the entrance, one meant for Sicarius, not only for disobeying Sespian's order, but also for leaving them to deal with these ancestors-cursed cubes by themselves.

Up ahead, the tunnel opened into a chamber, and Maldynado veered to the left. Amaranthe ran in on his heels, the others pounding in after her. Maldynado climbed into the cabin of the steamroller and seemed surprised when Amaranthe popped in right after him.

"Scoot." She shoved him to the side. There was a control wheel instead of levers. Good, that'd be easy. And the engine and boiler were in front, between the cab and the roller. Also good. So long as she and Maldynado could get out fast enough.

Amaranthe shoved the throttle lever and grabbed the wheel. The steamroller lurched forward more quickly than she expected.

"Emperor's warts, boss," Maldynado blurted. "What're you doing?"

"Driving." Amaranthe yanked the wheel as far left as it would go and cursed under her breath at how slowly the vehicle lumbered in the desired direction. "Clear the way," she yelled to the others, though, given the wide-eyed way they were backing up, it might not have been necessary.

If she could reach the entrance with the steamroller before those cubes entered the chamber…

"They're coming," Akstyr yelled. "Where's the back door?"

"There is no back door," Yara said.

"Maldynado, you dolt," Books yelled. "You led us into a dead-end!"

In front of the cab, gray plumes of steam escaped the stack. The vehicle picked up speed.

"If this works, be ready to jump out fast," Amaranthe said.

"If what works?" Maldynado demanded, his hand clenched on the bar supporting the cab roof.

With her eyes focused on the tunnel entrance, Amaranthe didn't answer. She held her breath, hoping…

They reached the tunnel and turned into it only to smack right into one of those cubes. Amaranthe flinched in surprise but didn't release the wheel. The cube bounced off the massive roller without being harmed. It leveled itself, and a red hole on its nearest side flared with light. Four more cubes were lined up in the air behind it. Their holes burned with crimson energy as well.

"Get out," Amaranthe cried. "Now!"

She coiled to jump out the side of the cab, but Maldynado grabbed her, throwing her under his arm like a toddler, and leaped over the seats and out the back of the vehicle.

Crimson beams lanced through the air. Before Maldynado's feet hit the ground, one of the fiery rays struck the steamroller's boiler. Even expecting it, Amaranthe was caught off guard by the power of the explosion. The shock wave hammered into her and Maldynado, tearing her away from his grip. She flew through the air and smashed into someone, taking the other person down with her. Locked in a tangle of limbs, they rolled several feet. She came out on top and grimaced when she realized Sespian was the one flattened beneath her.

"Apologies, Sire." Amaranthe rolled off, hoping he'd spent enough time with the team now that he'd be used to being manhandled by commoners.

"Do many weeks pass without you blowing something up?" Sespian's tone was light, though the joke didn't reach his eyes. He was either worried about those cubes or what he'd heard in the meeting. Or both.

"Not many," Books said, offering both Sespian and Amaranthe a hand up.

Amaranthe checked the tunnel entrance before accepting his help. Dust and smoke clogged the air, and the steamroller had disappeared beneath a pile of rubble. There was no sign of the cubes, but, given the hole she'd seen one incinerate in pure rock, she doubted it would take long for them to burn a way through.

Maldynado pointed at the blocked tunnel. "That was the only way out."

A drop of water splashed onto Amaranthe's nose. As she lifted her eyes toward the source, an ominous snap emanated from within the rock above them. A jagged crack ran across the chiseled ceiling from wall to wall. Beads of moisture kissed that jagged line.

Amaranthe could only stare. In the back of her mind, she calculated that, based on the height of that window-ceiling above the crater and the length of the vent they'd crawled down, there had to be thirty or forty feet of rock above them. She hadn't been thinking of the roof when she'd blocked the tunnel—there hadn't been time for that.

"Dear ancestors," Books whispered. He'd noticed the drip and the crack too.

*Everyone* had noticed, and everyone was staring at the ceiling in as dumbfounded a manner as Amaranthe. More beads were forming and dripping now. No escape, her mind whispered. After all they'd survived, after all her crazy schemes, *this* was going to be the one that killed them all.

"Get in the vehicles," Amaranthe said. It was stupid advice. As if the metal roof of some steam wagon could protect them from thousands of tons of rock caving in on their heads.

"In or *under*?" Maldynado asked.

"It's not going to matter," Books said, but, like everyone else, he ran to jump into one of the cabs.

Another crack sounded in the earth above them. The drips turned to a steady stream pouring onto the stone floor.

"Maybe the cave-in will take out our enemies too," Yara said.

She, Amaranthe, Sespian, and Basilard had climbed into one lorry while the others had leaped into the second. Nobody responded to her comment. It wasn't much of a consolation. Even if they buried Forge with them, they'd be taking out Sespian too. Who'd be left to spearhead the next iteration of the empire? Some backstabbing relative of Maldynado's? Amaranthe shook her head. What had she done?

"My shoulder feels like it's been dipped in acid," Akstyr growled. At least he'd revived enough to stand. Not that it'd matter in a moment.

"We have another problem," Yara said.

"Oh, good." Amaranthe couldn't hide the high-pitched squeak to her voice. "We didn't have enough to worry about."

Yara pointed at the tunnel entrance.

Beyond the water pouring from the ceiling crack, smoke was rising from somewhere. At first, Amaranthe thought it was from the buried vehicle, but it couldn't be. It had to be those cubes, burning their way through that rubble. In a few seconds, they'd be inside.

A slab of rock snapped away from the ceiling crack and crashed to the floor. Water poured through the gap.

"Maybe those cubes aren't waterproof," Amaranthe said bleakly. She doubted it.

"Maybe the chamber will flood," Books said from the other lorry, "and we'll drown before they incinerate us." Indeed, thanks to the increased flow, water smothered the floor and was creeping up the walls of the chamber. In another foot, it'd reach the bottom of the cabs.

"Better than being smashed by the roof collapsing," Maldynado said.

Sespian cleared his throat. "Can't we just swim out?"

Amaranthe blinked. He was right. Right now, there was no way anyone could fight the current of the descending water, but once the chamber filled, everything ought to equalize. Shouldn't it? She looked at Books.

He lifted a shoulder. "If those cubes don't break in first. And if the route isn't too twisty and narrow for human bodies to pass through. And if the surface isn't too far up."

"Don't overwhelm us with your optimism, Booksie," Maldynado said.

Basilard tapped Amaranthe. *If necessary, I will distract the cubes so the team can escape.*

"Noble, Basilard," Amaranthe said, "but I'd prefer it if we all lived." She'd prefer it if Sicarius were there too. She wanted to kick him for abandoning them. Not that she wanted him to die with them, but he knew more about those cubes than anyone.

Water crept higher, flooding the cab. The cold currents tugged at Amaranthe's legs.

Across the chamber, a fist-sized piece of rock tumbled down the cave-in hill and splashed into the water. More smoke wafted from the hole.

"That's it," Amaranthe said, certain the cubes were about to burst through. Running away from them would have been hard enough, but swimming?

Another thunderous crack came from above. This time, the boulder that dropped away was the size of a steam vehicle. The lake gushed in. Before Amaranthe could do more than suck in a gulp of air, tepid water engulfed her. It extinguished the lanterns, and blackness swallowed the cave.

Fear surged through her limbs. All she could think to do was push away from the lorry and swim in the direction she *thought* was the hole. She bumped someone's leg, or arm, or who knew what? So long as it wasn't one of those cubes.

Her fingers scraped against rock. The ceiling? The water seemed brighter ahead. All too aware of how deep they were and how little air she had, Amaranthe angled in that direction, hoping her eyes weren't tricking her. As she swam, she kept one hand on the rocky surface, using it as a guide. It ended in at a jagged edge. The hole leading upward, she hoped. What else could it be?

With that optimistic thought, Amaranthe angled her body into the passage. All of the edges were jagged, and she had to twist and writhe to find a route upward. At least she *hoped* it was upward. Maybe she'd merely found the tunnel, and she was swimming deeper into the complex and farther from the surface. And air.

No. The tunnel wouldn't have any light, and those sharp, jagged edges hadn't been formed by erosion or machines. They were fresh.

Again, Amaranthe bumped against someone—this time her knuckles brushing a boot. Someone was above her. That gave her further hope. If others were going that direction, it had to be the way out. As she continued on, the brightness grew stronger. There was no current in the crevice, but she could feel her natural buoyancy helping her ascend as well.

Finally, the dark stone walls disappeared. The water made her sight blurry, but she could see reds and greens—seaweed. She'd reached the bottom of the lake. None too soon either. Her lungs were pleading for air.

Not sure how many feet down the bottom was, Amaranthe kicked for the surface. Her long dress tangled about her legs. Had she the breath, she would have snarled at the impractical garb. She kicked harder and stretched her arms toward the surface, longing to break through and gasp in fresh air.

A dark shadow blotted out the light coming from the sky. At first, Amaranthe thought she might be coming up under a log, so she veered to the side. Then the "log" dove down and slammed into her.

The force drove her several feet to the side. Her last vestiges of air escaped in an explosion of bubbles even as she tumbled through the water, head over feet.

Amaranthe clawed for the short sword that usually hung at her waist, but only found a knife. It'd have to do. She yanked the blade free. The dark shape had come around; it swam straight toward her. It looked like a giant eel. It had to be the creature from the underwater pool, the one that had feasted on the guard.

Her lungs ached to suck in a breath, and the surface waited, tantalizingly close, but she dared not turn her back on the eel. At this depth, plenty of light filtered down to reveal its maw as it neared, how it opened up, displaying two fences of fangs bigger than swords....

Amaranthe gripped her knife tighter, the short blade paltry in comparison.

The eel's tail undulated, and the beast surged forward. She tried to fling herself to the side and lash out as it swam past, but it was too fast. This was the eel's milieu, and that maw whipped about to follow her as quickly as one of Sicarius's sword strikes. It would have—*should* have—chomped down on her, but the creature halted mid-attack. It reared back, and Amaranthe didn't question her reprieve. With her lungs screaming for air, and blackness encroaching at the edges of her vision, she swam for the surface.

When she burst through, her desperate gasp drew in as much water as air. Coughs wracked her body. Dagger still in hand, Amaranthe spun in a circle, trying to spot the creature—or nearby land so she could sprint to a beach where it couldn't reach her.

"You all right, boss?" came Maldynado's voice from twenty meters away. He was treading water and supporting Yara. She'd succumbed to a bout of coughing as well. Closer to shore, Basilard lifted his arm. Thank his ancestors, Akstyr had revived enough to swim out; he treaded water with Basilard's support.

"I think so," Amaranthe answered.

Something churned beneath the surface, agitating the water.

"Find the others," Amaranthe called. "Get everyone to land."

Afraid one of "the others" was down below, fighting that creature to help her, Amaranthe took a breath and dropped below the surface again. When the giant eel had been above her, its dark shape contrasting with the light from the sky, she'd had no trouble making it out, but she struggled to see anything against the dark depths.

Though her muscles were reluctant to comply, Amaranthe stroked downward. Swim to the beach, the sane part of her mind said, but if some comrade had come to help her, and now needed her help...

The water grew still. Uneasiness swam into Amaranthe's stomach. What if her unseen savior had sacrificed himself to distract the creature from eating her? If it had been Books... He'd come a long way in the last year, but he still wasn't a natural fighter. Dealing with powerful, inhuman monsters surely wasn't his forte.

When she didn't spot anyone—or anything—Amaranthe turned a circle, afraid she'd misjudged the source of the agitation.

Something dark floated in the water a couple of meters away. Amaranthe almost dropped her knife. Swearing at herself, she recovered, bringing it to bear in case the eel attacked. But it wasn't moving. Blood clouded the water.

Amaranthe swam back to the surface. She spotted Books in the distance, paddling toward shore.

A few feet away, Sespian bobbed, treading water. He waved a knife. "It's dead, right?"

"*You* did that?" Amaranthe asked, then, realizing that might sound offensive, added, "I mean, yes, I believe it's dead. Thank you for your help."

Sespian smiled, though it didn't reach his eyes. "I thought I should practice proving myself useful, given that I'm unemployed now."

"Ah, yes. Well, let's find someplace dry and talk about that." Dry and *safe*, Amaranthe thought. There might be more of those giant eels about.

The rest of her team had paddled for Marblecrest Island, the nearest piece of land. Amaranthe counted heads and accounted for all but one. A blond one.

She tried to lock her emotions away, reminding herself that *he* had chosen to leave the group against her wishes. If he hadn't found a way out, it was his fault. Except it wasn't. Not really. He had been trying to protect Sespian, and probably her as well, the only way he knew how.

Amaranthe wiped water out of her eyes. Don't get maudlin yet, girl, she told herself. He'd find another way out.

"I must apologize for dragging your team into this," Sespian said. "You must believe me when I say I had no idea about... I had no idea."

"I know, Sire."

He sighed. "At least you were paid well for your time."

"We were?"

"I gave your men the money I promised." His laugh sounded forced. "Better spend it before Forge's plan goes into effect and it's worthless."

"I'm sure they're only planning to inflate the currency a few percent a year. Besides Maldynado probably already spent it on hats."

Amaranthe ought to swim to shore—Basilard had already crawled out and was waving the others over—but she kept expecting Sicarius to pop up. Unless a passage led to an exit on Marblecrest Island somewhere, anyone who didn't come up soon... wouldn't ever. Though maybe he'd made it back to the underwater vehicle. All of the Forge people were probably trying to escape that way—if they'd had time. It wouldn't take that water long to flood everything. A grisly thought came to Amaranthe. What if her explosion had, however inadvertently, killed everyone down there?

Sespian mumbled something.

"Pardon, Sire?" Amaranthe asked, glad for a distraction.

"I'm having a hard time believing this and wondering if they might be wrong. Maybe they made it up." Sespian shoved his bangs away from his forehead. "I mean, I knew my fa— Raumesys and I didn't have anything in common, but I'd never heard any speculation… I wouldn't have guessed…"

Amaranthe didn't mean for her face to give anything away, but Sespian was watching her and frowned at something he saw there.

"You aren't surprised by any of this," he said. "You didn't… *know*, did you?"

Avoiding his eyes would be suspicious, but Amaranthe couldn't help it. She'd *always* feel guilty about being the one who had given up the information to Forge.

"You did," Sespian whispered. "For how long? Did you know when you decided to go through with my kidnapping request? I know you didn't do it for the money." He waved toward the cove where the steamboat had crashed. "You didn't even ask about it."

"I believe you're a good man, Sire, and that your ideas are what the empire needs going forward."

"You can stop calling me, Sire. If I'm not Raumesys's heir, then I've no claim to the throne. *Goodness* doesn't matter."

"It should be the only thing that matters."

"Very few in the empire will agree with you. Unless my real father has warrior-caste blood and a link to one of the old imperial lines…" Sespian was watching her again. "You don't know who it is, do you?"

Raindrops splashed onto the lake. We really ought to get out of the water, Amaranthe thought, but she didn't make a move to the shore. They were alone. Maybe it was time to tell him. She'd always thought Sicarius would be the one to do it, but he'd had opportunities and hadn't. Maybe he couldn't. For all the dangers he'd fearlessly faced in his life, he'd never had to deal with the crushing feeling of disappointing a family member—a loved one. As long as Sespian didn't know, Sicarius could imagine… Who knew what he imagined? Some noble future with Sespian ruling the empire and him at his shoulder, guarding his back against anyone who might do him harm. A chance to be a better man at

Sespian's side than he ever was before? Whatever notion he had in his head, the dream could only live so long as Sespian didn't squash it.

Sespian touched Amaranthe's shoulder. "Please, Amaranthe. If you know, you must tell me."

The others were all on the beach now. When Amaranthe looked that way, Maldynado held out his arms in a what's-the-delay gesture. Nobody was in earshot, unless one counted the dead eel, which had floated to the surface, its bloated body dark beneath the cloudy sky. Movement stirred the water near the mouth of the river, a flash of gray, and then it was gone. One of the Forge submarines escaping? If so, then the world would soon know of the Turgonian emperor's flawed heritage. Sespian had already heard enough from strangers. Time to tell him the truth.

"Sicarius," Amaranthe said.

Sespian jerked his head around, checking behind him.

"No, he's not there," Amaranthe said. "That's who your father is." She refused to contemplate that the tense on that verb might be incorrect.

Sespian's head swiveled back to her, and he shook it, denial taking up residence behind his eyes. "That's not very slagging funny."

"I know." Amaranthe waited to see if he had questions, but he merely stared at her in silence. "We better get out of this water," she said and paddled for the shore.

Sespian didn't follow.

Epilogue

When Amaranthe walked onto the beach, water sloughing from her drenched clothing, the men were arguing. She would have preferred someone be standing watch, but, given the topic of conversation, she could understand how they wouldn't find security the priority.

"He's *not* the emperor?" Maldynado asked. "What're you talking about, Basilard?"

Amaranthe ignored the flurry of hand signals in favor of squeezing water out of her hair and re-tying her bun. She didn't want the rehash. Out in the water, Sespian had finally started swimming toward shore, though he was angling for a landing spot farther up the beach. Amaranthe wanted to talk to him eventually, but he needed time to digest what, in his eyes, must be an extremely unpalatable meal. There was still no sign of Sicarius. They'd come ashore near the cliff underneath the hot springs, and she watched the trees near its base, expecting him to stroll onto the beach at any moment.

"We don't know that those Forge yokels were telling the truth." Yara propped a boot on a log.

She'd retained her footwear, though not everybody had. Akstyr was wandering around in sandy socks, gripping his injured shoulder. Maldynado had lost his shirt. Though that might simply be an excuse for him to show off his physique in front of Yara.

"Did the emp—Sespian say anything to you out there, boss?" Maldynado asked, and all eyes turned toward Amaranthe. "Did he *know* anything about this?"

"Nothing." She didn't elaborate. She didn't want to discuss this. Not with them, not now. She eyed the trees again.

"Has all our work been for nothing?" Maldynado asked. "This was all about helping *him*. And getting our names cleared. Cursed ancestors, boss, he won't have the power to remove your bounty now, will he?"

If he brought up his stupid statue, Amaranthe didn't think she'd be able to keep from smacking him. Wasn't anyone else concerned that Sicarius hadn't reappeared? He'd saved all of their lives before. They owed him more than disinterest. She caught Basilard looking around, a hint of concern in his eyes. That was something at least. And Maldynado didn't mention the statue. Maybe he was genuinely more concerned about her and her bounty.

"What are we going to do now?" Akstyr asked. "If he's not the true emperor, do we even care who's on the throne?"

"We care," Books said, joining the conversation for the first time.

Amaranthe remembered the look he'd given her up on the ledge. He'd seemed to know about the Sespian-Sicarius link.

"We want someone in charge with the foresight and wisdom to manage the future's changing currents in a manner that will empower the people, not impoverish them." Books glowered at Maldynado, as if he, because of his older brother, was responsible for Forge's scheme.

Maldynado lifted his hands, pointing a finger at Akstyr. "He asked, not me."

*Now that it's possible there are choices*, Basilard signed, *are we certain a nineteen-year-old boy is the person with the 'foresight and wisdom' of which Books speaks?*

"Perhaps not," Books said.

Akstyr scowled at Basilard, perhaps objecting to the notion that young people couldn't have foresight and wisdom.

"Let's not abandon him yet." Chin up and back stiff, Yara appeared miffed at how quickly people were dismissing Sespian.

Amaranthe shared the feeling, though she wasn't sure it mattered. Would Sespian want anything to do with the throne now that he knew he wasn't the rightful heir? What if he simply walked away? Though she didn't know him well, she had a hard time believing he'd do that. Even if Sespian knew he couldn't be a part of the ruling future, she thought he'd want to try and thwart the Forge and Marblecrest scheme. Besides, he still had a claim to the throne, albeit a muddled one.

Books came over and touched Amaranthe's shoulder.

"Wait," Maldynado said before Books spoke, apparently in response to Basilard, "who *is* Sespian's father? Does anybody know?"

"Some kitchen boy, probably," Akstyr said.

"Don't be crude," Yara said.

When Amaranthe didn't speak, Books's eyebrows rose. "Are you going to say anything?" he asked.

"How long have you known?" she murmured.

"I've had a hunch it was something like that for a while, but the exact puzzle pieces didn't snap into place until Sicarius threatened Maldynado if he didn't keep the emperor safe."

"Ah." At least she hadn't been the one to give it away. Right, Amaranthe told herself, you can keep secrets from friends, just not from enemies.

"I have been working on ideas," Books said, "for a new form of government."

"A new *government*?" Amaranthe had only ever wanted to help Sespian retain his position. Now Books was proposing… she didn't even know what. Revolution?

"It was only an exercise until this information came out," Books went on, "but the antiquated notion of an empire might not be what Turgonia needs as it goes ahead into modern times. So much of the strife between the old warrior caste and the new entrepreneurial class is born out of mutual resentment, which never would have been a factor if land

and power were not hereditary, gifts given to those loyal families who have been willing to support totalitarian rule over the centuries."

Maldynado strolled over, and, for once, Amaranthe was glad. She wasn't ready to think about spearheading a revolution.

"What are you two discussing?" Maldynado asked. "Some sort of…" His gaze shifted over Amaranthe's shoulder.

Sicarius strode out of the trees, as grim and deadly as ever. Relief flooded Amaranthe, though, with so many witnesses present, she didn't run to him. He wasn't looking approachable anyway. He wasn't wet, so he must have found a back way out, but Amaranthe wished he *were* wet, as the water might have washed the blood stains off his hands and out of his hair. She'd seen him gore-covered before, but, given Sespian's new knowledge, she wished he looked less like a soldier straight from the front lines. An assassin, she thought, not a soldier.

Sicarius spotted Sespian further down the beach, and a hint of the starkness faded from his eyes, though an uncommon stiffness accompanied his gait. It might have been an injury or simple tension.

"Glad you could join us." Amaranthe forced a smile. She didn't want to open with accusations, but she had to know what he'd done down there. "Did you, ah…"

"There was a translucent barrier further protecting their meeting area," Sicarius said. "I found another way around, but they sent their bodyguards to delay me. I dealt with them and was catching up with the Forge people when the tunnel collapsed."

"Tunnel collapse?" Amaranthe asked, her heart sinking.

"There were several after an explosion sounded." Sicarius looked at her, as if he knew she'd been responsible. And why not? Who else did he know that was crazy enough to blow up tunnels from within? "Water flooded inside, causing structural damage. I reached the docking pool too late to retrieve our vehicle. I had to find another way out."

A swollen bruise on his temple made Amaranthe wonder if, for once, the blood spattering him *didn't* belong to someone else. Dust caked his black clothing, and numerous scrapes abraded his hands.

"Sorry about that, but you *did* choose to take an alternative route out." Amaranthe felt like a heel implying that he would have been safe had he stuck with her—she'd nearly gotten her entire team killed—but wandering off to stalk Forge people had been his idea, and she refused

to pity him for the bruises he'd obtained. "You said you made it to the submarines. Do you know if, ah, did all of the Forge people get out?"

Sicarius hesitated. "Unknown."

That uncharacteristic hesitation made Amaranthe probe deeper. "Truly?"

Sicarius clasped his hands behind his back. It wasn't the first time she'd received silence in lieu of a response, and she'd learned to read some of his silences. He was protecting her. Her actions *had* resulted in deaths. Not all of the Forge people had escaped in time. Amaranthe stared at the ground, stung by the cosmic unfairness. She'd accidently achieved what an assassin had wished but failed to do. Sicarius stood there, stained by blood, while the water had washed any such stains from her. Visible stains anyway.

A few meters away, a boot crunched on pebbles. It sounded loud on the quiet beach. Amaranthe hadn't realized how still it had grown, or how many eyes had been turned toward her conversation.

Assuming one of the men was simply moving about, Amaranthe didn't turn to see who it was. Only when Sicarius's hand dropped to his dagger, halted halfway there, and hung in the air, did she turn.

Sespian stood there, a loaded pistol in his hand. Aimed at Sicarius.

Stunned, Amaranthe could only gawk.

"Uhm," Maldynado said, summing up her thoughts.

Amaranthe had expected a reaction from Sespian, but not this reaction. She lifted a hand and stepped toward him.

He skewered her with a hard gaze so similar to ones she'd received from Sicarius that it stopped her in her tracks.

"Don't move." Though Sespian spoke to Amaranthe, the pistol never wavered. Its muzzle pointed straight at Sicarius's heart. When Sespian looked at him again, anger seethed in his eyes. "How?"

Sicarius lowered his hands, not toward his weapons, but to his sides. He didn't say anything. He did glance toward Amaranthe, and she cringed, knowing she bore all the responsibility for this moment.

"How did it…" Sespian took in several deep breaths that did nothing to lighten the tension bunching his shoulders. "Did you rape her?"

The blunt accusation startled Amaranthe, but she abruptly understood the pistol. In case Sicarius was going to answer with silence again—silence that might be misconstrued as an admission of guilt—Amaranthe said, "No," for him.

Ignoring Sespian's earlier warning, she walked toward Sicarius. She didn't lunge to protect him, fearing a quick action would surprise Sespian into shooting, but she strode across the intervening distance and planted herself in front of him. Sespian moved the pistol so it didn't point at her, but he didn't lower it.

"Your mother chose him," Amaranthe said, keeping her eyes toward Sespian, though she was aware of the slack-jawed stares from the rest of her team. "Raumesys got rid of his first wife for not producing an heir. Your mother intended to make sure she wouldn't suffer the same fate. She could have seduced some kitchen boy, but she wanted you to inherit athleticism and intelligence." She looked at the pistol in Sespian's hand and over her shoulder at Sicarius, who ought to be saying something by now. "*Some* intelligence, anyway."

That earned her a brief slit-eyed look from Sicarius. She tilted her head toward Sespian, implying that Sicarius could take over the explaining any time.

"How does the boss know so much about this?" Maldynado muttered to Books.

Amaranthe didn't hear the answer. She was focused on Sespian. He was doing a good job of being just as stony and hard to read as Sicarius.

"That's the story he gave you?" Sespian finally asked. "And you believe it? Without any proof?"

A grimace wanted to find its way to Amaranthe's lips, but she forced herself to smile and keep her tone light. "If you had any idea how much prying I had to do, you wouldn't doubt that I'd finagled the truth out of him."

"You're wrong. My mother was a good person. She *never* would have slept with a psychopathic murdering monster." Sespian threw the pistol down. "If you want to protect him, fine, but I want nothing to do with him or anyone who chooses to be around him."

Sespian sent a dismissive glower toward the others before turning his back and stalking down the beach. Not down the beach like someone who needed time to think, but down the beach with the determined stride of someone who never planned to come back.

Amaranthe sighed. At least, with nothing except rowboats left un-crashed, he couldn't go anywhere quickly. She faced Sicarius, whose expressionless façade was firmly affixed. "Please note, for future reference, when someone asks you if you've raped someone else, the appropriate answer is a prompt no."

Though Sicarius's expression never changed, Amaranthe was close enough to catch the long, soft exhalation. It had a deflationary effect on her as well as him. "Saying something would not have mattered," Sicarius said. "He would not have believed it."

Probably true. With no peers and so few allies growing up, Sespian must have loved his mother a great deal. Imagining her as someone who had willingly sought out a man that he considered a monster couldn't be easy. Maybe he wouldn't be able to do it at all. No, Amaranthe couldn't accept that. Sespian might never come to care about Sicarius, but he *would* know the truth. After all the times Sicarius had saved her life and backed up her silly schemes, she owed him that.

"Don't worry," Amaranthe said, "I'm not giving up."

She gazed out over the lake. The serenity of the water belied all the craziness that had gone on beneath the surface. She didn't know what she'd say to Sespian, but she had best go after him before he found a way off the island.

"No," Books said, in response to someone's murmured comment. "Sociopath is more applicable than psychopath, though I don't believe either is wholly accurate."

Amaranthe rubbed her face. Leave it to her men to focus on the inane and unimportant. Sicarius didn't seem to have heard. He was gazing in the direction Sespian had gone, his face—to most—unreadable, but Amaranthe sensed the bleakness beneath the mask.

"There are enforcers out there," she told the team. "We need to leave soon. Please gather whatever gear might be useful from the steamboat. Oh, and that money too." She had a feeling they'd need it to fund… She wasn't sure yet. "I'm going to talk to Sespian."

"Where will we be going when we leave?" Books asked.

"I'm not sure. I need time to think of a plan."

Amaranthe heard Akstyr saying, "I hear the Kyatt Islands are nice in the winter," as she walked away. She might have to do some extra persuasive talking to keep everybody from going their separate ways now

that they knew backing Sespian wasn't a path to having their dreams fulfilled—or bounties lifted.

After several minutes of searching, Amaranthe found fresh footprints on the sandy beach near the dock. They led to the boathouse. She paused in the doorway to let her eyes adjust to the dim interior. She expected to find Sespian readying a canoe or rowboat, but he was merely sitting on the worn wooden deck, his face resting in his hand. He must have heard her walking in, but he didn't lift his head.

Amaranthe sat on the end of an upturned canoe. "I don't know if you know this, but that day in Stumps when we first met, it brought me to Hollowcrest's attention. I guess you mentioned me in a… romantic light." She watched Sespian for a reaction, and thought there might have been a wince, but his face remained covered by his hands, and she couldn't be certain. "Since he thought I would be an inappropriate choice, he figured he'd deal with the matter by having me killed. He created a ruse of an assignment, sending me off to kill this notorious assassin and promising me a promotion should I succeed. I was uncomfortable at the idea of assassinating anyone, wanted murderer or not, but I didn't think I had a choice. Who refuses the Commander of the Armies?

"Well, I wasn't as clever as I thought, and Sicarius saw me coming. He was a split second away from killing me. Literally. He had his hands around my neck—but he stopped just shy of breaking it."

Though Sespian didn't lift his head, his fingers shifted, so he could see her.

"You see, this young man had given me a bracelet. For luck, he'd said. And luck caused that bracelet to slip free of my sleeve at that moment so that Sicarius saw it. That's what made him pause. He knew it was something you'd created, and he figured I must mean something to you if you'd given it to me."

Amaranthe paused for a moment, to see if Sespian wanted to say anything. He didn't.

"I can't claim to know everything that's in his head," she went on. "You've probably noticed he's a slightly reticent man. But I know he wants a chance to know you. And for you to know him. I'm sure he doesn't expect any sort of loving, hugging father-son relationship—" that finally drew a reaction, if only a snort, "—but your mother forbade

him from having anything to do with you, and he regrets that you grew up fearing him. I know you think he's a monster, and I'm not going to try and defend what he's done in his life, but I believe that's entirely a result of how he was raised. He's only given me glimpses into what had to have been a nightmarish childhood, but I'm sure the dastardly details are there in Hollowcrest's old office somewhere if you were ever inclined to search for them. Given what he went through…" Amaranthe winced, thinking of Pike and wishing that she could burn him from the pages of her memory. "*Knowing* what he went through first-hand," she amended, "even if I only had to experience it for a week, I find it remarkable that he's capable of caring about you or anyone else."

Sespian shook his head stubbornly.

Amaranthe prodded at mold fuzzing a crevice between two boards and reminded herself that they weren't staying long enough to need to clean anything. Though she would find this conversation easier if her hands had something to do.

"Whatever your opinion is of him," Amaranthe said, clasping her hands in her lap, "Sicarius is very professional and practical about his… career and the way he lives his life. I know you're thinking I have no way of truly knowing what happened with him and your mother, but he's not a rapist. Had he been raised by a couple of nice, loving parents, I sincerely believe he would have been a good man." She felt it important to mention that, even if Sespian wouldn't believe it, because he was probably thinking his own blood was somehow tainted now—as if Sicarius could be any worse than Raumesys, a man who'd apparently thought nothing of hiring Pike as his master interrogator. "From what he told me, I inferred that your mother chose him much like you'd choose a stud for breeding a hound. You must grant that he's exceedingly skilled and gifted at what he does, and they're the same traits that would have made a superior soldier or athlete or even the type of emperor Turgonians are used to." The corners of her mouth quirked upward of their own volition. "I guess your mother wasn't counting on there being an artistic bent in there."

Sespian had been patient, or at least silent, thus far, but at this he rolled his eyes, looking every bit like a teenage boy for a moment. "Oh, please, you're not trying to tell me I got *that* from him."

"Ask him to draw something sometime."

"He does *not* draw."

Amaranthe couldn't tell if there was any curiosity behind the flat denial. She decided not to admit that Sicarius's only interest in art had apparently come from a cartography class where some tutor had suggested that an assassin ought to be able to draw maps of areas he'd spied upon. Instead, she smiled again and asked, "Who do you think drew the ranmya designs for our counterfeiting scheme?"

"Tracing isn't drawing," Sespian muttered. "Though... I suppose the engravings would have to be in reverse..."

At least he seemed thoughtful over the idea. Amaranthe wouldn't try to elicit promises or ask for his opinions, not at this point. If she'd started him thinking that his mother had chosen Sicarius, and that there might have been good reasons for that choice, that was enough. She had a feeling she couldn't do much more anyway. If Sespian and Sicarius were to have any sort of relationship at all, Sicarius would have to figure out the rest.

"We'll be leaving soon if you want to come," Amaranthe said.

"To what ends? I'm not the legitimate emperor. As soon as the Forge people get the word out about that, it'll be true in all senses. And... I would not wish to live a lie, regardless."

"Well, I've been thinking about that..." Not really, but she needed to start. If they were going to oust Ravido Marblecrest and keep Forge from implementing their new money plan, they'd need some sort of alternative to push forward. She thought of Books's words. Creating a new government was a little more comprehensive of an alternative than she'd meant to push forward, but maybe... Maybe the idea had merit. Knowing Books, he'd designed some sort of republic or meritocracy, so there'd be a lot of opposition from those entrenched in the warrior-caste way of life, but all those up-and-coming entrepreneurs would surely love a system where one could reach the highest levels in society and government no matter to whom one had been born. And perhaps a radical change in government might assuage some of the anti-Turgonian sentiment out there from those the empire had conquered or otherwise mistreated over the centuries.

*Audacious, girl*, she thought. Was she truly contemplating going back to the capital and trying to change a seven-hundred-year-old form of government? Whether it worked or not, it'd probably get her that

place in the history books she craved. She chuckled. The men would accuse her of being a megalomaniac. They'd say she was crazy, and this time they'd be right. Maybe she could blame Books. He'd started her ore cart down this track.

"It looks terribly entertaining in there," Sespian said.

"What?" Amaranthe forced her mind back to the moment.

"In your head."

"Oh." This time, her chuckle was more self-conscious. "It's, uhm, a fascinating place for sure. At least I think so." Amaranthe stood, extending her hand. "You better come along. This is going to be interesting."

Sespian regarded it thoughtfully for a moment before accepting it. "Promise?"

"Oh, yes."

THE END

# AFTERWORD

Thank you for reading the latest Emperor's Edge novel. I hope you enjoyed the story! I'll be taking a break from EE to write the sequel to *Encrypted* next, (I'm planning to tie the two story lines together at the end of Book 6), but I hope to have both books ready for you in 2013. In the meantime, if you haven't read *Encrypted*, it explains where the alien technology (and that black knife) comes from. Also, a young Sicarius makes an appearance in the latter half of the book, for those interested in seeing more of him.

As always, I'd love to hear from you; you can get in touch with me on Facebook, Twitter, or my blog. If you'd like to chat with other readers, there's an Emperor's Edge forum now (some of the members have posted EE fan art, and you can see the collection on my Pinterest account). If you visit the forum, watch out for Maria Bender McConnaughy and Alex Baird, the leaders of the Naughty Brigade. They might wish to... recruit you.

# ALSO BY THE AUTHOR

## the Emperors Edge Universe

**Novels**:
*The Emperor's Edge, Book 1*
*Dark Currents, Book 2*
*Deadly Games, Book 3*
*Conspiracy, Book 4*
You just read: *Blood and Betrayal, Book 5*
*Forged in Blood, Book 6 (coming in 2013)*
*Encrypted*
*Decrypted*

**Short Stories:**
*Ice Cracker II (and other short stories)*
*The Assassin's Curse*

## THE FLASH GOLD CHRONICLES

*Flash Gold*
*Hunted*
*Peacemaker*

## THE GOBLIN BROTHERS ADVENTURES

# CONNECT WITH THE AUTHOR

http://www.lindsayburoker.com

http://www.facebook.com/LindsayBuroker

http://www.twitter.com/GoblinWriter